Don't miss any of the exciting books in
Curt Benjamin's *Seven Brothers*:

The Prince of Shadow

The Prince of Dreams

The Gates of Heaven

THE PRINCE OF DREAMS

VOLUME TWO OF *Seven Brothers*

Curt Benjamin

DAW BOOKS, INC.

DONALD A. WOLLHEIM, FOUNDER

375 Hudson Street, New York, NY 10014

ELIZABETH R. WOLLHEIM

SHEILA E. GILBERT

PUBLISHERS

www.dawbooks.com

This book is dedicated to my mom and dad, who get excited every time a book comes out. To the Hoffmans, especially Bethany, who plays the flute and helped me out in a really important flute scene! And to the Greenspans, especially Bonnie, for the new computer just in the nick of time. Cathy and Tom, and Barb and David and Erik for support and critique—you helped to get it right, but I made the mistakes myself. Charlotte keeps me fed while we do corrections at her dining room table. How can you say thank you enough for comfort food after a long day of proofing, or all the other ways she treats me like one of her own kids?

Fantasy is half imagination and half research, so a big thank you to the Free Library of Philadelphia. Without you there would be no book. Libraries rule!

PART ONE

THE ROAD TO DURNHAG

Chapter One

"SO THIS is dying."

Llesho strained against his bonds, tormented by the fire burning in his gut and the icy sweat dripping from his shivering body. In his brief moments of lucidity, he wondered how he could burn and tremble with cold at the same time and where he was and how he had come to be a prisoner again. In his delirium, Master Markko came to him as a winged beast with the claws of a lion and the tail of a snake, or sometimes as a great bird with talons sharp as swords tearing the entrails from his belly. Always Llesho heard the magician's voice echoing inside his head:

"Among the weak, yes; this is dying."

No escape. He knew, vaguely, that he cried out in his sleep, just as he knew that help wouldn't come. . . .

"Are you waiting for someone?" Master Den rounded the rough wooden bench and sat next to Llesho, quiet until the confusion had cleared from his face. "Your eyes were open, but you didn't answer when I called."

"I was dreaming," Llesho answered, his voice still fogged with distant horror. "Remembering a dream, actually."

A low waterfall chuckled in front of him, reminding

him of where he was. The Imperial City of Shan had
many gardens, but the Imperial Water Garden in honor
of Thousand Lakes Province had become Llesho's special
place, where he came to sort out his thoughts. Like him,
the Water Garden had taken some damage in the recent
fighting. A delicate wooden bridge had burned to ash,
and Harnish raiders had trampled a section of marsh
grasses beside a stream that had flowed red with the
blood of the fallen for many days. At the heart of the
Imperial Water Garden, however, the waterfall still
poured its clean bounty into a stone basin that fed the
numerous streams winding among the river reeds. Water
lilies still floated in the many protected pools and the
lotus still rose out of the mud on defiant stalks. The little
stone altar to ChiChu, the trickster god of laughter and
tears, still lay hidden under a ledge beneath the chuck-
ling water.

Like the garden, Llesho had survived and healed. He
sat on the split log bench just beyond the reach of the
fine spray the waterfall kicked up, contemplating the
altar to the trickster god—a favored deity of an emperor
fond of disguises and mentor to a young prince still learning how to be a king—as if it would give up the secrets
of the heavens. In his hand he held a quarter tael of
silver and a slip of paper, much wrinkled and dampened
from the tight grip he held on it. With a sideways look
at Master Den, who was the trickster god ChiChu in
disguise, he placed the petition on the tiny altar with the
coin inside it for an anchor. Then he sat back down on
his bench and prepared to wait.

Master Den said nothing, nor did he reach for the
offering on his altar. If it came to a contest, the trickster
god had eternity to outsit him. Llesho gave a little sigh
and surrendered.

"He comes to me in my dreams. Master Markko. He
tells me I'm dying, and I believe him. Then I wake up,
and he's gone, and I'm still here." Still alive. But the
dreams sometimes felt more real than the waking world.

"And you want to know—?"

"Is it real? Or am I going mad?"

"Ah."

Llesho waited for Master Den to go on, fretfully at first, but as the silence stretched between them, he found that his fears, all his conscious thought, for that matter, drifted away. He heard the merry chime of water dashing on stone, and saw the bright flick of the light bouncing off the droplets in myriad rainbows. He felt the sun on his back, and the breeze on his face, and the rough split logs of the bench under his backside. The sun moved, and he turned his head to feel its heat on his closed eyes, on his smile. Without realizing it was happening, the moment stole through him, sunlight filling all the chinks and crannies of his fractured existence. He was aware only of a profound peace settling in his heart and his gut, pinning him to his bench in a perfect eternity of now.

"As long as you hold the world in your heart, he can't touch you." Master Den gave a little shrug. "But if you ever tire of the world, have something else to grab onto."

His mind went to Carina, the healer with hair the color of the Golden River Dragon, and eyes like Mara's, who aspired to be the eighth mortal god. But he knew instinctively that wasn't what his teacher meant. He already had a purpose to hold him: to free his country and open the gates of heaven. Now he needed a dream more powerful than the ones Master Markko sent to trouble his sleep. His questions, about the brothers still lost to him that he had pledged his quest to free and the necklace of the Great Goddess that the mortal goddess SienMa had charged him to find, would keep for another day. This lesson, to store up the sights and sounds and smell and touch of peace against the struggle to come, he finally understood.

They sat in comfortable silence together until the sun had reached the zenith, and then Master Den swept up the petition Llesho had placed on his altar.

"You are wanted at the palace." He flipped Llesho's

silver coin in the air, and when it had landed in the palm
of his hand, he tucked it into his own purse with a wink
and a lopsided grin. He was, after all, a trickster god.
"It's time to go."

Llesho had already put on the disguise he would wear
for the next part of his journey, the uniform of an imperial militia cadet. Hmishi had stowed the gifts of the mortal goddess—his jade cup, and the short spear that
seemed to want him dead—in his pack for the road. He
had only to find his companions and be gone. Still, he
doubted their plan.

"I don't know who in their right mind would hire me
to protect their camels," he grumbled. Merchants would
expect a cadet of his age to have the skills and reflexes
of a soldier, but no real experience of combat. "I explained that to Emperor Shou, but you know how he is."

Shou had simply raised an eyebrow and asked when
had he ever left anything to chance.

"I'm sure he has something in mind. After all, he had
a very good teacher." Master Den winked, sharing the
joke. He was, of course, that teacher, which didn't reassure Llesho at all.

Their horses awaited them at the rear of Shou's palace,
in a cobbled courtyard milling with servants and stable
hands, with friends staying behind and friends who would
continue the quest, though not as many of the latter as
Llesho had hoped to see. Kaydu was crying openly. Little
Brother, her monkey companion, offered what chittering
comfort he could from his perch on her shoulder.

"If I were a better witch, I could send an avatar of
myself to ride with you." She gave him a hug, which
dislodged Little Brother and made Llesho wish they *had*
been more than friends on the road.

"Her ladyship needs you here." He understood that.

Master Markko, the magician who had betrayed the empire to the Harn, had escaped: none of them were safe until he was found and taken prisoner. After Llesho, Kaydu and her father had more experience with the traitor's evil than anyone else alive.

"I'll come after you, when we find his trail," she assured Llesho. "The gods know that you can't take care of yourself on the road."

Llesho smiled weakly at the joke. He would have told her how the magician came to him in dreams and threatened all he loved, but they were only dreams and didn't change anything. "I'll watch for you along the way," he promised. He wished he'd had the nerve to ask ChiChu to watch out for her. Asking anything of the trickster god was . . . tricky . . . however, and secretly he had hoped the god of the laundry would come with him to Thebin.

"I'm letting you down again." Bixei kept himself a little apart from the crowd. Stipes, a patch over the empty socket where he'd lost an eye in battle, stood at his partner's side. Bixei wouldn't meet Llesho's gaze, but stared at his feet as if overcome by his own failure to put duty ahead of Stipes. "The old man needs me."

Stipes gave him a jab in the ribs. "I'm no old man, though I can't deny I need the young'un here." A smirk escaped him at the description, Bixei being no child but a young warrior, and himself still muscled from battle. But he admitted, half ashamed, "It tore my heart out when Lord Chin-shi sold him to her ladyship. Now that we are free, we'd not be split apart and, together, we'd be a hindrance to you. Who would hire a guard with just one eye?"

Llesho wanted to answer, "I will hire you, one eye or none," but he couldn't be that selfish. Stipes wasn't fit and the trek they had ahead of them might kill them all as it was.

"It's not like you have abandoned the fight," Llesho reasoned with him. "Shokar needs you to help train the recruits. You'll still be working against Markko and the Harn. And who knows? You may get a chance to save my ass again." Llesho smiled in spite of his anger. It wasn't Bixei or Stipes he was mad at.

Shokar wasn't coming either. With the slaves freed, the oldest of the seven exiled princes had set himself the task of finding their Thebin countrymen carried into bondage by the Harn. Bixei and Stipes would train the Thebin recruits into an army, and they would follow later, when, or "if," Shokar had said. He had escaped the Harn attack, being out of the country at the time, and had spent the years of exile as a farmer and a free man.

"If there are enough of us left to make a difference, we will follow.

"But there are a thousand li of Harn between Thebin and this, our only safe retreat. If we have to fight our way, march by march, there may not be enough of us left to do more than die on our own home soil."

Shokar had grieved for his brothers, but he had a family and a home in Shan, and he hadn't come looking in all the seasons that Llesho had suffered on Pearl Island.

He felt Shokar's absence at his side like a missing weapon. The ghost had told him to find his brothers. He was not sure it would be possible to take Thebin back from the Harn if they didn't stand together. But he could not change his brother's mind. And Shokar, who had wanted him to stay safe in Shan, would not watch him go.

Adar waited patiently, however, a hand on his mount's nose, and Lling and Hmishi both sat astride the sturdy little horses that had carried them from Farshore Province. Mara, who had traveled to battle in the belly of a dragon, had declared herself too old for such goings-on anymore. She had returned to her cottage in the woods with the explanation that adventures belonged to the young; the old needed more naps than a quest allowed. Her daughter, Carina, had joined them in her place, which suited Llesho just fine. During his recent convalescence, he'd had plenty of time to contemplate the color of her hair—the same burnished gold as the scales on the great back of her father, the Golden River Dragon—and her smile, which reminded him of her mother. Now he would have the weeks of their journey to debate the color of her eyes.

Shou hadn't come out to see them off. His ambassador had informed them that the emperor was occupied elsewhere. So, that was everybody. With a last look around to set the memory of old friends in a stolen moment of peace, Llesho raised himself onto his horse.

"It's time." With a jerk of his chin as farewell, he turned to the open gates. Adar moved up beside him, and Master Den took up a position on the other side, his stout walking stick in his hand.

"You don't think I'd send you off on your own, now, do you?" he asked gruffly. "Not after all the work I've put into you."

Some of the tightness over Llesho's heart loosened. *I can do this,* he decided. *We can do this.* "Let's go, then."

Chapter Two

WITH Carina and Hmishi in the lead, and Lling following at the rear, Llesho's party left the Imperial City of Shan by the kitchen gate at which they'd entered. He'd been asleep when they'd arrived, and it had been dark at the time, so the narrow, rutted supply lane that took them away from the palace came as a surprise. Apple trees crowded them on both sides, their branches growing so low in places that he had to lean over in his saddle to keep from hitting his head. The lush growth cooled their passage under the two full suns, but Llesho wondered at how poorly kept the road seemed.

"Not what you expected?" Master Den eyed the dense foliage with appreciation.

"I thought . . ." Llesho paused, trying to put those thoughts in order. He didn't want to criticize Shou, but he had to wonder what manner of leader would conscience such neglect at the very gates of his own palace. "I thought the empire was rich and prosperous. But this—"

"Who would believe such a ramshackle lane would lead one to the very heart of the empire, eh?" Master Den grinned as if he knew some hugely entertaining secret. "Wait a bit before you condemn our friend too severely."

They had journeyed no more than a li when they came to a crossing. Even paving stones, broken here and there by the roots of trees burrowing near the surface, showed that once the road had been better tended. Like the lane before it, however, the new road suffered from neglect.

The crossroad seemed to be a signal for their party to reshape itself. Hmishi left them with a word over his shoulder about scouting ahead. Llesho would have moved up to take his place next to Carina, but Master Den held to the bridle of his horse. Adar, however, had no such restraint. There he was, riding next to Carina as if it were the most natural thing in the world, and she was looking over at him and smiling. Llesho sneaked a glare at Master Den, who caught him at it with a trickster's gleam in his eyes. Fortunately, he didn't say anything.

"Where is everybody?" Lling had moved up to replace Adar at Llesho's side, and she cast a worried look about her. Fewer trees hemmed them in here, but where were the travelers?

"Do you think it's a trap?" Llesho's hand went to the sword at his side, reflexes honed in battle immediately on alert.

"This road sees more traffic at dawn," Master Den waved a hand at nothing in particular, as far as Llesho could see. "And sometimes, after dark."

"Spies?" Llesho asked. He knew the emperor's penchant for slipping out of the palace undetected, and for sneaking secrets in after dark.

"Maybe. But vegetables for certain, and rice and coal and perishables for the larder. You are on the kitchen road, after all, and most of its usual traffic is home growing the crops that will come through the gate when the daylight fails."

As an answer it almost made sense. But a few mo-

ments later a farmer passed them heading back the way
they had come with a wagonload of yams. The man had
an unusually military bearing for one of such lowly rank,
as did the herdsman they came upon who watched them
pick their way around half a dozen sheep milling in the
road. Both gave short bows to Llesho's party.

"They're not . . ."

Master Den twitched an eyebrow, but said only,
"Look—"

The road they followed ended, spilling into the great
Thousand Li Road to the West, and Llesho silently apologized for doubting Shou's powers as emperor. The
builders had drawn from quarries all across the empire
to construct a patchwork of colors and textures underfoot. The stones had been carefully dressed to fit together
smoothly, and Llesho realized that they'd been laid out
in a pattern of light and dark in grays and greens that
mimicked brush strokes on pale green paper.

"It's as wide as the market square in the city," Den
said, urging him forward. Transfixed, Llesho watched all
of Shan passing before him in the shadow of the Great
Wall of the imperial city. Traveling merchants and bellowing camels and covered wagons that served as homes
on wheels for the hapless souls who pulled them followed
the great trade road west. The emperor had released a
division of his regular militia for hire to the merchants
who rode or walked the Thousand Li Road. Even Stipes
might have felt at home among some of the more grizzled bands that marched purposefully forward to their
private cadences.

There should have been dust from the tramp of so
many feet, but the stones of the road showed patches of
damp where a sprinkler wagon had passed. On the far
side of the road the trees had thinned. Between them
Llesho could see softly rolling fields of green topped with
bright yellow flowers in rows like ribbons floating over
the dark brown earth.

On the near side, the city wall raised its massive stone shoulder high above his head. Each green block in the Great Wall would have come up to his chin if stood on end instead of lying on its side. He saw no mortar between the stones, but the wall didn't suffer for the lack—hardly a chink showed for as far as Llesho could see.

"Does this please you more, my prince?" Master Den asked, pausing only for an ironic bow as he walked.

"I take it all back," Llesho admitted, although he had spoken few of his doubts aloud.

Master Den looked very pleased, as if he were responsible himself for the Imperial Road. Which he might be, Llesho figured. If asked, the trickster god was as likely to lie about it as not, but one could never tell with a powerful being which way the lie would go. Would he claim a feat he hadn't performed, or deny a feat he had?

"It's a wonder," he finally offered. The god could take it as a comment or a compliment as he chose. It seemed the right thing to say, because Master Den's eyes twinkled with pleasure.

"Yes, it is. Travelers' tales mention the Thousand Li Road to the West as one of the great wonders of the world. The Great Wall of Shan they count as another. Three guards can walk abreast along the watch-path at the top, and a fast messenger can run from one end of the city to the other within the wall itself. There are cuts carved high overhead to give the inner passage light during the day, and torches light the way by night."

"Kungol had no wall." Llesho stared up at the mass of stone that towered over them. His mother and father might still be alive if they'd had any defenses at all. But Kungol was a holy city, her people given to prayer and meditation—and to the daily struggle to survive the barren, airless climate of the heights. They had not concerned themselves with battle strategy.

Master Den nodded, as if he followed all that Llesho did not say. Then he went on, telling a story as he had so many times in the laundry on Pearl Island. As he had back then, Llesho figured there was a lesson Den meant him to learn, and settled in to listen.

"Shan first rose as a city in the time of the great warlords, before there was an empire or an emperor," Master Den explained. "The lands that now make up the independent provinces of the empire waged war against each other. Thieves and bandits plundered their neighbors and dashed across each other's borders to safety, only to return the next time they got hungry. The warlords built their walled cities as a defense against each other and the bandits.

"Shan had won more of its battles than most, however, and for a while its ruthless warlords imposed their iron control over their own people and their surrounding neighbors. In the deceptive peace that followed, the city grew like wild blackberries outside the walls that were originally built to protect it. The old city inside the defenses turned to administration and governance and left the work of providing food and clothing and shelter to the provincial citizens who gathered at the foot of the Great Wall. The officials thought they were safe against any attack, but the seemingly impossible happened. Those neighboring warlords banded together against their more powerful oppressor. They burned the city that had grown up outside the walled defenses, but no fire or hurled stone or wizardry could penetrate the stones themselves.

"During the siege that followed, the barbarians attacked from the west—not the Harn, but the people we know as the Shan today. They drove back the warlords, but the wall still stood, protecting the rulers who cowered within. Fortunately—" Here, Master Den gave Llesho a hard-eyed glance, "—a wanderer among them knew the secrets of the tunnels through the city walls. By night the barbarians crept into the city. By morning they held it all and had driven out those comfortable ministers and politicians and false priests. Since that time, the wall has grown with the city. The old foundations make good roadbeds."

"I suppose it was the false priests who prompted the wanderer to reveal his secrets," Llesho gibed, more interested at the moment in the fall of the old city than the rise of the new. He had no doubt who that wanderer had been, almost expressed aloud the thought that crossed his mind—that only a fool would trust a trickster with the plans to one's defenses. Since he was doing the selfsame thing, he had to wonder if there was as much warning as history in the story.

Master Den fell still, a dark sorrow carving lines around his mouth. "Actually, it was the false generals. When the neighboring warlords put the new city to the flame, no general, no politician, nor any priest rode out to rescue their dying people. Armies, grown fat on the taxes of those tradesmen and skillsmiths, hid themselves behind their wall for protection while outside the children screamed and the mothers begged for help and with their husbands beat their lives out against the flames."

Llesho could hear the anguish of the parents, even the crackle of the flames. He could feel in his throat the cries of the children, and the tight pain of holding back his own screams, waiting for his moment. Almost he imagined the slick glide of blood on a fist much smaller than the one he clenched now, the knife slipping between ribs, and the raider falling under the weight of Llesho's seven summers. It hadn't been enough. They'd murdered his father, killed his sister and thrown her body on a pile of refuse like yesterday's garbage, scattered his brothers, and sold them into slavery. His beautiful, wise mother was gone, dead.

"What was Thebin's sin?" he asked, his voice rough as if he was still holding back his screams today. "What did we do that was so terrible that our country had to die?"

"Nothing." Master Den shook his head slowly from side to side, as if trying to rid himself of the taste of ash in his mouth. "Sometimes evil wins, that's all."

Sometimes, evil wins. Llesho stared up at the wall that marched beside them, li after li of stone between the city and the fields that stretched away from it. "When I am king, Kungol will have a wall, and watchful guards, and an army," he decided.

But posing as traders and merchants, the Harn had entered the imperial city through her open gates as easily as they had entered Kungol. The fields that lay around him might be put to the torch just like that long ago city. Master Den already knew, of course. A wall could imprison its builders inside their own fears, but it could not keep out a determined enemy.

"There has to be a way to protect my people, or why am I going back at all?" he demanded. The goddess' people. "If all I can do is bring more death, what is the point?"

Master Den gave him that scornful look that he'd seen too often in the practice yard. So he ought to know better. Fine. If he didn't get it, was it his fault, or his teacher's?

"What protects Shan?"

Not the wall.

The emperor. Emperor, general, trader, spy. Friend. Judge. Not the office, then. "Shou. Emperor Shou."

"What is in here—" Master Den placed a hand over his heart. "Not the robes, the man. Can you be that man, Llesho?"

"Not yet." He didn't speak his doubts aloud—Shou was twice Llesho's age, and he had a heart for adventure, while Llesho just wanted to go home—didn't want to make his fears real in the world, as speech would do. But Master Den knew the uncertainty that curled like a worm in his gut.

"You will be."

Llesho didn't trust that confident smile. Master Den was his teacher, but he was also the trickster god. And trusting Thebin's fate to such a god seemed . . . unwise. It worried him that he couldn't seem to help himself, though the story of the Great Wall warned him against trust. Finally he shook his head. The story would simmer in the back of his brain somewhere, until the moment when need and understanding came together.

The sun was warm on his skin, however, and if nothing else, Master Den's stories were good to pass the time. He realized that they'd been riding for several hours and, with a shiver, that the Great Wall of Shan still tracked them on their way. He'd known the imperial city was big, but he hadn't quite wrapped his mind around *how* big.

They were coming to an end, however. From a distance the sound of the caravansary drifted softly on the wind. The lowing of camels, and the clanging of their bells, the general uproar of drovers and grooms and loaders and merchants and acrobats and beggars released a flood of happy memories. Llesho urged his horse to a faster pace, leaving his teacher behind with his concerns about the future. Master Den dropped back to walk with Carina, who smiled her welcome while her horse continued its slow amble. Llesho felt a sudden flash of temper that confused him before the smells of camels and cooking and dust pushed whatever thought he'd started out of his mind. Adar caught up with him and rode at his side as he had when Llesho was a child, with Lling and Hmishi following tight on his tail. A stranger would have mistaken Adar for the focus of the guards' protection. Llesho himself did not realize that his brother, as well as his companions and his teacher, all set their guard for him.

Chapter Three

TUCKED behind a screen of slender pine trees at the side of the road, the first inn came into view. Then another, then both sides of the street were lined with stables and lodgings for the grooms who smelled like the stables and, beyond them, open fields of camels that smelled the worst of all. More than a thousand brown and tan hummocks dotted the landscape surrounding the caravanserai. Only their dignified heads rising on tall necks showed they were not themselves part of the rolling earth, but pack camels resting peacefully on the grasses of the pastureland.

A little farther on, the road widened into a market square much larger than the one inside the city walls where Llesho had battled Master Markko and his Harnish allies, but just as crowded. Food vendors hawked their sweet and savory wares behind counters decked with ribbons in the colors of their provinces. Scattered among the food shops, small traders called out prices from behind heaps of lesser grade silks and tin pots and incense, while street musicians and puppeteers vied for the dregs of the market-going pocketbooks. Just as Llesho had seen inside the city, however, great trading houses of dignity and power lined the square. Sturdy pillars carved from the trunks of fine hardwood trees framed these "temporary" residences of the wealthy merchants. Windows of real glass looked out onto the world of commerce, and silk banners with the names of their houses floated on the breeze in front of brass doors beaten in elaborate designs. One banner, over a house of modest design but elegant execution, said, "Huang Exotic Imports Exports" and Llesho wondered if the owner bore any relation to the emperor's minister, Huang HoLun.

At the backs of the great houses, along side streets wide enough to accommodate the flat carts used for moving merchandise, counting houses and storage warehouses and money-changing establishments rose in support of the wealth of the caravan merchants. Llesho mulled over Master Den's story about the fall of the old walled city as he guided his horse through the market. The settled part of the Imperial City of Shan now lay protected behind the great city wall, but too much of the wealth of the city had moved out among the inns and stables and marketplaces. As in the story of old, the caravanserai had become a city of its own sprawling into the countryside on the outside of Shan's defenses. He couldn't help but wonder if the emperor committed the same mistake as his ancestor. If he'd understood the story aright, though, Shou's ancestors had been the barbarian invaders, not the self-serving officials who had let their people die rather than risk battle.

As evening softened around them, the crowd thinned. Imperial citizens packed up their wares and returned to the illusion of safety within Shan's walls, leaving only the strangers to tend their camels and their trade. "The barbarian is once again at your gate," Llesho muttered to himself as he guided his horse around jugglers and past vendors who reached for his stirrup with bits of food upraised to tempt the traveler. "But this time he's brought his shop and money counter with him."

A hand brown as his own thrust at him with a skewer

of meat cooked over coals in the Thebin style. The wonderful smell of woodsmoke and food made his mouth water, but Llesho kept his head turned forward and gave no sign that he recognized what he was offered. Adar had the look of the North about him, and Llesho was supposed to be on guard. He stole a glance at the vendor as they passed, however, and bit back the disappointment when a lined old face he didn't know stared up at him. Foolish, to expect his brothers to fall over his horse on the road, especially on the caravan road at Shan. Shokar would have found any brother in the area. Still, he had hoped for a moment, and he felt the disappointment like a loss.

Adar led them to a small inn of modest frontage, suitable for one of careful means and a delicate nose. The sign on the door announced the inn as "Moon and Star: rooms to let by the evening." They entered through a small dining hall, much cheered by the thought of food and sleep. A window screened in oiled parchment let in the light but kept the dust of the road out of the public room, which was decorated in quiet tones of pine and oak polished to a respectable sheen.

The proprietor—Llesho identified him by the huge apron that wrapped twice around his thin form—dozed on a low padded bench in the corner. His occasional loud snorts interrupted the drone of his snoring, but his brood of energetic children seemed to manage perfectly well without his assistance. A girl about Llesho's age swept the rush mats scattered on a floor of wide, short boards while another with a few more summers scrubbed the small, low tables until they gleamed. A son with a round face and complacent smile stood duty at the taps, surrounded by the crockery and glassware of his profession. The inn offered no entertainment, but did a passable meat pie, so a comfortable number of the small tables were occupied.

Adar set his hands palm-down on the teak counter. "Two rooms, if you have them, and supper all around."

"Supper we have, for a fair price to any traveler." The tappy waved his hand at a small boy who scurried out from behind a folding screen with a tray of the richly seasoned pies. The boy delivered his steaming treasures to a table of hungry soldiers laughing in the corner and stopped for Adar's order. When he had disappeared again into the back of the inn, the tappy wiped his hands on his apron and considered the man sleeping in the corner.

"As for rooms, Pap has a caution, there, what with daughters in the house."

One of those daughters stole a glance at Adar and blushed before scurrying into the kitchen. Her step grew decidedly more pigeon-toed beneath her long wrapped tunic and dress. The tappy gave Adar a sharp look, but Adar smiled blandly, with no sign that he noticed the gentle suggestion in the girl's walk.

With a little shrug, the tappy made his decision: "The emperor trusts all of Shan to his militia, I suppose I can do no less with the inn. A quarter tael for pies and ale. Rooms are one tael, but there aren't two to let. If you take the one, you'll find clean covers and a fresh mattress. If your guards wish to hire companionship, they will have to look elsewhere, however, as this inn does not provide such entertainments." Llesho suspected that the pigeon-toed young daughter feathered her nest with the gifts of her admirers, but said nothing of this to her brother, who continued to explain the house.

"We have four rooms occupied besides your own, all men and one room a large party, so your lady should not go wandering during the night." He gestured at Carina when he spoke. Whether he did not know that Lling was also female, or assumed that she could handle any unwanted attentions from fellow lodgers, Llesho couldn't quite tell. Neither could Lling, whose expression closed down while she tried to figure out if she should consider the omission an insult or a compliment.

"Your man sleep in the stables?"

The innkeeper jerked his chin in Master Den's direction, and Llesho bristled at this casual dismissal. *This is no servant but a god,* he thought, *and you are not worthy to serve him in your house. Pray he doesn't curse your pies with burned bottoms for your insolence.* But he knew their safety depended upon the ruse.

Adar had a cooler head, and a purse to back his demands, however. "I am never parted from my servant, or my apprentice," he insisted blandly.

"Of course, my good sir." The tappy shrugged a shoulder—the ways of foreigners were no concern of his—and led them to a pair of low tables inlaid with elaborate leaf swirls of black and red lacquer. The three guards and the "servant" he directed to one table. The master and his apprentice shared the second.

From where he sat, Llesho could scan the entire public house, and he did so carefully, noting patrons scattered through the room as varied as the milling crowd outside. The table at their right was unoccupied. On Adar's left several burly men dressed in modest but well-repaired coats and breeches, and with a family resemblance about the eyes, dug into a dinner of eel pie in thick green gravy. In the far corner, two men with golden skin and dark hair shared a table. The younger reminded him of Bixei, and he wondered how his sometimes friend was faring on Shokar's farm. He shivered in spite of himself when his gaze fell upon the older man, who might have been Master Markko himself, except for the scar that crossed his face, and the humor that lit his eyes. Master Markko had never smiled, never laughed like that, in all the time Llesho had known him. But the presence of members of the magician's race at the inn reminded Llesho that his enemies could likewise travel in disguise.

Llesho and his friends were the only Thebins, but not the only patrons who wore the imperial uniform, although they were the youngest and wore insignia of the lowest rank. Several widely scattered tables of officers sat with dignity in quiet conversation over their dinners.

As Llesho's gaze passed over them, each officer's table paused in mid-word or bite to return his study before picking up their own business. Adar's presence as their employer explained why a table of young recruits might stop at an inn that would exceed their pocketbooks and sorely disappoint their search for the pleasures of the caravan marketplace. If deeper calculation went on behind those experienced eyes, they gave no evidence of it.

A boy and a girl each wearing a brightly patterned apron moved about their tables to offer water for washing and warm towels for drying their hands and faces before they began their dinner. The servers departed again, the boy to disappear behind a painted screen that hid the door to the kitchen. He returned with a tray full of pies. Eel had given way to a filling of questionable ancestry that took a bit of chewing, but the roots used for flavoring had a savor to them that brought tears to the eye and a smile to the lip.

"Wine, sir?" The tappy had returned with two small earthen vessels filled with wine in one hand and a candle set in a small wire basket in the other. He set one crock of wine on the table between the guards—they must content themselves with cold wine. To Adar he gave a bow calculated to the station he had measured them to fit, and set the wire basket on the table. The girl lit the candle, and her brother the tappy set the wine vessel into the basket which held the earthen base just above the flame.

"And some cider for the ladies," Adar amended. Lling, of course, would drink as much wine as any of the men at the table, while Llesho preferred cider. He had already scandalized the house by sitting down to supper with his servants, however, and felt no need to burden the kitchen boy with this intelligence. As they settled to demolishing their own dinners, a rumble of voices filled the open door of the public room.

". . . slaves . . . trade . . ."

The Harn who piled into the public room wore native

dress, still red with the dust of the grasslands. Secure
in the knowledge that no one so far from Harn would
understand their language, the traders went on with their
animated argument, speaking freely among themselves.

". . . dead . . . money . . ."

They were almost right. Llesho had never learned
more than a few words of Harnish, but picking the few
he did know out of the conversation in the doorway sent
a chill down his spine. Now that Shan had outlawed the
sale of prisoners in the slave market, the Harnishmen
had to decide between smuggling in the illegal slave market or finding a new business. Their debate seemed to
hinge more on the penalties for breaking the law than
any change of heart about the trade.

Unconsciously, Llesho's fingers went to his knife. Before he could draw, however, a larger hand wrapped his
own. Master Den held him firmly but gently in place,
giving him a twitch of his head imperceptible to anyone
but Llesho, who knew his teacher's methods very well.
"Not now," that almost not there gesture said, and "No
danger . . . yet." Harn on the attack would approach
with greater caution. Llesho relaxed back into his seat, a
wait and see promise in his eyes that satisfied his teacher.

When Master Den removed his hand, Llesho's awareness opened up to take in the silent room around him.
All attention was concentrated upon the strangers. Terrified, the innkeeper's daughter gasped and dropped the
empty wine jug she had collected from their table. The
crash of breaking crockery snapped the attention of the
room like the crack of a whip.

They don't know who we are, Llesho repeated silently
to reassure himself. *They can't know who we are. They
carry the dust of the eastern road on their clothes and
could not have been in Master Markko's army when he
attacked.* The leader among them said something in his
own language, out of which Llesho caught the word for
a child-slave and another that meant incompetent soldier,
but he gave no sign that he recognized the Thebins in

their militia uniforms by anything more than their nationality. His comrades' answering laughter died, however, when the senior militia men began, one by one, to rise from their seats.

"We are full up, gentlemen," the innkeeper informed them with a shaky voice and a desperate glance at the scattered soldiers coming to attention throughout the public room. "And we have just run out of pies."

The leader of the small group considered the innkeeper's words and the battle-nervy veterans ranged against him. "We are not welcome here," he conceded. "We will bother you no further." Raising his hands to show that he was weaponless, he gestured to his companions. Following his lead, they made a solemn bow to the room and filed out of the inn much more quietly than they had come. Once outside, the argument began again, this time in grimmer tones. Llesho heard only well remembered curses that faded as the party moved away.

"They will find no warmer welcome anywhere in Shan Province," a grizzled old soldier asserted from the corner. "Treacherous bastards will sleep with the camels tonight."

Agreement murmured throughout the public room and Adar seized the moment of camaraderie with the poise of an accomplished liar—a skill Llesho had never known him to possess.

"Probably looking for protection," he sniffed, "As if a decent goddess-loving man would attach his party to the company of barbarians!"

This brought a laugh from the room, as Adar was taken for a fool who did not know how useless his youthful guards would be.

"It's no cause for laughter," Adar chided them. "I have purchased the services of the empire's great militia to protect myself and my apprentice on the journey and already they have served me well—note how our intruders withdrew upon recognizing the military presence in this room. With such success I should have no trouble

in trading their services to a likely merchant in exchange
for passage with a party heading West by the southern
route.

"Though not," he added, "a Harnish party."

Someone at a nearby table snorted his disbelief, and
Llesho tried to look both foolish and attentive as an
untried cadet might. He noticed bland calculation in the
eyes of the officers, however. The danger, if it existed,
came from the men who did not doubt at all the skill of
Adar's young cadets, but wondered what experience they
might have gained in the recent battle with the Harn.

By the time the broken wine jug had been swept away
and a new one brought, the soldiers in the room had
returned to their pies, Adar and his young company just
a lingering joke among them. The barkeep kept his opinion to himself, but offered what assistance he could to
his customer:

"You've come to the right place, if you are looking to
hook up with a caravan party, stranger." He wiped his
hands absently on his apron, lost in a moment of calculation. "There are two such caravans forming now for the
high mountain passes in the west. Bargol Shipping is first
out tomorrow morning. Old Bargol takes the long way
round, through Sky Bridge Province and down the Thousand Peaks Mountains, but you'll be wanting to talk to
the agent who deals for Huang Exotic Imports Exports,
I think. Huang's caravans take a more direct route. They
sometimes cross into the Harnlands in bad seasons, but
not so far as to expect trouble. Huang agents favor this
inn, the Moon and Star, so you are in the right place."

Huang. Llesho had met an ambassador Huang HoLun
at the border between Thousand Lakes and Shan Province, right after the emperor, in one of his many disguises, had brought Shan's provincial troops to their aid
in battle against Master Markko. Master Jaks had died
there. Llesho did not believe in coincidences, so he was
not surprised when the barman added,

"Just this afternoon I overheard a trading man with

twelve camels and three horses who said he wished to travel with the Huang caravan to Guynm. You're too late to talk to him tonight, but he expressed an interest in obtaining protection for the journey."

Adar did not believe in coincidences either, and he was prepared with his foolishly eager expression to inquire, "Do you know if he has already engaged suitable guardsmen for his journey?"

"I can't rightly say. You might ask him yourself. He has a room upstairs for the night. You will have the room next to his and can make your own arrangements as you wish."

Adar offered his thanks to the barkeep, who scurried away with a word for the serving lad to show them their room.

Lling watched him leave with a worried frown. "I'll bed down with the horses," she said. "Those Harnish traders might come back and try something while the inn is asleep."

Hmishi shook his head. "I'll do it. You should stay close to Carina, for propriety. We don't want the innkeeper telling tales after we leave." He gave her a rueful smile of farewell, and was gone before the innkeeper's son returned.

Chapter Four

"FIRE! Fire!"

The dreams latched onto the frantic voices, heat of remembered wounds painting orange flickers behind his eyelids. Then a hand grabbed his shoulder and shook it.

"Llesho! Wake up!"

He flinched awake at Adar's voice to find his brother still shaking him. "What?" But he didn't need an answer. Light and shadow danced on the walls in the unmistakable pattern of fire. Bells clanged in the courtyard, and someone pounded urgently on a door.

"The stables are on fire," Adar explained while he tore through his pack, shifting ointments and cloths into a smaller sack.

Hmishi had been sleeping in the stables.

Llesho, reacting with the speed of his military training, was up and dressed by the time his brother straightened with his healer's bag ready in his hand.

"Where is Master Den?" Llesho asked as he belted on his sword. Lling was already heading out the door with Carina on her heels, but the trickster was nowhere to be seen.

"He left while I was trying to wake you."

The dream hadn't wanted to let go.

Adar grabbed up some additional supplies for tending burns, and they ran for the door.

"That way!" The innkeeper stood at the head of the staircase that led to the public room, but he was pointing in the other direction, to a door at the far end of the hall. "Able-bodied men to the courtyard!"

To help fight the fire. Llesho turned to go, but Adar grabbed his sleeve. "Injured?" he asked, holding up his healer's supplies.

The innkeeper moved aside. "Below,"

Adar pulled Llesho after him. "I need you here."

"No, you don't." He stopped, refusing the offered protection, and whispered urgently. "What kind of king rides from a crisis?"

"Survive long enough to *be* king and we'll discuss it." It was really no argument at all. They both knew safety was an illusion, and they had attracted the notice of the innkeeper, who strained forward in an attempt to eavesdrop on the argument.

"I have to go." Llesho freed his sleeve and ran. He'd apologize later, after he'd found Hmishi.

He'd thought that in the Long March and in the battles against Master Markko he'd experienced the worst that the gods could throw at him. When he tumbled, running, into the courtyard of the inn, Llesho realized that he'd been wrong. Fire was the Devourer, more terrifying by far. Searing heat burned the sweat from his body, leaving him dry and blistering, sucking the superheated air out of his lungs and burning when he managed to gulp a gasping breath.

The stable was engulfed in sheets of orange-and-blue flame that towered high in a moon-drenched sky, roaring like a typhoon. Timbers exploded, sent sparks rocketing into the night sky, falling back to earth in showers that landed on the roof of the inn and on the firefighters toiling in the face of the destruction. They'd given up on saving the stable; brigades of bucketeers worked frantically to wet down the red clay tiles of the inn's roof and

to put out the fires that smoldered in the bits of straw
and debris scattered in the courtyard.

Reacting to the maddened cries of the horses and more
purposeful calls directing the bucket brigade, Llesho
quivered with battle nerves. Tensed, he waited only for
a order to unleash action.

"Here, boy, grab a bucket!"

He knew that voice—it got him moving again toward
the lines of men and women hauling water from the well.
A bucket found his hands, was passed on, replaced by
another. He fell into the rhythm of the brigade, freeing
his mind to wonder if the voice that set him to work had
been a figment of his imagination. Needing a com-
mander, had his mind supplied the voice that he would
follow? If not, what was the emperor of all of Shan doing
in the courtyard of a moderately priced inn on the great
caravan road to the West? And what did Shou's presence
have to do with the fire blazing at his back? He couldn't
very well ask the camel driver who handed him the next
bucket, or the innkeeper's daughter, who took it and
passed it on.

Shou himself was nowhere in sight or hearing, and
gradually, the strain on Llesho's arms and the heat on
his back grew to fill all the space his mind had for thinking. He became a blank, moving out of habit when his
mind abandoned the field. He'd go on until the bucket
ceased to find his hand or he dropped where he stood.
Or until somebody pulled him out of line and handed
him a cup of water.

"Rest," Shou told him. Llesho blinked, realizing only
then that the red haze flung against the smoky cloud
was the dawn. The stable had sunk to blackened ruin,
shattered support beams lying at crazy angles in the ash.

"Hmishi?" Llesho asked over his cup of water. "He
was sleeping out here."

"He's around somewhere," Shou told him, "and well
enough to rouse the house with the alarm."

Llesho craned his neck, but couldn't make out anyone he knew in the milling throng of dazed firefighters.

"Let's get you inside, let Adar have a look at those hands—"

Llesho dropped his gaze to stare at his hands. "I'll be fine," he dismissed his injuries. They could have been a lot worse, but some of his calluses had torn. Blood seeped around the edges of blisters he would have thought it impossible to raise on hands so used to weapons craft.

"You can't hold a sword, let alone fight with one, in that condition."

True enough. He was just so tired. "Okay."

Shou hadn't waited for his answer. With a firm grip on his shoulder, the emperor of Shan was guiding him through the milling crowd, into the public room where Carina and Adar had set up their aid station. Hmishi was already there, getting a bandage for his forehead while Lling fussed at his side.

"What happened to you?" Llesho asked, just as Hmishi said the same thing. Relief as much as anything else made them both laugh.

"You first," Llesho insisted. "What happened out there?"

Hmishi shot a wary glance at Shou, and then answered with a deliberate misunderstanding of the question. "A bit of flying debris hit me in the head—cut and cauterized at the same time—Carina just had to clean it up a bit. What about you?"

Llesho held up his hands, his tired mind catching up at last. Someone had burned down the stables. They'd nearly killed Hmishi, and might have intended to murder everyone sleeping at the inn. And whoever did it might be hiding among the victims.

"That's nothing," Hmishi boasted.

"It needs some salve and a bandage nonetheless," Adar interrupted their conversation, drawing Llesho over

to the table where his supplies were laid out. He gently
cleaned the blisters while Hmishi and Lling watched with
detached interest.

"You should have seen my head before Carina put
that bandage on it," Hmishi continued his boasting.

"Fortunately, it was your head, and nothing important." Lling snickered, but her eyes hadn't cleared of
their panic.

"How is he really?' Llesho asked her. He wanted to
know, but he was equally grateful for the distraction.
Adar was cutting away dead skin, cleaning back to the
healthy flesh. He winced, but didn't miss Lling's helpless shrug.

"What happened?"

"He was unconscious when I found him. I thought, at
first, that he was dead."

"Then I woke up." Hmishi poked experimentally at
his bandage, unhappy at the result.

"You scared me!" Lling punched him on the shoulder
and Hmishi had the good sense to look contrite.

"I won't do it again."

"You'd better not!"

"You're done." Adar tied off Llesho's bandage with a
flourish. "Someone else can keep watch for a while. The
master of this house will reopen for business soon, and
I want you both to go upstairs and get some sleep."

Llesho nodded, wanting nothing more than a bed or a
bit of floor to sleep on. Shou was coming toward them,
however, wearing robes well made and of fine cloth, but
in the plain Guynmer style. His apparent wealth had
come down several notches from the elegant dress of a
Shan merchant he had used to travel undetected through
the streets of his own imperial city. He gave Adar a
little bow of politeness between not-quite equals with the
blandly purposeful expression that caused his opponents
to seriously underestimate his intelligence.

"If you have a moment, healer, I have business I wish
to discuss. We may converse in my room?"

"I—" Adar hesitated briefly before returning the bow. "Yes, of course—"

"Then, if you are finished here, my man will find something to temper our thirst."

It did seem, then, that the worst of the injured had been cared for. Grooms and servants who had fled their beds in the stables were finding corners to curl up in for a few hours of sleep before the first wave of customers dislodged them in the morning. Adar packed up his sack, but a last look around the room for any wounded who had been overlooked reminded Llesho that he hadn't seen Master Den since he'd woken up to find that the fire was real this time.

"Where . . . ?"

There he was, coming toward them with long, sure strides, trailing a stranger in his wake. He didn't stop at the aid station, but passed them, presenting the stranger to Shou.

"This is the man I mentioned to you." Master Den bowed to Shou with scarcely a hint of irony. "May I recommend to you Harlol, a Tashek camel drover out of the Wastes. His master lost much of his load in the fire, and so he seeks a new position."

"I have a drover," Shou answered slowly. Like Llesho, he studied Den's face for a sign of what was expected of him. Unlike Llesho, the necessity of doing so set his mouth in a thin line of annoyance.

Harlol bowed deeply and spoke up for himself. "Not anymore. Your man was seen running away from the stables. I don't think he'll be back."

"He wasn't chased by a Tashek drover by any chance?"

"None that I saw, good sir." He couldn't have missed Shou's meaning, but Harlol met the emperor's gaze with a level innocence that Llesho didn't trust at all.

Shou, however, was looking at Master Den, not the Tashek drover. Master Den gave him a slow, lazy blink that said nothing useful.

"On your head be it," Shou answered the unspoken challenge in a tone that said more clearly than words how much he doubted the wisdom of trusting the trickster.

But Master Den grinned and bowed and clapped a hand on the drover's back. "There you are. Didn't I say it would work out?"

Harlol wriggled out of the trickster's grasp to give Shou a bow even deeper than Master Den's and with a great deal less irony evident. "I will make my bed among the camels, since your man no longer tends them."

"Indeed." Shou dismissed the man with a warning glare at Master Den. Bowing hospitably, he led his guest's entourage to a room next down the hall from the one where they had begun the night.

"Come in," Shou said, "I won't keep you long, but we have to talk." The emperor stepped aside and Hmishi entered first, blocking the doorway until he passed a quick glance over the room in search of an ambush. When he gave the "all clear," Llesho entered, with Carina, Master Den, and Lling right behind him. Adar entered last and closed the door tightly after them.

A brass lantern from Shou's travel pack lit the room, where a man in the tunic and breeches of a servant busied himself setting out a camp chair for his master. Llesho noticed that, in spite of his low station, he carried himself with the bearing and muscles of a soldier.

"Sento," the emperor called. Ignoring the camp stool, he made himself comfortable on the rug spread out on the floor, squatting on his haunches in the Guynmer style. "Bring a bottle, please, and cups from my pack."

"Yes, sir." Well trained or unaware, Sento gave no sign that he guarded an emperor. He dug into a pile of rugs and tents heaped in the corner and returned bearing not one bottle but two, and a stack of small tin cups. Llesho hesitated, unsure how much the servant knew or how to begin the conversation they needed to have.

"What are you doing here?" he finally asked, leaving

it to the emperor to specify. He'd grown accustomed to speaking to Shou as the disguise of the moment called for, rather than with the formal court address due an emperor. Even when he hadn't figured out exactly what the disguise was. Then he thought about the standard saddle pack and larger bundle of tents and rugs of a caravan merchant dropped in the corner.

"*You* are the trader with twelve camels?"

"Of course. Who else could I trust to see you to the border?"

Llesho remembered his earlier question—where would the emperor find a trader foolish enough to take on three Thebin pearl divers as his only protection on the Thousand Li Road to the West. The answer, he realized, had a Shou sort of logic.

While Llesho dealt with his shock, the servant filled the tin cups and took up his position outside the door.

Hmishi made as if to follow. "How much do you trust him?"

"Enough. Sento has accompanied me before," Shou motioned them to take a seat. "No one will overhear us while he guards our door."

Llesho wasn't ready to trust the man—servant or soldier—yet. Master Den had already seen one of the emperor's party acting suspiciously. But then, trusting the trickster didn't make a lot of sense either. He was confusing himself, so he took a drink to settle his nerves and puckered up like a fish.

"Cider," Shou explained. "As a Guynmer trader, I honor the beliefs of that place, and neither serve nor indulge in spirits."

Llesho generally liked cider, had been drinking it with his dinner in fact. The Guynmer sort had a sour bite to it, though, and Llesho set aside the cup after just a couple of mouthfuls. He had too many questions to get through before he fell over, and he was in no mood to play Shou's spy games—not even with the cider.

"We could have been killed tonight."

"That's always a possibility," Shou agreed at his most irritating.

"Are we up against a plot to harm the empire?" Hmishi asked, almost hopefully, it seemed. That, at least, would mean it hadn't been meant for Llesho. Since he seemed to be asking the right questions, Llesho let him take the lead.

"What about that man Master Den saw running away from the fire? I saw him, too—didn't know he was yours, but he certainly wanted to put as much distance as possible between himself and the burning stable."

"He was mine, all right." Shou punctuated his assertion with an emphatic nod. "And with any luck he has made his way back to the palace, where he will advise the Lady SienMa of what has occurred here."

"Oh." Hmishi looked from the emperor to the trickster god and back again. "Master Den knew that?"

"Probably," Shou admitted.

"So you must have wanted this man Harlol for some reason."

"Not that I knew."

Master Den interrupted with a sigh. "Yes, I recognized an intelligence officer when I saw one. But we were still left without a camel drover. The Tashek are famous for their way with the miserable beasts, otherwise they're pretty mysterious. I thought it would be interesting to have one around."

Picking the elements of truth out of that story would take more time than it was worth. Llesho figured that Master Den had some reason for wanting the drover in their party, and the emperor seemed to have decided to let further explanations wait as well.

"Did you find out who set the fire, or why?" Shou asked the trickster god.

"Take your pick." Master Den shrugged, denying higher knowledge of events. "The Harn who came in earlier in the evening might have wanted revenge for their hostile reception, or they may have recognized Llesho and used the fire to create a distraction, hoping to snatch him for the magician in the confusion. Or it might have been a personal vendetta having nothing to do with the Harn or our party. More than one merchant had stored his goods under the stable roof. It could have been a competitor, or even an accident with an unstable element in the trade goods." The trickster's eyes twinkled with mischief at the last possibility, but they all agreed to ignore the awful pun.

"If we wait to find out more, we'll raise suspicions about ourselves." Lling didn't look happy about her contribution to the debate, but there didn't seem to be much point in objecting.

"I guess if it happens again, it's us, and if the trouble stops here, it's not." Llesho didn't look any more convinced than his companions, and Master Den stated the obvious:

"We are bound to meet trouble on the road, whether or not it has anything to do with tonight."

"Her ladyship will not let it be," Shou assured them. "If we are in danger from this, she'll find a way to warn us."

That pretty much ended the conversation for the moment. But Llesho wasn't finished with his questions for the emperor.

"I would have thought you were needed in the imperial city," he hinted.

"The Lady SienMa sits on the throne in my place." The emperor's eyes seemed to focus far from the room in which they sat, and Llesho wondered about that meeting, and what had put the mortal goddess of war in command of an empire. Shou gave his head a shake, clearing it of the thoughts he kept to himself. "Markko and his followers proved the empire has taken its own power too much for granted. Harnish war bands came into the imperial city from somewhere."

Llesho knew that—they'd both suffered losses in the

recent fighting, and the emperor's habit of traveling his empire incognito was one of Shan's few closely guarded secrets. In his many disguises, Shou heard and saw much that would otherwise remain hidden from an emperor. It didn't explain what he was doing on the caravan road this time, however.

"But why Guynm?" Llesho had no choice. The northern passage through the Gansau Wastes was impassable even in early summer. Already the springs and watering holes that made the trek possible just after the winter thaw would have dried up. Even the nomadic Tashek people, who clung to the brief-lived oases in the spring, would have packed up their tents and moved farther south, searching for water.

Like the route out of Guynm, the Sky Bridge Road led south before turning west to the passes above Kungol. Longer than either the passage through the Gansau Wastes or through Guynm and the Harnlands, Sky Bridge was considered the safest route precisely because the Harn had no trading presence there. If they were going to find his brothers, however, they needed to go where the Harn had been. And that meant Guynm, whether they liked it or not. But Shou had no such constraints. Taking a sip of his drink, however, the emperor explained:

"Guynm is Shan's most vulnerable border with the Harnlands. If Guynm Province falls, the empire stands open to its very heart. The Imperial Gaze has fallen elsewhere too long—it's past time I took a look."

Adar frowned, troubled. "So what are we likely to find when we reach Guynm?"

"If we're lucky, a stalwart governor and a Thebin prince or two, happy reunions, and a formal visit. Then I return to Shan in state, and you continue your journey."

The emperor gave a little shrug, as if to acknowledge his own doubts. "It is more likely that we will find a province that clings to the empire by a thread while it takes care to see nothing when Harnish raiding parties pass through. But I didn't expect trouble this soon."

The plan made sense if one assumed they didn't carry the spies and saboteurs with them. That wasn't a certainty right now. Llesho decided he should object, just as soon as he managed to pry his eyelids open again.

Adar's voice distracted him from his efforts to look alert. "More discussion can wait. If we are to be ready to go, we all need an hour or two of sleep."

Llesho agreed. His fingers and toes seemed to be a long way off and the distance between filled with a mist where his body ought to be.

"Help me get Llesho into his bed before he falls asleep where he sits," he added, and muttered, "I knew he wasn't ready to travel."

Llesho dragged his eyes open enough to catch a bleary glimpse of Master Den looking back at him. Then Adar had his left elbow and Carina his right, and he discovered that his legs did still work even if they didn't feel connected to his body. Before he knew it he was in their own room—he could tell because he recognized the baggage heaped behind a screen like the one in Shou's chamber. Then Adar was tilting him onto the bed and he let himself fall into the stiff mattress. Adar tucked in beside him with a kiss on the forehead and a quick prayer for a peaceful night.

Lucky for them that they journeyed with a god. Their prayers had so little distance to travel. The thought drifted away into the dark of Llesho's sleep. In his dream it was his seventh summer, and he lay in his small bed in the shadow of the great mountains of the gates of heaven, listening to the call of the caravans. His body remembered the thin air and the smell of pack ice melting on a summer breeze in the great passes to the West, and he struggled against the heavy air of the lowlands.

"Mother!" he called in his sleep, in the high tongue of Thebin.

"Hush. Hush." Adar's hand stroked a cool path across his forehead. It was okay if Adar was there. He'd be safe. He slept.

Chapter Five

"OH, GODDESS!" Llesho woke with a snap just as the first rays of the great sun gilded the windowsill. He didn't notice the second sunrise, however, but made a dive for his travel pack, berating himself under his breath for how stupid he'd been the night before.

"Llesho? What's wrong?" Standing guard at the door, Lling came to attention with her sword in hand. Urgency sharpened her voice, waking the rest of their party who felt about them for their weapons. But there was no enemy to fight.

"We're not under attack," Llesho assured them, "at least not right now. But we forgot to consider a possible motive for the fire last night—" He dug into his pack, searching for the gifts that her ladyship had given him on the road from Farshore.

Master Den rose and stretched, the tips of his thick fingers brushing the ceiling at its highest peak. "You mean, that Master Markko might have wanted to clear the inn so that his thieves could have a go at your luggage?" he asked as he watched Llesho scramble on the floor.

"Do you think I'm wrong?"

"Not necessarily." The trickster god shrugged off the

question. "No matter the diversion, however, the emperor would never have left these rooms unguarded. Luckily for Sento, the fire didn't take the inn as well as the stables."

Llesho shuddered. He'd known the man was more than a servant, knew that as soldiers they might all be called on to give their lives in battle. The idea that Shou's man might have stood fast, burning with the inn rather than abandoning his post, brought back memories of his own personal guard dying on the sword of a Harn raider in Llesho's seventh summer. He didn't want the people around him dying to protect his life and property, but it was going to get worse the closer they got to Thebin.

He found the wrapped shapes in his pack and pulled them out, took off their bindings to make sure that they were indeed safe. The jadeite bowl, a wedding gift in a former life, he took in his hands and turned in the morning light. Captured by the warm gleam of promises shining through the translucent jade, he spent a moment in quiet study. Something stirred in the back of his mind, like old forgotten memories, but they refused to come into clear focus. Wondering about its secrets, he set the bowl back in its wrappers and grasped the short spear by the shaft. The weapon had taken his life once and still thirsted for his blood. He hated the thing, but it came to his hand with the easy fit of long usage, and he marveled over how natural it felt there.

Master Den nodded at the spear. "Markko will know the legends. He'll want the spear because it is supposed to hold a deadly power over the king who wields it. That power goes two ways, however. You injured him with it before. Like yourself, he's had to heal, and he'll be wondering what control you now hold over the weapon."

Llesho hadn't considered that the bond might influence the weapon, but he *had* hurt the magician with it. Markko would be wondering, now. He'd want to protect himself from the legendary spear as much as to turn it against Llesho.

"We can use that," he said, and set the spear aside to carry on the road.

"If you're right that Markko is behind this—" Adar gestured at the window which opened onto the ash-drifted courtyard, "—carrying that thing openly will look like a direct challenge."

"And?" Llesho gave his brother a level stare.

Adar tilted his head back, eyes closed, and heaved a frustrated sigh. To Llesho's annoyance, Carina rested her hand on his brother's arm. "Adar is only worried about your safety."

The healer opened his eyes with a grateful smile. "Of course. How can we keep you safe, Llesho, if you make yourself a target?"

"Master Markko knows I have the spear. That makes me a target already. If he considers me a threat as well, it will slow him down, make him cautious, and that can work to our advantage."

"Listen to your king," Master Den interrupted before the disagreement could grow any more heated. "When it comes to a contest, we have to know which will rule— the weapon or the boy. Better to find out now than at the very gates of heaven."

"We need a living king, not a dead sacrifice," Adar snapped, though he let Carina soothe him.

"I don't intend to let it kill me." Llesho rose from his place on the floor with the spear in his right hand. His left he wrapped around the three black pearls—gifts of goddess and ghost and dragon—in the small leather pouch that lay on his breast. Hmishi and Lling gave Adar a polite bow, but followed Llesho from the room without a word or question, which seemed to please the trickster god immensely. Finally, with Carina's encouragement, Adar surrendered, bringing up the rear with a last objection: "We are going to regret this."

Llesho knew that, he just didn't see a lot of options. He wondered if he might win Carina's sympathy with the admission, but he didn't want her pity, and wouldn't accept it as a substitute for the care she seemed to offer his brother. So, he chided himself, chalk up another one to experience—or lack of same—and get your butt moving before the caravan leaves without you.

In the night, the fire that had burned the stables of the Moon and Star Inn had seemed all consuming, and Llesho'd expected signs of the disaster all over the caravanseray. Except for a thin gray mist that seemed to leave a gritty coat over everything, however, the broad square bustled with its daily business as if nothing had happened. Huang agents pushed their way through the crowd, bargaining final agreements while a thousand camels, annoyed to be rousted from their pastures and hemmed in on every side by the inns and counting houses and storehouses, milled and bellowed and spat thick, stinking gobs at their handlers. Drovers cursed their animals in a dozen languages, their voices blending with the shouted commands of the merchants and the smell of dusty camel and incense and bits of meat roasting on sticks. Through it all cut the high tenor clang of camel bells on harnesses and the deeper call of brass pots clattering where they were tied along the sides of the camel packs.

Surrounded by the familiar uproar of caravans gathering for the journey to the West, Llesho found himself caught up in memories both old and new—the present overload of sensation colliding with the memories of the great plaza of Kungol, where the caravans paused before daring the high mountain passes. Suddenly, images of the Harn raiders attacking the palace and killing everyone he knew mixed in his tired mind with the chaos of the night spent fighting the fire, freezing him in mid-stride. But Lling and Hmishi flanked him, their mouths hanging open and their eyes wide and shining.

The two ex-slaves had come to Shan from the poorest of the outlying farms of Thebin, packed in carts for the journey among the dour and threatening Harnish raiders. Nothing in their past, not even the marketplace at the center of Shan, had prepared them for the smells and sounds and crush, the sheer excitement of the greatest caravan staging area of the Shan Empire. Although they maintained the proper positions to guard Adar and Carina at the center of their party, they would convince no one who saw them now of their battle-hardened competence.

Their wonder was contagious, and Llesho caught their excitement, letting go of the past to grin back at them through the uproar. They might have stood there longer, gaping like bumpkins, but Emperor Shou's voice cut like a scythe through the din: the three cadets followed the sound of his curses down the slowly untangling line.

"Tighten that strap! Can't you see that beast is blowing out his ribs? We won't get two li down the road before he dumps five hundred tael of silk and pigments in the dirt!"

Experienced drovers looked up from their own work to watch the show, sneering behind their hands and with their own rude suggestions. The emperor nudged aside an inexperienced young groom and poked the camel in the ribs. The animal complained with a bellow, but his barrel grew noticeably thinner. Shou tugged on the cinch with a sure and practiced hand while he cursed, "The damned camel is smarter than you are."

If not for their meeting in Shou's rooms the night before, Llesho would have sworn the Guynmer trader with the dull clothes and the sharp tongue was a stranger with a vague likeness to the emperor. He even spoke differently, his voice higher and accented with the brisk twang of Guynm Province, though he hadn't changed his name.

"Shou, like the emperor," he announced, clasping Adar's arm as if they'd just met.

Llesho thought his heart would stop on the spot. The logical part of his mind knew that few of the emperor's

subjects had ever seen their monarch, except in the ceremonial mask he wore on state occasions. But the battle-
scarred part of him that sent Llesho skittering for cover
whenever a servant dropped a tray reminded him that
Markko's spies could be anywhere. At any moment he
expected a pointed arm and a raised voice from among
the camel drivers and hangers-on, exposing their true
identities to the bustling crowd. Sento, Shou's personal
servant and equally disguised guardsman, rolled his eyes
behind his master's back, however, and the drivers and
laborers smirked their sympathy.

"And I'm the Golden River Dragon," muttered a passing drover in a sarcastic aside. This was an old masquerade, then, taken up with the skill of a true caravanner
at the emperor's need. His servants had heard the story
many times, had grown weary of their pompous master's
pride in an accident of naming, and even the other merchants who traveled this route knew the bragging of the
Guynmer merchant.

"Where is that drover you recommended to me,
healer?" Shou demanded of Adar. "I need someone who
knows what to do with a camel or we will never leave
the imperial city."

Before Adar could answer that he hadn't recommended anyone, it had been Master Den, a voice piped
up between them.

"Right here, good merchant Shou." The Tashek
drover, who had introduced himself by the name Harlol,
wandered forward then, brushing straw and black mud
from his hands. "Zephyr had a cut on her knee, but I've
put a plaster on it and she should heal well enough on
the journey."

"Zephyr?"

Harlol twitched a shoulder, dismissing the question
with a bland, "She needed a name, and seemed to like
that one. It suits her." The nomadic Tashek were bred
to the camel, slept with their beasts and fed them with
their own hands in the desert. A man who did not know

his beast didn't survive. Hearing this young drover talk
about a camel as if it could understand and even choose
its own name convinced Llesho beyond doubt that the
nomads were stranger even than reports had named
them. Shou, however, seemed surprised only by the
choice of names. "She never struck me as being that light
on her feet."

The Tashek drover smiled. "Perhaps she was only
waiting to be asked."

"We'll see . . . What's wrong with you, boy?" The
emperor turned the sharp edge of his tongue on Llesho,
who jumped as if he'd been bitten by an adder. "Posing
for a statue on my time?"

"No, sir!"

"Then get ready to move out! There're five hundred
camels and as many horses in this caravan, and the front
of the line is already halfway to Guynm by now. They
are not going to wait for one daydreaming cadet!"

Chastised, Llesho snapped to attention, acutely aware
of the short spear strapped to his back and the imperial
militia uniform he wore. He turned with a will to hitching
his pack to the back of his horse, just one among hundreds of militiamen hired out to guard the many caravans
journeying to the West. Squads passed up and down the
ranks, finding their places at the sides of their temporary
masters. Old campaigners of rank, they took up positions
in the parties to the front and rear of Shou's camels.
Llesho recognized in their number several who had dined
at the Moon and Star. They were elite imperial
guardsmen, he suspected, and no more at home in their
militia uniforms than his own cadre. They passed Shou's
party with no acknowledgment, but Llesho felt a great
pressure lift from his shoulders: the emperor did not rely
on their band alone for his defense.

He was more than grateful for their presence when a
handful of Harnishmen in the shaggy breeches and
coarse shirts of the plains people rode by on their short
horses. In their midst, a trader with the same look but

much finer garb rode on a taller, more elegant steed. He'd known that small parties out of Harn sometimes traveled with the larger caravans, but hadn't considered the possibility that they might join *this* one. With a tight grip on the hilt of his Thebin knife he watched them make their way to their position at the rear. None of that party gave Shou a backward glance; they didn't know who he was, or they were skilled spies. Either way, Llesho figured he would need to stay on his guard. At their best the Harnishmen were mischief, at their worst, deadly.

The Huang agents had divided the caravan into parts: two units, each of a hundred camels and as many horses, had already departed. Shou's small party had drawn an inconspicuous slot toward the middle of the third unit. If raiders came at them from the front they'd have plenty of warning, but they were not so far to the rear that they would fall into the hands of bandits sweeping down on stragglers.

The emperor, disguised as a Guynmer merchant, offered Carina a pallet on the back of a camel, but she declined, insisting that she would ride. She wore the robes of a healer with a wide split skirt under and a thick swathe of veils that covered her from head to foot, protecting her from the sun and the dust. Adar had pulled a short veil over his eyes but left his face uncovered, as did the three Thebins in the full uniform of imperial military cadets. Master Den wore his usual loin wrap and an open coat that fell below his knees. In his right hand he carried his long staff with an umbrella stuck in it for shade, and over his back he carried a small pack which might double as a change of clothes, Llesho figured.

The call sounded for their party to move out, and Llesho scrambled into his saddle. He had expected Shou to ride horseback as well, but the emperor climbed onto the bent leg of the lead camel and slid effortlessly into a padded seat built up for him in front of the camel's pack.

Harlol stood ready. "Up, Zephyr. Up!" he shouted, and gave the camel an encouraging slap on its haunch. The camel rose, rocking her passenger who rolled with the motion as if he'd been born to it. A second camel remained on its knees. The Tashek drover scanned the crowd, cursing under his breath in a language thick with harsh consonants that Llesho did not understand. "You are certain he is coming?" he finally asked in Shannish.

Shou nodded, squinting in concentration as he looked over the sea of beasts and people. "There he is now—" He pointed, but Llesho saw no one paying them the least attention.

"Ah! I see him!" the drover's attention locked on its target, and Llesho followed his gaze to the most incredible figure he had seen all morning.

A dwarf in the exotic dress of Thousand Lakes Province struggled toward them through the milling press of food vendors and trinket sellers hawking their last-minute wares to the forming caravans. In one hand he carried a pair of cymbals, and on his back was strapped a quiver full of flutes. Behind him, he dragged a small stepladder. "Harlol!" the dwarf addressed the new drover by name, "You seem to have landed on your feet. I thought you'd be begging your way home!"

"A Tashek drover never stays unemployed for long." Harlol steadied the ladder against the waiting camel's pack, demanding, "What kept you? The master is growing impatient to be gone."

The dwarf climbed up and plopped himself in a small chair with arms and a gate that he latched across his front. When he had settled his instruments and fluttering garments about him, he drew a deep breath and nodded a signal for the drover to bring the camel to its feet.

"There was this maid from Sky Bridge Province who, noting the diminutive size of my visible parts, was curious about the size of my other parts." He explained his tardiness with a sly smile and a careless wave of his hand to take in his lower body. "I proved to her that small messengers can carry big packages, but she insisted I repeat the experiment, to be certain." The dwarf shrugged with mock innocence. "I could not leave the lady unconvinced, and in faith, she took almost more convincing than I had strength to devote to the debate."

"Tell that to the master when he takes a whip to your hide for holding up our departure."

As far as Llesho knew, Emperor Shou didn't own a whip. That doubtless explained why the dwarf showed no sign of fear or contrition, but laughed merrily at Llesho, as if they two shared some secret joke at the drover's expense.

Harlol latched the ladder to the camel's pack with a twitch of a smile that quickly vanished when the camel reached around on his long neck to take a nip out of his backside. Harlol gave her a sharp smack on the nose. "Behave yourself, Moonbeam!" he warned the animal, which offered an opinion of this new name in the wad of spittle it flung at Harlol's departing feet.

"Enough!" The drover made a rude gesture at her and turned on his heel to run down the row, checking the tether line that tied each of Shou's twelve camels to the others. Shouting in the Tashek language, which the beasts seemed to understand best, he prodded at their flanks with a goad that he carried for the purpose.

"Evil-tempered beast," the strange newcomer said, but he was watching the departing drover, and not the camel, as he said it.

Curious about the new addition to their company, Llesho settled his horse beside the camel on which the dwarf rode at his ease. As their party moved forward, he stole a glance upward, only to find the dwarf staring down at him.

"And who might you be, squirt?"

"I'm called Llesho, and I'm a cadet in the imperial militia," Llesho answered with his cover story. "And I think, sir, that you have no room to call another names that belittle his stature. What—who are you?"

"I am called Dognut, though my parents named me Bright Morning at my birth. And as you see, I am court musician to His Majesty's travels."

Llesho had no practice at subterfuge; a blind man might read the horror that slackened his face at the dwarf's words. The little man gave him a wink that, on the surface, said he played the same game as their neighbors in the caravan, mocking their master and his pompous affectations. The gleam sharpening his grin spoke of deeper knowledge and more dangerous ironies. They had not yet left the city wall behind, and already Llesho was tired of the joke.

"I have never met a man of your race before. Where are your people from?" he asked, trying desperately to change the subject.

"Like our employer, I am a king—king of the short people."

Llesho was about to commiserate with the shoddy treatment the little king received from his companions when a braying cackle, like a donkey in heat, erupted from the dwarf's mouth. Dognut held his sides and laughed until the tears ran down his cheeks and Llesho wished a lion would jump from the bushes and kill him just to put him out of his misery.

"My 'people' farm the Thousand Lakes Province, and surpass your own length, pygmy lad. My looks are a mere accident of birth—the bones of my arms and legs break easily, and refuse to grow, which the wealthy find amusing. When it became clear that this body had reached its full height before its hands could reach the plow, I was offered to the governor to be trained as an entertainer. Unfortunately, I did not live up to expectations in that regard either. With one thing and another, fate cast me adrift upon the mercy of our current master, who has no great ear for music and therefore prizes a musician with a similar lack of sensibility."

Llesho blushed furiously, feeling every word out of his mouth was another foot in the camel dung. "I'm sure you jest with me about your skill with your instruments," he stuttered in a lame effort to appease the situation.

His brother rode ahead with Carina and he kneed his horse to a faster pace to join them, leaving the laughing dwarf's ridicule behind. The two healers were deep in a conversation about poultices, but Adar paused with an expression of patient inquiry on his face. Llesho had no conversation to offer. Unfortunately, he had now reached the head of their party, hobbled to the slow but steady pace comfortable for camels and horses.

"Can't we go any faster?" he asked his brother.

"I don't know much about camels. The horses could manage a brisk trot for a little while, but on a trip this long, a faster pace would kill them."

Adar meant no harm, but his words dropped Llesho into the past as if it were all happening again. The sounds of the caravan blended into the memories of another journey filled with hunger and thirst and exhaustion, his people dying between one step and the next. Clammy sweat sprang out all over his body, chilling him to the bone, and he gasped as if he'd been shot with one of his own arrows.

"Llesho! Llesho!"

Adar's voice reached him through the fog in his mind. They had drawn to a halt while the caravan plodded by, drovers he did not know and guards he thought he vaguely recognized turning curious glances on him as they passed. Adar was on foot, his hand on Llesho's arm.

"What are you doing here?" Llesho looked at his brother, confused in time. "We've fallen behind, don't let the guards see—" But no, the Long March was over. They were going home. Llesho closed his eyes for a moment, centering himself; Adar's hand was like an anchor holding him in the present.

"Where's your horse?"

"He's right here. Will you be all right if I let go for a moment?"

Llesho thought about the question. He'd been impatient, embarrassed, and suddenly he'd found himself a thousand li away, crossing the grasslands again. He gripped his brother's arm, hard, couldn't let go for all the silk in the Shan Empire.

"Nine thousand died," he whispered. The Harnish raiders had driven ten thousand out of the holy city of Kungol. All but one thousand had perished on the forced march to the slave market in Shan. It wasn't the answer Adar was looking for, but it opened his eyes, blurring them with tears.

"Dear Goddess, Llesho. How did you survive?"

He hadn't told his brother how he'd wound up on Pearl Island, a continent away from his home in the mountains of Thebin. They'd scarcely found each other again when they were plunged into battle, and it had all seemed so far away. Now, however, something inside of him demanded release. He had to tell Adar, even if his brother never forgave him for what his life had cost them.

"I was their prince, and so they died for me. Starved to feed me, went thirsty so that I would have water. Carried me until they dropped, then passed me on to the next until he died as well."

He sighed and turned his anguished gaze into the blue, blue sky of Shan. "I wish I could turn into a bird and fly home right now." Llesho leaned forward in the saddle, his muscles bunched under him, poised to leap into the air with the faintest puff of wind. Nothing happened. He had expected that. Kaydu could have done it, but he didn't have her gifts.

"I'm sorry, Llesho. I wish I could do something to make this easier for you."

That sounded like forgiveness, or maybe even as though his brother didn't blame him at all. If he thought about it logically, as Adar seemed to be doing, there hadn't been much he could have done about it anyway. But if it wasn't his fault—the blame spilled from him like an open sore.

"I am the favored of the goddess, right?" Sarcasm oozed around the words. If this was favor, he could not imagine what it must be like to incur the disfavor of the gods.

"Believe it, no matter what has happened." Adar gave his arm a shake to fix his attention. "The goddess has some purpose for every step of your path, brother, the evil of the Long March, and even testing your patience with the pace of a caravan."

"As the goddess wills." Llesho held out his hand for his reins. He didn't believe it, and that scared him more than coming unstuck in his memories had. He felt the need to reach Kungol as an ache in his bones and a bitter taste in the sweat that crested his upper lip. The light touch of the short spear at his back mocked him with whispers in the voices of his enemies: "Going to die, going to die."

He had come to imagine himself as a great general, the liberator of his people, but distance and his own weaknesses set insurmountable obstacles in his way.

"I'm afraid we will be too late," he said. All of Thebin lay under the yoke of the Harnish raiders, and he still had four of his brothers to find as well as the pearls of the goddess' necklace.

"A husband must show great patience as well as the determination to battle fiercely for his lady," Adar began, but Llesho stopped him.

"I am no husband," he bleakly reminded. "I kept vigil, but the goddess did not come."

Adar's gentle laughter did not even startle his horse. "She came. Her mark is on you, Llesho. I see it in your eyes."

"She didn't come. I would have known."

The last of their unit had passed them, the following one approached out of the caravansary. Adar remounted with a final word of homely advice: "She came to me in the shape of a priestess I had known in the Temple of the Moon. I don't know how she came to you—perhaps

you can ask her one day. But we will have to wait to
find out. The gates of heaven are far from Shan, and the
caravan will travel at the pleasure of its beasts, not its
masters, or it will not travel at all."

With that they nudged their horses into motion, past
the curious glances of strangers—the emperor's spies
and the Harnish traders—and reclaimed their place in
line. Master Den seemed not to have noticed their absence, but Lling and Hmishi exchanged a worried frown.
Carina watched them return with concern in the crinkles
at the corners of her eyes, but a little smile curled her
mouth and her eyes never left Adar's face as they
approached.

It hurt that Carina had picked Adar. The two shared
so much in common, even temperaments, that he felt
foolish when he thought about how little he had to offer.
Embarrassed, he separated himself from his brother,
choosing Dognut's company again. Let them have their
discussions of powders to cure bladder irritations—he
wouldn't wear his heart on his sleeve any more. The
dwarf, however, continued to look at him like he was a
lovestruck fool in search of a shoulder to cry on.

"It's going to be a long journey if you insist on wearing
that face," Dognut commented, gazing down on him
from high atop his perch on the camel. "I am not sure
I have enough songs about broken hearts in my
repertoire."

Llesho glared at the dwarf. Yes, he wanted Carina—
or, wanted her to want him. But when he really thought
about it, disappointment in love didn't haunt his soul.
The Long March did. The truth was, now that they were
actually going home, he couldn't shake the anger he'd
been too young to understand the last time he'd made
this journey. He wanted to weep, to scream, to tear at
his enemies with teeth and claws and cut their hearts out
to feed his subjects dying on the road. But there were
no enemies near, just the warm sound of camel bells and

the jostle of goods and men and animals settling in to the long trek. And there was nobody he could tell.

Suddenly, a voice sang out over the curses of the grooms and the bleating of the beasts. The emperor of Shan, sitting atop a camel loaded with bolts of silk and dangling brass pots off his sides, was singing a Guynmer hymn. Dognut drew a flute from his quiver and added its high, quavering voice to the simple tune.

In the shadow of the dark night
I come to you
When the wind sweeps the dunes of Gansau
I huddle at your feet.
You who protect the camel and the date tree
Can you do less for your child
Lost in your desert?

Harlol gave Shou a troubled look, as if he was trying to decide whether the merchant mocked or believed. But Shou's servants had taken up the hymn, and after the first verse so did the new drover, raising prayer to the spirits whose believers had come out of the Gansau Wastes spreading word of the desert faith to Guynm Province. Even Master Den, the trickster god ChiChu in his human form, joined in singing the prayer to the foreign spirits:

We offer dates and honey
We sing praise and
Burn myrrh and incense
At your altar
You who protect the camel and the date tree
Lost in your desert
Can you do less for your child?
Gifts of gold and silver
We give you

With paint we decorate
Stone images of your faces

After a few verses, Adar joined in, and soon all along
the caravan the hymn had been taken up.

Drover of the sun and the moon
Spirits of camel and the goat
We ask your protection
In this great journey.

When the song finally came to a halt, a new hymn came
down the line to them, a merry song to the trickster god,
who joined in with great relish:

A farmer let a stranger in
And fed him rice and leavings
The stranger shat upon the hearth
And left the goodwife screaming.
When strangers come up to your door
And ask for food and liquor
Treat them as you wish yourself
For ChiChu's sake, the trickster.
A trader took a stranger in
And sold him shoddy trinkets
The stranger slipped out late at night
Taking all the blankets.

From his place at the side of the emperor's camel,
Master Den grinned at Llesho, inviting him into the
trickster's sly enjoyment of his secret identity. Llesho returned the smile, though his own felt forced. The wink
that followed was all ChiChu the trickster, reminding
him: "This is not the Long March; stay in the now."

Llesho returned a quick nod. But it was hard to be
cheerful when Carina's eyes, bright and adoring, fixed on
his brother.

When the laughter died away after the trickster prayer,

the Harnishmen at their rear began a Harnish anthem. Only a scattering of voices added to the song, but angry muttering thick with the threat of bloodshed rustled through the caravan. Then Shou raised a competing voice, carrying a Harnish hymn of thanks to wind and rain and earth, the Harnish natural deities, with no challenge or boast in it. Dognut gave Llesho an uneasy shrug, but raised his flute to strengthen the melody line. Grudgingly the Harnish traders gave their own voices to it. Few others along the length of the caravan joined in, but the blood had gone out of the moment. Only the wary tension of an oncoming storm remained. When the hymn had ended, Dognut put away his flute, and the caravan returned to its private chatter. The singing was over, and Kungol was still very far away.

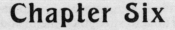

Chapter Six

THE round, full light of Great Moon Lun hung low in the sky—Lun chasing her smaller brothers Han and Chen, already touching the zenith. Habiba moved about his workshop with precise, studied motions. The magician once had told him that Lun was no moon at all but a dying sun smoldering in the dark, and somehow Llesho knew that he was waiting for Lun's faint light to shine more fully through the window that overlooked the workbench.

He took a shallow bowl of polished silver from a shelf and carefully wiped it clean with a soft cloth. From an earthen pitcher he poured pure, cold water, filling the bowl to the brim.

"What's that for?"

The magician bent over so that his nose almost touched the water in the bowl but gave no answer.

"Habiba?"

Llesho wondered briefly how he'd come to be here, and why Habiba didn't seem to hear him or even notice his presence, but the youth couldn't seem to muster much worry about it. He stretched on tiptoe to peer over the magician's shoulder. As Great Moon Lun rose, its glow filled the sky in the silver bowl with pearly light. It overpowered the lesser shine of little Han Moon, which floated like a black pearl in the reflection. The pattern from the silver bowl drifted on the water, so that the pearl of Han seemed to hang suspended from a silver chain.

"Ah! But where are you?" Habiba asked the image in the water. The magician was looking for the String of Midnights, the pearls of the Great Goddess lost in the attack on the gates of heaven. Llesho had three of them; it seemed that Habiba had found another.

As if some spell had taken control of his body, Llesho's hand reached out for the dark moon-pearl floating in the bowl. Part of him expected to close his fingers around the pearl while another part braced for a cold wet hand.

Instead, he fell headfirst through the water, which parted like a mist around him.

"Help!"

"Grab hold!" a voice answered.

Llesho reached out and grabbed onto the wide silver chain he was passing as he fell. The chain pulled him up short and he swung for a moment over an abyss before he managed to wrap his legs around the broad flat links and pull himself up on them.

"Who's there?" he asked. It wasn't Habiba's voice, or Kaydu's. He might have expected ChiChu to show up at a moment like this, but it wasn't the voice of the trickster god either.

"It's me." The moon swimming in Habiba's silver bowl began to jump like a fish on a hook, nearly dislodging Llesho from his perch. He peered more closely: the moon was no pearl at all, but almost manlike. Round in the body and naked, his skin was black as pitch and gleamed like the pearls Llesho carried in the pouch at his breast. The pearl-man sprouted tiny arms and legs that he flailed in his effort to escape the chain that ran through a hook set in his back. The creature snuffled through a round, upturned nose that was pink around its flaring nostrils. His mouth, lined with pearly white teeth, shouted, "Get me down from here!" in a voice far too large for its pearly head.

"Stop that!" Llesho shouted as the chain that held them both swayed dangerously. "How can I get you down anyway? I'm stuck here myself, and about to fall if you don't stop rocking the chain."

"I beg your pardon," the creature apologized politely. "I let my anxiety overcome my good sense."

"Pardon given," Llesho returned with equal grace and added, when curiosity would allow silence no longer, "What magical creature are you? And," he thought to ask, "why are you hanging around like this, naked like a pearl from the goddess' jewel chest?"

The creature sniffed indignantly. "My name is Pig. I'm a Jinn in the service of the Great Goddess, chief gardener in her heavenly orchards." The pearl-man, who called himself a Jinn, stopped struggling and allowed his body to swing slowly on its chain. The whole situation should have disturbed him more, Llesho thought in passing. But the Jinn was waiting patiently to tell his tale, so he tucked his left foot into the open loop of one of the links and grabbed hold of another with his right hand. Securely anchored against a fall, he settled in to listen.

"Ever since the demon invader laid siege to the gates of heaven, I have searched for a way to escape and seek help for my lady, the Great Goddess. Finally I devised a plan; I would make myself small as a pearl from her lost necklace and slip through the cracks, so to speak. I thought to fall to earth far from the gates where our enemies lay in wait, and then I hoped to raise an army and march to the rescue."

"Doesn't seem to have worked out that way." Llesho felt it needed to be said.

The Jinn puffed out of his cheeks and gave Llesho a sour glare. "I didn't need you to tell me that. Now, if you will just release the pin in my back, I can go about my business. Heaven can't wait forever, you know. There's planting to be done."

"You should have thought of that before you turned yourself into a pearl. What if you're lying to me?" The question added an unwelcome note of reality to the situation. Jinn were a notoriously untrustworthy caste, which even Pig had to recognize.

"You can make me promise to give you wishes," Pig suggested with a trustworthy smile. "You can use your wishes to make me tell the truth." His efforts to look dependable were thwarted by the way he swayed hypnotically, like a pendulum, which made Llesho very dizzy.

Pig's present state suggested that ideas were not, perhaps, his strongest game. This one seemed fairly simple, though. Foolproof, even.

"I'll do it." Llesho stretched over the abyss to grasp the pin in the Jinn's back, but Pig wriggled out of reach.

"I have to promise first."

"You just did."

"No, I said I *would* promise. You haven't asked me to do it yet."

Llesho was growing more annoyed with the strange pearly creature by the minute. When he stopped to consider this strange situation, none of it made sense, least of all his own patience in dealing with the captive Jinn. He was in it now, however, and could see no way out except through to the end.

"Promise me three wishes," he insisted, and started pulling himself closer on the chain even before the words "I promise" left Pig's mouth.

Suddenly, a hand big enough to hold Llesho and the Jinn together in its palm swept him off the silver chain and held him up to the face he most dreaded in the world. "Welcome home, Llesho."

"Master Markko!" he shouted, and woke up in a cold sweat, with a hand clamped over his mouth. Struggling against the strong arm holding him down, he almost missed the words whispered in his ear.

"You were calling out in your sleep."

Hmishi. Friend, then. When he thought about it, all

the signs of a dream were there, but he hadn't questioned anything while it was happening.

He nodded once, to show that he was awake and paying attention. Hmishi removed his hand and sat back on his heels, waiting for Llesho to return to the present.

He remembered now. They had stopped at a way station with one small inn at the far end of a staging area for the caravans. Long, open stables flanked the square on either side. Adar and Carina had gone to the inn with Shou, as would be expected of persons of their apparent rank, with Dognut the dwarf as their entertainment. Lling had accompanied them to stand first watch over their master's sleep, maintaining the ruse that they traveled with Shou's party as guards for hire. The rest of their party bedded down with the travelers of lower station among the animals in the stables.

Nearby, sharp eyes gleamed with curiosity out of the late-night darkness. Harlol, the Tashek drover, had kept to himself during the day's travels. Now, he propped his chin on the palm of his hand and watched the Thebins.

"It's nothing," Hmishi assured the man, an undercurrent of threat a low rumble in his voice.

The drover took the hint and rolled over in his blankets. He only pretended to go back to sleep, Llesho figured. The veterans working as paid guards, who lay scattered among the sleepers for their protection, were doubtless fully alert behind their closed eyelids as well. Nothing like an audience when nightmares decided to make a performance of his sleep.

"You were calling out Master Markko's name," Hmishi whispered. "What was that about?"

Llesho shook his head. "Not here."

Thinking about this particular dream sent a shiver through his body. The logic of it fell apart in the light of his waking mind, but a seed of truth at its core worried him. What did it mean?

"Where is Master Den?"

"Privy, or maybe the pump," Hmishi answered. They both knew that could mean anywhere.

Llesho rose and gestured for Hmishi to follow. They made their way quietly past the huddled sleepers and those whose bodies lay unnaturally still as they listened. A cool breeze soothed their heated skin when they passed out of the stable under one of the many elaborate arches that pierced its long face. The cloud-streaked sky gave them no stars to see by, but enough light from one moon or the other filtered past the drifting tissue strands of mist to cast the long row of arches into darker shadows crossing against the night.

The Huang caravan had stopped at a reputable resting place inside the borders of Shan Province, but Kaydu had trained them well. Both of the young Thebin soldiers scanned the great echoing square for stealthy bandits and sneak attack. Shoulder to shoulder, hands at sword belts, they peered as deeply into the shadows as they could see. When a hulking clot of darkness detached itself from under one of the stable's great arches, Hmishi stepped between his prince and the approaching threat. Both drew their swords, but Llesho's blade shook in his hands.

"You are greatly troubled." Master Den's voice issued softly from the darkness before them. He moved a hand and the clouds parted before the great moon's glowing disk, pushing back the shadows.

"A dream, Master."

Master Den nodded and motioned him to a bench that curved around an ornate column holding up a gracefully curved arch. Master Den urged him to sit, then asked, "Tell me what you saw."

"It was more than a dream, wasn't it?" Llesho risked a glance at his teacher, but Master Den gave one of his typical shrugs, offering no useful advice, but demanding much of his supplicant.

"You could be suffering the ill effects of a dinner left out too long in the sun. Only a dream reader can tell for

certain. The Tashek have the most revered dream read
ers, but I don't expect to meet up with one on ou
journey."

"Has anyone ever seen a Tashek dream reader?"
Hmishi asked, "I thought they were a myth, like the
Gansau Wastrels, used to scare little children."

"They are real," Master Den confirmed. "But they are
a religious caste, and enter the dreams of sleepers only
when invited, to give aid to the troubled. They are not
as the tales suggest, the cause of night terrors."

Hmishi blushed, and Llesho wished he knew what they
were talking about. He'd seen Tashek drovers in the
streets of Kungol, had even watched, from a hidden cor
ner of a balcony, when Tashek tribal chiefs had paid
their respects to his lady mother. But servants did no
frighten the palace heirs with stories of mythical mon
sters. Sometimes he thought that a great fault in his edu
cation. He might have fought more wisely as a child i
he'd known of such things as Harnish raiders and thei
hunger to snuff out life. And he might even know wha
Hmishi and Master Den were talking about.

"Not a myth," Master Den informed them, "though
we are not likely to find one to advise us on our pres
ent road."

"If it wasn't just a dream, what was it?" Llesho trusted
Master Den's opinion more than he would a stranger'
anyway.

"I won't know until you tell it, now, will I?"

"No." Taking a deep breath, he pinned his gaze to the
pale disk of Great Moon Lun so that he didn't have to
look at Master Den while he spoke, but that reminded
him of the dream. Han and Chen had set while they
were talking, and Lun had followed past the zenith.

"I was watching the magician, Habiba, catch the moon
light in a silver bowl filled with water. He was searching
the moons' reflections for the black pearls of the goddess
I looked over his shoulder and fell in. That's when
met Pig."

Master Den settled a listening expression over his human face, but he offered no encouragement beyond his puckered frown as Llesho told the tale of his dream. When the telling had wound down to the last chilling words, Master Den nodded.

"Did you recognize anything else? Anything in Master Markko's surroundings that will give us a clue about where he is now?"

Llesho shook his head. "I saw Habiba's workshop well enough. I think he must have been in the imperial palace—I'm pretty sure I recognized the view out his window. Once I fell into the water, nothing seemed real. All I saw, beyond the chain and the Jinn who calls himself Pig, was Master Markko himself.

"There was something strange about him, though." Llesho paused, staring at Great Moon Lun while he tried to recapture the feeling of the dream. "Markko talked to me, and I talked to the Jinn. But Markko didn't seem to notice the Jinn or the silver chain, and Habiba didn't see me. It was like our dreams had touched, but only at the edges."

"If we are very lucky, you are correct," Master Den agreed. Llesho would have preferred an answer that didn't confirm his own suspicions.

"But it was a dream, right?"

"I know this Jinn," Master Den said. "Pig has served the goddess through many ages, and has been her favorite for most of those lifetimes."

"It seems a strange name for someone loved by the goddess."

Master Den's fond memories crinkled a smile at the corner of his eyes. "Not at all. Pig really is a pig. He was, in his mortal life, a great hunter of truffles. The goddess invited him to heaven and offered him any shape he wished, just so that he would provide the heavenly table with truffles as wonderful and pungent as those he had sought out in the mortal realm. He agreed but, being a pig, could imagine no greater calling than to be what he was. So the goddess raised him up on two feet, and gave him speech, which he finds amusing, and the rank of chief gardener, which he takes very seriously. In all else, however, he remains a pig. As for names, like his shape, he seems to feel a need for no other."

Llesho shivered. When he was a slave on Pearl Island, Master Markko had threatened to feed him to the pigs, and he could not help but find an omen in the dream. Master Den had also served on Pearl Island, however, and followed Llesho's thoughts with sorrowful ease.

"He is my friend," the trickster god reminded him. "Pig has never, to my knowledge, eaten either frightened slave boys or weary old men, no matter how hungry he might have been."

"You must think that I am a fool."

"A fool knows no fear, and needs no courage to go forward," Master Den corrected Llesho with wry humor. "A brave man understands his fears, but does what he must in spite of them."

"Then I must be the hero of this tale," Hmishi complained, "because I am terrified most of the time, of just about everything."

Master Den laughed, as he was meant to do, and slapped a hand on the back of each Thebin boy. "Go back to sleep," he ordered them as he might two mischief makers.

"Not me," Hmishi grumbled. "It's time I relieved Lling on guard duty anyway."

When he had gone, Llesho took a minute to ask a final question. "Whose dream was it? Was I in Habiba's dream, or he in mine?"

"Perhaps you dreamed each other." Master Den gave Llesho a comforting pat. "We'll figure it out. In the meantime, try to get some rest. I want you up early for prayer forms."

"Yes, Master." Llesho rose and bowed his gratitude to the trickster god. In simpler times he had learned the prayer forms and their defensive counterparts as combat forms. Master Den's reminder soothed his fretful soul: even on a caravan, far from anything he knew, he carried the ordering of his own existence within him.

Llesho was not so pleased when Hmishi shook his arm to rouse him from his too short sleep well before the sun had risen. "Master Den is waiting for you in the courtyard. I get a free pass today, because I've just come off duty, but he wants you up and out on the double."

Llesho groaned and rolled out of his blankets as Hmishi fell into his own. Lling was nowhere in sight, her pack already stowed for the next stage of the journey. Llesho followed her lead, and stumbled into the square just as the gray false dawn of the little sun washed the straggling line facing Master Den.

Lling was there, and Dognut, of all people. The dwarf stood at rest with his feet settled apart on short, bent legs and his equally shortened arms clasped around his belly. He almost appeared comical, until Llesho looked into the centered calm of his eyes. Then he found himself wondering what role the little man actually played in Shou's court.

Carina had cast aside her veils and joined them in her long split skirt. Adar stood with the emperor in disguise and a small cluster of senior guardsmen who gathered in front of the inn. A handful of merchants paused in their preparations for departure to watch as well, while a denser knot of the lower ranks looked on curiously from across the courtyard. A lesser number of Harnish merchants stood among the onlookers with their own guards in the dress of raiders.

Ignoring the curious audience as much as possible, Llesho took his place next to Carina. He shook his arms to loosen his muscles; perhaps he could impress the healer with his skill at the exercises, since nothing else seemed to be working for him.

Master Den gave the ritual bow, and their little line

returned it. Then the laundryman and trickster god called out the first of the morning forms. "Red Sun."

Llesho moved his body into the gentlest of fire signs to greet the dawn. Each bend and stretch reminded him of all the times that he had performed the prayer form in the past. Warm as sunlight, the faces of companions lost or left behind came to him in his prayer: Bixei and Stipes, and Kaydu, alive and training their troops on Shokar's farm. The gladiator Radimus, sold to the enemy to pay a dead man's debts. Madon, who had sacrificed his life to stop a war and Master Jaks, who had given his life in fighting that war anyway. Lleck, who had grown old and sick in the service of the kings of Thebin, following Llesho into slavery to keep faith with his duty. Out of a storm-tossed life, memories of passing comforts squeezed his heart with a desire to see his comrades again.

The form brought them back to rest, and several of the guardsmen joined them. A groom or two followed, and even a few of the merchants abandoned their coats to servants and joined the ranks of those in prayer.

"Flowing River," Master Den called.

Personal memory emptied into a greater consciousness as muscle flowed into muscle. The Way of the Goddess, the exercise taught, did not resist, but pursued its course with unrelenting gentleness. Only now exists; time is the present in motion. The past flows into the future like the river which flows eternally yet remains always in the present.

"Still Water," Master Den looked to Adar when he called the next prayer.

Adar acknowledged the summons. He moved away from the inn and joined the teacher in front of the now-substantial rank of worshipers. With a bow to the mortal god, he took a stance and returned the trickster's welcoming smile with a grin of his own, as though they shared a secret. Master Den raised his arm, and Adar, facing him, mirrored the movement so that their upraised hands almost touched. Adar bent deeply into the opposite knee and brought his free hand forward in a sharp, taut move that stopped just short of Master Den's hand reaching to meet it. The form passed through a series of sharp movements each poised in stillness before moving to the next, and each restrained a hair's breadth from its reflection in his partner.

Llesho followed the moves with a scattered few who practiced the advanced forms. None but the two masters completed the "Still Water" form with a reflecting partner, however. Llesho gave up on the idea of impressing Carina. Though he hadn't known of it, his brother's mastery did not surprise him. Adar had received the favor of the goddess as one of her spiritual husbands. Her gifts had included Adar's great skill as a healer. He wondered how his brother could believe the goddess had likewise come to him, when he was clumsy and unskilled and had received no gifts at all on his vigil night.

When they completed the form, Adar bowed his whole body into a deep obeisance, as if the form had been meant as a rebuke.

"Butterfly," Master Den called, but a second voice challenged him.

"The journey to the West requires stronger gods than these." Harlol, the Tashek drover, swaggered into a cleared space in the square, pacing back and forth in front of the massed crowd of grooms and drovers and lesser guards.

Llesho felt a jab at his hip and looked down to see a troubled frown on the dwarf's face. "The master has been too long away from the caravans," Dognut whispered. "I hope he doesn't pay dearly for taking up with strangers for this journey."

Like the dwarf, Llesho had a very bad feeling about this.

Having made his challenge, the Tashek drover began to sway in a desert dance. Soon he was whirling madly, his heavy coats flying out around his ankles. From somewhere in the crowd a sword flew at him and he plucked it out of the air. Another, and he likewise grasped it, swinging both in counter circles as he twirled like a madman. Bending low, then leaping high into the air, he jabbed and thrust with both swords, and twirled them over his head in a choreographed dance of death. When he finally came to rest, his lungs blowing like bellows, the swords rested on Adar's shoulders, crossed in an X at his throat.

"I am a healer." At first, the Tashek seemed to take the words as a plea for mercy, and his lip curled in contempt. Then Adar finished his promise—"I won't hurt you."

"Read your fortune in the fire of the blades, healer."

Adar smiled at him, a warm crinkling welcome; the swords on his shoulders rose and fell when he shrugged. "I don't think the goddess wants me today. But if she does, she can have me."

Llesho came to the immediate conclusion that his brother had lost his mind. He wondered if the emperor had done the same, letting the trickster god persuade him to hire on a madman as a drover. Would Shou really let a common drover murder a healer-prince in cold blood, and right in front of his eyes?

"No!" Llesho was so busy damning the lot of them to the outer reaches of hell that he didn't realize he had drawn his knife and sword until he stepped out of the line.

"No," Shou agreed, in a hushed voice so that only Llesho could hear. He took Llesho's sword from his hand, and Lling's, and approached the drover with both weapons held in a loose, easy grip.

"I know this dance." The emperor of Shan stood in front of his drover, his plain but rich clothes a reminder that this character he played studied the Guynmer version of the Tashek religion. He stamped his foot once, twice.

"Come, Wastrel, dance with me."

The term "Wastrel" was a complex one to turn on a Tashek. Outsiders used it as an insult, to mean that the race had neither ambition nor any inclination to work when they might beg or steal or trick a mark out of a day's bread. To the Tashek who came out of the Gansau Wastes, however, a Wastrel was a holy wanderer and, above all, a survivor. Shou could have meant either, or both. Neither tone of voice nor expression of face or body gave up his meaning. So a Gansau Wastrel would have done it.

"As you wish, merchant." Harlol drew his swords away from Adar's throat, leaving a thin trail of blood as a reminder, and turned to face the emperor-in-disguise. Stamping his own foot twice in the dirt, the Tashek accepted the challenge.

Gazes locked, the two men circled each other. Swords flashed and clashed in time to feet beating out the pattern of the dance in the dust. Whirling, leaping, dropping to the ground again, sweeping out a leg to upset his dancing opponent, the emperor met the Tashek move for move. The dance had a ritual meaning; swords flew and slashed about the body of the dancer who held them or met over the heads of the combatants. The worship form meant no harm to its practitioners, although accidents could prove fatal at the level these two prayed. A slip of the foot, a lapse in concentration for a fleeting second, could bring death to either man.

Feet beat a faster rhythm and the dance picked up speed. Shouts from the crowds encouraged first one champion, then the other. Shou was older, the Tashek sword prayer one of many forms he had learned over the years of his travels through his empire, though only Llesho's party among the crowd could know that. Harlol seemed much the favored dancer; he had the endurance of the young and the single-minded purpose of one who danced the only religion he believed. Shou had set his life against a thousand contests, however, while the Tashek drover had danced only for bragging rights among his age-mates.

Gradually, Llesho noticed a change in the pattern of the contest. Like the prayer forms of the Way of the Goddess, the dance had a combat style that dealt murder in every pose and action. So Llesho was not surprised when Harlol reached out with his swords aimed at his opponent's heart. A glance at Dognut's tense, watchful expression confirmed his suspicion: the Tashek drover had adopted the deadly style.

Llesho held his breath in a turmoil of indecision. He saw in his mind a vision of Shou dead in the caravanserai square, his blood spilling into the dust as his empire came apart like bricks in a wall without mortar. Harlol had dictated the shape of the combat, but Llesho blamed Shou for the aftermath his death would bring. The drover thought he was fighting a Guynmer merchant and certainly could not anticipate the destruction he called down on his people if he unwittingly murdered the emperor. But any move Llesho made to help might distract the very man he wished to save.

He took half a step forward, not certain what he would do next, and a hand fell on his shoulder. Master Den held him fast in a tight grip.

"He had a good teacher," the trickster god reminded him. Den himself, that was.

He would have objected, that Master Den taught the prayers and combat of the seven mortal gods, the forms that shaped the Way of the Goddess, and not this savage game of press and thrust. But even without any training in the Wastrel's dance, Llesho had seen when the prayer had turned deadly. Shou had seen the same, and moved seamlessly to adapt to it. A slash, another, and the drover lay at his feet, breathing raggedly and bleeding from cuts in his arm and leg.

"Dawn," Shou noticed, his voice steady and his breath calm. Great Sun had come up while they fought. "Friend

Adar, can you help my drover? And I will need someone to take his place on the journey."

"I won't hold you back." The Tashek drover staggered in Adar's grip, but managed to hold himself upright. "I need just a stitch or two, and I will be back at my post by midmorning. Who will you find in a place like this to learn your ways as quickly?"

"I have certainly invested more in your education already than you deserve," Shou commented acidly. He returned the swords he had borrowed and raised a questioning eyebrow at Adar.

"The young have amazing recuperative powers of the body," the healer prince gently cuffed the ear of the wounded man he supported. "One wonders if his brains have not been addled in the sun, however."

"Dress his wounds, then, and pay for two days' keep." Instructions for the Tashek's care disposed of, Shou addressed his next order to Harlol: "Rest. You can join the caravan again in Durnhag when your leg will support you. In the meantime, we have need of additional hands, or we will never be ready to leave with the rest of our caravan."

Satisfied that the Guynmer merchant had settled accounts for the foolishness of a boastful young drover, the crowd broke up into small clusters of gossip before moving on to the day's work. A stranger with a family resemblance to the injured drover left one such knot to present himself to Shou.

"I'm Kagar, Harlol's cousin. For the honor of our family, I offer myself to take his place in your service, sir." Kagar bowed very deeply, shamed by the dishonor Harlol had already brought on his house.

"Is this some plot against my camels?" Shou demanded with all the indignation of a merchant who feared thievery and none of the censure of an emperor foiling an attempt at assassination. "Did you follow your cousin hoping to plunder my cargo between you?"

Harlol glared at the youth who had declared himself

a cousin. "By my honor, I have no such intention, nor does my cousin, who is guilty of bad judgment only."

"I did follow you," Kagar admitted, "but not to steal from you. I had hoped that I might persuade you to take me on as a groom to assist with the horses. I did not expect my cousin to disgrace our family. Now I wish only to repair the damage he has done on this field of battle."

Kagar stood very erect, with only a scathing glance for the humbled drover. "I beg you, kind merchant—I ask no payment but the repair to our good name."

"Free is a good price," Shou agreed. "Though you will need to be provided food and shelter." He passed a thoughtful frown from the Tashek youth to Master Den, who gave no sign what he should do about this most recent supplicant. "Very well," he finally decided, "but if you make me regret my decision, I will leave you behind—even if that means abandoning you in the desert."

The young groom bounced a little on the balls of his feet, suppressing a grin with great effort. "Yes, sir!" he said, and with a final bow made a dash for the stables.

Llesho would have liked to leave them both behind. He was glad they were abandoning Harlol, at least for the present, but wondered why the emperor hadn't discharged the man who had tried to kill him. At the moment, however, Shou had turned his wrath from the Tashek who had attacked him and was targeting it on Llesho instead.

"I am capable of protecting my own guests against upstart challengers," Shou informed him with the steel of a blade in his voice. Llesho heard the silent rebuke that would have broken their cover identities if spoken aloud. Others could have rescued Adar. He was too valuable to Thebin to risk in a plaza brawl.

Which was fine, because Llesho was just as angry right back. He had the advantage of the emperor, however, that he was right in their true identities as well as by the parts their disguises gave them.

"My good sir." He bowed, rigidly formal as one accustomed to parade manners might to a merchant—with no great respect but with attention to the forms. "Please remember that your life is worth more than the guards who are paid to protect you. Let us do our jobs, for our reputations if for nothing else."

Shou saw the fear in his eyes, not of combat, but of losing the emperor of Shan in a stupid street challenge. "He wasn't that good," he assured with a grin, but promised, "I'll take your advice in future." The crowd had dispersed, giving the merchant and his guard no more than passing interest. No one would have noticed the narrowing of Shou's eyes when he added for Llesho alone to hear, "If you had fought him, you would have died. I couldn't allow that."

Apparently the Tashek drover was that good.

"At some point you will have to trust me to live or die by my own skills," Llesho countered. He was right, they both knew it, but Shou's struggle to accept it churned in his eyes.

Llesho nodded to acknowledge the conflicting emotions the emperor revealed. "That's how I feel when you do something as stupid as answer a challenge to mortal combat from a hotheaded drover," he said. With a sharp salute that belied the heartfelt nature of their disagreement, he turned and walked away.

Chapter Seven

HOW do you transport two deposed outlander princes through an uneasy empire and enemy territory, and into the heart of their captive nation? Llesho asked himself. How do you sneak past forces that would see those princes dead or captive at any cost? According to Emperor Shou, you made a public spectacle of yourself as a merchant with more self-importance than means, and added those princes to your already eccentric caravan. You identified three callow cadets as your only visible means of protection. Then you paraded said princes before a cheerfully mocking crowd who would never imagine the movers of empire could be so stupid.

The emperor had great skill as a tactician in battle, and he'd shown equal competence as a spy. Even the mortal gods favored Shou. From Shou's very throne SienMa, the goddess of war, guarded his empire. ChiChu, the trickster god, traveled at his side. Llesho had serious doubts about Shou the strategist, however. Only a trickster could love the current plan; Llesho had the uncomfortable feeling that he was walking around with one of Lady SienMa's archery targets on his back.

The plan had worked so far, of course. With his songs and hymns Shou had declared himself a practitioner of the Gansau religion, so no one had seemed particularly surprised when he accepted the drover's challenge in the sword dance ritual. Few among the Tashek themselves had the skill to recognize how expertly Shou had moved from prayer to combat form as he responded to Harlol's attack. The attack had been no accident, however. No simple drover working for a minor merchant would have such skills of mortal combat. Harlol had brought the subtle craft of a warrior and a spy to the contest, and whoever had paid the young groom to maim or murder Shou must now wonder how the emperor would react to the attempt on his life.

Their neighbors in the caravan readied their camels for the next stage of the journey with an equal, though less lethal, curiosity. What would the Guynmer merchant do next? Shou didn't leave them in doubt very long. With a nod of his head, he signaled Dognut, his dwarf musician, and began to sing. The lively hymn recounted the droll tale of the first Gansau Wastrel to bring the sword dance to the faithful of Guynmer. At the chorus, the wary caravanners joined in as if the hymn were a drinking song, their worry about a vendetta on the road set aside. It seemed natural that the party ahead of them should answer with the long and ribald chant about the exploits of the trickster god. Llesho sang along when a clash of Dognut's cymbals marked the chorus.

By the time they had reached the end of the tale, with a stolen fig and a Jinn named Pig in a tree pelting the trickster god with rotten fruit, the camels were bellowing their mournful counterpoint to the raucous drovers. Even the Harnishmen had entered into the laughter, though Llesho couldn't tell whether they joined the spirit of the song or jeered at the foolish Guynmer merchant at the heart of the singing.

The hundreds of li they traveled had shaken loose the tightly ordered structure of the caravan, however. Boundaries of ownership and hire bent to loyalties seen and unseen. Hmishi and Lling ranged up and down the

line, a hundred camels linked nose to tail in gangs that
told the numbers of each merchant's wealth: Shou's
twelve, led by the Tashek, Kagar; the Harnishmen's
twenty-five at the rear; fifteen between; and another fifty
or so ahead that belonged to a rich merchant of Thousand Lakes Province. According to Hmishi, the Harnishmen at the rear rode with one eye ever looking behind
them, but seemed more nervous than scheming. Perhaps
they worried that the emperor would reconsider the
mercy he had shown to the merchants who had not par-
ticipated in Master Markko's raid on the imperial city,
and that he might yet send soldiers to stop and kill them.
Or, perhaps they awaited their own reinforcements before murdering their fellow caravanners. Hmishi couldn't
tell Llesho which was more likely.

Llesho tried to stay alert, but the regular clang of the
caravan bells and cries of the drovers, the warmth of the
sun overhead, the smells of camels and leather, of spices
and incense and horses of the caravan, all lulled him
with the joyful memories of his early childhood. The land
reminded him how far he was from home, however. As
the days passed, the water-rich fertility of the Shan Province gave way to gently rolling downs furred over in
tough, gray-green grasses.

"What do you think of your first caravan journey,
young militiaman?" Dognut asked him from his superior
position atop the camel Harlol had named Moonbeam.

"I thought we would be crossing desert," Llesho
admitted.

"Not yet. We've come what? Three hundred li? No
more, give or take a day. Even when we reach Durnhag,
the seasons will disappoint you. In the winter, when the
rains come, the grasses grow thick and green, and the
whole floor of the Guynmer track is afire with flowers.
It's still early in the dry season. As the days grow longer,
however, the water will grow more scarce, until you will
find little enough to sustain a caravan of this size. The
grasses will shrink back, leaving nothing but scattered

patches where hidden springs survive the summer underground.

"At the height of the dry season there is more life than meets the eye. Where there is water there are living creatures, hiding sensibly in their burrows through the heat of the day. The farther south we go, however, the shorter the water season, and the more violent and poisonous the life that survives there. Once we have passed Durnhag, take a care to your shoes and blankets!"

"Will we pass close to the Gansau Wastes?" Llesho asked, his gaze crossing the landscape that was not as barren as he had expected it to be.

"Not this trip." Dognut trilled a few notes and, satisfied, put the flute away with the others in its quiver. "The water has retreated into the depths and the oases have dried up by now. Even the Tashek will have moved on," he said with a sharp sweeping glance that took in the flat land to the east. "No one will return to the Waste until the monsoons come in the fall."

Llesho's gaze fixed on Kagar, who was swearing at the lead camel while he dragged at the creature's head with a thin but strong arm. In summer, the Tashek migrated into Harnish lands. Some years they fought, but mostly they pretended not to notice each other. He wondered what they were doing this year, and what it meant to the Harnishmen traveling in their caravan, the Tashek drovers riding at their side.

Near nightfall their guide called a halt at a small byway. No more than a well and a rough corral for the animals, it would serve while they awaited the rise of Great Moon Lun to go on. As they moved toward hotter, drier country, they would begin to take their rest by a different set of customs than the towns: in the heat of the day, and in the deep dark between the setting of the true sun and the rising of Lun. Since they would be moving on after just a few hours, they left the tents in their packs, but broke out the cook pots and the blankets.

While the rice for dinner simmered over a low fire,

gossips passed among the parties offering their wares in trade for a cup and a story in return, or an opinion if the merchant had no tales in stock. It surprised Llesho that Harlol's attack upon the "Guynmer merchant" had caused very little concern. Most cup-gossip said that Harlol had let the bravado of youth overcome him. In this version, the jovially bombastic Guynmer merchant had simply turned an inexpert display of the sword dance into a lesson from the drover's elder and social better. Few in the camp had given a moment of uneasy sleep to the Tashek grooms and drovers bedding down with their camels. Of course, the scoffers didn't know the true identity of the merchant in question. They couldn't move against the Tashek drovers or the Harnishmen they suspected of hiring the attack without exposing the emperor, however. Llesho was pretty sure that the senior militiaman in the employ of the Thousand Lakes party shared his concern. He pretended not to recognize the officer who had kept a sharp eye on the public room at the Moon and Star, and who always seemed to be nearby when trouble brewed. He'd bet this one twitched at the feel of Tashek eyes focused between his shoulder blades, though.

"I'm Captain Bor-ka-mar, released from the emperor's service and hired on, like yourselves, to provide safe passage for this caravan." The soldier squatted in front of Hmishi, addressing him as their leader, though he stole quick glances at Llesho out of the corner of his eye. Lling nudged up against Llesho's side, her hand on the knife at her belt, but left the next move to her companions.

"Well met, Captain." Hmishi clasped the captain's arm in friendship, accepting the charade that took the attention of strangers and enemies away from the prince traveling among them. In Shou's personal service as a captain of the Imperial Guard, Llesho guessed, and not released from that service at all, but he took the man's arm in his turn and waited for Lling to do the same before Bor-ka-mar explained his presence at their cook fire.

"This plodding pace is making my men lazy," he began. "We need a bit of exercise to keep us sharp. You three are welcome to join us if you've a mind. And who knows—you might even learn something." The man's grin revealed several levels of meaning in the statement. He meant by that not only hand-to-hand combat training and weapons craft, but the lay of loyalties in the camp, and the intelligence of Shou's military spies.

Llesho looked to his companions, who were waiting for his decision. "We might at that." He threw a pat of camel dung into the slow flame of their campfire, letting his own many meanings sink in.

Then he stood up, leaving the task of cooking a supper to the grooms and Master Den, who puttered about the camp on errands suitable to his disguise as a lowly servant. After only two days in his new identity, Llesho was taking the god's service for granted. He couldn't decide if he committed sacrilege against the trickster ChiChu or betrayal of his teacher's honored place in his heart. Master Den would call it spycraft, of course, but it still made Llesho uncomfortable.

Hmishi and Lling accompanied him with no questions. They took their positions with unthinking attention to his safety—Lling in front and to his left, with Hmishi following at his right like an honor guard.

"Your friends are telling your enemies which among you is of value." Bor-ka-mar slapped Hmishi on the back with a hearty laugh to mask his businesslike comment.

Lling took his meaning at once and flung an arm around Llesho's waist. Tucking herself in all along his side, she protected him with her body while giving the impression that she had more seductive plans on her mind. Hmishi scowled at the two of them.

"Better," Bor-ka-mar muttered under cover of a lewd grin. "Though it would have more effect if you would at least pretend to enjoy the lady's seduction, Llesho. You look more in need of rescue than a private place for love-play."

Llesho blushed a deep mahogany right to the roots of his dark hair, but flung his arm around Lling's shoulders as they walked. He'd have apologies to make later, he figured. Hmishi knew it was an act, but if things had worked out differently he'd have meant it enough to make apologies necessary.

Captain Bor-ka-mar led them to a bit of pasture land marked off as a makeshift exercise yard by half a dozen torches thrust into the red marl soil. Clumps of grass threatened to trip them up, but real battles seldom took place in an arena with sawdust underfoot. News of the practice had spread, and a small crowd had gathered to watch, ready to trade wagers and cheer on their champion of the moment. Llesho recognized the dress and countenance of several Harnishmen wandering the edges of the circle of flickering torchlight, but he let them slip to the back of his mind.

At the center of the exercise yard, two hands of guardsmen tried their hardest to look less experienced than they were. Their battle-ready postures, so much a habit that it must have become instinctive long ago, gave them away, at least to Llesho and his companions, who fell into the same stance as they waited to begin. He wondered if any of these men had fought in the battles against the magician, Master Markko, that had deviled his journeying since Pearl Island. Shou would have his head if he asked; knowing the emperor trusted these men with all their lives would have to be enough.

The captain separated the cadets and matched each with an older partner. He ignored the short spear Llesho carried on his back as if someone had warned him not to draw attention to it. Instead he tapped the sword at Llesho's side and motioned that he should take up a fighting stance against a battle-scarred veteran who gave him a wink as he hefted his own sword in a callused

hand. Then the workout began. Bor-ka-mar called out
the weapons formations, simple, basic skills that shook
off the worst of the rust but would scarcely compete with
a lesson from Master Jaks or Kaydu.

"You have a good arm, young cadet." Llesho's partner
countered his move and returned a smart follow-through
of his own.

"And you, good sir." Gliding around a clump of coarse
grass, he pressed the fight with a quick jab that Master
Jaks had taught him. The soldier deflected the point of
his sword with no great skill apparent to the onlookers,
but they both knew what it took to counter that move.
Something about the man's style of fighting reminded
Llesho of Madon, the gladiator who had died at the
hands of his allies for the honor of a broken lord. The
memory hurt too much to think about for long, though,
and the fight gave him no time for brooding. There was
a message in the pairings, however. Shou's guards as-
sessed the skills of the young cadets and they, in turn,
judged their safety in the hands of the soldiers they traveled with. These were Shou's picked troops, hidden in
plain sight. That notion would offer more comfort, however, if the emperor hadn't taken on his own Tashek
drover in a one-on-one sword battle. Much good his
guards would do any of them if the emperor got himself
killed maintaining his disguise.

When Captain Bor-ka-mar decided they had had
enough, he called a halt to the exercises. The onlookers
dispersed to settle their wagers, leaving the soldiers to
straggle, gossiping, back to their cook fires. Someone had
heard that Harnish camps were massing on the border
that divided the Shan Empire from Harn, they said. Just
gossip, but given the source Llesho figured they could
take it as army intelligence. Rest did not come easy
after that.

Chapter Eight

ONE day was very like another on the trail: waking at false dawn to prayer forms and breakfast, slogging forward, li by slow li, until the caravan broke in the heat of the afternoon to rest and graze the animals. Then up with Great Moon Lun for weapons practice while the camp packed up, and on again until the moonlight failed them. Shou hadn't been the only merchant with musicians in his train, and the players came together by the light of the cook fires for a song or two before they all tumbled, exhausted, into their bedrolls.

The caravan had grown more tense since they had passed over the border into Guynm Province. Gossip and rumor swept through the caravan as regularly as the tides in Pearl Bay. If Harn wanted to take the capital city, their massing hordes would have to sweep through Guynm to do it. And the Huang caravan stood directly in their path. The audience for weapons practice grew as the caravanners sought reassurance over entertainment.

"Mind on what you're doing, boy!" Bor-ka-mar's commanding voice latched hold of Llesho's wandering attention and pulled him up sharply to discover his sword resting at Sento's throat.

"Easy as you go, there." Sento took a wary step back.

Shou's servant never tried to hide his military background and regularly took weapons practice with the soldiers on private contract. Those who gathered to watch weren't likely to notice, but he could hold his own against their best, one of two or three Llesho figured he wasn't likely to kill by accident. Looked like maybe he'd figured wrong.

"My apologies." Llesho dropped the point of his sword and bowed humbly, trying to mask his confusion. He'd let his mind drift and his sword arm had carried on without him, not a matter of skill but of battle experience. Muscle and bone continued to act long after the mind had grown too numbed and broken to rule them.

"Accepted." The man discreetly did not inquire where Llesho had picked up such reflexes, but handed him a water bottle to share along with the most recent intelligence. "Have you heard the tale told by the Harnish merchants?" he started in a bland voice that suggested nothing more than gossip. "They say that the Harn have an ally, a terrible magician who searches for his familiar, a small boy lost in the desert. Some add that the ground bursts into flame beneath his feet, others that it means death to look on him." He gave a shrug, as if not really believing the stories. As Shou's servant, of course, he knew full well who this unnamed menace was and so his next statement had more meanings than it seemed.

"Whatever lies behind the stories, it frightens the Harn among us as much as it frightens their neighbors."

So the Harn among them did not, on the surface, share an allegiance with Master Markko's followers. "There's always something behind stories like that," he agreed. Llesho knew it from his dreams, but Sento confirmed that those followers were still looking for him.

"Always," Sento warned him before leaving to find his own bivouac.

For Llesho, the stories confirmed what his dreams had told him: Master Markko was still out there. That the Harn of their caravan feared the magician didn't neces-

sarily mean anything. The raiders who had invaded
Thebin hadn't needed the magician to goad them into
action; the promise of wealth without effort had been
enough.

"What news?" Lling joined him, wiping the sweat of
her own mock battle from her brow. Absently, she swung
her sword in lazy circles with one hand while she reached
for the water bottle and drank with the other. When she
was done, she wiped her lips with the back of her wrist
and handed the bottle off to Hmishi, who was still blowing like a bellows from his own practice.

"The Harn at the back of the caravan grumble at their
position in line."

"So I hear," Hmishi confirmed when he had drunk his
own fill.

Strolling easily through the resting caravan, they
weighed how much trust to give anything the Harn said
in the hearing of others. Lling had come to the conclusion they shared and voiced it: "They have their own
reasons to be where they are. I think Bor-ka-mar expects
they will attack before we reach Guynm."

"Are they working with the Tashek?" Hmishi asked.
"That's what I'd like to know."

The tribesmen out of the Gansau Wastes were scattered throughout the caravan, which made Llesho wonder if they didn't plan some assault independent of the
Harn. Harlol hadn't given Llesho any reason to trust the
Tashek even before he attacked the emperor. Kagar, who
had replaced his injured kinsman in Shou's service,
hadn't pulled a sword on anybody—yet. He did his job
with the grim determination of one who wished himself
in other circumstances.

"It's like he had his own plans and Harlol made a mess
of them." Llesho explained the feeling he had about the
groom. "Now, he seems to be trying to work the situation
he's stuck with."

"I don't trust him." Hmishi ran a thumb thoughtfully

along the edge of his Thebin blade. "Don't know that I trust that dwarf fellow either."

Lling snickered at him. "You don't trust anyone who rides that close to Llesho."

Hmishi ducked his head, embarrassed to be that easily read but not at all ashamed of his devotion to his prince. Lling felt the same way: they would protect him with their lives, and even their reputations.

The easy camaraderie between his two companions reminded Llesho of the old days in the pearl beds, but then he'd been part of that bond. Now he was its purpose, but outside of it. That hurt, but it would hurt his friends more to let them see the ache in his heart. He left them with an easy joke to find the slit trench before he gave himself away.

"**P**lay some music, *please*, Dognut! I'm about to fall asleep in my saddle here."

Llesho adjusted his seat impatiently and pulled the desert veil over his eyes to filter the dust and the light. The climate had grown hotter and drier the farther south they traveled. And more boring: no trees, clumps of dusty grass so sparsely scattered that for a while he'd entertained himself by counting them. Nothing but brown dirt below a sky pale with dust. Caravan life, he had discovered, came with all the hardships of a military campaign, but with none of the basic terror. He didn't miss the fear, but would have welcomed anything, even Dognut's songs, to occupy his mind. The dwarf was sleeping, however, and answered Llesho's plea with a gargling snore before settling back into his cushions.

So wrapped up was he in the complaints he muttered under his breath that he almost missed the subtle shift in the gait of his horse. But he heard it, the clop of hooves against stone.

"Dognut! Wake up! We're there!"

"What? What?" The dwarf's head shot up on his fragile neck and he stared all around him for a minute before subsiding again into his chair. "I thought we were under attack!"

"We've arrived!" Llesho explained. "Beds and baths and fresh food!" They had finally reached the outskirts of Durnhag.

"Oh. Well, that's different." The dwarf sat up, observing their surroundings with sharp interest. Quickly, however, his excitement turned to nose-wrinkling dismay.

Llesho agreed with the silent judgment. He hadn't envisioned anything as opulent as the Imperial City of Shan. As the center of trade and governing for Guynm Province, however, Llesho figured Durnhag would be at least as grand as Farshore. He'd hoped for something more exotic as befit its place along the caravan route, but at the least had assumed they'd find a decent inn with good food and mattresses free of bed ticks. First impressions didn't promise even that much.

A jumble of mud houses and tin sheds settled drunkenly against one another on either side of the road dusted with sand by the wagons that carried trade wares in and out of the city. As they passed, the inhabitants of the ramshackle dwellings ran after them, grabbing at their packs, stealing brass lanterns, tin pots, anything that they could snatch or cut from the pack strapping. "It's not what I expected," he muttered.

"I think Shou did, though." Dognut looked worried.

Before he could say anything more, a mother swathed in veils that covered her hair grabbed onto Llesho's stirrup with one hand. With the other she held up a starving baby for his inspection. "My baby!" Her dark eyes bled her despair as she cried to him, "Help for my baby!"

Llesho slipped her a copper coin and was instantly besieged by beggars who cried out in half a dozen languages for food, or money, or milk from the udders of their camel mares. Street toughs intercepted the mother and stole her coin before she could escape the crowd.

Here was the point of the story Master Den had told him at the beginning of their journey. The emperor would never allow something like this in the imperial city, and he didn't look pleased to find it in Guynmer. Shou grew quieter, more brooding as they neared Durnhag proper. He scarcely looked up when the camel drovers, screaming at their beasts and slashing with their camel goads, joined the soldiers to push back the beggars.

"There's going to be trouble." To emphasize his words, Dognut gave an eerie trill on a flute not much bigger than his hand. He didn't seem surprised when, passing a dark and ill-favored inn that marked a divide between the shantytown and the lowest accommodations the caravansary offered, Shou called a halt and pulled his party out of the caravan. Llesho wondered what the dwarf knew about this place that the rest of them didn't.

Captain Bor-ka-mar, forced to break his cover or leave Shou to the protection of three cadets, gave his emperor a sour glare. Shou offered him no encouragement, but signaled him to continue with the party his cadre had hired on to protect as a cover for their real mission. Bor-ka-mar seemed almost on the brink of mutiny, but the emperor silently turned his back, closing the subject.

Out of Shou's hearing, the captain's vocabulary demonstrated a knowledge of swearing both wide and deep, in languages rich in obscenity and in others Llesho would have sworn had no such terms at all. But the soldier followed orders. He nudged his horse into motion with his knees and followed the caravan as it moved away from the man that Bor-ka-mar, like all Shan's imperial guard had sworn on his life to protect. Llesho felt an overwhelming urge to call him back, but he kept his peace and followed the emperor. Shou had a plan. Again. Which comforted Llesho not at all. He discovered that his own unsavory vocabulary had developed depths he didn't know he had.

At the door to the disreputable inn, Master Den aban-

doned them as well. The trickster god gave Adar a little
bow in keeping with the role he played as servant.

"If you'll lend me a guard, I'll check out the stables.
We'll bring the travel packs back with us," he declared
in a voice loud enough for the innkeeper to hear. Harlol
hadn't caught up with them yet, but Kagar still warranted
watching. Shou sent Hmishi and together they followed
the Tashek groom back out into the dust.

Desperate to understand Shou's reckless action, Adar
looked to Llesho for an explanation or an argument that
they continue with the rest of the caravan to the city.
Llesho didn't have one either; he shrugged, and entered
the inn after Shou.

Inside the thick mud walls, the inn was dirty but surprisingly cool. A small fire burned in the huge hearth at
one end of the rough-timbered dining hall, with a teakettle hanging over it by a metal arm. A tripod next to the
kettle held a cauldron that bubbled like a potion and
released odors almost as foul. Llesho hoped some medicine was cooking, but he had a bad feeling it was dinner.
Not surprisingly, the room was nearly empty, so there
were more than enough benches for their company to sit
together at one of the long plank tables. Shou led them
to a place in a corner, with a wall at his back and a
window to the side. They could watch the street as well
as the innkeeper from here. He nudged Llesho in first,
and drew Lling after himself, lounging back against the
wall while Adar helped Carina to a seat facing them and
Dognut settled his bag of flutes at his feet.

A barkeep with no belly to speak of wiped his hands
on a dingy gray rag and approached their table with the
rag slung over his arm. Close-up, they could see that the
corners of his mouth turned down almost to his chin in
an expression that appeared sour by habit.

"What can I get for you, sir?" He addressed Shou with
a quick knowing scan. He didn't need to recognize Shou
to know what a modestly dressed Guynmer merchant
would want with his establishment.

The emperor set a worn purse on the table. "Whatever you are serving this evening, for myself and my companions."

The barkeep barely stifled a sneer at the thinness of the purse, but motioned to a sooty young girl at the hearth to bring plates for the customers. Llesho had hoped against good sense that a real kitchen with roasting fowl and fresh bread hid behind the door in the rear. They would never find out with the purse Shou had offered, however. While the girl was dishing lumpy gray goo from the pot over the fire, the barkeep turned his attention back to his customers.

"We'll be staying the night," Shou said, "If you can meet our needs.

"I think we can manage that," the barkeep said with a smirk. "We have one room to let upstairs. The bed is sturdy and large enough to accommodate the gentleman and his pleasures, male or female."

Llesho doubted that the inn had anyone else staying the night. What money the beds brought in came from hourly rates, and he didn't even want to think about the condition of the blankets in a place like this.

With a glance up at the railing that ran the length of the gallery, the barkeep continued. "Our boy is so skilled that poets have written odes to his name, and our girl is a true find, hardly used at all. Was a servant in the great house in the city, so her manners are city-bred. Got herself turned away for refusing to do for free what she asks good coin for here on the paying side of the city towers. The governor's loss is your gain, good sir."

A servant in the governor's palace. That went a good way to explaining why they had stopped in this place. Llesho'd had enough experience with Shou's spies so that the realization never reached his face. When he followed the direction of the barkeep's gaze, however, he couldn't take his eyes away. A man and a woman well past the bloom of youth advertised by the barkeep perched on the railing. Except for the open robes thrown carelessly

over their shoulders and the tall wooden shoes with high
thick heels on their feet, they were both naked.

Llesho had seen naked women working in the pear
beds—had seen Lling that way most of the days of their
lives. Modesty had prevented him from thinking of them
as anything but workmates, but this was completely dif
ferent. The woman noticed that he was looking and
nudged her partner in the ribs, sharing a joke at his ex
pense. Holding his gaze, she opened her robe further and
circled her hips in a lewd dance. Llesho felt the heat of
her body in spite of the distance between them. He
blushed. With a grin and a wink, her male companion
leaned over and licked her belly, then blew him a kiss.

"For a modest fee, your help can sleep here on the
floor once the tap patrons have gone home."

Tearing his eyes away with an effort, Llesho found
the innkeeper looking speculatively from Shou to Carina.
Adar wrapped an arm protectively around her shoulder
and the man moved on to the three young Thebins in
their cadet uniforms. He smirked before adding
"Though perhaps the gentleman prefers the young one to
warm his bed."

The emperor played the part of his disguise. With a
careless shrug, he flicked a glance over the pleasures dis
played above them on the gallery. "Send both your peo
ple to me after our supper. Perhaps they can teach my
pets a trick or two."

So, not just the woman, but the man as well were the
emperor's spies. The barkeep seemed unaware of what
covert negotiations he might be transacting, or with
whom, but called the girl from the fire.

"My girl will air the room, good sir."

"Good. We'll want to retire early." For emphasis,
Shou ran the tip of his thumb down the side of Llesho's
face. They'd played this masquerade before, but this time
Llesho felt a less accommodating reaction was called for.
He shuddered, pulling his head away with just a touch
of fear in his eyes.

"Good boy." The emperor smiled indulgently at Llesho. He approved the way Llesho had played the part.

The innkeeper said nothing at this exchange. Guynm Province kept to a strict religious code, but the poverty on the outskirts of the caravansary and this inn on the edges of the city proved that Durnhag had come to terms with its own corruption by moving it out of sight. He understood his patron's vices now, or so he believed.

Adar hadn't known the emperor very long, however, and didn't share the innkeeper's worldliness. He neither accepted nor trusted this disguise. Shoulders pulled back, his spine snapped to rigid attention, but he kept silent. Protective instinct warred with the caution any slave learned in order to survive. He wasn't a slave now, though, and Llesho held his breath, afraid that his brother would take no more from the emperor or the trickster god himself if it came to Llesho's safety. Adar had always been sensitive to the mood around him, however, and Llesho's tension seemed, paradoxically, to calm his brother. Or to put him on his guard, as Llesho wanted him to be.

Shou answered the healer's indignation, and his protective arm around Carina, with sophisticated boredom belying his modest Guynmer costume but not surprising the innkeeper, who had seen the same many times before. "I'm not a greedy host. You can have her if you want her.

"I ask only for your services as a healer to return my property to good working order when I am done with them," Shou added. "It's sometimes difficult not to break one's playthings."

Memory of his battlefield dead passed behind Shou's lidded gaze, and Llesho thought that some truths were worse than the masquerade. Dognut, however, seized the moment of Adar's stunned silence to rest a small hand on Lling's breast. He waggled his eyebrows and leered at her. "Pretty soldier. Want to see Dognut's blade?"

Lling gave him an icy smile and drew the long Thebin

knife from the sheath at her hip. "Would you like to compare?" she asked, all teeth. When she wiped a speck of blood from the blade on a corner of his blouse, Dog nut removed his hand. When Lling's knife disappeared into its sheath, the innkeeper gave the dwarf a wink.

Llesho still worried about Adar. When it came to his youngest brother, the healer-prince didn't trust Shou and might ruin whatever plan the emperor was hatching with a misguided attempt at a rescue. But slowly, soundlessly Adar brought his reactions under control. Maybe he'd figured out there was more going on than he understood or maybe he was biding his time. For the moment, a least, disaster was averted. Shou beamed at the healer as if he had performed a trick his master had despaired of teaching him. Llesho closed his eyes in silent prayer that the two men would not come to blows before they had deposited the emperor at the palace of the governor

"Now that we have settled the arrangements, I am in the market for information." Shou turned his attention to the innkeeper. He'd get a complete report from his spies soon, but never gave up the opportunity to sound out the locals on conditions under their daily view.

"What did you want to know?" The innkeeper gave a doubtful look at the purse on the table.

Shou shrugged in the vague way of one who preferred not to speak his business aloud and emptied the purse onto the table. The innkeeper's eyes widened at the coins that spilled out. Small, but purest gold, the coins were worth ten times the man's earlier estimation and went far toward calming his suspicious nature.

"Strangers coming by in the past fortnight or so?" Shou prodded.

"Besides yourselves?" The innkeeper counted the value of secrets in the gold coins on the table and substituted another question. "Such as?"

"Dangers to a merchant on the road again with the sun?" Shou gave a wave of the hand, as if it went without saying, but the coin between his fingers ended up in the palm of the innkeeper.

"Too many Harn." He growled out the name as if he would hawk it up out of his throat. "And the Tashek have been sneaking around, looking over their shoulders at every creak of a floorboard."

"Trouble brewing." Shou didn't quite ask.

The innkeeper took a deep breath and reached back to rub at a tight spot at the base of his skull. "I reckon so," he admitted, and bit into the small gold coin to test its purity. Purer than the man could imagine, Llesho suspected, and straight from the stamping yards of the emperor who sat in disguise in his very inn.

"Safest to keep your head down and stay clear. There's going to be action between 'em, I'm betting, what with the dry season come on early, and Harn on the move." The innkeeper stepped away with a second coin and a nervous backward glance. Llesho found he had lost his appetite—just as well it wasn't a roasted fowl in front of him.

Stretching out with a catlike sprawl, Shou draped one arm across Llesho's shoulders and the other around Lling. "Jung An is a servant of her ladyship," he muttered into Llesho's ear with a tilt of his head to signal the woman, who moved back into the shadows of the gallery.

Llesho had figured the spy part on his own and wasn't surprised to find the hand of the mortal goddess of war stirring this pot. "Was it Lady SienMa's idea to send Bor-ka-mar away with his men and meet with your spies alone in this den of thieves?" he asked, keeping his words low so that their import didn't pass beyond their table. The resistance in his tone carried anyway.

Shou got him by the hair and shook him, a warning both real and acted out for their small but avid audience. "And how much attention would a squad of veteran troopers draw in a house like this one? Learn a lesson. It's safer to play a small man with large vices than a powerful man on a mission." He let go with a final shake and a reassurance given like a threat: "When I've taken Jung An's report, we can get out of here."

"If we haven't run out of time already."

Hmishi and Master Den should have joined them by now; the hairs on the back of Llesho's neck were standing up like the gods were passing at his back. Trouble.

Shou was dragging him from the bench, however, and didn't seem to hear. "We'll have that room now, and—"

The front door opened. They had time only to register the voice, "I heard there were Thebins—"

"Balar!" Adar rose from his place at the table, a broad grin on his face and fell on the newcomer with a crushing embrace that nearly cracked the three-stringed lute Balar carried on his back.

They had no more time for greetings. A shout from a table at the rear alerted them seconds before Harnishmen came pouring in through the back door. At the same time, raiders burst through the front. More had entered through the upstairs windows and they now joined the attack, rushing down the stairs and leaping from the gallery. Her ladyship's spies had disappeared from the railing, but blood dripped to the hall below giving evidence of their fate. Llesho drew his sword and fended off his attackers, trying to make his way to his brothers who stood unarmed at the center of the swirling battle.

Balar swung his three-stringed lute about him like a stave, sweeping the legs out from under a Harnish raider but breaking the neck of the instrument. He dropped the pieces and fell into a fighting stance that Llesho recognized. Master Den had taught him the same moves in Lord Chin-shi's gladiatorial compound, a lifetime ago it seemed. Master Jaks had shown him that he'd already known some of it from early childhood, but Balar, for all his gentleness, brought the grace of the dancer to the deadliness of one who had trained long in the Way of the Goddess.

The battle closed in around him then; Llesho lost sight

of his brothers, lost count of his attackers, knew only the rise and fall of his weapons. He felt unstuck in time, fighting for his life in the Palace of the Sun while he did the same, again, on the road from Farshore, and again, in the market square of the imperial city. Fighting with all his skill, he found the place inside where action replaced thought and move followed move like instinct. He would not die, would not be taken prisoner in some grimy inn. But the Harnish raiders kept coming.

He was scarcely aware of the strange wailing cry that had joined the din around him, but he felt the strike of a hilt against the back of his head, and he was falling, falling, into a black pit that closed over his head like Pearl Bay.

PART TWO

AHKENBAD

Chapter Nine

HMISHI was screaming. From the raw sound of it, like sand caught in a mill wheel, he'd been at it for a long time. Llesho's head beat with each cry as if it were going to split his skull open.

"Lling?" he whispered, but even that slight movement jolted a searing stab of pain through his head—just a dream, except that it felt real. Somewhere, Hmishi was being tortured, and it was his fault, because he'd gotten away. But how? And where was he? He blinked a moment to clear his vision and wished he hadn't—the ground was surging like a restless ocean.

"Are you awake, Llesho?" Dognut's voice called from above his butt and Llesho realized that he was the one moving, not the ground, and that Shou's dwarf musician was the traitor among them.

Someone—it had to be an accomplice, because the dwarf couldn't have managed it on his own—had trussed him up and slung him over the back of a camel. He had his backside in the air, his face pressed into the flank of the animal, and a pair of elbows digging into his kidneys. When he tried to right himself, he discovered that his captors had tied his arms and legs to the pack strapping that wrapped under the animal's belly. When he opened his eyes, he saw camel. When he took a breath, he smelled camel. Which would have been bad enough without the camel bouncing him like a juggling ball.

Running. The camel was running. He'd seen camel races a few times as a child; he'd wanted to go right out and try it himself. Khri, his bodyguard, had put an end to his aspirations with a firm hand on the back of Llesho's court coat. His plans back then hadn't included traveling like a bedroll, but he wondered why camels moving at high speed had ever seemed like a good idea. This one was making him very, very sick, and he groaned before he could stifle the sound.

"He's awake!" The elbows shifted from his back and presently Llesho heard the sound of a reed flute, trills and whistles only, since it was impossible to play anything recognizable on a camel at full gallop.

Llesho pretended to be asleep while he tried to figure out where he was and who had taken him, and why. Dognut was having nothing of the pantomime, however.

"The question was a courtesy," he said, smacking Llesho soundly on the butt with the flute. "I know you're awake in there."

He stirred, wriggled, but there was no way of getting comfortable. "Where's Hmishi? What are you doing to him?" Pointless to ask. He knew it had been a dream, but maybe they were in the same camp, or part of the same force. He could tell them what they wanted to know and they would leave Hmishi alone.

"The boy isn't here. What do you remember?"

A fight. Someone hitting him on the head. If Hmishi wasn't here, where was he? If Dognut had known the answers, he wouldn't be asking questions.

Llesho didn't know anything, except, "I'm going to vomit."

Fortunately, Dognut was pulling on the reins of the beast they rode, and calling in Tashek to someone over his shoulder. So, the dwarf was in league with—

A drover leaned over and grabbed the bridle of the

skittish camel, bringing the beast to a halt. Llesho turned his head enough to see—

"So you found us after all. Traitor!"

Harlol glared back at him, and they both tensed for action, though Llesho was in no position to move, let alone attack.

"Don't."

Goddess, what was he going to do now? That was his brother Balar's voice snapping at him from somewhere out of sight behind his right ear. Llesho didn't want to believe his own brother had sold him into captivity, but it was hard to ignore the fact that he was trussed up like a pig for the fire pit.

"How much did the magician pay you?"

"Nobody paid me anything." Balar shook his head and stooped low to cut the strap that looped under the camel's belly, securing Llesho's tied ankles to his bound wrists.

"Right. That's why I'm hanging upside down from a camel with my head ready to explode." Llesho wasn't surprised when his brother let him slide off in a heap. Traitor or not, Balar was really angry.

Hands planted on hips, his brother watched him pick his face up out of the sand- -definitely sand. Where were they, anyway? Llesho rolled over, which gave his brother some signal to go into full rant mode.

"A full complement of imperial militia traveled on private contracts with that caravan. If your damned Guynmer merchant had gone on with the rest, you would have been perfectly safe. We'd have had our happy homecoming at a decent inn, played a few songs, and we could have gotten you away from there before the Harn knew what we were doing. But he didn't. The fool left himself fully exposed in the most disreputable fringes of the city."

Shou wasn't, generally, a fool and you couldn't figure his motives based on his disguises. Their stop on the outskirts of Durnhag was about trouble in the city and her ladyship's spies, not about saving a few tael on lodgings, though the emperor wasn't here to support his claim. Neither was Adar or Hmishi or Lling, or Master Den. He had no intention of telling the brother who had kidnapped him any of that, however, which left him to listen as Balar lost his temper.

"The Uulgar had spies among the Harn in the caravan, of course, and they were looking for you."

"Who are the Uulgar?"

"The Harnishmen from the South. Your caravan had a group of Tinglut, Eastern clans. Not friends of the empire, but not under the magician's thumb either. The Uulgar, however, have a general order to take Thebin males of your age and let the magician sort you out."

"Is that where we are going now? To Master Markko?"

"Don't be more of an ass than you can help." Balar glared at him, as if Llesho were somehow responsible for the position he found himself in. Llesho glared right back.

"Fortunately for you, little brother, the Tashek have spies as well. Kagar got word to Harlol that you had stopped at that damned cesspit of an inn, and what was supposed to be a warm family reunion turned into a mad attempt at a rescue.

"We had to get you out of Durnhag, but you were fighting like a demon. Kagar tried to attract your attention and when that didn't work, . . . he . . . hit you over the head."

Now that he could actually see around him, Llesho noticed the Tashek groom lurking on the far side of the camel.

"He panicked," Balar continued, "hit you too hard, and maybe cracked your skull. It was the best we could manage under the circumstances. If the Harn hadn't divided their efforts between you and the other boy, we wouldn't have had a chance at a rescue."

If that was the truth, it didn't bode well for Hmishi. As bad as it was to be the object of Markko's search, how much worse to face his wrath as the wrong hostage? The memory of his friend screaming sent a fine tremor shivering through Llesho's body. Just a dream. But he knew it was more than that.

"By the time we pulled you out of there," Balar finished, "you were in no condition to ride, so we did the best we could."

Llesho cocked an eye at Dognut, who rode at his ease on a secure chair on the camel's back rather than tied down like a saddle pack.

"It seemed the easiest way to haul an unconscious body," the dwarf explained.

If Balar was lying, well, he wouldn't be the first prince in history to sell out his birthright, though from the look of him he'd made a poor bargain of it. Llesho probed for the lump on his head with his bound hands, winced when he found it.

"I'm not unconscious now," Llesho argued. "But I'm still tied up."

Balar had the grace to look embarrassed. Then he pulled his Thebin knife—a weapon which, Master Den had once told Llesho, a Thebin royal drew only to kill. So. Treason and murder it was. Llesho waited until his brother leaned over, blade poised, and then he kicked with all his might.

"Oof!" Balar didn't fly through the air as he should have, had Llesho been in better shape, but he did drop to his backside in the dust. And the kick knocked the knife out of his hand. Since his legs were still tied together, Llesho was no closer to escape, but it felt good to strike a blow in his own defense. Or it did until Kagar flung himself belly first over Llesho's legs and Harlol ground his shoulders into the sand beneath him. He gave up the struggle then. If he were going to be skewered, at least it wouldn't be on his brother's knife.

"I wish I had a stylus and paper." From his perch on top of the camel's pack, Dognut peered down at him with an avid grin. "I feel a comical song coming on."

"Traitor!" Llesho struggled to escape his captors.

Common words, like "betrayal," covered the actions of the Tashek drovers and Shou's double-crossing musician. His brother's actions went so much deeper that it almost didn't matter what they did to him next. Balar had already done the worst there was.

Brushing the dust from his robes, Balar cast about for his knife, but he put it away without making any further threats with it. Well out of Llesho's reach, he dropped into a Tashek squat, his elbows on his knees with his hands hanging loosely between them.

"No one is going to hurt you, Llesho."

Llesho snorted in disbelief. They'd already cracked his head or he would be giving them a decent fight, and his brother had just come after him with a knife.

Balar read the look he cast at the sheath on his belt. "I don't know what they've told you, but it's not magic. It's just a knife. I'm careful in a sparring match, but it cuts my beard—or a knot—just fine."

He knew that, and it reassured him more than it should have, that truth from his brother.

Balar gave him a lopsided smile. "You were in a battle fugue, fighting like a madman—or a god—"

They both understood the irony of that statement. All of the princes of Thebin shared in the divinity of the royal family. But as seventh son of the king, himself the seventh son of his own father-king, Llesho was, to his people, a god indeed.

"I'm sorry we had to hit you, but I can't apologize that you're here, with us, and not on your way to Harn." Balar drew in a deep breath and visibly calmed himself.

"Let him go." He reached out then, rested a hand on Llesho's knee, and gave a nod as a signal. "Kagar is going to cut your legs free so that we can get you on your horse."

Kagar drew his knife and slashed through the leather strap that held Llesho's ankles together. Oh. Not murder, then. Llesho had the humility to blush as his brother grabbed him by the collar and dragged him to his feet. At least, Llesho supposed he was standing. He couldn't feel anything below his knees and his legs bent under him like young bamboo. The two Tashek took his weight at shoulder and knee, and between them, they flipped him into his saddle.

"Harlol will tie you onto your saddle for your own protection," Balar explained in low tones that were meant to be soothing, but just made Llesho angrier. "Tomorrow, or the next day, when your head is a little clearer, you can ride without restraints. Until I'm sure you can manage without landing in the dirt, we'll do it baby-style."

Llesho remembered that reassuring smile, almost remembered the words. No more than a year or so old, he'd ridden his first pony strapped into a training saddle, much as he did today. But he knew treachery when he saw it. Harlol, the man who tied him onto his horse, had attacked the emperor's person, might have killed Shou if he'd been a better fighter. Where was Shou now? Or Master Den, for that matter, or—

"Where's Adar?"

Balar didn't answer right away. He mounted his own horse, staring out into the desert as if he could see something Llesho couldn't, which was likely given his gifts. "Adar will be all right. He was fully grown when the Harn attacked Kungol, and he didn't make the Long March." Guilt stirred in eyes grown damp with some old regret when Balar looked back at Llesho.

"He'll survive until we free him. You." He shook his head, unable, for a moment, to continue. Then he seemed to gather himself together for a last effort.

"The dream readers were not all agreed that you would survive the Harn again. They were afraid that you would throw your life away, fighting past hope until the raiders killed you. And that couldn't happen."

They were using the high court dialect of Kungol to keep their conversation private, and it took Llesho a moment to process the meaning out of the old, almost forgotten words. When he did, he gave his brother an icy glare. "I'm not that fragile." Or hadn't been, until Kagar had whacked him over the head. He was still unsteady from the blow, which made him sound less than convincing even to himself, but he wasn't about to let Balar treat him like a child. "The Harn took them, didn't they?"

Balar wouldn't even look at him, and Llesho remembered the sound of Hmishi screaming in his dream.

"Are we following them?" Pressure at his back told him no, but he waited for his brother to answer him. "We have to get them back."

"We are taking you to Ahkenbad. The dream readers will decide what to do next."

"Not good enough." Llesho wheeled his horse around, though weaponless and bound he could do nothing but make his brother chase him. "Master Markko will kill Hmishi out of spite, just for not being me. And you don't know what he will do to someone like Adar." Markko would take him apart, dissect him looking for the organ where the healer's gifts might reside. Llesho didn't say anything about Shou. Only the truth might move his brother to action there, and he still didn't know if Balar was his betrayer or the savior he claimed to be.

"We'll find Adar." Balar looked away, but not before Llesho saw the guilt fleetingly cross his face.

"What have you done?" he asked, determined to know the worst. His hands were still bound in front of him, his reins held on his right by his brother on horseback, and on his left by Harlol on foot. Kagar had taken his place on the camel, at ease on a pad of cloth folded into a seat in front of Dognut, who perched atop the creature's hump. Like the others, he furtively turned away when Llesho looked to him for answers. Dognut answered his question with a little dirge he played on his flute, but no one appreciated the humor. The mournful tune faded away into an uncomfortable trail of random notes, and the dwarf found something fascinating about the fingering of his instrument to study.

"Balar! Look at me!"

The musician prince gave a guilty start, but composed his features and faced his brother. "What do you want to know?"

"Why are you dragging me across this goddess-abandoned waste if this is not the direction they have taken Adar? And don't start babbling to me about dreamers and mystics. I've had my fill of the lot of them and I won't sacrifice the brother I have only just recovered to chase after some old hermit with a crystal ball."

"A powerful magician is looking for you—"

"Master Markko, I know. We have danced this dance many times. What of him?"

"Do you know why he wants you?"

"He thinks I have powers. I don't. So he's in for a disappointment either way it goes."

"You do, actually." Balar gave him a cool, appraising look.

Llesho smirked annoyingly at him, daring his brother to find any magic about him. When the dreams flitted through his mind, he banished them, refusing to believe they were anything more than a bad mix of anxiety and old memories rising out of his sleeping mind.

"I don't see it either." Balar shrugged. "But the dream readers swear it is true. This magician, they believe, will offer to free Adar if you set yourself in his place. He may include others of your companions in the trade if he must. They felt certain that you would exchange yourself for Adar, possibly for this Shou, definitely for the old servant who travels with Adar. To prevent your foolhardy sacrifice, I will take you to the dreaming place, bound if I must. When you are safely stowed, the dream readers will decide what to do about Adar."

"I'm not going to leave my brother's life to the visions of a stranger. He doesn't have time for that."

Harlol might have objected, and Llesho belatedly remembered that the drover practiced the religion of dreamers and Wastrels. Balar spoke up first, however, his eyes pleading, his expression ashamed.

"I'm not a soldier, Llesho. I know the forms; all the princes learned the Way of the Goddess, but I never used them to hurt a man until I had to pull you out of that inn. I just can't do what you expect of me."

Grumbling, Llesho gave in. He couldn't do much either, with his head swimming this way. Balar didn't have much to say after that, which left a lot of time with nothing to do but think.

"Adar is a healer. Balar centers the universe. Lluka sees the past and the future." He'd said those words to Kaydu, explaining his painfully failed vigil at the start of his quest. Six of his brother-princes before him had spent the night of their sixteenth summer waiting for the Great Goddess to show herself. Three of his brothers she had rejected, leaving each to his life of lesser gifts and no great destiny. Three she had found worthy: Adar and Balar and Lluka she had showered with gifts of the spirit, but none of them had been a soldier.

Llesho had ended his vigil with more destiny than he could handle, and no gifts to help him. Out of the blur of memories, his aching brain latched onto one unquestioned truth, however: *Balar centers the universe.* Was that what this trek across the desert was about? And, if so, why? He already had more quests than he could handle. The universe was just a bit more than he felt ready to take on for a Tashek hermit's dream.

On the other hand—which was still tied to the first, he balefully reminded himself—Master Den had said he needed a Tashek dream reader and here he was, suddenly off to see one. He'd never explained what the dream readers were, or why they might be important, but Balar, who centered the universe, seemed to think they were important, too.

"Who are these dream readers anyway, and what do they have to do with me?"

Balar gave him a sideways glance, not trusting this reasonable conversation.

"The dream readers are the holy seers of the Tashek people. In their dreams, they move freely between the world of their people's dreams, where time and distance run differently, and the waking world. When they awake, they bring the knowledge of their dream travels into the day, to guide the Tashek people. Lately, though, dreams about a young Thebin prince have spread throughout the camp, and with them the Great Goddess has sent a compulsion, to find the prince, her husband.

"You have to understand, they do not worship the Great Goddess here, and the intrusion of a strange deity into the dreams of the Tashek mystics has upset them greatly. I don't understand all of it, but it has something to do with her gardener, the Jinn."

"Pig. I know. Your dream readers are not the only people currently plagued by visions of talking pigs."

Balar nodded as if Llesho had just confirmed a suspicion he hadn't yet spoken aloud. "The Dinha has seen this magician, Markko you say his name is, searching for the gardener of heaven. But in the dream, the gardener he seeks is not Pig, the Jinn, but a great black pearl on a silver chain around the throat of that prince."

Llesho didn't know what a Dinha was, but raised his bound hands and looped a finger over the neck of his tunic, tugging the fabric out of the way to expose his throat. "No silver chain," he pointed out, though he knew the chain his brother spoke of, had seen it in his own dream.

"No chain," Balar agreed, "but three black pearls."

They had searched him while he was unconscious, which he should have expected. That he still had the pearls on their cord around his neck surprised him.

Llesho shrugged in mock indifference. "I'm collecting them. It's part of the quest. Lleck's ghost gave me the first one when he sent me to find my brothers. He stole it from the dragon queen who lives in Pearl Bay with her children, which turned out all right. She would have given it to me herself, she said, if I didn't already have it. Lady SienMa, mortal goddess of war, gave me the second."

He did not mention the other gifts he had received from the mortal goddess; he wondered if he had lost those relics of his past self in his brother's harebrained kidnapping. "The third I received from the healer Mara, beloved of the Golden River Dragon, and aspirant to the position of eighth mortal god. And mother to Lady Carina, apprentice to our brother, Adar."

He did not need to tell his brother the consequences of leaving Carina in the hands of the Harn. Balar had grown quite pale.

"I'm supposed to find them all—the pearls, not the gods—but no one bothered to tell me how many there are. I've collected three brothers as well, but I'm not as good at keeping my hands on the Thebin princes as on the pearls."

"You travel with such creatures and receive gifts of the mortal gods, and still insist you have no magical gifts?" Balar demanded, wary in his turn. "I think, perhaps, you do not listen to your own tale. But I am one brother, and Adar is a second. Who is the third?"

They were Balar's brothers, too. Llesho didn't see any reason not to answer. "Shokar has a farm in Shan. He was raising crops when I found him, but when I left, he had changed his agronomy to soldiers, and now raises troops."

"Make that four, then."

It was Llesho's turn to show both his pleasure and his surprise. "Who?"

"Lluka awaits our return among the dream readers of Ahkenbad."

Lluka was the third husband of the goddess, and had received the gift of knowing the past and the future, so he

probably fit right in with the Tashek mystics. Llesho wasn't
certain he was ready to hear about his future, though, even
if it did insist on cropping up in his dreams. Especially
since that future seemed to be taking him into the Gansau
Wastes. Even the desert-hardened Tashek had fled into
the Harnlands to survive the dry months. Or so Dognut
had said. Dognut, of course, had lied about many things.

Balar seemed to read the doubt in his face, though he
had no way of knowing the cause. "The Holy Well of
Ahkenbad is no myth."

"Holy Well?"

"It is the most sacred place in all the Gansau Waste,"
Balar explained, "and whether the water flows because
the Tashek dream it so, or the dream readers dream
because the water flows, even the dream readers cannot
say. You can ask Lluka about it when you see him."

A holy well in the desert. No wonder the people of
Ahkenbad had strange dreams. Master Markko could
probably tell them exactly what poison had seeped into
the water from the surrounding soil to give them their
visions. Then he'd torture them to death studying its
effects.

"I'd rather know where my pack is," Llesho replied
tartly. "I need my weapons. Kagar and Harlol might as
well be riding backward for all the attention they are
paying to the road ahead. The raiders won't be happy
that you stole their prize, however wrongheaded they are
to put so great a value on my hide. I don't give much
for my chances if I'm unarmed and tied to my saddle
when they catch up to us."

"We brought your pack." Balar gave him a penetrating
look. "The spear you carry in it burns me when I touch
it. Kagar suffers no such rejection and has taken your
possessions in safekeeping."

His jade cup, his spear. He found himself growing suspicious and defensive when they were out of his control.
"I want to check my property."

"The Tashek wouldn't steal from you, Llesho; they

think you are their personal savior. I couldn't even if I wanted to, so whatever you have in there is safe. But if I return your weapons, will you give me your word as a prince and brother not to run?"

The sun rained hammer blows on Llesho's head in spite of the covering someone had flung over his brow for the desert crossing. He looked out through the protective mesh, stained now to the dun color of the sand, into the sand-clouded sky.

"Have we been on this trek minutes or days while I slept on my belly over Shou's stolen camel?" Laughing bitterly, he surrendered, biding his time. "Is there any direction to run in this hell that doesn't end with me dead of thirst?" Water, he dreamed, in a jade cup green as the sea.

Balar gave an uneasy look behind him; Llesho felt the pursuit as well, like heat pressing against his back. Harnish raiders of the Uulgar clans thundered at their heels, goaded into the desert by the devouring hatred of the magician.

"If it comes to that, kill me," Llesho said. He wouldn't be a prisoner of the Harn or the subject of Markko's experiments again.

"If it comes to that, I won't. So don't let it come to that." Balar gave a sharp whistle between his teeth, and Kagar trotted up beside them.

"Give him his sword and his knife. Hold onto the bow and arrows, and especially the short spear. Lluka will want to look at them."

"You are speaking of the gifts of the Lady SienMa," Llesho warned his brother. "She will not take kindly to their theft."

"Theft again, Llesho? Is that what you think of your brothers?" Balar's stare burned his skin more surely than the sun, but finally he gave a fractional lift of his shoulder. He reached over with his knife and cut the bonds that tied Llesho's wrists to his saddle. "Return these gifts, then. We don't want to anger the goddess of war."

Kagar reached behind him and unlashed the pack resting on his horse's haunches. He took out the sword, the knife, and handed them over. Attaching them to his belt, Llesho held out his hand for the short bow which he strung and tested before sliding it into the saddle-scabbard behind his right leg. The quiver of arrows with her Ladyship's own fletching he settled across his back. When Kagar drew out the short spear, Llesho shivered, suddenly cold in spite of the sun. Pain cut deeply into his breast, shadow-memory of past deaths, but he refused to give the weapon power over his present.

"Give it to me," he commanded softly

Moving like a sleepwalker, Kagar held out the spear. "The cup is safe, Holy One," the Tashek groom offered in a high, light whisper.

Llesho took the spear with a nod to accept both the assurance and the weapon. The groom trembled, wide-eyed with terror, but his hands were unhurt. Adar had blistered when he'd held the spear; Llesho didn't know how, but the weapon must be able to recognize the blood of a Thebin prince, and would accept only the chosen one.

"You travel with wonders about you, Llesho." Dognut the dwarf gestured at the spear with a twist of distaste around his mouth. "And they don't like you very much."

The dwarf's comments murdered any hope Llesho had that the connection he felt to the spear came from his own imagination. Kagar had felt it, but only when he touched it. Dognut hadn't needed the contact to be affected by it. Llesho resolved to pay closer attention to the dwarf.

Balar watched him expressionlessly, waiting for an answer that Llesho didn't understand himself. He said nothing, but nudged his horse into motion. "How long until we reach this holy well?"

"Too long," Balar admitted, and urged them to a faster pace.

Chapter Ten

WITH the sun on their backs like the ever-present fear of pursuit, they pressed deep into the Gansau Wastes. Maybe the blow to his head had done more damage than he'd realized, or the spear whispering at his back had driven him mad. It seemed to Llesho that the desert itself, growing more impossibly bleak with each passing day, had bled his thoughts dry, leaving nothing but the dreams growing steadily more powerful that plagued his sleep: Hmishi screamed as though his captors had torn out his liver for the birds while Lling, pale and dreadful, looked on and Shou rattled his chains in helpless rage. Habiba followed on a great white horse, with an eagle perched on his pommel, but even his subtle powers could not show him the way. Master Markko appeared in none of these visions, but his presence filled them like a poisonous vapor.

Llesho grew to dread any rest. When he refused to sleep, however, the twilight dreamscape spilled into his waking mind like a hallucination, and he felt the anger and terror of the Harn in his own heart. Images assailed him, and he knew that the Harnish raider whose mind leaked into his both loathed and feared the magician whose will drove them from a distance. For the power

of his clan, however, and in dread that Master Markko
would kill them all if they failed, the man followed his
chieftain deep into the desert. The Harnishman feared
the Wastes as well, for the myths that Hmishi had talked
about—the Wastrels, and the dream readers and the spirits that walked the deep desert. Equally he dreaded that
they had lost their way in the parched wastelands. When
they ran out of water, the sun would bake the flesh from
their bones while their brains boiled in their skulls.

The raider's thoughts were so like his own that the dis-
tinction between them blurred. Llesho felt the pressing fury
of the pursuer, only dimly aware that he was the focus of
that rage. The Harnishman didn't resent the chief of the
Uulgar clan who had led him into the Wastes, but hated
the prey that drew him more deeply into the land of his
nightmares. The man pictured in his head the tortures his
raiding party would inflict on the Thebin prince when they
caught him, and Llesho cried out in his dream. The imagin-
ings of the raider raised bruises and welts on his skin, as
if the blows were real. They would make him talk and turn
him over to their master a broken, beaten slave.

Llesho pulled on the bonds that tied him to his saddle,
lost between the torment of the dream and the throbbing
unreality of his own trek through the desert. Dimly, from
a distance he could not cross, he thought he heard Balar
calling to him, but this time he couldn't escape the tortured visions that circled in his aching mind.

"Llesho! Wake up! It's just a dream!"

They had come to a halt, or Llesho thought they must
have since Balar was standing at his side.

"Drink, please!" A waterskin, evil-smelling and nearly
empty, poked at his chin. He remembered a caution
about poisoned wells and pushed it away, at the same
time doubting everything he saw—the waterskin and the
dead oasis long gone to sand, and the failed shade of
dying date palm where they had stopped for rest.

"You have to drink, Prince Llesho, or you will die!"
Dognut urged him, still atop his snappish camel.

"Please, brother." Balar lifted the waterskin again.

Llesho gave him a shove, "You're not real!" he cried, surprised at how hoarse his voice had become. The skin fell, water drooling into the sand. He could smell the moist promise of it with a desperate desire. Even a hallucination could tell the truth once in a while, and Dognut was right; he was going to die if he didn't drink.

Harlol, who had tried to kill the emperor, snatched the skin up again before too much was lost. "Damn it, Kagar, did you have to hit him so hard?"

"I didn't!" Kagar insisted. "It's the dreams. They've addled his brainpan!"

"Tell that to the Dinha when she asks us why we've come home with the dead husk of the prince of dreams."

Harlol was angry. Good. Well, not good if it meant Llesho was dead, but at least the Tashek had begun to show his true colors. They had kidnapped him to give to this Dinha. Balar said to trust him, but maybe he'd been duped.

"The prince won't die," Balar grabbed the waterskin and Harlol grunted a noncommittal answer before going off to check the feet of the camel.

He had no intention of dying. Llesho could have told them that, but he didn't trust them with the only truth he clung to: the minions of his old enemy, Master Markko, had taken Adar. He would stay alive, whatever it took, until he got his brother back. If they chose to poison him, well, their dream readers survived it and so could he. After all, he'd been through it before with Master Markko.

"Please, Llesho. You've fought so long, don't give up now." Balar poured water into his hand and offered it like a supplicant. "Drink."

This time, he drank. It tasted stale, and a little bit like leather and Balar's dusty hands, but otherwise untampered with. That didn't mean he could trust them; it just meant they wanted him alive for the time being. He could deal with that.

"Good boy."

Llesho would have hit him for the condescending approval, but it seemed like a waste of effort to punish a hallucination. "You're not real." He'd already said that, but couldn't figure out anything more original to add. It must have worked, though, because Harlol cursed imaginatively as he climbed onto his horse. Balar said nothing, his expression closing in around his bleak desperation. Then they were moving again, and Llesho lost himself once more among the worlds of his dreams.

When the pressure eased, he thought that he had died, or that he would waken to discover that everything since the vigil of his sixteenth summer had been a dream. Afraid of what he'd find when he did so, Llesho opened his eyes to find himself in her ladyship's orchard in Farshore Province. The mortal goddess SienMa had taught him to shoot a bow here, by taking aim at the stems that held the peaches to her trees and afterward they had dined on the fruit he had plucked with his newfound skill. In the dream, he woke to the green pattern of leaves overhead and the prickle of grass beneath his backside. The smell of peaches filled his nose with memories of his last moment of peace, and he would have wept, except that he didn't believe in any of it, not even for a moment.

"My gardeners cannot reach the top of the tree, where the best peaches have ripened—can you shoot them down for me?" The goddess SienMa nudged his shoulder, and Llesho peered out at her through an eyelid slitted open in the hope she wouldn't notice that he was looking.

"I know you're awake, and I'm hungry for that peach."

"You can't be real." He surrendered to the dream, drawing himself up so that his spine leaned back on the slender trunk of the peach tree. "Master Markko burned this orchard to the stone."

That was when the killing had started in earnest—Llesho's first true battle, but not the last. He'd forgotten the beauty of this orchard, though her ladyship was as he remembered her: beautiful and terrible at the same time, with a smile colder than the snow in the mountains high above Kungol.

"Even a dream can get hungry. I'd really like that peach." She was, he reminded himself, a mortal goddess and the patroness of wars. And Shou had left her on his throne to defend the Shan Empire in his absence.

"Is there trouble?"

"Of course there is trouble. The emperor has got himself captured by his enemies along with that trickster ChiChu, and I still don't have that peach."

Llesho considered for a moment. He couldn't do much but apologize for the one, but his dream self knew how to bring down a peach. He stood and bent low from the waist in respect. When he thought of it, his bow appeared in his hand, and he drew, aimed, sent his soul flying into the treetop, and opened a hand to receive it just as the peach fell. "My lady."

"Thank you." She took the peach from his outstretched palm and began to eat. Her lips barely seemed to move. Llesho saw not even a glimpse of her teeth or any juice of the peach on her chin, but still the fruit was disappearing. When the yellow flesh was gone, she flipped the stone into the grass and settled her eyes on him again. Llesho found her full attention daunting but felt he owed her more than one of her own peaches for all the trouble he'd caused.

"My lady," he repeated. With a graceful nod of her head she gave him permission to continue.

Llesho took a deep breath. "I don't deserve your forgiveness, but I beg your pity."

"For what, boy?"

"It was my quest, but the emperor has suffered for it, and with him his whole empire. Master Den is a prisoner as well, and Adar, and Carina, whose mother aspires to be a mortal god." He gave a bitter smile. "I have angered more gods than I ever imagined I would meet, and at least one dragon as well. As quests go, I couldn't have made a bigger mess if I'd intended to screw up from the start."

Everyone who ever tried to help him had suffered or died for it, including the goddess whose orchard had burned in Markko's pursuit of him.

Her ladyship tilted her head, as if she needed to study the problem of Prince Llesho from a different angle. "You are assuming that yours is the only quest on this journey," she finally pointed out. "Shou also has trials to suffer and lessons to learn."

"But Shou is old!"

"Not *so* old."

The protest had escaped him before Llesho could stop it. At the goddess' wry reply he blushed and fidgeted, trying to keep his mind away from questions like, "How old is a mortal goddess anyway?" and "What are you testing Shou for?" On consideration, he figured Shou could probably use some lessons at that. The emperor showed great bravery and daring in matters of battle and espionage, for which Llesho took him as a model and teacher. But he didn't seem to spend a lot of time on statecraft and diplomacy, which Lleck had always told Llesho were the trusty tools of a great king. That was before the old minister had been reincarnated as a bear, of course, back when he had advised Llesho with greater subtlety and better pronunciation.

So, giving Shou a quest made sense. Maybe so did leaving him to figure it out for himself, though doing it as a prisoner of the Harn made it a whole lot harder. It left Llesho with a problem, however. Master Den had followed Shou to teach those lessons, he guessed or, knowing the trickster god, to keep the emperor alive while he learned them on his own. It didn't help Llesho.

After giving it enough thought to make his head ache even in his dream, he admitted, "Master Den was *my* mentor. Without him, I don't know what to do."

"Look around you." The mortal goddess reached into a bowl that Llesho hadn't seen before and pulled out a plum, which she handed to him. "There are many teachers in the world if we pay attention, and none at all if we don't."

Llesho was pondering the meaning of that when he noticed a huge pig rooting at the base of a peach tree. He remembered another dream with a pig in it, and he reached for the three black pearls that hung at his breast. "Is that—?"

Before he could finish the question, Lady SienMa answered it with laughter in her voice. "Not a teacher, but possibly a guide." Then she called the creature to her, "Master Pig!"

"Not 'Master,' my lady, as you well know. Just Pig." The Jinn stood on his hind legs and bowed politely, then swiped another plum from the lady's bowl. "We've met." He grinned at Llesho around huge, sharp tusks, then gobbled down the fruit, pit and all, in two powerful snaps of his teeth. "You're going the wrong way, you know. You'd have done better to stick with Shou—at least the Harn are carrying him closer to the gates of heaven."

"Closer to Master Markko as well," the lady added.

"And I have brothers still to find, and pearls."

"Ah, well. You have a point there." Pig's nose twitched and he gave the ground a sharp glance. "Still, we'll find a use for you, I suppose." Sniffing attentively, he wandered away with the words, "Keep in touch," tossed over his shoulder.

"How am I supposed to do that?" But when he turned back, Llesho discovered that the mortal goddess of war had disappeared and her orchard lay in ashes. He awoke with a start to the realization that a barely sensed pressure between his shoulder blades had not returned. The Harn no longer followed them.

It took a moment for Llesho to realize that something

had actually wakened him. They had left the desert sand for a road winding between hills stripped clean to the rocky bone. High on either side cliff faces rose above them, layers of soft stone folded in on themselves like the leaves of a hastily abandoned book or stacks of broken plates. Color slashed across the dun layers, rust-red and gray, with veins of lichenous green and sulfurous yellow running through the cave- pocked sandstone. He wondered what forces had cracked the hillside, and how a road had come to exist between.

"Welcome to the Stone River of Ahkenbad, boy." Dognut waved a flute at the cliffs on either side.

"River?"

Dognut waggled his eyebrows in a display of mock amazement. "Did I say river? Yes, I did! The Gansau Wastes weren't always a desert. That was before the time of the Tashek and their nomad cities, of course. Now the riverbeds make fine roads in a place nobody wants to go."

"What happened to it?" Llesho stared about him with amazement. Some giant hand might have taken hold of the earth and ripped it from its moorings here.

"Many things. Ages laid the stone, and ages more the great river wore the stone away."

"But where did the water go?"

"Ah, well, there was a dragon. Isn't there always? There used to be a song—"

Llesho didn't know about real life. In all his seventeen summers he'd only met two dragons, and those had been under extraordinary circumstances. He had to agree that dragons showed up in an awful lot of songs, however.

The dwarf drew out a flute no bigger than his thumb. He played the first few measures of a tune, and when he was satisfied that he'd set the melody in his ear, he began to sing:

Now when the summer reeds grew tall
and sun shone on the water

Lord Dragon sallied from his hall
The fisherfolk to slaughter.

"My hall!" he cried, "is not for men,
Their nets, their lines, or sinkers
And if I must warn you again
I'll stave in all your clinkers."

Llesho's confusion must have shown on his face, because Dognut paused to explain, "Clinker-built is a way of making the bottom of a boat so that the water can't get in."

"Like Master Den's traveling washtub," Llesho remembered out loud.

"Exactly." The dwarf swept his explanation past the point before Llesho could ask how he knew about battle-field laundry tubs. "The dragon was threatening to sink the fishing boats."

The farmers of Golden Dragon River lived in peace with their monster. They revered the worm beneath the water and respected his right to the fish that swam in the silty currents. He had a bad feeling about the Stone River, though.

When he nodded that he understood, the dwarf picked up the song again, and Llesho found himself drawn into the tale of a Gansau that was no waste at all, but a fertile land where rivers used to flow and lush jungles grew on the hillsides. In spite of the wealth the river brought to the land, however, the fishermen wanted the fish as well. Unfortunately, so did the dragon. When they couldn't come to an agreement, the fishermen hired hunters and mercenaries to rid them of their dragon. At the height of the story, with murder hinted just ahead, Dognut ceased to sing.

"You can't stop now!" Llesho protested, and he noticed that Balar and their Tashek guides had likewise turned to the dwarf for an ending to his tale. "What happened next?"

"That depends on who tells the story. Some say the fishermen succeeded in murdering the dragon, and the mourning river refused to flow. Some say the dragon grew tired of the harassment and left, taking his river with him. In that version of the tale, Lord Dragon found a new ground to water and a new bed to sleep in where the people knew how to honor a river. As for the fishermen, well, some say they died, and wanderers took their place in the waste they left behind. Others say they remained, clinging to the wells and oases until their children had forgotten that any river ever flowed here, or any fish swam in it."

The dwarf made a sweeping-broom gesture, a past to be brushed aside. "The only truth that matters is that no river flows here now."

Llesho figured the story might be true, but Dognut's conclusion likely wasn't. His own experience of dragons had proved them difficult to kill, hot-tempered but of a legalistic temper. And they didn't like to stir from their homes much. Thoughtfully he slipped from his saddle, wanting to feel the land through his own feet. Did it shift under him like an old dragon stirring in its sleep? Or was that just the beat of the horses' hooves on the drum of the road?

The heat, he decided, had driven out logic and left only fancy and a dry drift of yellow dust blurring his senses. Somewhere in the hills, he felt the presence of people he could not see and water, like a siren call, stirred deep beneath his feet. Light blazed in the distance, but he stood in a place of darkness. Lifting the gritty veil from his eyes didn't help.

"Am I blind?" he asked himself, and only realized that he'd spoken aloud when Balar answered him.

"It's just the dust," his brother assured him, but that wasn't it. He could see well enough, but what he saw seemed at odds with what he felt around him. A veil lay across his mind, not his eyes, and he shook his head, determined to clear his clouded thoughts. And he saw it, the gritty corner of a sandstone ledge jutting from the cliff face. Focusing down on the individual grains of sand fused into stone, he forced the haze from his mind.

Ahkenbad. Somehow, they had entered the city itself and stood in the shade of a rocky overhang. Llesho blinked, a cry of surprise escaping—

"How?"

His mouth was hanging open, and he closed it with a snap of his teeth. Ahkenbad was like no city he had ever seen. For one thing, it seemed to be no city at all—he saw no buildings, no walls like those that made the cities of Shan or Farshore, no gardens. Rather, artisans had carved the whole city into the towering cliffs that rose high above the riverbed that wound between them. Set along narrow paths that zigzagged to the top, the mouth of cave after cave gaped down on them between glinting streaks of jade and lapis fused in tortured waves that rippled across the cliff face.

Simple carvings of pillars and trailing vines that drew the mineral colors into the designs outlined the openings into the caves at the heights. Rows of heavy curtains hid the chambers behind heavy embroidery worked on red cloth: elaborate twining vines, and nests with brightly feathered birds standing guard over huge eggs stitched in blue and yellow. Flanking the road at its own level, the caves of Ahkenbad were larger and more elaborate. Figures carved in bas-relief seemed to writhe in sinuous dances around each entrance—strange, stern desert spirits glaring over an abandoned marketplace that lined the road with just a few tattered awnings draped on poles. Beneath the faded canopies, among the empty bins and broken bits of oil jars, aged Tashek nomads stared into a distance that had nothing to do with the handful of paces between themselves and Llesho's party.

"The chamber of the dream readers." Balar directed his attention to a cave with an entrance more elaborately decorated than the others. With an effort, he let go of his tense contemplation of the Tashek elders who lined the streets more terrifyingly than the great stone dancers, and looked where Balar pointed.

Set at the very center of the mountainside, a jagged cave entrance stretched like the gaping mouth of a monstrous dragon out of Dognut's songs. Around the yawning arch of its mouth, open wide as if to swallow the road, artisans had carved the stone into sharp, curved, dragon teeth. A broad flat nose flared over the mouth, the smoke of fires perfumed with sandalwood and cedar drifting from its deep nostrils. The plates and horns of a dragon's ruff made a halo around the entrance. On the top of the carved head, great horns rose like columns flanking the entrance to a cave that opened atop the dragon's head. Great eyes had been carved in the half-closed position of a sleeping dragon, with deep blue flashes of lapis just hinted at between the lashes. They reminded Llesho too much of the Golden River Dragon's impersonation of a bridge, stirring a creeping terror in his heart.

While he stood transfixed, wondering if he would survive a meeting with yet another legend, someone pushed aside a cloth of heavy silk and came toward them out of the dragon's mouth.

"Balar, did you find—"

Except for his shaved head, this man could have been Llesho himself in another ten years. They were of equal height and had the same dark coloring, though he paled when he saw Llesho.

"Sweet heavenly Goddess, you have found him."

To Llesho's consternation, his newfound brother fell to one knee and bowed his head at Llesho's feet. Then, all along the road they had travelled, the aged Tashek mystics followed his example, bending aching joints to kneel in the grit, their heads bowed to the young prince.

"Lluka?" he asked in disbelief, "What are you doing down there?"

Chapter Eleven

"HONORING the prince of dreams." Lluka stood slowly, his glittering eyes dry in his weather-pinched face. A strange mix of calculation and emotion seemed to pass behind that searching gaze.

In the slaver's office, where they'd met to rescue each other, neither Adar nor Shokar had succeeded in hiding their anguish and the love they felt for their youngest brother. In the fleeting moment before the Harn attacked the inn at Durnhag, Balar's joy at finding his brother had shone in his face. When he stared into Lluka's eyes, however, Llesho felt only the slow glide of secrets rising out of darkness. Lluka wanted something from him, and he wasn't sure Llesho would give it.

"I don't understand—" He turned to Balar for his answers, trusting at least his own powers to read the man who'd kidnapped him and dragged him across the desert.

"The Dinha said to bring the prince of dreams, so I did." Balar shrugged, clearly hiding something.

"And Lluka is the Dinha?"

Balar shook his head. "No. We are both simple students in the service of the Dinha."

That answer didn't satisfy him at all. He scanned the

crowd, looking for a less guarded source of information. Harlol had stopped to embrace an aged crone with a wrinkled, leathery face. She handed him a pair of curved swords suspended from a tooled leather belt and he buckled them under his coats, low about his waist. He stood taller, balanced over his knees like a soldier, and met Llesho's gaze steadily.

"The merchant Shou called you a Wastrel," Llesho answered the challenge. They both remembered when Shou had taunted the Tashek drover over poised swords.

Harlol dropped his head once in acknowledgment. "The Dinha sent Wastrels to bring you here before the Julgar Harn could take you to the magician. I had the advantage of our Harnish friends, however. Lluka and Balar have studied with the Dinha for many years; the family likeness stamps you like a coin. Adar, I was not so sure of. I meant to test him, but I would not have killed your brother."

"His blood stains the blades you drew on him." The memory squeezed like a fist around Llesho's heart. So much he might have lost on that morning—a brother, a friend. The emperor of Shan. The world had almost come undone. "Did you know that our host would answer your challenge? If not Adar, did you plan to murder Shou?"

"Your merchant should have stayed out of it."

Stubborn. Llesho was unimpressed. "And for defending his guest, you would have killed him?"

"I might have tried." Harlol laughed softly. "I hoped only to scare him a little, but there is more to our pompous merchant than he seems."

He wasn't laughing now, but settled those uncanny sharp eyes on Llesho, as if he could find his answers in an unguarded emotion. "He fights like no fool but rather like a man whose life has dangled on the point of a sword many times. And I had worried him. Among the Tashek I'm considered one of the best, but I count myself lucky to have survived the encounter."

"And your Dinha wished this because . . . ?" Llesho
sidestepped the question of Shou's identity, referring instead to the testing of Adar, and his own kidnapping.

Lluka interrupted before Harlol could answer. "If you
will come with me, she'll tell you herself." With a clap
of his hands, he called out, "Shelter for our guests, and
water—"

Several of the Tashek scurried to do his bidding, with
the dwarf's grumbling from atop Shou's stolen camel
only adding to the general commotion. "About time,"
he muttered, and grumbled at Kagar to: "Let me down,
before my legs fall off up here."

As if released from the spell of Ahkenbad, Kagar
raced to Dognut's side and unhooked the ladder from
the saddle pack. When the dwarf had made his painful
way to the ground, complaining with each step about the
sting of returning life in his legs, Lluka gathered them
up in the sweep of his arm.

"Come in out of the heat. You are safe now—from
discovery, at least."

"The Dinha wants to ask you some questions." Balar
fell in beside him with wry gloom written on his face.

Llesho nodded. The exhaustion he had fought for so
long would have felled him if his brother hadn't taken
him by the arm. "Some great power muddies the flow of
dreams. She thinks it may be you."

With more effort than he had to spare, Llesho mus-
tered a retort. "I didn't do anything. The Dinha would
do better to concentrate on Master Markko. If he finds
us unprepared, we are doomed."

"The magician failed, at least in this—the magic of
Ahkenbad turned his forces aside. You, however, found
the hidden city in spite of all its protections. If nothing
else, it proves the city wants you here."

"I just followed you," Llesho objected. "I didn't even
control the reins of my own horse for most of the
journey."

"Ah, but we didn't know the way." His voice kept

very low, Balar murmured for only Llesho to hear. "We followed you."

"You live here, and so do Harlol and Kagar. Of course you knew your way back."

"We couldn't find the way." Balar gave a little shrug, accepting the strangeness of it. "We'd still be lost in the desert if we hadn't followed you."

He didn't believe it for a minute, and suspected that Lluka didn't either. Balar did, though, so there wasn't any point in arguing it with him. "And what was that bending and kneeling about anyway? The last time I saw Lluka, he refused to speak to me because I broke one of the screws on his lute."

"He has his moods, but he loved you. More than that I will leave for the Dinha to explain."

Llesho felt the past tense of that like a sharp cut. He said nothing, however, but followed his brother into the mouth of the dragon.

Whatever he had set himself to expect, it wasn't the dim but opulent chamber that he discovered there. A single lantern rested on a table fashioned from a rocky outcropping at the center of the massive cave. Skilled artisans had plastered the soft rock of the walls and ceiling until they were as smooth as fine paper. They'd decorated every surface with elaborate paintings of date trees with birds nesting in them and curious spirits with tongues of fire dancing above their heads. In the flickering lamplight, the spirits seemed to nod their heads at one another, their eyes reflecting the lantern's flame with otherworldly purpose.

Amid the spirits dancing on the walls at the back of the cave, a staircase carved from the living stone of the mountain ascended into the darkness. The floor was covered in a thick layering of carpets, and cushions lay scattered about for people to sit upon. Most were taken up by silent figures who sat perfectly still with their eyes open but unseeing, like the dead. For a brief, irrational moment, Llesho imagined that life had fled those human

shells to take up residence in the more lively gazes of
the spirits painted on the walls above them. He shivered
even as he rejected the notion. No mystical transference
of life essence, but the skill of the artists and his own
imagination brought those images to life. Or so he hoped.

Several old Tashek trailed them into the cavern and
found their own places on the floor. Lluka directed him
to an empty cushion and Balar took a place at Llesho's
right. Dognut settled himself in a corner that seemed to
be fitted out for his special use. Harlol, the last to enter,
took up a position as sentry at the entrance to the cave.

Llesho found that he was sitting across from a crone
who slept, barely breathing, sitting upright with legs bent
in the lotus. Her eyes were open, like the others of her
kind, but covered by cataracts that turned the orbs in
her head to milky pearls and he shuddered with some
supernatural dread. Even blind and asleep, the old Tashek woman seemed to be studying him. It felt like she'd
stripped him naked in front of all the gathered company.

With a touch on the shoulder, Balar distracted him
from his momentary discomfort. "Dinha," he said, dropping his gaze in a respectful bow, "I have brought my
brother-prince, as you spoke the dream."

"You have done well, my child."

Llesho trembled at the shock of her raspy whisper. "I
thought you were sleeping."

"We are," she answered, "sleeping. You are our
dream."

She smiled at his consternation, though how she saw
his frown remained a mystery to him.

Lluka handed Balar a plain silver cup, but to Llesho
he held out the jade cup of the Lady SienMa before
seating himself at Llesho's left. A Tashek youth followed
with a tall pitcher in his hand. He knelt before them,
carefully pouring a scant inch of water into each cup. No
one offered refreshment to the old Tashek dream readers
seated together in the dragon's mouth, although each sat
dust-covered and with parched lips.

"As you see, however, even the holy city has little hospitality to offer." The Dinha gave a nod in Lluka's direction, and the prince accepted permission to speak.

"Too much has happened since you left us, Balar, and little of it has been good."

Balar sighed and drank his scanty portion. "The situation outside is worse than we thought as well," he warned the gathering. "Our enemies are close behind us. We lost them as we approached the city, but they will not have gone far."

Llesho cocked his head, looking within himself for the sensation that had lately preyed upon his mind. He found nothing.

"They're gone," he said.

"Who?" Lluka asked as Balar pressed, "Are you sure?"

"I'm sure," Llesho insisted. "For now, at least. I felt it when they lost our track, like a stone lifted from my heart, but waiting to fall again."

He did not say, "It was during a dream about a pig in her ladyship's garden," but he thought perhaps it would not surprise the Dinha. "Now, the stone has turned to dust. Something turned them away."

Silent but watchful behind her unseeing eyes, the Dinha listened carefully. Then, with a languid gesture that seemed to arise out of dreams, she raised a hand to halt the questions. "Our guest needs rest."

She subsided again into trance, while Lluka took up duties as host. "You will want to sleep. I regret that we have no bath to offer you, but the spirits of the desert have struck Ahkenbad a terrible blow."

"Then it has happened—" Balar frowned. "The holy well no longer flows?"

"It fell to a trickle soon after you left us, and for days now the bucket has brought up only sand. We have a day or two in reserve, if we are cautious, but not enough water to hold Ahkenbad against the dry time, nor sufficient to take the old ones out of the desert. That supposes they would leave or had a safe place to go if they could travel. The dream readers of Ahkenbad have withdrawn into the dreaming way. They've given their share to the acolytes who stayed behind to serve them, but their sacrifice gains us just a few hours."

"I'm sorry." Balar let his head fall.

Llesho reached a hand to touch his brother's shoulder, as if he could somehow take the weight of desperate knowledge from him. So this explained the parched creases of Lluka's face. How long had he gone without water so that Llesho could drink? It reminded him too much of the Long March. He couldn't say that he liked these newfound brothers yet, but Lleck had told him to find them all, not just the ones who loved him. And he'd lost too many already—his people on the Long March; his teacher, Master Jaks, in battle; and now maybe Hmishi, too, sacrificed so that Llesho could complete a task he'd never asked for. He would not lose these brothers and the chance to know them again, to gain another day or two of life without them.

"If you die for me, I won't forgive you for it, ever," Llesho swore at his brother.

"I'll do my best to keep us all alive," Lluka assured him in return. "But the Dinha insists that you hold our fate in your hands, and in your dreams."

"And the goddess, your lady wife? What do you see with her gifts?"

"I see light reflecting off tears, and locked gates that have lost their keys." Lluka rose to his feet and offered him a hand up. "And maybe—after long seasons of searching—we have found the great key."

Llesho would have objected, but he had grown tired of making denials that no one believed anyway. He scarcely recognized this man whose voice managed to convey both irony and hope without letting any of his secrets go. Hard to remember that Lluka had been no older than Llesho himself was now when last they'd seen each other. His brother hadn't suffered the Long March, the battles, or the years of captivity to lay calluses on his heart, but his own hardships had changed him into this distant stranger with the farseeing look of the desert. Llesho missed the young idealist, the musician who glowed with the blessings of the goddess in his eyes.

"Do you still play the lute?" he asked.

"Often. I like to think the goddess accepts my music as the offering of a devoted husband. I hope that I give her some pleasure, and some peace, in these terrible times."

Llesho nodded, satisfied that this at least had not changed.

"You'd better rest while you can. Tomorrow we'll keep you busy performing miracles." The sun had set, casting the dragon cave into greater darkness, and Llesho felt the pull of sleep. Wearily he followed his brother to the back of the cave where Dognut sat watching with quick, dark eyes. As Llesho passed, he picked up a reed flute and played a simple lullaby, softly so that the sound barely reached beyond the niche where the stone staircase began. He wondered if the tune were meant to mock him in some way, but the dwarf looked troubled, and he finished with a sad smile.

"Sleep safely, young prince. Don't let the dreams steal all your rest."

Master Den had spoken with respect of the dream readers of Ahkenbad. Llesho had gotten the impression they were councillors of some kind, and his brothers' presence in the holy city inclined him to trust them. But Master Den was, in his true form, a trickster god, and his brothers had kidnapped him, abandoning the emperor of Shan to capture or death. So he answered, "I won't," and determined to stay on his guard even in sleep.

"No one will hurt you here," Lluka assured him with a glare for the dwarf.

Dognut gave no reply, so Llesho figured they were

both telling the truth. He didn't know how that could
be, but he followed up the stone staircase anyway, to the
chamber that opened between the horns of the dragon.

There was no lantern, no plastered walls or paintings
in the tiny cave, just a few rugs scattered on the rough
stone floor and a pallet in the corner with his pack lying
beside it. But the chamber seemed to glow with a faint
light gleaming from the frozen crystals that pulsed like
living veins in the rough walls.

"Sleep well. The Dinha will guard your dreams tonight. Not even Ahkenbad can promise safety beyond
that. I wish . . ."

Llesho heard the unspoken good-bye. So this was his
brother's secret, or part of it. The goddess had given her
husband the gift of past and future. But in all those mil-
lions of tomorrows, Lluka saw himself in none.

"The spirit of our father's minister charged me to
gather all of my brothers." Llesho gripped Lluka's shoulder and shook him, as if he could rattle some sense into
him. "Without you, there is no hope."

Lluka smiled. "It shall be as the goddess wishes." The
serenity of his expression seemed at odds with the blood
that beaded on his cracked lips.

"Just make sure it's the goddess you're listening to,"
Llesho warned him. "We don't know what these Gansau
spirits may want of us, or what they will do to get it."
Superstitious fear kept the name of Master Markko from
his lips. He would not bring his enemy into this holy
place, although he feared the magician's hand in his
brother's despair.

"Don't worry about me." Lluka left him with a bloody
kiss at his brow. "Sleep in peace."

It didn't take a seer to realize the prince had made no
promises. Deep in his troubled thoughts, Llesho dropped
to the pallet, though he was certain he would not sleep.
The conversation with the Dinha had sapped the last of
his energy, however; his lids fell heavily, draping lashes
like a curtain over his dreams.

Chapter Twelve

SLEEP drifted in layers through his clouded mind. In one dream, his brothers brought him to the Dinha, who questioned him and bade him sleep. In another, the searching gazes of two magicians crossed like knives in the dreamscape. One magician looked for him with concern turning into panic, the other cut through his resistance as he sought the images that would lead him to Llesho's hiding place. In his dreams, Llesho fled from the dark rage of Master Markko, but he couldn't reach Habiba through the sightless night thick with the sounds of captivity—Hmishi, weeping brokenly, and harsh cries with the timbre of Emperor Shou's desperate voice.

"I don't want to be here," his mind told him, and cool fingers touched his brow, fading the terror to nothing. In the darkness that remained, relieved only by the faint light of the distant stars, Llesho stumbled on a narrow path. This was not his bed. He felt his way with a hand pressed against the cave-pocked cliff rising up on his left. To his right the empty dark of a blind fall to the valley floor lurked in wait for him. As it had in the desert, the huge black pig entered his dreams unbidden. The night was too thick to make out the creature clearly; Llesho saw only a mass of darker shadows swallowing the night

ahead, blocking the way. Little piggy eyes glittered at
him with a hard black light, like the pearls of the goddess
that Llesho wore at his breast. He nodded to accept the
visitor to his sleep, and the pig dipped his head in acknowledgment. The massive bulk on the path flowed and
reshaped itself, and the pig began the steep ascent.

Llesho followed ever higher into the hills. The caves
they passed were hung with cloths that crawled with
shadows in the dark, but the stillness from their depths
was complete. Whoever had lived or worshiped here had
fled long ago, leaving only the sad reminders of their
passing in the tatters covering the entrances to the caves.
After a while even these abandoned coverings fell behind. The blind and empty mouths of the deep upper
caverns whispered to him with the ghosts of winds passing through unknown cracks in the mountainside. The
cave city of Ahkenbad lay below, while above only darkness and the holy, hidden places awaited. Llesho climbed,
following the pig who waited patiently on the path and
led him forward again when he caught up.

"You can't exactly lose me," Llesho complained.
"There's no place to go except up this merciless goat
track."

The pig, not surprisingly, said nothing, but trotted
ahead, until they came to a turning where a date tree
clutched desperate roots into the hillside. The creature
pushed at the roots of the tree with his tusks, then gave
Llesho a speaking look.

"You want me to dig?" Llesho asked, and when the
pig continued to stare at him, he fell to his knees and
cast about him for a stick or flat stone with which to dig.
He had no need for tools, however. As he leaned into
his search he felt his back twist and stretch, his fingers
grow together until, looking down at them, he discovered
that his hands had become the pink feet of a pig with
sharp hooves at the ends.

'What is happening to me?' he tried to say, but the
harsh oinks and squeals of a pig came from his throat.

Dropping his head in misery at the foot of the date tree, he moaned in mournful piggy tones while his guide stamped at the ground above him.

"What do you want?" The words came out in pig grunts, as Llesho feared they would. The creature seemed to understand, though he said nothing in return. He stared deeply into Llesho's own piggy eyes, and pawed the ground again.

"All right!" Llesho snuffled around the roots of the withered tree, seeking out a hint of a scent. There, right there—he pushed his snout into the dirt, trying to get closer to the elusive smell, and tusks at either side of his mouth drove deep gouges into the baked ground. He dug at the root with his hooves, snuffling his snout under the tree when he had cleared space enough. There . . . there . . . trapped in a hole beneath the date tree, he found the black pearl bound in silver wire he remembered from his dream on the road, and nudged it free with his broad flat nose. He reached for it; his forehoof stretched, became fingers again, and he snatched the pearl up in the palm of his hand and clutched it tight in his new-made fist. The smell he had followed was stronger now. Water. He'd found water, could hear it maddening him with its call. When he tried to bring a handful to his mouth, however, he woke to find himself still on his pallet in the cave of glowing crystals.

"Lluka!" he called.

When nobody answered, he struggled onto his feet and staggered to the staircase, determined to find the path of his dreams and uncover the sleeping pearl. Cross-legged on their pillows, the dream readers remained as they had been, staring into their mystical visions with eyes that saw past the material world. Llesho gave them only the briefest glance as he headed for the entrance. When he pushed the silk curtain aside and wandered out onto the road, he discovered that dawn had come to Ahkenbad, and with it a stir of excitement and hope that he had not seen on his arrival.

"Llesho! Wake up!" Lluka tapped him cautiously on the shoulder.

"Where am I?" Llesho blinked, embarrassed, and squinted into the sunlit road.

"Ahkenbad. You were walking in your sleep."

"Now I remember." But it didn't feel like a true memory at all. How much of it had been a dream?

Balar was walking carefully toward them, a plain earthen cup in his hands and a broad grin splitting his lips.

"Water!" He held up the cup for Llesho to see. "The spirits of the desert favor you. The holy well has begun to flow again. Drink!"

Water. Aged Tashek mystics wandered out of their caves, giving praise to the spirits of the Wastes for the return of the holy well. The smell of it reminded Llesho of his thirst. He hadn't had a chance to drink at the spring above the city, and he reached for the cup only to discover that his hand remained clenched in a fist pale as a pig's hoof. Dried dirt crusted his nails and plastered the cracks between his fingers.

Balar rubbed the pad of his index finger across Llesho's nose, bringing it away again with mud on the tip. "Where have you been roaming in your sleep—" He frowned, staring thoughtfully at his finger, then his head came up abruptly, eyes wide and his mouth round as he gasped, "Oh!" Lluka glanced from one brother to the other, then took Llesho's clenched fist in his hand and carefully pried open each finger. There, on Llesho's dirty palm, lay a black pearl.

At Lluka's gasp, the Tashek passing nearest them came closer and when the brothers dropped to their knees, the Tashek did likewise.

"Get up!" Llesho colored like a berry, overcome with embarrassment. "This is ridiculous!"

The brothers stood, but they seemed only to be humoring him. The Tashek came more slowly to their feet. Whispers spread out from their center, and the crowd of devotees grew around them as Llesho explained. "The black pig led me to a date tree up in the hills. The pearl had blocked a spring at the base of the tree. I thought it was a dream, but I must have walked in my sleep." He did not mention turning into a pig. They would probably believe it, and he wasn't ready for that.

"There are no pigs in Ahkenbad," Balar informed him. "And no date tree in the hills."

Lluka nodded, rejecting Llesho's effort to make sense of the pearl in his hand. "I watched through the night, and you never strayed from your bed in the acolyte's cavern until just now, when I woke you," he insisted. "If anyone had come in or gone out, the guards would have alerted me."

Llesho remembered fingers on his forehead, but said nothing about them. He reached inside his shirt instead, and drew out the pouch in which he had carried the black pearls since leaving Shan. All three lay inside it. Neither of his brothers looked particularly surprised, but it bothered Llesho. It was one thing to dream of a place and find it afterward, and quite another to bring a pearl out of a dream and into the light of day. And, if he could believe his dream, he held no pearl at all but the transformed person of Pig, the beloved gardener of the Great Goddess' heavenly orchards.

"Let me through!"

Reprieve! Harlol blustered his way through the crowd, drawing up in front of Lluka. "The dream readers of Ahkenbad have awakened," he announced. "The Dinha requests the presence of the Thebin princes."

Llesho shook his head, seized by the notion that the mouth of the Dragon Cave would snap shut and swallow him up forever. He didn't have a rational explanation for the feeling, so he mumbled something instead about being hungry to divert their attention.

It didn't work. Lluka had grown more determined in the years since his childhood in Kungol. "The Dinha will feed you," he insisted, and drew Llesho away from the curious Tashek who followed, tugging at his coats as he passed.

"Why are they doing that?"

"They believe your touch will confer blessings, even healing, on their families." Balar looked as if he ought to know this, but Llesho didn't know why. Thebins didn't put much stock in talismanic magic, and certainly no one in Shan had looked upon his person as sacred. It might have saved him a few nasty practice sessions with knife and sword if they had.

"They've got the wrong brother," he grumbled. "Lluka's the mystic around here. If they need a healer, you should have rescued Adar instead of me."

"They needed a dreamer to bring back the water," Lluka reminded him, "You saved them—all of us, actually. The dream readers of Ahkenbad wish to thank you, no doubt."

"Nothing to worry about—" Balar clapped him on the back, but Llesho didn't find it reassuring. "The dream readers of Ahkenbad are perfectly civil when they're awake. They'll probably pinch your cheek and cluck at each other about what a fine young man you are. It likely won't make a bit of sense, but it will keep them happy. Once they've checked you out, you can ask them questions if you want."

"The Dinha's answers didn't sound very useful last night," Llesho reminded him, to which Balar nodded enthusiastic agreement.

"Oh, the answers won't make any sense when you hear them. When it's too late, you'll realize what you should have done, if they'd been more straightforward about their warnings in the first place."

It sounded like every bit of advice he'd ever gotten— straight-forward enough until it turned out you hadn't understood it at all.

But Lluka was looking at him as if he'd grown a second head, and it was speaking in tongues. "Be quiet, Balar! He didn't see the Dinha last night."

"What? Oh. No, the dream readers haven't woken in weeks," Balar agreed. "You must have the Dinha confused with one of the acolytes, though that hardly seems likely. Of course, if you haven't met the Dinha, you wouldn't know that."

"She was old," Llesho said, "and blind. And you, Lluka, led me to a chamber above the cave of the dream readers, lit by seams of natural crystals running through the walls."

"The Dinha is not blind, though it is said that dreaming, her eyes turn inward." Lluka searched his face, as if he could pierce Llesho's soul and spy out the mysteries hiding there. "You had a dream, and in your dream, you had another dream, and in that nested dream, you saved all our lives."

The mystery is in my hand, not my eyes, he thought. The gifts of the sleeping world were supposed to vanish with the rising sun, but the black pearl still lay in the palm of his hand.

His brothers did not speak for a moment, though they said much to each other with glances. Gifted with the sight of past and future, Lluka did not look pleased when he admitted, "The futures I've seen are unclear. That doesn't have to mean anything, of course. Seeing the future is an imprecise art; but this, I did not see at all."

"Sounds like a pretty useless gift to me." Llesho wasn't really asking—the answer to his own question was plain in his tone of voice, that they were not gifts at all, but a major inconvenience. Shokar thought so, too. He'd received no gifts, and often declared himself the happier for it.

Lluka raised a wry eyebrow. It was hard to deny the charge, after all. "The gifts of the goddess are like a garment cut to the shape of our older selves. As we grow in the spirit, time and the use we make of our gifts improve the fit."

"And you, Balar, have you grown into your gifts?" Llesho wanted to know.

Balar shook his head. "Sometimes," he said, "I think that they are not gifts at all, but a madness that comes of approaching too closely matters that are beyond our comprehension."

"Sounds like a husband to me," Lluka commented tartly. "The Dinha awaits us, however. I suggest we do not leave her to cool her heels like a supplicant while we debate family history."

"I have plenty of questions for the Dinha, like why they sent you to steal me from my quest and drag me across the desert. And why we abandoned Adar and our companions to the enemies who wish our whole family dead."

Lluka tried to stare him down, but that hadn't even worked for Master Den, who was himself a god. It surely wasn't going to work for his brother, however much a mystic he had become.

"If you really see the past and the future, you know that glaring at me never changed my mind or my course of action."

"Use caution, at least. You cross the dream readers of Ahkenbad at your peril." Lluka's warning clashed discordantly with Balar's assurances, but Balar was the brother who looked uncomfortable.

"They won't strike you dead or anything," Balar protested, but had to concede, "but they can make you squirm like an ant under a lens if you try to hide the truth from them."

"Some secrets are worth even my life to keep."

Lluka shook him roughly by the shoulder. "Don't even think it, little brother. Yours may be the only life we can't afford to lose."

"You don't know that."

He'd faced death and wonders alike in his journey, and apparently he'd learned a thing or two from his masters about glaring. Lluka dropped his sleeve and took a step back, which brought a pleased smile to Balar's lips. "For my sixth natal day, I asked the goddess to gift me with a new wonder every day. She hasn't disappointed me yet."

Llesho suddenly found himself in common cause with Lluka—the two of them glared in unison at their brother. Then Lluka turned on his heel and followed Harlol a short distance up the Stone River Road, toward the cavern where the Tashek dream readers awaited them.

Harlol stepped aside as the brothers entered the dragon's head cavern between the stony dragon's teeth. Then he took up his position as guard, exactly as he had the night before, with his hands crossed on the swords at his waist. The Dragon Cave looked the same, the spirits painted on the walls even more lifelike in the filtered light of the Great Sun than by lantern. Dognut still slept in the corner by the stone staircase and Lluka again took the cushion at Llesho's left, with Balar to his right. Unlike in his dream, however, busy acolytes brushed by with whispered apologies to set up low tables and load them with food and drink. As Balar had said, most of them, dream readers and acolytes alike, were women, though a few were men. He recognized a boy his own age who had offered him an inch at the bottom of his jade cup to drink in his dream. The flick of a glance told him that the servant shared the memory.

"Welcome, Prince of Dreams." The Dinha gestured with a jut of her chin at the waiting food spread out before them, "Join us, please, in breaking our fast while we talk."

Llesho recognized the Dinha immediately from his dream. She looked the same except that her eyes were brown, with glints of amber that twinkled her amusement at him. He wanted to deny it, to pretend he didn't know this woman, this place, but the black pearl clasped in his fist gave physical proof of the impossible and no comfort at all.

The Dinha seemed to follow his thoughts. She reached

to touch the jewel, and Llesho clenched his fingers more tightly, drawing it reflexively to his heart. Around them, from a noose of lives, rose a single breathless gasp.

"My lady." He bowed a deep apology, but found himself at a loss to explain his unwillingness to open his hand.

"I beg your pardon, young prince. It was ill thought. No one will take the pearl from you."

"What do you want of me?"

"We would only honor your gift with one of our own. Weightier discussion can await a full stomach, however." At a gesture, a young Tashek knelt before him with a basin.

"You will want to wash."

Drying mud still clung to the pearl in his grubby hand. He saw no head, no tail, no piggy feet, but felt a superstitious dread of drowning the goddess' gardener in his own bathwater. The Tashek acolyte seemed to understand his problem. She dipped a cloth into the basin, and wiped the back of his hand carefully with it, until he took it from her and cleaned the pearl with equal care. When the mud was gone, a fine tracery of silver wire was revealed, wrapping the familiar black sheen. Each thread-like curl led to a central keyhole loop: a setting for a jewel or a prison for a Jinn? Dreams and reality had tangled themselves so closely together that he scarcely knew one from the other any more.

The dream readers of Ahkenbad nodded approval in unison, and one of them, an old man whose knees squeaked when he levered himself upright, came forward with a silver chain offered in his outstretched hands.

"I know this chain." Llesho shuddered, and clutched the pearl more tightly in his hand. "In dreams, it hung around the neck of my enemy."

"A warning," the Dinha agreed. "But did you fear the chain, or the enemy who held it?"

Both, and more. Memories of other chains tangled themselves in the silver links: Lord Chin-shi's chain in

Pearl Bay, his imprisonment in Master Markko's workshop, and Farshore's lighter bondage. He would have refused the gift if it hadn't echoed in all his dreams, like fate. But Llesho had no intention of sharing that with strangers. He let the old man slip the chain over his head, but hid the pearl itself in the pouch with the others he had collected.

After waking to find all his memories of Ahkenbad were dreams, and then sparring with the Tashek Dinha over the meaning of the pearl he had discovered on the mountain, breakfast seemed a mundane letdown. But Llesho had spent the greater part of his recent journeys on a diet of unidentifiable boiled fodder for humans that made him wonder if he wouldn't do better to forage with the camels. With its supply of water refreshed, Ahkenbad dug into its store of supplies to feast the visiting prince, and the wonderful smells drew him to the table as if a spell had been cast on his taste buds.

Vegetables, cooked just enough to bring up their colors and their aromas, dominated the spread, with a variety of pickles served over a millet dish cooked to tenderness but not to mush. Some dishes the acolytes served warm, and others came to the tables cooled by the waters of the Holy Well of Ahkenbad. Flatbreads and other grains supplemented the main dishes.

The lay of the table jogged a memory from deep in Llesho's childhood. It drifted out of his past with the image of his mother's reception room so sharp in his mind he thought he could reach out and touch her chair. He had sat at her feet and quietly watched and listened as a delegation from the caravans out of the Gansau Wastes had stopped to pay its respects. When his mother had called for refreshments, she'd explained that the religious among the Tashek would eat only cooked food. The most holy castes among them took only plant material, never animal.

He'd seen Harlol eat meat when they'd had it, and with gusto, of course. Perhaps there were different rules for Wastrels, or spies. Whatever recipes those dancing gods on the walls demanded, the Tashek had made the best of them, however. The food gave up wonderful smells, pungent and sweet, that brought water to the desert of Llesho's mouth. He filled a bowl with vegetables and round slices of pickle, and gave only half a glance at the young woman who approached him with a tray on which sat an elaborately wrought urn of tea and his own jade cup taken from his pack. When she set the tray down in front of him, a flash of eye, an ironic twist of the lip drew his attention for a second look. Kagar!

"You're a girl!" he whispered, trying to keep the secret in spite of his shock.

"Since I was born," Kagar whispered back her admission.

The acolytes who attended them gave no sign of hearing the hushed conversation, but the Dinha drew away the veil of illusion with a wry smile. "Tashek women do not wander in the world as Wastrels. Though called to the dream readers' cavern, our Kagar wished to challenge the ordering of such things."

"I did it, too. No one ever suspected, except Lling, who kept my secret."

Llesho wasn't sure he was more surprised by the idea that Kagar was a girl or the notion that Lling had kept such a big secret from him. He consoled himself that it hadn't been her secret to tell, but he still felt like a fool for being the only person in the room who couldn't tell a girl from a boy.

"Now you are home," the Dinha continued with a gentle smile, "And a better acolyte for your experience of the outside world, I trust."

"Until the next time."

Kagar gave the promise that the Dinha seemed to expect, but the dream reader's smile faltered.

"Until the next time," she agreed. Her eyes became suspiciously bright, and Llesho wondered if only the parched weeks without water kept the tears from falling.

But his brother's awed, hushed tones drew his attention to the table, where Lluka reached hesitantly to touch the cup Kagar had set in front of him.

"Surely wonders have returned to walk among us," Lluka whispered with a shake of his head.

Balar's gaze quickly followed. "Have you lost your mind?" He took the bowl carefully in his two hands and lifted it for a closer look, his face paled and suffused with dark blood by turns. "Do you know what this is?"

"It's a bowl." Llesho felt an ages dead self looking out of his own eyes. The world he saw differed little from the one he had known many deaths ago, and he lowered his eyelashes to hide that knowledge from his companions. He wondered if that long-gone self had ever been wiser than he was now, and felt an echo of laughter skitter along his nerve endings. Who was to say what was wise, his past self asked him, and he had to admit he didn't know.

Llesho thought he had moved quickly enough to hide the lives that echoed within him, but his brother dropped his head in awe, and held out the bowl like a supplicant. "The universe turns on the head of a pin," he prophesied, "and you are that pin. Tell us what to do."

"Try not being an ass," Llesho advised him in a tart whisper, "and let me have my tea." He retrieved the bowl and held it out to Kagar, who filled it with a dare in her eyes. The drover warranted more thought, but not now, with his brothers asking questions and the dream readers of Ahkenbad watching every move he made.

"Where did you find it?" Lluka asked.

"A gift," he said, and sipped from it before setting it aside in favor of a plate of food.

"There is a room above this chamber." Between bites, Llesho pointed to the staircase at the back of the cavern, and the Dinha nodded to confirm the memory.

"I slept there last night, and dreamed of the black pig."

"You slept in the guest quarters on the outskirts of

Ahkenbad," the Dinha corrected him gently, with a smile. "Sleeping, you joined the dream readers of the holy city. And in your dream, you had a dream in which the honored Jinn led you to the hidden spring that feeds the Holy Well of Ahkenbad."

"That's what I thought." Llesho licked the sticky pickle sauce from his fingertips. "You said you wanted to help me," he reminded the Dinha. "What did you mean?"

"We are the Tashek dream readers," she began, needlessly at this point. "From your brothers we understand that young bridegrooms who receive magical gifts of your goddess find their own way to mastery. This was not always so, however. The royal family of Kungol once received tutors from all the lands that made use of Thebin's high passes. Although the passes are now closed to us, the dream readers of Ahkenbad offer themselves as tutors to the princes of Thebin, a post they filled for your father's father, many summers past and which they have filled for your brothers since the fall of Kingol. Stay with us a while, until you learn the art of your gift."

Llesho helped himself to a serving of dates and figs in honey while he considered the offer. "You haven't helped my brothers much," he pointed out.

Balar pinched him, a reminder of royal manners. But it was true, and the Dinha took no offense.

"We have taught your brothers patience, and a mastery of their own minds, but their gifts are not those of Ahkenbad. You are the prince of dreams; in gentler times, our tutors would have sought you out in your own holy city. Now, we have but a brief reprieve to do our duty before you must continue your journey."

Llesho wondered what she meant by a brief reprieve. Master Den had advised that he needed a dream reader, but that was before the Harn had taken their company prisoner. Even if he accepted that his dreams had more meaning, more power, than he knew, how could he abandon his friends and brother to the tortures of Master Markko while he developed his inner gifts? And Shou was himself a favorite of the mortal goddess SienMa. She would doubtless take offense if he allowed the Harn to murder the emperor, whose death would also plunge the Shan Empire and its neighbors into chaos. As his first act of statecraft, making an enemy of her ladyship while unleashing havoc upon the civilized world seemed a poor choice.

"The times do not call for patience," he pointed out.

"I understand." The Dinha bowed to acknowledge the truth of his words. He suspected that the dream readers understood more than he would have liked. The Dinha gave him a rueful smile, as if she read his mind. "We cannot regret the good you have done for Ahkenbad, however, and would repay the service you have done us. You have seen one in your dreams, a magician on a white horse—"

"Habiba," Llesho agreed, while an acolyte poured water over his sticky hands and offered him a soft cloth to dry them.

"You are right that he can help you, but so can the dream readers of Ahkenbad. Soon you will need us both. Don't reject our aid because you don't like the manner in which you were brought to find it." With that the old ones closed their eyes.

"We've been dismissed." Lluka rose effortlessly to his feet, something Llesho did with considerably less grace. Balar followed, and together they made their way out of the cavern of the dream readers, and found themselves once again bathed in the heat and light of the Stone River Road.

Master Den's words in the dark of a caravanary carried the force of a prophecy. "The Tashek have the most revered dream readers," the master had said. But had he spoken as a wise teacher or as trickster? For the good of the dream readers or for Llesho's own quest? The universe seemed to turn under him in the yellow dust, tumblers falling into places he still couldn't see. The almost-vision of it made him dizzy.

Chapter Thirteen

"ARE you all right, brother?"

Lluka tightened a hand on his shoulder. He brushed it aside and wandered farther into the road, staring up at the cliffs where waves of color broke against a sea of sandstone bleached pale in the sun. Somewhere beyond the cliff city a presence wandered; he cocked his head and listened for a change in the wind that would tell him the storm was coming. The wind stayed quiet. Llesho dug deeper, into the place where dreams and hunches lurked, for an explanation. Not the dark oppression of Master Markko's questing eye; he'd recognize in an instant the magician's pressure on his mind. A little thrill of anticipation ran through him. Llesho walked out to meet it. Troubled, his brothers stayed where he left them, but Harlol was right on his heels, nervous, with his hands on his swords' hilts.

"Where are you going?"

"To meet my destiny," Llesho gave him the flip answer. He hadn't figured out what was drawing him into the desert, and likely wouldn't have told the Tashek warrior anyway. He just knew he had to go out to meet it, whatever it was.

Harlol fell in step beside him.

"Why are you following me?"

The Wastrel cut him a sideways glance, indicating with a raised eyebrow that he didn't, in the strictest sense, follow Llesho. Having made his point, he answered the spirit of the question. "It's my job. The Dinha charged me to defend the prince of dreams, so where you go, I go. It would be a lot easier on both of us if you would just stay put."

"Not going to happen," Llesho advised him. He didn't slow down.

"You could at least tell me where we're going."

"I would if I knew." Llesho kept walking.

"Then you'll probably need this—" Harlol didn't expend his energy on argument. He reached into his coat and drew out Llesho's sword. "If we will need more than our blades, an army, for instance, tell me now."

"It's enough, thanks." Llesho attached the weapon to his own side. Then, pulling hoods and veils over their heads to protect them from the elements, they marched in step, out past the cave city and into the desert.

They walked for an hour or more in companionable silence. Sweat beaded at Llesho's pores and dried before the drops could fall, but the call across the wide expanse of desert kept him moving. During a pause to catch their breath, Harlol offered a waterskin.

"I hope this is more than a whim," he said.

"Something is out there." Llesho jerked a shoulder in the direction they walked, away from Ahkenbad. His companion did not look pleased with the answer.

"Ahkenbad has protections against strangers, but we are about to pass beyond their reach. If we don't turn back, whatever you feel out there will find *us*."

"Perhaps I want to be found." Llesho's step suddenly felt more buoyant. Sunlight found a corner of his heart that had lain in dreaming shadows. They had passed outside of Ahkenbad's defenses.

Harlol glared at him. "The likelihood that good will come out of the desert looking for you in this exact spot is vanishingly small. Our enemies, however, have the power to find a single pebble in the gravel pits of Dhar."

"You underestimate our friends," Llesho assured him with a sudden grin. He knew this consciousness pressing toward him. When the cloud of dust appeared on the horizon, he ran to meet it.

"No!" Harlol grabbed his arm and swung Llesho around to face him. "Distance in the Gansau Waste is deceiving. The heat reflects the image of what you see like a mirror, over many li. Your friends may be coming this way, or they may be on a different heading altogether. But even if they sense your presence, as you sense theirs, they have a long way to go before they reach us. Hours still, and they have horses while we are on foot." He gave Llesho a shake, snapping the hypnotic grip of the dust cloud on the horizon.

Llesho shook off his arm, took another step. But Harlol was right. Between them they had no provisions—the Wastrel, in desert fashion, had carried a bit of water for emergencies. That was almost gone, and neither had picked up food before they left Ahkenbad. They were ill prepared to go any farther.

If the newcomers didn't change course, they would ride right into Llesho and his companion, anyway. Better to conserve strength and wait. "We will stop here," Harlol repeated, "make a tent of our coats, and wait."

"A tent?"

"If you don't want to bake your brains out in the Gansau Wastes, we will make a tent, yes." Harlol gave him one of those superior Wastrel looks, like the one he'd given Shou before he'd tried to slice and dice him. "It will take both our coats. And your sword."

He undid his own scabbard from his belt and began to undo the ties on his coat, so Llesho followed his example. Letting his coat fall to the dust was easy. He held onto his sword long enough to try the Tashek's patience.

"You still mistrust me for the fight at the caravansary.

I told you before, I never intended to hurt the healer, Adar. I *didn't* hurt him, you know."

"And Shou?" Llesho asked.

Harlol shrugged, the color rising in his face. The Wastrel was embarrassed, Llesho realized, and he knew how that felt. "I meant it as a test, of sorts. He shouldn't have been able to counter the prayer moves." Harlol sounded indignant. "When he did, I had to see how deeply his skills ran. I was just . . ."

"Showing off?"

"Yes." The air seemed to leave the Wastrel like a punctured bubble. "I underestimated him, badly. The next thing I knew, I was fighting for my life, or so I believed. He could have killed me at my own discipline. I would have thought no outsider could do that."

"I know exactly what you mean," Llesho admitted. And he did. "Shou is full of surprises,"

They were alike in a lot of ways, and it was easier to forgive the warrior, not much older than he was himself, for doing his duty than to make sense of his brothers' part in his abduction. He had a feeling that was all going to be irrelevant when the cause of that dust cloud arrived, however. Llesho handed over the sword.

With a quick, sharp, downward stroke, the Wastrel drove the points of the scabbards into the dry ground, so that the swords stood upright, separated by the span of his arms. One coat he looped over the pommels and draped facing east, and one he stretched from the swords in a westerly direction, creating a small tent with the swords as low tent poles. They had no pegs to hold the ends in place, but Harlol crawled inside and reclined, his shoulder pressing down the edge of one coat tent cover. Llesho crawled in beside him and sat, hunched over his own crossed legs.

"The dream readers believe in your ability to foretell the future," Harlol said once he was settled. "I honor your gifts with our comfort, since we would be hard-

pressed to defend ourselves with our swords tangled in
our coats like this."

Llesho didn't think they were very comfortable, but he
wasn't worried about the oncoming dust cloud. If Master
Markko pursued that closely, he would feel dread like a
trickling poison. He had no such foreboding now, and he
realized that included Harlol. Whatever the Wastrel's
part in all of this, he didn't mean Llesho any harm. Unfortunately, he already showed signs of boredom.

"So tell me," Harlol prodded, "what brought you to
the Moon and Star Inn on the Imperial Road?"

"The Harn conquered my country. I am on my way
home to take it back."

Harlol looked, of all things, offended. "I am not unschooled," he sniffed, "but we have a long wait, and I
saw the way you handled yourself in Durnhag. You've
fought in combat before. I thought the story might pass
the time."

"I work hard at not remembering." Llesho didn't want
to relive his past with this young and inexperienced warrior, but Harlol reacted with shock to his admission.

"Other people give us our names," the Wastrel admonished him. "Who we truly are is recorded in our
histories. To give up your history is to give up your self."

"You didn't make that up yourself." Llesho meant it
as an insult, but Harlol solemnly shook his head.

"The Dinha sows wisdom in the desert soil of a Wastrel's heart," he said, "and, sometimes, her wisdom
takes root."

Llesho figured he had a choice: tell the Wastrel his
story, or listen to him preach the word of the Dinha or
memory. Better to do the talking than the listening, he
decided and began the tale.

"The Harn attacked during my seventh summer
They'd come into the holy city with the caravans, and
sneaked up into the palace through the kitchens. One of
the raiders killed Khri, my bodyguard, but he didn't see
me hiding on a chair behind the curtain. While he was

cleaning his sword on Khri's uniform, I pulled my knife. I wasn't strong enough for a killing stroke, but I fell off the chair, the knife slipped between his ribs, and the raider died. Later, when they caught up with me, I threatened to do the same to their leader. They were killing the children—too much trouble on the march— but my threats amused them, so they kept me alive for the slave pens."

"I heard you tell your brother that you made the Long March," Harlol said, and Llesho nodded.

"We left our dead on the wayside across half of Thebin and all of Harn, into the heart of Shan. In the slave market of the imperial city I heard the overseer tell the Harnish slave trader to slit my throat. "Too young for hard labor, too old for begging," he said, "and not enough endurance left to satisfy the perverts—I'd never earn back the cost of feed." I didn't know what any of it meant until later, except the throat-cutting part. By then I was grateful that Lord Chin-shi had come to the market looking for Thebin children to dive in his pearl beds."

"That's how you became a pearl diver?"

As he told his story, Llesho had fallen more deeply into the spell of his own past. Harlol's question tugged at him like a lifeline, and he followed it back to the present.

"Yes. Pearl Island wasn't too bad, really. There were people my age; that's where I met Lling and Hmishi. And old Lleck came later. I had known him at the palace, and he helped me."

"But you left the pearl beds."

"Lleck died. His ghost gave me a black pearl, and told me to find my brothers and save Thebin. I couldn't do that at the bottom of the bay, so I became a gladiator in Lord Chin-shi's stable. I had passed my fifteenth summer by then. I was wiry and strong, and my natural stamina had returned. Master Jaks and Master Den knew who I was from the start. They brought the Lady SienMa from Farshore Province to test me, and she warned me to keep my identity secret. Master Markko guessed something as well. He was a slave high up in Lord Chinshi's house, his overseer. When I look back, though, I think he was working against his master even then."

"Master Den was your teacher for the arena? So how did the healer Adar come to have as his servant a training master of gladiators?" Harlol asked with a mind to the trickster god's most recent disguise. He had curled his legs up under him, and listened avidly. Llesho wanted to hit him for treating his painful past like a campfire tale, except that it didn't hurt as much as he had expected. The words seemed drawn out like an arrowhead cut out of the flesh so that the wound could heal. But Master Den's story was his own to tell.

"It was a disguise. Master Den has many of them. Even I have never seen through all of them, and he has been with me as my teacher since Pearl Island."

Harlol seemed on the verge of making a comment, but something of what Llesho was thinking must have made it to his face, because the Wastrel said only, "What happened next?"

Llesho shrugged. "My first fight in the arena was my last," he said, taking up the story where he could. "The pearl beds failed, and Lord Chin-shi had gambling debts. Habiba managed to purchase some of us for Lady SienMa; the rest went to Yueh." Madon, a friend, had died at Habiba's hand that afternoon, a wasted sacrifice to stop a war that came on them anyway.

"Her ladyship kept no slaves. Under her direction, we became free soldiers. She gathered my friends and teachers, added Kaydu as our captain, and when Master Markko attacked, we were ready. The lady gave me the gifts that you have already seen—the short spear and the jade cup—and took her household to her father at Thousand Lakes Province. Our small cadre—me and Hmishi and Lling, and Bixei and Kaydu whom you haven't met yet—ran for the imperial city. On the way we met dragons and healers and gods and bears and we fought. Lleck is dead twice, and Master Jaks is gone. In the imperial city we battled in the streets and put an end to the slave trade in Shan, and discovered that Master Markko is himself aligned with the Harn, but I don't know why." He gave a helpless shrug. "I haven't been at this 'intrigue' thing very long, but the beings I've met along the way all seem to be pointing me at Thebin. In Shan I received more gifts of pearls which I am charged to return to the goddess who lost them. And to bring the tale back to the beginning, to do that I have to free Thebin."

He said no more about the "String of Midnights," the necklace of black pearls stolen from heaven. He needed to return it to the Great Goddess so that night could return to heaven, but he didn't trust the Wastrel with that much truth.

"For a short life, you have seen more battle and intrigue than the old men who chew their stories under canopies in the sun." With that brief comment, Harlol gave the tale a moment of silent contemplation before he asked. "Is that why we are out here waiting for an approaching dust cloud to resolve itself into friend or foe?"

"Friends, definitely friends." Llesho yawned deeply. Telling even a part of his story had exhausted him, but it had made him feel better, too.

"If that's the end of your story, you might as well take a nap," Harlol advised. "It makes the waiting pass more quickly." With that he tucked the tent coat under his hip to hold it in place and promptly went to sleep.

A nap sounded good, but the heat beating on their makeshift tent seared his lungs and the approaching party tickled at the corners of Llesho's mind. Not evil, certainly not Master Markko, but a mind he'd felt before and knew the texture of was out there looking for him.

And Harlol snored.

Llesho nudged at him with his foot, and the Wastrel snuggled down deeper into the small depression he'd dug with his hip. Llesho nudged a little harder, and the snor-

ing broke, became a grunted snort, before resuming
again. Llesho wondered how a man who slept like the
dead, but more noisily, expected to survive as a wandering warrior. He reached a foot out to kick again.

Fast as a striking snake, Harlol grabbed his ankle.
"Take a nap."

"I can't sleep. It's too hot, and you snore."

"This is going to be a long afternoon," Harlol moaned
to himself. "All right. You go to sleep first. Then, you
won't hear it if I snore."

"I told you my story." Llesho pushed out his jaw, belligerently. He was beginning to feel foolish for revealing
so much in his tale, and their close quarters, separated
only by the swords they used as tent posts, were making
him nervous. "So what is a Wastrel anyway? Are you
allowed to tell, or is it a sacred mystery?"

"You're not going to let me sleep, are you?"

Llesho shook his head. "I have a lot of questions, but
'What is a Wastrel?' is top of the list."

Harlol propped himself up by his elbow, with his chin
in the palm of his hand. He didn't look sleepy at all, and
Llesho figured the snoring had been a ruse, to avoid this
confrontation.

"A Wastrel is a warrior-priest, sworn to the desert
spirits. We don't choose, but are dedicated to the Dinha
at birth. Those who survive the training and the trials of
thirst and fire and solitude become the eyes and ears of
the dream readers in the waking world. We go where
the wind takes us. When our paths follow the caravan
routes, we work at the common labor available to our
kind. Other times, we wander as the stories tell, seeking
out the lost places in the desert. We are the protectors
of Ahkenbad. Always, however, we go at the will of
the Dinha."

"Is Kagar a Wastrel now as well?"

"No." Harlol laughed. "Kagar is no Wastrel, but my
true cousin, the child of my mother's brother. We owe
each other much filial love, and so I kept her secret until

I could bring her safely home. But sometimes Kagar can be very annoying."

"That makes two of you," Llesho muttered to himself. "Why did you attack Adar?"

"The Dinha told me to protect the prince of dreams at any cost." The typical Tashek shrug came off as ungainly in a reclining position, but Harlol didn't seem to care. "You didn't travel as princes—or as brothers. Adar looks not at all like the princes I knew. When I saw him pray the Way of the Goddess with the master, I knew he could ruin all our plans if he chose to fight against Balar in Durnhag. I meant only to test him, perhaps to injure him so that we could leave him behind. I would not kill any man unless he threatened you."

He wanted to resent the man, but couldn't. Harlol was too much like himself, in age, and even in the way his gods ran his life. Llesho would have seen it sooner if he'd been paying attention, the way Shou evidently had. For all his training, Harlol had seen far less of battle than Llesho's own cadre. He was a priest who spent much of his time alone in the desert or traveling with the camels, and hadn't crossed a thousand li of battleground to get here. So Shou hadn't killed him even after he had turned from prayer to battle forms in mid-demonstration.

"Had you ever used your training to deliberately harm another before that morning?"

"I am trained—" Harlol dropped his gaze. "I would not shame my training."

"Of course not." Quick as a thief Llesho had his knife out, point pricking just below the Wastrel's voice box. "I, on the other hand, killed my first Harn raider while still in the training saddle. I have seen men die at the hands of an ally for the honor of a shamed lord, and I have fought every li of the way from Pearl Island to Durnhag. Do not presume to understand those with whom I travel, Wastrel, and don't hasten to add my nightmares to your own sleep."

Harlol ignored the knife at his throat and met Llesho's

eyes with a level gaze that reflected no fear, but bragged not at all of Tashek bravery. "My life is a tool of the spirits. I will do as the Dinha requires in their service. Are you going to kill me now, Prince?"

"Of course not." Llesho put away his knife. "If I planned to kill you, I wouldn't warn you. And I am warning you. I know the mind that approaches. Don't put yourself between us, don't speak, don't draw a weapon."

"Who is it?" Harlol was pulling himself upright, taking apart their tent with the knuckles of one hand white around the scabbard of his sword. They could feel beneath their feet the rumble of the approaching horses.

"The Dinha told us at breakfast. It's Habiba." Llesho flashed a predatory smile and settled onto his side. "He is a magician, and the right hand of the Lady SienMa, mortal goddess of war."

Harlol paled, but his fear seemed reserved for Llesho rather than the approaching riders. "Surely you walk among miracles, my prince."

"It's not all it's cracked up to be," he assured his companion. The Wastrel's shock should have been a victory, but Llesho just felt tired. Together they stood, waiting for the horses to come to a halt in front of them.

Habiba remained in his saddle, his tall white steed still as a statue. Behind him, his army worked to control their skittish horses. At his side, three dressed as officers slipped from their mounts, drawing off their desert headgear so that he could see who they were.

"Kaydu!" With a grin he ran forward and grabbed her hands. At the sound of his voice, the pack on Kaydu's back began to wriggle, and out popped a small head, followed by a tiny body in the uniform of the Imperial Guard.

"Little Brother!" Llesho greeted the monkey, who climbed out of his pack and chattered ferociously at him. With a chuckle, Llesho stood still while the creature clambered onto his head, exploring for wildlife before returning to his mistress.

"What wonders are these!" Harlol whispered at his back.

"It's a monkey, Kaydu's familiar."

"I have seen monkeys before." Harlol drew himself to his full dignity. "But they are known to be fickle creatures. I had thought they would make poor soldiers."

Kaydu let it seem as though his words had caught her attention, but Llesho knew she did her father's bidding, drawing out the stranger while Habiba watched carefully from the distance of horseback and wizardly silence. "Little Brother is a paragon among monkeys. I would not count on any other to defend my back."

She made it sound like a joke, though Llesho remembered a time when Little Brother had saved all their lives, carrying a message to the Lady SienMa when Markko's forces had threatened them on the road. Some things would take too long to explain, and even longer to believe, so he laughed with the others, content to let the tension ease, if only for an hour. Soon enough they'd be back in the fray.

"So much affection for a cowardly ape, and not even a greeting for your brothers in arms!" Bixei, Llesho's onetime enemy and more recent ally, stepped away from his horse and received a companionable slap on the shoulder.

"Bixei! What are you doing on the march? You're supposed to be in Shan, helping to train a Thebin army. How is Stipes?"

"I am very well, Prince Llesho." Stipes himself came forward, letting Llesho see him. He wore a leather patch over his damaged eye, but otherwise looked sound and hearty. "And you see a part of that Thebin army before you, though we could not stop the emperor's own imperial guard from accompanying us."

Llesho glanced over the small company bristling with weapons. Fifteen Thebin faces stared at him in wonder as they sat the small hill horses like his own, while thirty tall warriors at the rear rode the warhorses of Shan. Scattered among them, Llesho recognized the mercenary garb of his childhood bodyguard, the same worn by the weapons master who had died to protect him in the war against Master Markko's villainy. He would have sent them home, the debt their clan owed a dead king long paid, but he knew they would not go.

"How is this possible? I left you only weeks ago—"

Bixei grinned wickedly. "With the Lady SienMa's assistance, and the fall of the slave trade in Shan, many potential allies found themselves at loose ends. And no few of them have trained in secret and waited for the chance Shokar offered them."

"With the arena in turmoil, your brother had his pick of trainers," Kaydu explained. "Now he raises armies, and husbands a bumper crop."

She gave a little shrug. "He has given the emperor the loyalty a guest owes his host, but trusted this particular plan of Shou's not at all. So he took the harvest of his labors to Durnhag. He was right. We arrived at Durnhag too late to prevent the attack, but Shokar tracked the raiders, who were heading toward Harn. We followed the signs of your passage into the Gansau Wastes until yesterday, when the desert seemed to swallow you up. We thought we had lost you. Then, suddenly, there you were again and here we find you in the empty desert in the company of one lone Wastrel."

"We are not as far from civilization as we seem." Llesho answered Kaydu's unspoken question, but he looked to her father as he did so.

"So you have found Ahkenbad." Habiba bowed his head in a thoughtful nod. "And you can find it again?"

"Waking or sleeping, whether I wish to go there or not." The magician understood Llesho's wry smile. "The dreams don't ask permission," he commented. To which Llesho added, "Neither does the Dinha of Ahkenbad."

"Respect, if you please." Harlol raised himself up to

his full height, his hands resting on his sword hilts in the way Llesho had come to recognize as readiness for battle.

"With understanding," Llesho countered. He did respect the Dinha; he just didn't trust her to put the will of a young Thebin ahead of the needs of her own people.

Habiba interrupted before the Wastrel could respond with a challenge, however. "We have traveled long and ridden hard. If Ahkenbad is as close as you say, perhaps we can finish this discussion out of the sun—"

"Of course." Llesho gave him a formal bow, but cast an uncertain look back toward the cave city. He had come out ill-prepared to accompany an army on horseback. Kaydu saw his indecision and offered a hand when she had mounted her own horse. "She can carry two, if it isn't too far."

"I'll take the Wastrel with me," Stipes offered. Bixei's glare changed his mind. "Or, Bixei will ride with me, and the Wastrel can borrow his horse?"

Bixei leaped onto the horse's rump with a surly growl and gave his partner a pinch under cover of securing a grip. Smothering a chuckle, Llesho shook his head when Harlol looked to him for guidance. The Wastrel knew nothing of his companions but their names, mentioned in passing as they shared stories to help the time pass. He wouldn't have understood the byplay, but he mounted the offered horse and let Llesho take the lead.

Kaydu nudged a little away from the others so she and Llesho could talk without being heard. "Where are Lling and Hmishi?" she asked, the pleasure of meeting falling away as the business of guarding a prince took over. "I trained them better than to let you wander off alone."

"We were betrayed." Llesho stared out into the desert, remembering a dream of anguish and despair. "The Harn have them."

"Damn. I'm sorry. But we'll get them back," Kaydu assured him, all levity now gone.

The pressure of Master Markko's search had not returned, but a superstitious dread of being overheard by magical means kept Llesho from saying anything more. Llesho's nemesis might not yet know what prizes his raiders held.

Kaydu turned in her saddle with a worried frown, but she said nothing more. Llesho could tell by the faraway look in her eyes that she, too, tested the air for more than the taste of dust. After a journey the longer for the exhaustion of the horses, they passed through the dream readers' barrier that blinded the eye to the presence of the cave city of Ahkenbad.

"By the Great Goddess, that's a trick," Kaydu muttered when the carved cliffs of the cave city appeared around them.

Inside the warding defenses that protected Ahkenbad from her enemies, Llesho braced himself for another confrontation. How was he going to explain to Habiba that he'd lost the emperor?

Chapter Fourteen

THEY had come to the gaping stone mouth of the Dragon Cave. Worried acolytes and servants surrounded them, stirring up the dust with their feet. He recognized Kagar among them. Her avid, envious eyes locked briefly on Kaydu before she slipped into the chamber where the dream readers gathered. The Dinha trusted her; Llesho didn't. He still had the lump on the back of his head to remind him why that was a smart thing, but his brothers presented the more immediate problem.

Lluka and Balar stood side by side in the very teeth of the stone dragon as if they could hold off Llesho's new forces with their persons. From Llesho's seat atop Kaydu's horse, his brothers looked very small. He shook his head to rid it of a fleeting image: the jagged stone teeth snapping shut, the bloodied faces of his brothers ground against sharp edges come to life. Not a wish, but a worry— What part did the sleeping dragon of Stone River play in the dreams that tied the princes of Thebin to this place?

They could not know where his thought had taken him, of course, and watched their rebellious younger brother with matching stern frowns. "Only a fool goes into the desert unprepared," Lluka scolded him. "When you didn't come back, we thought you must be lost, or dead. You will have apologies to make to the Dinha, and to the search parties when they return."

"Harlol was with me," Llesho reminded his brother, but that answer just earned the Wastrel a scathing snarl of contempt.

"You move through the world wrapped in a no-sense zone, Llesho. It warps the judgment of anyone who comes in contact with you."

"Then don't come too close, or you might grow a backbone."

Lluka colored as if he'd been struck, and would have continued the argument but for Habiba's rumbled, "It's true, Llesho. Admit defeat with grace."

He didn't concede any such thing, of course, but Balar chose that moment to turn the attack on the magician, freeing Llesho from the unwanted attention of his brothers and the lady's witch.

"You have breached the Dinha's security." Balar said it as a fact, rather than an accusation, just as his will to protect the dream readers was a fact and not a show of bravado.

Habiba slipped from his horse and bowed a respectful greeting in spite of the surly introduction. Llesho was glad Balar wasn't carrying a lute. Experience had shown him that his brother wielded the instrument as well in battle as in song, but the magician had a tricky temper at the best of times. He might indulge a verbal challenge. In a physical attack, however, he was as likely to turn Balar into a camel first and apologize later. Not the best plan in a place that reeked of sleeping magic. Fortunately, his brother had come out unarmed even with music, and Habiba's courtbred manners guaranteed his good intentions.

"You have nothing to fear from me—Prince? I honor the Dinha and her dreams." With that very proper greeting, Habiba gave the signal for his army to dismount. "I beg hospitality for my troops—water for their horses, and a place to rest out the heat of the day. I would pay my respects to the Dinha, and we will be on our way with the rising of Great Moon Lun."

The brothers could not help but recognize, among the soldiers massed at Habiba's back, their own countrymen and the clan dress of the honorable mercenaries who had guarded them as children. Lluka surrendered with a lowering of his eyelids and gestured for a Tashek groom. Kagar had put off her disguise here, among her kinsmen, and Harlol had taken up his role as a warrior, so the task fell to a stranger. Experience told Llesho not to trust the man out of his sight, but Harlol cast him a challenge in a glance. He had to accept the aid Habiba had requested or pay for the insult to the Tashek people. This time, he conceded the point.

Kaydu arranged for a soldier to take her horse. With Stipes and Bixei at her back, she gave the princes a cool examination. Llesho shook his coats into order, pretending to a disinterest he didn't feel when the princes returned her disapproval with watchful glares.

"These must be brothers," she declared with a satisfied smirk. "They look more like you than Shokar or Adar, though I can't say much for their dispositions."

Llesho would have returned Kaydu's grin, but he dreaded his coming report on the Harn attack. He didn't want to compound his offenses with poorly timed humor.

"Indeed," he therefore answered as neutrally as he could manage, "May I introduce the youngest of my older brothers, Prince Balar, who would hold off our army with the daggers of his eyes—or his five-stringed lute, which felled no few of our enemies on the outskirts of Durnhag. And Prince Lluka, who would still have me taking naps in the afternoon with my favorite hound sneaked into my bed."

His brothers' hostile glances turned to surprise and awe when he reversed the introduction: "Princes, may I introduce the loyal servant of her ladyship, the mortal goddess SienMa: Habiba the magician-witch, and his daughter, Kaydu, who is the captain of my own cadre. You know—the Imperial Guards you left in the hands of the Harn."

"My Lord Habiba," Balar began, but an angry roar interrupted his greeting.

"You what!" Bixei, who had remained silent but watchful at Stipes' side, strode forward to place himself between Llesho and the threat of his brothers. "I'm amazed Shou didn't strip the skin off your hide after a fool stunt like that!" he shouted into Balar's face.

In spite of his rage, Bixei retained enough sense not to blurt out the emperor's title. Llesho did the same.

"Shou had no say." This was the moment he had dreaded since Durnhag. "The last time I saw him, Shou was holding off three Harn raiders, trying to reach Adar's side. Neither Adar nor the Lady Carina bore any weapons. Both are skilled in the Way of the Goddess, but they could not hold out against so many. While I fought the raiders between us, one of our Tashek grooms struck me from behind, and I fell."

Harlol, who had taken a position of defense at Llesho's side, jumped at the mention of his cousin's part in the kidnapping, but carefully avoided eye contact. After only a brief, scathing glance, however, Llesho continued his story.

"When I recovered consciousness, I found myself half-way to Ahkenbad in the custody of my brother and our Tashek drovers. They left the others, including Adar and Shou, Master Den, and Carina, to the hospitality of Harnish murderers."

He exchanged glares with his brother over Bixei's shoulder. Balar still owed him for the lump on his head, and perhaps for much more if the worst had happened to Emperor Shou. Or their brother: the ghost of his adviser, Lleck, had said nothing about getting his brothers killed while gathering them to his side.

Habiba's eyes opened wide. Briefly, Llesho thought the princes of Thebin were about to die. Maybe Habiba would kill him, too, for arrant stupidity, though he doubted it. Llesho was starting to figure out the part he played in the grand scheme of this conflict. Habiba needed live bait to catch Master Markko, and he was it.

He had begun the move to his knife, instinctively ready to protect his brothers, when Habiba brought his expression and his temper under control with a long cleansing sigh. "We should take this discussion under cover," he advised with a quick scan of the road, "And I have yet to pay my respects to the Dinha."

Balar fumbled indecisively in their path, but Habiba set him aside with a casual sweep of his arm and entered the sacred cave of the dream readers. Harlol followed close on his heels, hands perched dangerously on his hilts. Llesho figured he had more right to his place there than the rest of them, so made no objection. The magician wasn't through with him yet, though.

"Could you have angered more of our gods with one foolish act if that had been your intention?" Kaydu spat at the bemused princes before following her father into the gaping mouth of the dream readers' cave.

"Master Den will protect them," Llesho offered as comfort. It didn't help.

"Master Den might, but what about ChiChu?"

"They go back a long time," he reminded her, "before either of us were born."

Behind him, Balar's voice whispered anxiously in his ear, "ChiChu. A nickname for a fickle master?"

Llesho's baleful glare told him otherwise.

"Gods, Llesho! What have we done?"

Kaydu's face closed up around her thoughts with a muttered curse. Llesho knew the answer she would have given: brought down the empire and angered the trickster god. Made an enemy of the mortal goddess of war, left your own brother and a sacred healer to die at the hands of our enemies. Insane to talk about it in the middle of the road, though, where a stray word might escape even the protections of Ahkenbad. He followed Kaydu with just a brief comment for his brothers, "I think you're about to find out."

Only a hand of the dream readers remained in the dragon's mouth. Attendants had cleared away breakfast hours ago, and now they laid a light supper for their guests. Llesho recognized Kagar among the women setting out plates of fruits and flatbreads, and noticed again how she studied Kaydu with quick, darting glances. He had no opportunity to question her even with a look, however. Dognut stirred from his corner, a wide grin on his face.

"Lord Habiba! I knew Llesho would find you! Is that your lovely daughter?"

"Bright Morning, greetings. Yes, Kaydu has grown since you saw her last. I haven't come this far to reminisce, however, but to consult with the blessed Dinha of the Tashek people on a matter of great urgency."

It made sense, now that he thought about it, that these two would know each other. Bright Morning's family lived in the Lady SienMa's province and, like Habiba, the dwarf was in the confidence of the emperor. But Dognut had abandoned Shou and aided the kidnappers, even if they were Llesho's brothers; the association tainted Habiba as an adviser Llesho needed to rely on.

"Child of the desert." The Dinha released her attendant with a touch on his shoulder, and rose to greeted the magician with the rueful smile of familiar associates. "You find us well, thanks to your young prince."

Habiba bent to one knee in front of the Dinha and bowed his head. "Mother Desert, greetings. Meet your grandchild." Without looking up, he took Kaydu's hand and extended it to the Dinha's embrace.

"Granddaughter." The Dinha took both of Kaydu's hands and drew her into a kiss on each cheek. "Your father is a fine man, but he has kept us too long from his child!"

Only Llesho stood near enough to Harlol to see the

avid excitement on his downturned face. "Truth?" he asked. "Or a courtesy?"

Harlol gave an affronted snort. "All Tashek are the children of the Dinha. As for the magician, anyone can tell that he has Tashek blood."

A little of both, then. Habiba and his daughter shared an exotic look of foreign lands. Part of that—the shape of the eyes, the sweep of the brow—might indeed be Tashek, though the sum of their features remained a mystery. *So the circle is completed,* Llesho thought, with himself bound into the plots of those who had no care for Thebin.

He had little time to brood, however. At the Dinha's welcoming hug, the pack on Kaydu's back let out a screech that drew terrified gasps from the acolytes hovering anxiously in the shadows. Harlol's swords hissed out of their scabbards. The Wastrel checked his motion with an annoyed roll of his eyes when Little Brother crept onto Kaydu's shoulder and peered anxiously about him out of wide monkey eyes.

"Pardon my enthusiasm, sir monkey." The Dinha offered Little Brother a star fruit, lightly poached, as a peace offering. "I mean no harm to my granddaughter's familiar." When Little Brother had accepted the gift, the Dinha gestured for the rest of the party to eat, herself taking a light selection of vegetables that her attendant brought her.

"The dream readers have been troubled these many days, Habiba, and you figure in our prayers. But let me first bless you for the loan of young Prince Llesho."

Llesho filled a flatbread with fruit and ducked his head. If he pretended to be invisible, perhaps they wouldn't notice him. He might just as well have disappeared, however; Habiba spoke about him as he would an absent and unruly cadet.

"I can't accept your gratitude, Dinha. I don't command the young man." Habiba dipped a ball of grain-meal into a spicy sauce and popped it into his mouth, chewing thoughtfully before explaining, "Had I done so, little of what has happened would have come to pass."

"And yet," the Dinha informed him, "before he found his way to Ahkenbad, the Holy Well of Ahkenbad had failed. In his dream, the Great Goddess' Jinn led Prince Llesho to its source where he released the waters from their prison. Without his help, only ghosts would have remained to greet you."

"The Jinn has come to him?" Habiba darted a glance at Llesho, returning his gaze quickly to the Dinha.

"In a dream," she nodded confirmation, "and not for the first time, I judge."

With his free hand, Llesho drew out the newest pearl with its banding of silver. "Pig led me to the spring, where I found this."

"We are on first-name relations with the servants of the Great Goddess now," Habiba commented in a deceptively offhanded tone. His avid gaze on the pearl gave away his real interest, however. Even Little Brother abandoned his star fruit to sniff the air for danger. The pearl caught his monkey curiosity, and he snatched at it in Llesho's hand.

"No, you don't, little thief!" Llesho closed his fingers around the pearl and looked up to see Habiba's hand reaching toward him as if he, too, would have seized the pearl. The moment stretched, frozen in the gleam of the magician's hungry eyes.

Finally, as though waking from a trance, Habiba let his hand fall. "My apologies, young prince—to you, and to the Great Goddess you serve." He dropped his head, horrified by his own action, while his daughter watched for the tic of an eyelid or the twitch of a muscle that would offer a clue how she should jump.

The Dinha gave Habiba's hand a comforting pat. "Perhaps you should start from the beginning?"

"Which beginning?" Habiba shrugged. "The birth of a seventh son to the king of Thebin? Or the fall to the

Harn raiders of the mortal kingdom most beloved by the Great Goddess, and the scattering of her people? Or the perils of one boy through hardship and slavery and battle to free his home from tyranny?"

"There are some," the Dinha remarked acidly, "who would have argued that the king, this boy's father, lavished too much attention on his goddess and too little on his people, which may be tyranny itself. When one loses sight of the smaller things, disaster often follows in the large. But I did not mean to speak of the politics of the dead."

Llesho wondered for a bitter moment if she expected him to object. Well, he didn't. He'd come to the same conclusion himself, and somewhere between Durnhag and Ahkenbad he'd started to wonder if Shou didn't need a reminder of that as well. Maybe, if the emperor survived, they would sit down and talk about fathers and wild-hawk adventures and the people left without their king. The Dinha hadn't removed the arrow of her attention from Habiba's breast, however. "Perhaps you can begin with what our young prince was doing in Durnhag?"

Llesho sneaked a glance at Harlol. The Wastrel was the Dinha's man—how much that Harlol knew could be hidden from one who claimed his loyalty and could enter his dreams? For that matter, the Dinha herself had read Llesho's dreams. But he hadn't dreamed of the companions left behind at Durnhag; he'd dreamed of a magical pig. And Harlol, it seemed, believed Shou to be a simple merchant, with extraordinary skill with a sword but no greater connection to Llesho's team than the contract they had signed as part of their ruse.

"I knew it was a foolish plan from the beginning," Habiba muttered.

Her ladyship's magician was going to tell the truth. Llesho had a bad feeling about this.

"I expected Captain Bor-ka-mar's troops to contain any emergency."

"Shou was concerned about developments in Durn-hag," Llesho offered. He didn't want the soldier taking the blame for his emperor's decisions. "He stopped out-side the towers to meet with the spies of the Lady SienMa and sent Bor-ka-mar into the city, where an am-bush seemed most likely. Somehow, the Harn found out." And it struck him, not for the first time, that the goddess of war had wanted them there.

Little Brother had curled up for a nap in Kaydu's arms. She clasped her familiar close, braced for the terri-ble news she expected to hear. Balar had found them at the inn as well—their security had leaked worse than a pair of old sandals, but he'd been hauled off over a cam-el's back before he could discover anything about the conspiracy that had attacked them. Llesho shrugged, helpless to ease her fears.

"Dinha," Habiba said, and Llesho had never seen her ladyship's witch at such a loss. "It seems we've lost the emperor of Shan, beloved ally of Lady SienMa."

Llesho saw the dismay in the witch's eyes, the dread he felt to return to his lady with the report of Shou's death. But they had lost others as well. "And with the emperor, the trickster god Chichu," he added to the tally, "and Carina, the daughter of Mara, who aspires to as-cend into heaven as the eighth mortal god, and Adar, the healer prince of Thebin."

"The emperor?" Lluka asked. "How have I so mis-taken the future in my visions?"

"Shou, the merchant," Llesho explained. "He travels in disguise sometimes."

"I didn't know." By the door, Harlol's eyes widened in shock. "You left this out of your tale, dreamer-prince," he muttered under his breath, but Llesho heard.

"It wasn't my story to tell."

"What tale is this?" Habiba asked. Harlol took the question as an invitation to throw himself at the feet of the magician. "I raised a blade against the emperor," he confessed, "and for my crime, my life is forfeit. May justice come swiftly, and sweet death end the torture of the guilty."

"Don't be foolish," Llesho poked him in the side with his toe for emphasis. "If Shou had wanted you dead, he'd have killed you."

Habiba looked down at the groveling Wastrel with wry exasperation. "You didn't know you fought the emperor, did you?"

"No, my lord."

"And would you have fought him in a public square if you had known?"

"No, my lord." This second answer came muffled from the carpeted floor where Harlol lay prostrate, punctuating each answer with a kiss on the magician's foot.

"And did you inflict any wounds on the emperor, intended or otherwise?"

"No, my lord. He beat me soundly, and sent me off in the hands of the healer-prince, who also traveled incognito."

"Then I don't see that we have a case here. Why don't you go back to the door and keep guard as you were doing?"

Harlol lay stretched between the magician and the Dinha for another moment. Then, softly, he answered, "Yes, my lord," and raised himself to his feet. "With the blessing of the Dinha, I pledge my skills and services to the coming battle, and will give my life to win back the life of the great emperor."

Llesho thought the "great emperor" was a bit much, even allowing for the natural respect Harlol had for the emperor's skills. But they could use all the help they could muster, and he'd grown used to having the Wastrel around. Best, therefore, not to mention the attack on Adar that had started the whole thing. The Dinha, however, had other plans for her Wastrel.

"Do you give up your charge so easily?" she asked him, and Harlol blushed.

"No, Dinha—" he pleaded with his eyes to be let off this rusty hook, but the Dinha did not free him.

"Hold to the task you start with," she said, "and it will bring you to what you must do. Even this."

Llesho didn't understand it, but it seemed to satisfy Harlol, who went back to his post with renewed fervor.

When the matter of the attack on Shou by his own party had been settled, Lluka extended his hand, palm up as if to soothe troubled nerves. "Surely these bandits won't hurt their prisoners," he suggested. His own voice quaked with doubts, however. "They will keep them well whatever course they take, in case they need to negotiate a surrender."

"They've already hurt him."

No one asked Llesho how he knew. The Dinha didn't even look surprised. A groan from another quarter, however, greeted the dire announcement. Balar, stricken with remorse, curled in against his knees. "I didn't know," he whispered, unwilling to draw attention to himself, but unable to stanch the flow of his grief. "We made a terrible mistake."

"Would the presence of this one boy have saved this precious party of emperors and princes, when the gods themselves did not, child?" The Dinha spoke to Habiba, but she meant it for them all. She held the witch's gaze, relentless but kind, until he surrendered to her logic.

"No, Dinha." He sounded much as Harlol had, on being chastised for taking on more than his burden of guilt.

"And did not the boy's own goddess send her familiar, the heavenly gardener Pig, who led the boy to the holy spring of Ahkenbad? And did not this Pig entrust to him a great pearl from the goddess' lost and broken necklace as a token of the quest he undertakes to free his kingdom and the very gates of heaven from the enemies of the Great Goddess?"

"Yes, Dinha."

Llesho sneaked a glance at Kaydu, who watched her father with the stillness of a cobra.

One tear fell from Habiba's eye. "But my ladyship has lost so much."

"Your ladyship is the patroness of wars, and gathers to herself only what she has sown in the fields of others. This boy you blame for all your tragedies has suffered at the hands of your lady war, and yet you blame *him* for her losses?"

"No, Dinha," he said, with a sigh that released the anger he had suppressed but not let go of until now.

Llesho had thought it might please him to see the powerful magician brought down a notch, but now he realized how much comfort he had taken in that strength. If Habiba could be humbled like any man, what protection could he give against Master Markko and the armies of the Harn? Llesho remembered Master Jaks lying dead in a battlefield tent, all his strength and cunning spent so early in the struggle, and did not want to think that he could lose another defender.

"Apologies, my prince."

"Accepted. The important thing is getting them back before Master Markko, or his minions, do any more damage."

Habiba had treated him like a student and like a soldier in his command, and on occasion, even like an inconvenience, but the witch had never addressed him with the full weight of belief in his title before. Llesho found that it worried him now. If Habiba looked to him for direction, they were in deeper trouble than even he had thought.

"You're not making any sense, brother. You can't risk your life and your quest to save the emperor of Shan. He has soldiers and the gods to take care of him. Your responsibilities lie elsewhere. We will need you when the time comes to bring freedom to our people. The Great Goddess herself depends on you."

Lluka's objection came as no surprise. That didn't mean Llesho appreciated fighting with his brother over

every decision, and his voice had an edge of frustration
to it when he tried to explain again to his stubborn
brother why he couldn't sit out the coming storm.

"That time is already here. If Shan falls to Master
Markko, what chance do any of us have?" He gestured
to the assembled company, to show that he meant not
only Thebin but Ahkenbad and the mystics of the Gansau Wastes as well. "We need a strong Shan to back us
if we are to have any hope of defeating the Harn." He
didn't mention the demons that his dreams told him were
laying siege to the gates of heaven. He didn't think Lluka
was ready to hear it.

Habiba agreed. "Markko will have to eliminate anyone
with the power to oppose him. Llesho is at the top of
his list of targets. I'm certainly on that list and Ahkenbad
will be soon, if it isn't already. When you intervened in
Durnhag, you put yourselves forward in his eyes as well."

"I got them into this, I owe them my best effort to
get them out." Llesho gave a little shrug. It went without
saying, except that Lluka needed to hear it. "We are
none of us safe, however, if we don't stand up to him
now." Nobody needed to know that the torments of the
captives echoed regularly in his dreams.

He suspected the Dinha already did know, though. She
touched her forefinger to the back of Lluka's hand, as if
reminding him of something he had known for so long
that the awareness of it had fallen out of use. "You can't
go back and prevent that small boy in your past from
suffering the loss of his home and the murder of his
parents. You can't roll back the Long March or erase
the years of slavery.

"The young prince of Thebin has become a tool of the
gods, and you can only love him and find your own place
on the juggernaut."

Llesho recognized his own life in the Dinha's rebuke,
but he didn't understand what she was telling his brother,
except to let him go. Lluka didn't like it, but he bowed
his head, in submission to what will Llesho was uncertain,

except that Balar wasn't happy about it. And Dognut—Bright Morning—had a satisfied gleam in his eyes that didn't make sense on the face of a simple musician. He'd always known the dwarf was more, of course, but he was reminded of why that made him nervous. At the moment, however, he had more immediate worries, like the need for a plan.

"When do we leave?"

"The horses are exhausted," Kaydu reported, "and so are the troops that came with us."

The Dinha agreed. "So is Llesho."

"We rest then until sunset and ride with Great Moon Lun," Habiba decided.

With a gesture, the Dinha summoned an attendant and dismissed them with courtesy. "Quarters await you in the cavern of the acolytes. Balar can lead you."

But when Llesho rose to leave with the rest, she set a hand on his sleeve, her eyes fixed on the stone staircase set into the back of the chamber.

"I believe your Master Den suggested that you might better understand the course you take if the dream readers of Ahkenbad visited your dreams and gave you counsel."

He hadn't ever told her that, exactly, but it didn't take a special ceremony to have the Dinha enter his dreams. She must have seen his answer in the set of his mouth, because she accepted the rebuke with a bow of her head. "It is, however, an honor to sleep between the horns of the dragon. And sometimes, the dragon himself whispers in the sleeping ear of his guest."

She smiled when she said it, so that he could dismiss it as a jest or a fireside tale if he chose, but the glint in her eyes promised more if he believed. He wasn't sure how he felt about the Stone River Dragon, but he'd met enough of the creatures in his short life to know that, true or not, he didn't doubt the tale was at least *possible*. He gave the shadows at the top of the stone staircase a long look, then, with a bow of thanks, he went up. No

surprises—he had visited this chamber in dreams, and
found the pallet set there for his rest as he remembered.
He didn't think he would sleep, but a heavy curtain he
hadn't noticed before shut out the heat and glare of the
afternoon sun, and soon his eyelids shuttered the glow
of the dragon's crystals.

Chapter Fifteen

IN a dream he left his bed and went not to the staircase he had ascended to this place but to the beaten path that passed in front of the dragon's horns, above the head of the stone dragon. When he pushed aside the curtain, he found that Great Sun had set, leaving only the dim, dim glow of the lesser moons, Han and Chen, to light the trail to the cave shrines above the city. Centuries of Tashek pilgrims had made this path, carving shrines like a string of prayer beads out of the soft rock of the hillside. Close up, Llesho could see how varied were the hands that had created these offerings to the Gansau Spirits. Some caves were no more than shallow holes in the cliff, roughly finished in mud, their entrances covered by coarse curtains stitched with trembling fingers. Others cut deeply into the hillside, hollowed around elegantly carved pillars of rock, their walls smoothly plastered and decorated with jeweled images of the Gansau Spirits. The rugs at their entrances showed a fine hand in the weaving, shot through with precious threads.

The greatest of the cave shrines hid secret chambers filled with prayers written on paper and silk cloth, knotted in rags or wrapped in tooled wooden boxes. Nuns and priests made this pilgrimage from all over the Wastes to deliver the prayers they wrote down for a penny on the backs of older prayers or supply lists or letters of safe-passage, if their clients could not afford fresh paper. But all who found their way here—rich or poor, scholar or unschooled—made the trip up to the shrines on foot.

The trail was steep in places, in others passable only by ladders set along the cliff face and hard to find or follow in the dark. Llesho stumbled and caught his balance—the wrenching pain in his knee made it all more real than a dream had any right to be. Just as he began to wonder if he really did travel the pilgrim way through the waking dawn, however, the patchwork of rugs and curtains shrouding the mysteries of the mountainside came to writhing life. Against a faded backdrop of hills streaked with rust the color of blood, gods and goddesses and impetuous spirits moved through landscapes of thread.

Trying not to return the looks of the woven figures who stopped and watched out of the tapestries as he passed, Llesho moved more carefully through his dream. He had little understanding of the beliefs that had created monuments out of mountains, and he did not wish to intrude where he did not belong. His dream created caves out of his own mind, however: not Tashek designs, but something more familiar drew his hand. The embroidered scene on a background of pale blue reminded him of her ladyship's gardens in the governor's compound at Farshore Province. Those gardens had themselves been an artful rendering of her ladyship's home, Thousand Lakes Province.

Did such a thing as home exist when one lived through the ages as a mortal god? The Lady SienMa had carried a bit of Thousand Lakes with her to Farshore, as if that reminder had mattered to her. His memories of that time contradicted one another, however. Sometimes he saw her as the woman who loved a husband and honored a father, and who taught him how to use a bow. At others, he remembered the icy goddess who had judged him at weapons and who had given him gifts that whispered to him of his own past deaths, and perhaps his death to come.

If he thought about it too much, it made his head hurt. With careful fingertips, therefore, he traced the flow of a stream across the tapestry, caressed banks thick with rushes on either side of the ripple of green thread. Little wooden bridges, their planks marked in shades of sepia and tan, crossed to a knotted island very like the one where Llesho and his cadre had learned to fight as a team. Llesho remembered weapons training with Lling and Hmishi, led by Kaydu and chivied on by Bixei and the others, with a warmth almost of home.

He pushed aside the curtain and entered. Inside the sacred cave a flame burned like a ghost. Gases escaping the thinnest crack in the floor of the cave fed the eternal flame in honor of spirits Llesho did not know. By its light he made out a pillar of stone at the center of the shrine, carved in relief from top to bottom with a scene of whirling warriors. The figures stirred in the dim light, and sounds and smells of the battlefield came faintly to him, as if from a distance. He'd lost Master Jaks to the armies of Markko the Magician in a battle like that. They'd buried him in an unmarked grave so that his enemies couldn't find him to mock his body. Llesho hoped he'd made his way to the warriors' last home and the comfort of his brothers.

"All debts are paid," he muttered to the dream figures on the pillar. He knew enough to dread what the cave would reveal to him next, but still he reeled with shock when he saw the scene painted on the plastered walls. Her ladyship's orchard.

If he hadn't remembered the trees, laden here with amber peaches and amethyst plums, the figures in the painting left no doubt. A small, dark boy with worshipful eyes lay at the foot of a heavy-laden tree, his head in the lap of a lady with a face white as a ghost and with ruby tears of blood falling from her eyes. A bow lay abandoned next to a bowl of jeweled fruit on the soft green grass. The boy, he saw, lay dying. A short spear pierced his heart and yellow light spilled from the wound.

Llesho knew he was the boy painted on the wall, and recognized the spear. Somewhere in the city below, the weapon waited for him, a fearful thing to keep so close, but too dangerous to trust in the hands of anyone else. He hoped this wasn't a prophetic dream.

As if reaching for a lifeline, Llesho slipped a hand inside his shirt and grasped the small bag that held the pearls of the goddess resting over his heart. The one with the silver scrollwork was missing. Slowly he backed out of the shrine, would have backed right off the hillside if he hadn't bumped into a tall dark figure on the path behind him.

"Not to your liking?" Pig wore no clothing, but was wound about with thin chains like the silver wires that wrapped the pearl.

"Are you responsible for this?" Llesho gestured at the cave he'd just exited. Only a plain and dusty rug of Tashek leaves and flowers covered the entrance when he looked at it again.

"It's not my dream," Pig reminded him. "I'm only here because you called me." He nudged Llesho up the mountainside a pace or two before nodding at a rug covered in Thebin embroideries in rich mountain wool. Brushing aside a fold of the tapestry, he disappeared into the darkness. Llesho followed and found himself in a small cave.

The tinted plaster copied the yellow mud that gave Kungol its golden glow in sunlight, but no other sign of the pilgrim who had made the shrine remained. Llesho wondered if the Thebin cave existed in the waking world or if Pig had created it out of dreamstuff, but the Jinn said nothing. Whoever had hollowed out this space hadn't meant it for strangers. It felt unbearably private. Stroking one hand down the nearest wall with all his yearning—for his lost mother, his sister, his home—in his fingertips, Llesho turned away.

"Don't you want to see what's here?" Pig asked him.

"There's nothing to see." Nothing but smooth, cool walls of Thebin gold. The back wall did have a painting on it, though, in subtle colors so like the yellow of the plaster that he hadn't made them out in the dim light. As the light grew stronger, however, the mountains that rose above Kungol appeared like a whisper on the back wall: pale and shrouded in mist at their peaks, fading at their lower reaches into the yellow mud of the city.

The light, he realized, was coming from the painting, and he couldn't turn away, had to reach out. A cold, thin wind off the mountains touched his face, and he shivered. The mist on the mountaintop seemed to clear for a moment, and a gate made of golden pillars appeared. Llesho walked toward it, passed through into a place he'd never seen before, but knew instantly.

"The gardens of heaven," he whispered, and Pig, beside him, nodded.

"They need tending," the Jinn answered more than the question. His little piggy eyes held such a complexity of emotions that Llesho could not bear to look at them. Longing, he knew, and the delight of coming home, but also dismay, and a great sorrow, as if in the moment of greeting Pig braced himself to bid the beloved gardens good-bye. From somewhere Pig had materialized a rake, and he wandered off with a nod of farewell, his mind already on the work that needed his attention.

Abandoned to the vast gardens that existed nowhere in his own plane of being, Llesho shivered and searched behind him for the gates by which he had entered. Common sense told him he didn't belong here. He needed to wake up, to get back down the hillside and into his bed. But the gates had disappeared. He saw only gardens run to weeds and tangles of thorny scrub in every direction he looked.

Nowhere could he find a sign of friendly life. Llesho reached for his sword and remembered he had come out in a dream, unarmed. He wished for a spear or even a rake, but had only his bare hands to protect him from the teeth and tusks of the creatures grumbling threats in the rustling undergrowth.

Resisting the sudden need to curl up in a tight ball in the fork of a tree until Pig came to find him, Llesho looked around for a landmark to guide him through his terror. He found himself looking into the eyes of a plain woman of middle years in the simple clothes of a beekeeper.

"You've come."

She lifted the thick veils that draped her beekeeper's hat and her smile seemed to light her up from the inside, like a party lantern. Llesho found himself uncertain, suddenly, of all the assumptions he had made in his first look at her, as if two images shared the same space and vied for his fractured attention. One, the beekeeper, he understood. The other made him tremble, and he didn't dare name it to himself.

"Pig brought me." He addressed the beekeeper, and gradually his awareness of the other, stranger presence subsided.

"Pig." She nodded, and he shivered with aftershocks of something he refused to see. "But you've come. At last."

"It's just a dream," he reminded himself, or answered the unspoken question in her words. "I can't stay." Not really here. Gone with the moonrise, into a waking reality a thousand li away from Kungol and the gates it had guarded for so long.

"Don't dismiss your dreams. All of heaven is counting on them." She held his gaze another moment, gave him a little nod to emphasize her words, and then she was gone, slipping away into the foliage. He followed, thrashing around in the underbrush like a wild boar, but he could find no sign of her except for the hive that buzzed with wild bees in the branches overhead. He remembered his first impulse, to hide himself in that tree. At least her appearance had saved him from the painful discovery that there was no hiding in heaven. By the time he stopped looking for her, he had lost his bearings completely, and couldn't tell which direction he had come from or where he had seen Pig go.

Nothing at eye level gave him a clue, but the roof of a garden pavilion rose above the treetops in the distance. An overgrown path led in that direction, and he followed, it seemed, for hours, though the bright light of midday never varied. That was part of his quest, after all: to find the String of Midnights— the goddess' scattered necklace of black pearls—and bring the night back to heaven. If anything, that knowledge made the constant daylight more ominous instead of less, however.

He struggled forward, against his own fears and the dense growth. Once or twice he thought he caught a glimpse of someone through the bushes ahead, but up close, he found no sign that anyone had been there. Toward what must be afternoon in the world where sun and moon brought night and day, storm clouds boiling on the horizon gave the illusion of nightfall to the gardens. Lightning stabbed from thick black clouds and rain came on fast, pelting him with hail that left bruises on his arms and beat down the grass. Llesho ran for cover through rain-black tangles of thorns that caught at him as he passed. He hoped the beekeeper had found shelter, and prayed that no bolt of lightning strike him down, no flood drown him. When rescue from the storm did not come, he offered up his misery to the goddess and struggled on.

Eventually, the storm passed. The sun came out, sucking the steam out of the muck to curl around his slipping feet. He was afraid he'd fall into quicksand, but the ground remained solid enough under a soupy film of mud. When he no longer needed the protection, of course, he stumbled upon the pavilion he had seen from afar on the other side of the storm.

Once it must have graced the garden with its soaring beauty. Now, rain-swept leaves rotted against the risers and the excrement of predators raised a greater stink than the mud-rot. He hesitated at the bottom of a short flight of steps, embarrassed to mark the pale treads with his muddy footprints, even though there wasn't much more damage he could do the decaying structure. Picking his way carefully through the debris, therefore, Llesho made his way inside.

Trees, driven by the terrible storms, had crashed through the roof, strewing broken limbs and shattered tiles on the floor. A divan, chewed and defiled by nesting vermin, sat in a far corner. Llesho made his way toward it past the debris. He had thought he might find the beekeeper sheltering from the storm, but the pavilion stood abandoned. Without her there to ask directions, he didn't know how he would find his way back to the gates or to Pig. Nudging the shreds of draperies aside, he sat heavily on the smelly divan.

"What has happened here?" he asked, softly because he was only talking to himself.

"Too much despair, not enough attention to duty."

At the sound of a voice behind him, Llesho leaped to his feet in fighting stance, his leg raised for a side kick. Pig. The Jinn had found clothes, the rough pants and shirt of a common worker bound by a cloth belt and streaked with mud. Mud clotted between the teeth of his rake and the toes of the cloven hooves he walked on. Llesho relaxed his striking leg, so that he had both feet on the floor, but otherwise gave no quarter. "What happened here?" he demanded. "Where have you brought me?" He said nothing about the beekeeper, afraid that he'd created her out of his own imagination.

"We are in the gardens of heaven, as you well know." Pig leaned on his rake, exhaustion carved into his smooth round face. Llesho saw blood on the rake handle and blisters on the thick fingered black hands where a proper pig would have a second set of hooves. "As for what has happened here, it is despair. I've shaken things up a bit among the under-gardeners, though, and we've had some rain."

"I'd noticed." Llesho wrung out his shirt, distaste twisting his mouth. "It soaked me through. I thought the sun always shone in heaven."

"You have seen what happens when the sun shines all the time, Llesho: the Gansau Wastes. Even heaven needs rain. Its gardeners sometimes need a kick in a tender spot to get them moving as well, but these gardens, at least, should be set to rights soon. For a little while."

"Why just for a while?" It seemed pointless to maintain a threatening posture when Pig looked like he could barely stand on his two hooves. Llesho threw himself down on the corner of the divan and cleared the spot next to him for the Jinn, who did not sit, but paced his anger out the length of the pavilion.

"Because, when you awaken from your dream, we will both be in Ahkenbad again. I have given my assistants the flat of my rake, but heaven remains hostage to the demon at the gate, and no help can come until Thebin is free of the Harn who called him. When we are gone, lethargy will reclaim the lesser gardeners, and they will soon return to the state in which I found them, gaming among themselves, drinking, and weeping.

"Fools!" Pig threw himself down on the divan, nearly toppling them both into a snarl of bat droppings and chewed satin. "Not a one of them has left heaven by choice since called to serve the Great Goddess in her gardens. Now that they cannot leave, however, they mourn a freedom they never valued when they had it."

"And the goddess?" Llesho asked. He'd expected to see her, thought she might come out to greet him. That she hadn't only confirmed his own belief, despite his advisers' insistence to the contrary, that she had found him lacking as a husband.

"I thought—" Surprised, Pig cleared his throat, squirming uncomfortably so that the divan they sat on groaned under his shifting weight. "No one approached you?"

"I haven't seen anyone but you. While I was looking for you, after you had gone off without me, I stumbled on a beekeeper trying to coax a wild hive out of a tree, but no one else."

"A beekeeper." Pig looked at him thoughtfully, and it was Llesho's turn to squirm. "Did she say anything to you?"

"She seemed to think that I had come to free heaven in my dreams. That isn't possible, is it?"

Pig shrugged his shoulders. "I've never heard that it could be done. Until I tried it, however, I didn't know that I could turn myself into a pearl, or that I could escape by rolling into a spring that flows between the worlds of heaven and earth."

"You're a Jinn," Llesho pointed out practically. "Magic comes with the territory. Until a handful of seasons ago, I was a pearl diver and a slave. I can fight now, but my real talent seems to be as live bait that Habiba can dangle in front of Master Markko." His journey to Ahkenbad slung wrong way over the back of a camel still rankled. "I excel as baggage as well."

"The . . . beekeeper . . . thought you were more though?"

"She said my dreams were important. Here." He gestured with a nod of his head to encompass the gardens that surrounded them.

"Believe it." Pig nodded, as if the words only confirmed something he already knew. "Though I'm surprised she hasn't changed her mind about you, now that she knows your wits are dull as a fence post."

Llesho pondered this for a long moment. "You don't mean—" Pig couldn't mean what he thought. The Great Goddess must be beautiful, or at least as terrible as the Lady SienMa. Not plain, in homely dress and at homely work. Before he could pursue the question with Pig however, a familiar voice broke into his reverie.

"Llesho!" Habiba's voice called from some distance he couldn't measure, "Wake up! Hurry!"

"We have to get back," Pig agreed, as he heard the voice, too.

"There you are." The sorcerer appeared at the edge of the foliage that encroached on the pavilion where he sat with Pig. "There's been an attack. We've got to get you out of here and let the dream readers close the portal."

What portal? And how did Habiba get into his dream? The magician's urgency brought him to his feet even as the questions bounced around in his head. "Lead the way, my lord."

Habiba gave him a very strange look. "It's *your* dream, Llesho. All you have to do is wake up."

"I can't, my lord." Llesho gave an apologetic twitch of his shoulders. "I'm lost."

"We're going to have to work on that. Later, though. No time now." The magician seemed to be speaking to someone Llesho couldn't see. He felt a sudden pinch that brought him up off the divan with a yelp. Then Habiba was gone, and he was standing alone, high on the sacred mountain of Ahkenbad.

Kaydu met him halfway down the trail that wound through the cliff of caves.

"Llesho!" she called to him. "Are you awake yet!"

She grabbed his arm and shook it anyway, and he realized that the shock of finding himself in the hills instead of in his bed must have shown on his face.

"I'm awake. How did I get here?"

"Walked in your sleep, according to my father. You nearly gave him a heart attack when he didn't find you between the horns of the dragon. The Dinha told him you'd be wandering in the caves."

She gave him a strange look, wide-eyed with the urgency of the moment, but still filled with secrets. "Father walks in his sleep, too."

"Oh." *He walks in other people's sleep as well,* he could have told her, but he thought she knew that already.

"This way. There's no time." At a run that should have sent them headlong off the mountainside she led him down, down, the cliffside path, into the dragon's chamber he had left in his sleep.

"What's happened?" he gasped as he followed her through the crystal cave.

"Master Markko attacked the dream readers. They held him off as long as they could, but he knows where we are."

"How'd he find Ahkenbad? I thought the city was hidden."

"The dream readers were holding the portal open to your visions. Master Markko stumbled onto the portal and slipped past their defenses."

He'd been looking for Llesho. At what cost to their own people had the dream readers defended him? Llesho stopped to pick up his spear and his sword, then he tumbled down the stone stairway behind her.

He expected to find soldiers fighting, the clash of weapons in the moonlight, but all was in silence. Too silent, he realized. The dream readers lying on their mats were dead. Acolytes moved among them in a daze, offering fumbling help their masters were beyond accepting. Bloody tear tracks streaking their faces gave the only sign of the violence that had left the student dream readers shattered within.

"This is my fault." Llesho reached out a hand, as if the evidence of touch might disprove what he saw. "I should never have come here."

"You didn't choose to come here." Lluka stepped away from a tight cluster of figures in the shadows, his face a mask of horror. "It was our idea to bring you here." His gesture included Balar, and Harlol, who wiped at the blood dripping from the corner of his eye as he followed the princes into the dim light. Llesho wasn't accepting the excuses his brothers made for him.

"I could have gone—"

Absently, Harlol brushed a streak of blood from his chin. "It wouldn't have made a difference. The magician was trying to find you when he attacked. If you were a million li from here, he would have attacked just the same. He only knows where you are now because of what he found in our minds. The dream readers resisted, but they had to choose between—" He stopped, his complexion turning green under the bronze, as if he had only that moment realized the import of what he had to say.

"They had to choose between protecting my dreams from him, or protecting themselves. And they chose to die." Llesho jerked his head in a sketchy nod, all he could manage of courtesy while he struggled to contain his grief and rage.

Not again. He couldn't take it again, not the deaths of more innocents on his hands. There was nothing, nothing he could do that could repay the lives sacrificed for him, and he resented it, resented the burden they put on him, the expectations they never quite spelled out. All those souls waiting between the worlds for him to do something or be something that would set them free, and he had to make it worth their sacrifice. But he didn't know how he was going to survive the weight of their deaths long enough to redeem them.

"Kagar?" Llesho asked, afraid to add another soul to his tally.

Harlol had that one bit of comfort to offer. "The Dinha had forbidden the acolytes to join in the dream reading tonight. Some are hurt, all are in shock, but Kagar and the others are alive. They'll need help."

Llesho felt the Wastrel pulling away and gave him permission to go with a quick nod. "Help where you can," he said, and added, "I'm as safe as I'm going to be," to Harlol's retreating back. When he had disappeared into the dim night, Llesho turned to his brothers.

"The Dinha—"

Habiba's low voice rumbled out of the dark. "She's alive."

There was little hope in his voice when he said it. Peering intently into the corner, Llesho saw the Dinha lying as still as the dead, huddled in a heap of drapes and robes. The dwarf, Bright Morning to the Tashek dream readers, sat with her head in his lap while he gently stroked the hair from her forehead. Habiba sat at her side, her hand wrapped in his long, skilled fingers.

As he watched in an anguish of remorse, the Dinha's eyes drifted open. "Take the boy," she said. "Run. Worlds hang by his life's thread."

"You should have let him have me," he accused. "It should not have come to this."

"We could not allow him to follow you through the gates," she whispered.

It was true. The mere thought of Master Markko tainting the gardens of heaven made him shudder. The beekeeper—at the thought, her image filled his mind, and the spear hummed with life at his back. He'd do anything to keep her safe. Oh. His eyes, shocked at the recognition, met the Dinha's warm understanding. Then, with a little sigh, her eyes drifted shut.

"Will she be all right?"

"Yes." Dognut kissed her brow and lay her down gently into the nest of pillows. "She's fine."

Liar! She was dead! But Llesho was beginning to understand, a little, what she had meant his dreams to teach him. The body died, the spirit went on. She would travel far and return again with wisdom to the wheel of life. He ought to believe that, and maybe in a hundred seasons he would.

Slowly, a tremor underfoot drew him out of his desperate reverie. The keening wail from everywhere at once, it seemed, started so low that he scarcely noticed it at first, but rose in pitch and volume until he thought it would deafen him. The acolytes couldn't raise that much noise. He threw his hands over his ears, but it didn't help. When he thought he could take no more, the ground rumbled and snapped beneath his feet like a flag in the wind.

"Ah!" the rugs on the cavern floor cushioned his fall, but his left wrist hurt when he tried to put his weight on it to get up again. Then a rough hand had him by the shoulder, and Balar was dragging him to his feet.

"Llesho. We have to leave." Kagar appeared between the stone teeth guarding the entrance to the chamber. She had washed and put on the robes of a dream reader, but he saw the faint tracks where the blood had leaked from her eyes and nose. Her eyes glittered with fear and wonder in the dark. "The spirits have awakened the dragon. He stirs."

Llesho thought she was talking in mystical riddles until a great gust of wind passed out through the gullet of the cave, rattling the roof and emitting a roar that singed the hair on the back of his head.

"Quickly! Quickly!"

The ground heaved. With Kaydu's hand pushing in the middle of his back and Balar gripping his shoulder, he stumbled out of the Dragon Cave, onto the Stone River road.

"Dognut!" he cried, "Did Dognut get out of the cave?"

"I've got him!" Habiba swept by, the dwarf looking alarmed but safe enough tucked into the crook of the magician's arm.

Servants and acolytes spilled out all around them. Still weak from the shock of Master Markko's spirit attack, they stumbled and ran, linking arms for physical support and to ease their terror as the horrific roar mingled with the shrieking cries of unearthly voices. Horses and camels added their screams to the chaos, fighting the soldiers who struggled to control them.

Rocks were falling and they hunched their heads low between their shoulders as they ran. Llesho bounced off an armored figure who grabbed him and spun him around, thrusting the reins of a horse into his hands. "Get up. We have to get out of here—the mountain is coming down!" It was Stipes, and Bixei was near, holding two more horses against the panic. He mounted, and saw that others were taking to horse as well.

"Go! Go!" The acolytes, running on foot, were a little ahead of them, but they caught up, were well past the most elaborate of the caves when the roar rose in pitch, and the whole mountain shook, throwing off dirt and rock and the offerings of centuries. The great Dun Dragon rose into the sky, belching fire and screaming in anger.

The mountain was gone, the voices fallen to a low moan. Llesho thought the dragon was going to kill them all, but it circled slowly and came to rest at Kagar's feet.

"Dinha," Dun Dragon said.

Kagar bowed. "Lord Dragon."

"Who is this creature who rouses the Gansau Spirits and disturbs my sleep?"

"His name is Markko, and he searches for this boy." She gestured at Llesho, and put a hand on his arm to lead him forward. "Prince Llesho, of Thebin."

"What does he want of this child?"

Llesho's experience with dragons had taught him caution, and he answered politely when Kagar looked to him for an explanation.

"I am on a quest, Lord Dragon, to gather my brothers and free my people from the bandits and raiders who oppress them." He bowed deeply to the creature, to show his respect even as he spoke. "As part of my quest,

I must find the pearls of the Great Goddess, the String of Midnights, free the gates of heaven from the demon who lays siege to them, and bring the turning of night and day to the heavenly gardens."

"If memory serves me well—and it always does—princes usually go hunting for princesses, or treasures, or alchemical formulae for everlasting life," the dragon commented. "Don't you think you've taken on rather more than you can chew for a first time quest?"

Llesho found it difficult to take his eyes from the trail of smoke drifting from the dragon's left nostril, but he managed a diffident shrug in answer to the dragon's curiosity. "I didn't choose my quest—it's been handed to me in pieces along the way."

"It may be time to add the word 'no' to your vocabulary."

The dragon studied him, and Llesho considered asking it to return the Dinha. He was getting tired of dragons eating his teachers. But this time, he knew it would be no use. The Dinha had been dead when the dragon awoke. She wasn't coming back.

"What of this Markko—why does he want you so badly he will kill my children to reach you?"

"I don't know," he answered as truthfully as he could. "He has only ever found me useful for testing poisons on."

"I suppose he has learned something about you we do not yet know. Like why the gods would burden a young prince with so onerous a quest. At any rate, it seems clear enough he wants to stop you from accomplishing your many sacred tasks."

Llesho had no answer to that, but he had a question, growing more pressing as the mournful lament rose to painful levels once more. "Who . . . ?" he began, meaning the voices wailing in the night.

"The dead weep for the dead." The dragon sighed a thin stream of ash. "The Gansau Spirits demand vengeance for the innocents who have died here." Something about the way the dragon said that made him shiver. Dragons didn't always live in the same present as humans did, and this one seemed to be answering a call out of the past as well as the present. He didn't think he wanted to know how those voices had become the captive spirits of the Gansau Wastes.

A trill on a reed flute announced the arrival of Dognut the dwarf and his intrusion upon the conversation.

"Lord Dragon!" He performed a sweeping bow. "The songs of this terrible night shall be sung from Thousand Lakes Province to the very gates of heaven!"

"We've had enough of songs, Bright Morning." The dragon's head rose on its limber neck, waving back and forth hypnotically. "I have my children to attend, those your Master Markko has left me. Grieving must be done, and rituals performed. Take your quest and go. But don't come back."

"Not my quest," Dognut objected, but the dragon wasn't listening. Llesho was, though: it sounded almost as though Dognut and the dragon knew each other, which was impossible. The Dun Dragon had slept under the cliffs of Ahkenbad for untold ages—had *been* the cliffs, more or less.

"I think we've worn out our welcome," Dognut said to the air, then looked around him. "Has anybody seen my camel?"

When he had wandered off again, the Dun Dragon rested his head on his claws and smoked quietly as Kagar said her farewells.

"I had hoped to have time to travel with you, to see the world as a Wastrel sees it," the new Dinha told him, "but I am called to a harsher duty much sooner than any would have thought."

Llesho bowed his head in agreement. "We are both called to duty too soon, Dinha."

She touched his hand to acknowledge the truth of that, and tears filled her eyes as she said, "We will send a party of our Wastrels to guide you. The sword of the

Tashek people will join the storm gathering at your back. Spend our children well."

"The Tashek people have lost too much for a quest they didn't ask for. I'd rather not spend them at all, Lady Dinha."

Harlol chose that moment to join them. He held out Llesho's pack in his hand. "I know you didn't want to lose this."

Llesho took it with a sour frown. "I only wish I could," he said. The gifts of the Lady SienMa had only brought him bad luck.

Harlol didn't understand, but the dragon seemed to. Smoke rose from between its back teeth, but the creature did not object to the Dinha's offer, and finally Llesho surrendered with a promise, "I'll try to send them back in the condition I got them."

"I know that's what you want." The look she gave him pierced Llesho to the heart, and he would have cut it from his breast and offered it to her in his outstretched palm rather than see what she had seen come to pass.

"Harlol, at least, stays here. You will need him."

"There is no 'here' anymore, no safety anywhere," she answered him, ignoring the spark of anger in the Wastrel's eyes that almost rivaled the dragon's in its fire. "Ahkenbad no longer dreams my cousin. Harlol has passed to your dream now."

If the look in her eyes was anything to go by, Harlol was dead at the end of Llesho's dream. He couldn't let that happen.

"It's time you went, before you lose the light of Great Moon Lun." Kagar closed her eyes against his silent entreaty and walked away, into the moaning night. Yet again Kagar had become someone he didn't know, and the audience was over.

PART THREE

THE ROAD
TO HARN

Chapter Sixteen

THEY rode into the silver night of Great Moon Lun with Habiba at Llesho's right hand and Harlol at his left. His brothers would have taken the places of favor at his side, but in his mourning he refused their company with a baleful glare.

"I don't need your protection, and I don't have time for your regrets," he informed them stiffly. "I have a magician to kill."

Habiba flinched at the dire threat. Llesho didn't mean him, of course, but he was angry enough to give even his friends second thoughts about approaching him. With more determination than good sense, his brother Balar ignored the warning to plead with Harlol, "Make him understand."

Harlol's face had become a mask, wiped clean of any emotion. Only his bitter words revealed the depth of his revulsion. "I'm done with driving the prince of dreams where he doesn't want to go. I'd have thought you'd had your fill of it as well."

The accusation struck Balar like a bolt from a crossbow, but Lluka responded with smooth reason: "The Dinha wanted to see him—"

"Not the way we did it."

If they hadn't dragged him by the chin to Ahkenbad, the Dinha and her dream readers would still be alive. Ahkenbad itself wouldn't lie in a ruin of shattered stone. No matter what Harlol said to make him feel less guilty, they all knew it. After a moment of tense silence, Llesho's brothers fell behind.

Harlol would not back down. "The Dinha will have my head in a bucket if anything happens to you," he insisted.

He meant Kagar, who had wanted to be a warrior before Master Markko had wiped out all the tiers of priesthood between the Dinha and her most rebellious acolyte. *What do you think of war now?* he wondered. Llesho could well imagine what she would say to her cousin if he failed her.

With a handful of the mercenaries lately come from Shan, Bixei scouted the dangers ahead. Behind rode a force in excess of fifty soldiers, including ten Gansau Wastrels the Tashek of Ahkenbad could ill afford to lose. Llesho didn't know what Harlol thought he could do that their gathered forces could not. He'd lost more than any of them in Master Markko's spirit attack, however, and seemed determined to fulfill whatever charge his Dinha laid on him as penance.

It was hard not to trust this man who had lost his home and everything he loved in Llesho's defense. Some debts transcended all possibility of payment, but he thought they might share the common goal of destroying Master Markko. That much he could give the Wastrel. But he expected Kaydu in Harlol's place, and craned around in his saddle to find her. Stipes led her horse, riderless except for Little Brother, who peeked out of a sack tied securely to the saddle pack.

"Where's Kaydu?" he asked Habiba.

"Scouting." Habiba cut his eyes skyward, by which Llesho understood that his captain was hunting information in the shape of a bird.

"Where are we going?"

"Toward Harn." Habiba gave a shrug. He was working

on little sleep and less information, and seemed to beg forgiveness for not seeing into the hidden heart of their adversary as Master Markko had looked into theirs. "We'll have a better idea of our course when Kaydu returns. For now, we are simply putting as much distance as possible between us and Ahkenbad."

No need to ask why. Llesho wanted to find the magician, but on his own terms, not wake up with Master Markko's teeth sunk in his throat. He couldn't do much to move their party faster across the Gansau Wastes, or to hold Great Moon Lun in the sky past her transit to light their way. But he could get his own enormous rage under control and do something about Habiba's unreasonable guilt. With a long, cleansing breath, he let go of his anger—for the moment—and looked to her ladyship's magician.

"How difficult would it be for an adviser who can enter the mind of his enemy to do the same to his allies?" he asked.

"Not difficult at all, my prince."

Llesho returned a measured nod, accepting the conclusion. "Would you advise a prince to trust a counselor who might steal through his mind at will?"

"No, my prince."

"Then you present me with a problem in logic, Lord Habiba. How do I condemn you for the very lack that makes it possible for me to trust you in the first place?"

The magician slanted Llesho an exasperated frown. "I had thought of that, my prince. The simplicity of the question belies the complexity of the answer. Which answer, I might add, I do not have."

Was that sarcasm pressing a thumb to the scale next to the respect that had weighted Habiba's use of his title of late? About time, Llesho figured. "Let me know when you've figured it out," he responded with equal tartness. They rode on in silence then. The tension still lay between them, but they'd come to an agreement of sorts, to set it aside as long as they needed each other.

When Great Moon Lun chased her lesser brothers
below the horizon, Habiba called a halt and had the tents
set up for a few hours of rest before dawn. Llesho settled
in the command tent with Bixei and Stipes nearby, a
barricade of restless, lightly dozing bodyguards between
him and his brothers. Harlol didn't rest at all, but huddled over a camp table at the center of the tent, where
they had spread a map in the light of a shuttered lantern.
The Wastrel's breathy voice rasped low in the night, answered by Habiba's deeper whisper. But there was little
of planning to do until Kaydu reported on the progress
of Markko's Harnish accomplices. Gradually even these
murmuring voices died away. Llesho had feared more
dreams, but the memory of soft fingers at his temples
settled his frayed nerves. The Dinha had died, but still
he recognized her touch, like a benediction and absolu-
tion. He rolled snugly in his blanket against the cooling
air and let his heavy lids fall over his weary eyes. Harmless, meaningless dreams wandered through his sleep. He
made no effort to banish or to follow them, and woke
to Kaydu's voice setting a forceful alto counterpoint to
the deeper tones of her father and Llesho's brothers.

"I found Bor-ka-mar on the road and took his report.
The Harn who attacked the emperor's party left Durnhag
with the prisoners in train, as we suspected. Master Markko wasn't with them, so Shou's identity may be intact."

"Kaydu." Llesho pulled himself out of his bed and
nodded a salute which his captain returned. After a visit
to the trenches to relieve himself, he took his place at
the map table and Kaydu continued her report. She
looked weary, he noticed, but her delivery remained crisp
and efficient.

"Bor-ka-mar followed with twenty imperial militiamen. He guessed wrong on the direction and lost the
trail and a day's march."

Llesho didn't notice his own hiss of dismay until Kaydu
had answered it, defending the man Llesho had thought
a sound and competent soldier. "I would have guessed

the same, that the raiders would head straight for the Guynm-Harn border. The captain's men had to turn back, but they are on the right track now, and have gained back some of the distance they lost." She pointed to the map with a fingertip to mark their own position, then sketched the path from Durnhag toward them rather than away. "We've had some luck there. The raiders are heading north by northwest, as the crow flies—"

Llesho gave her a wary look which she returned with a bland smile. She'd been the crow flying, then. He made a mental note to ask her how she did that some day and bent to the map. They would need luck and more to intercept the raiding party even heading straight at each other. On the desert, a man who wandered off to take a leak could lose his party and his life in the endless sameness over the next dune.

"And Shokar?"

"Shokar, too, has adjusted his course. At utmost speed, however, I don't expect either party to catch up until sometime tomorrow afternoon."

"How long before they pass into the Harnlands?" They all knew time was their enemy. The map compressed all distances. It had taken them weeks to cross the Wastes to Ahkenbad, a matter of finger-lengths drawn on soft leather.

Harlol had listened intently, not speaking until now he stabbed at the border some fifty li west of the position Kaydu had marked out on the map. "I expect they are following the Gansau track and will cross into Harn territory here."

Lluka and Balar had fallen quiet while Kaydu and the Wastrel talked, but now Lluka added a caution, "If the raiding party crosses the border at a place of their choosing, rescue forces will face whatever support they have waiting for them."

"Then we will have to find them before they can join forces. We don't have troops enough to wage a war against Harn." Llesho didn't tell them that he heard their companions crying out in his sleep, that even now it might be too late.

"Best not to bring war to someone else's doorstep," Harlol agreed, "but the Harnlands aren't like Thebin or the Shan Empire. Small bands follow their herds all across this map. They have no centralized government and only the most limited communication between the most powerful of the clan lords. Sometimes a few clans will make short-term alliances for specific goals, but there's hardly a concept of 'official' at all. The raiders turned away from the most obvious route, perhaps to make it more difficult to follow, or to draw attention away from movements gathering against Shan. Or they may be making a detour around their own enemies among the clans.

"The farther into the heart of the grasslands you go, however, the less likely anyone you meet will have any notion that their neighbors are waging wars in the name of the Harnlands. The clans won't know or care what the raiders are doing, as long as they themselves are left in peace. Their shaman may be troubled by a powerful magician in their midst, but the Shan Empire figures in the thoughts of very few. The raiders will doubtless have some number of their allies waiting to aid them at their intended crossing, but I'd warrant their numbers will be small, and their Harnish neighbors unhappy."

Habiba had listened silently, but he stirred at this intelligence. "Master Markko or one of his puppets will be close by, probably at the border where the raiders plan to cross. He won't want to wait to question the prisoners."

Harlol studied the magician with a troubled frown. "No, you don't want to meet this one in battle," Llesho tried to convey with the downturn of his mouth; and: "Kill me yourself if the choice is to fall into his hands again," he pleaded with his eyes.

Kaydu shivered, a combination of empathy and memory in the way she met his bleak gaze. He saw a promise there. Good.

"We have to intercept them before they reach the border," Kaydu agreed. Little Brother wrapped himself around her neck, his uniform hat in his hand, as if he would urge them on their way. "We have a good chance of success if we can limit the fighting to just the raiding party. If we cross in force, neutral clans would have to enter the conflict on the side of the raiders, to repel what they see as an attack on their territory." Like him, she did not mention the futility of taking on the magician in his power.

"So we ride," Habiba instructed.

Kaydu gave a low bow of salute, and Harlol and Bixei did the same. Together, they escaped to set their troops in motion. Llesho tried to follow, but his brothers blocked the way. Lluka was giving him that big brother look, a sign of trouble sure as a beacon. Lluka saw the future, except now, when none of his visions made sense to him. Must be driving him mad, not to *know* the right thing to do.

"What?"

"Let *us* go with the troops, in your place." Lluka gestured at Balar and then at himself. "Stay to the rear with your own picked guard. Once we've returned the emperor to his militiamen, we can bring Adar and Shokar back here with us and decide what to do next."

"And if I say 'no,' will you hit me on the head and leave me tied to a tent pole?"

"You're the seventh son, Llesho." Lluka held out a hand, as if he held the Thebin Empire in his palm and could offer it as a gift. "The goddess needs you alive to fight for Kungol, which you can't do if you die for Shan."

"You can't protect me from my own quest, Lluka." Llesho rejected his brother's plea with a slow shake of his head. "And you don't know what the goddess expects of me." Too much, he would have said, but he didn't want to undermine his own argument with his brothers. "If the disaster at Ahkenbad taught us anything, it is that there is no safety except to see this miserable quest through to the end."

"What happens to the empire, or the kingdom, when the true ruler expends his life like a foot soldier?"

"I don't have a kingdom to lose." *Where were you when the Harn came?* He gave his brother a long stare, trying to keep the accusation out of the memories of blood in the Palace of the Sun. "But I do have one to win. I can't do that cowering in a tent in the middle of the Gansau Wastes."

"Llesho's right," Balar interrupted with support from an unexpected direction.

His brothers had seemed a united front, not against him so much as opposed to what he had to do. Until now. "Bringing Llesho to Ahkenbad was necessary to maintain the balance between heaven and earth. We had to study his gift, and the dream readers died for what we learned. But the Dinha knows where his duty lies, and so do we."

Balar didn't look happy about what he said. Llesho wasn't sure he even knew why he'd spoken out, but he didn't back down when Lluka glared at him. Instead he held out his hand, reflection of his brother's gesture, but his fingers flexed as if they held within them something as fragile as it was precious. "Much rides in the balance—"

Habiba watched the brothers, sharp eyes flicking everywhere. His shoulders heaved with a quick breath of relief when Lluka bowed his head, conceding the argument. With a nod to accept his brothers' surrender, Llesho followed his captains out of the tent.

He found Bixei and Kaydu and Harlol each among the forces they commanded, and drew them away for a quick conference of his own.

"Before we go on," he said, "I have to know where your allegiances lie." In particular he looked at Bixei and Kaydu. "We aren't the cadre that the Lady SienMa set on the road to Shan together anymore. So tell me now, who holds your oaths."

They knew he meant, "How far can I depend on you? Will I look up during battle to discover that the winds have changed at the first uncomfortable command, and allies have become enemies?" It troubled them, what he must think, and more the reasons why he thought it.

"I never should have stayed behind." Bixei stripped off his brass armguards and extended them on his out-stretched hand with all the guilt in his heart written in the lines that creased his stricken face. "I thought only of myself. Our cadre was broken, and Shou has fallen to the enemy. We could have lost you both—"

Losing Emperor Shou to the Harn must have rubbed that old wound raw in the hours his broken cadre had to brood while he slept. But Llesho had no more use for his companions' guilt than he had for the armguards held out to him. It wouldn't save Shou or his fellow prisoners, and it could only destroy the hard-won rapport that had made their cadre work at all. Llesho wanted his friends back, wanted the backslapping and the bragging with which they had met him out in the desert, back the other side of telling them that he'd lost Shou to the Harn. He didn't think that would ever happen now. And Habiba had come out to watch what he would do next. Another damned test.

"I thought this army was worth something." He jerked his chin in the direction of the troopers mounting up for the march.

"They're good." Bixei's head came up at the challenge.

"But for whom?" Llesho asked. "Where is their loy-alty sworn?"

"I am sworn to the Lady SienMa, who has put me in your service." Kaydu spoke up, appropriately as their first captain and trainer. "The imperial militia ride in the service of their emperor. Fewer than I would have liked could be spared from the imperial city, but they will die to win Shou's freedom and, if they survive, will continue to serve at his pleasure. So you have us all until then, and me after, however Shou chooses."

Bixei answered next, "The Thebins who remember the Harn attack on Kungol have sworn life and limb to Thebin's king. I'm not worried that they'll panic when it comes time to attack, but that they'll throw their lives away rather than hear an order to retreat.

"For myself, I ride with the mercenaries, in memory of Master Jaks, to reclaim the honor of his clan lost at the fall of Kungol. We are yours to the Palace of the Sun, and will ride with you to the very gates of heaven if you demand it of us."

"I hope that last bit's not an idle boast." Llesho released a long sigh, feeling the reins of battle coming into his hands, if some more steadily than others. "The Great Goddess needs our help."

Bixei gave a little shudder, but they'd all grown accustomed to traveling with wonders.

He didn't have to ask Harlol. Kagar, the new Dinha, had given the lives of her Wastrels to Llesho for the spending. He knew what he would choose in commanding them. . . .

"Take your men home," he said to his kidnapper, who had become a trusted friend. "There's been enough death among the Tashek. Your dream readers need burying and your living need their brothers."

Prince and Wastrel studied each other across an abyss of culture. Shutting out his other captains and the army mounting up at a short distance, Llesho's eyes narrowed with the intensity of his purpose. He would cut through the Tashek's objections like a Thebin knife.

Harlol, for his part, answered Llesho's desperation with a serene smile. "We go where the Dinha sends us."

"Kagar—the Dinha—believes that you will die." Llesho's voice had fallen to a whisper. The very notion squeezed his heart. He didn't want to imagine a battleground littered with more Tashek dead, and his revulsion curled his lips back from his teeth.

"And so we will die, and heaven will take us in. Water will fall out of the sky on us and we will fill our stomachs with the fruit of lush gardens."

You don't have to die for that, Llesho thought. *The*

Lady SienMa has gardens and plenty in the imperial city, where rain will fall on your head as often as not. Harlol knew that, of course, had been to Shan and back again, and still believed in a heaven that looked like the orchards of Farshore Province.

"If I order you to go—" he began again.

"We will follow," Harlol answered. There would be no bending.

"Come if you must," Llesho told him to end the argument, "but I own you now. Die only at the risk of my displeasure." He turned to walk away, then threw a last warning over his shoulder— "And remember, I have some say in the heavenly gardens. It will not go well for you in any world if you cross me now."

He didn't know that it was true, but Harlol seemed to believe it. The Wastrel stared, unblinking, for a long moment before he dropped his head to accept the threat. *Don't die,* Llesho willed him. *How can I face the Dinha in my dreams if I have lost the children of her station, and the cousin of her blood?*

Habiba, crossed by the shadow of the last tent pole standing, was satisfied. Llesho didn't know how he knew, because the magician's mouth remained as thin and expressionless as ever, but the easing of the tension in those shoulders was, for him, the equivalent to a smile in another. He'd done all right, then. Wished Habiba had dealt with the situation instead of giving Llesho a headache trying to figure it out for himself, but he'd done it.

"It had to be you." Dognut had wandered up on the other side and jabbed him with an elbow to punctuate his muttered comment. "They hadn't done harm to Habiba, so he couldn't forgive them."

Llesho didn't know where that came from. Wasn't anything to forgive. He grunted some vague acknowledgment and went off to find his horse.

Chapter Seventeen

THEY had ridden through the morning, and after a stop at the heat of the day, had gone on when Han and Chen rose to chase Great Sun over the horizon. When it grew too dark to continue, Harlol directed them to a sheltered place off the road, with no water or grass for the horses but a bit of scrag for the camels to gnaw on. The rest of them would be living off what they carried until they reached the border.

While a handful of troopers raised the command tent, Llesho wandered out into the darkness. The slide of saddles and the thump of packs landing on the ground told of soldiers who would take what rest they could against their tack, but first they tended to their animals, feeding them by hand what forage they carried.

Some few of the soldiers recognized him, and they turned to watch when he passed, nodding an informal salute. Well trained not to demonstrate undue deference for the eyes of spies hidden anywhere, they couldn't hide their battle nerves. No one spoke to him, which was just as well, since he didn't feel much like giving inspirational speeches. The soldiers understood that the world as they knew it rode on their success. His own presence, a deposed prince of a ruined house, was lesson enough of the consequences of failure.

After an uncounted time of such directionless wandering, a dim light flared behind him. Llesho flinched, then settled. A lamp, nothing more, shaded by tent canvas. Llesho turned and retraced his steps. The troopers had departed to their own rest, leaving Bixei and Stipes on guard; Bixei trusted no one else with this duty. They nodded salute as he drew near and stood aside to let him enter.

Habiba had instructed against the laying down of rugs and the hanging of silk from the crosspiece. Their packs lay piled in the dirt of a corner, with Dognut sitting atop the heap like a prince of drovers, his flutes and music quiet for once. On the dwarf's lap, Little Brother slept peacefully, tiny monkey paws curled around the hat of the imperial militia the creature wore. Llesho wished his own rest came so easy.

At the center of the tent Lluka and Balar sat on camp stools. Harlol watched from a corner, his hands on his sword hilts and Habiba, with a dun-colored owl perched on his shoulder, paced impatiently between the dwarf and the Wastrel. The map, as always, lay open on the table like a silent accusation.

"Llesho," Habiba greeted him. A hand stroked the head of the owl, which returned the soothing caress with a head butt to the magician's chin. The owl peered solemnly at Llesho, then, with a ruffle of wings and a fluttering hop, Kaydu stood in front of them, still twitching in the way a bird settles its feathers.

"Spirits of storms!" Harlol made a warding gesture but stood his ground. The regard of Llesho's own brothers sharpened keenly, he noted, though more with scholarly greed than fear or superstition. Lluka gave him a searching look, measuring the ease with which he accepted the owl's transformation.

"You travel with wonders," Lluka reminded him as he had once before.

Yes, brother, he didn't say. *I've grown casual around miracles.* It showed on his face, though, an irony born of darker knowledge than his brothers could imagine, who had lost the understanding of their gifts when they were needed most. Knowing Kaydu as he did, Llesho wondered if Harlol's fear didn't show more sense than any of them.

Kaydu followed the unspoken challenge with her usual ease. She was his teacher, after all, and had long ago learned to gauge his reactions. When she thought the pissing contest had gone on long enough, she grabbed Llesho's arm and tugged him into the group around the map with a proprietary sniff.

"We were about to hear the young Wastrel's report." Absently, Habiba flicked a stray pinfeather from his fingers, commentary of his own laced with an obvious reminder of the powers gathered around them.

"We are here." Harlol came forward and pointed at a spot on the map that showed no human habitation, but a range of hills that folded into the high plateau of the grasslands.

"The border with Harn lies here." The Tashek's finger trailed up the map. "If we rest until Great Moon rises, we can travel through the bright of the night, into the morning. By high sun, we should be within striking distance of the Harnlands."

Habiba turned to Kaydu, who had scouted high above the fleeing Harnishmen and their pursuers.

"And you, daughter? What can you tell us?"

Kaydu studied the map for a moment, as if trying to convert her owl memory into the symbols burned into the leather.

"The Harn are here." A gesture pointed out the place where she had picked up sight of the raiders below her in flight. "Their party has grown since it left Durnhag; they now number a hand of hundreds, though scattered up and down the road for a li or more, each band trying to look like it has no interest in the others.

"They know they are followed now, and there seems to be a split in the ranks. Markko's supporters ride forwardmost and wish to reach the Harnlands and their master before attack on their rear can come. Others hope to trade the hostages for wealthy ransoms and lag behind.

"As an owl, I overheard their conferences. Emperor Shou continues to play the part of an indignant Guynmer drawn into events over his head, but they torture him for information to turn against his fellow travelers. Lady Carina and Master Den likewise hold to their disguises and travel under light guard as servants of no consequence. We will have help from that quarter when the attack comes."

"Attack?" Habiba raised a disapproving eyebrow. How much better it would be, Llesho thought, to cut the forces against them in half with the simple application of money. But Kaydu rolled her eyes in disapproval of the message she brought.

"Bor-ka-mar was closest, so I stopped at his camp to pass on the intelligence before I returned. I urged him to pretend surprise when the demand for a merchant's ransom comes, to pay it and quietly return the emperor to the capital city with none the wiser. He chooses battle. Honor is at stake, he claims, and a lesson to be learned."

Llesho wondered who needed the sharper lesson: Bor-ka-mar, who would surely feel the edge of his emperor's temper for taking the path more costly in lives, or the Harn, who would learn not to touch the citizens of Shan. A hostage wanted for his value in cash, however, would remain alive as long as his captors found a value for him. But . . . "What of my brother?" Llesho asked.

"Adar is well. For the most part," Kaydu added. "The prisoners ride. They fear he is magical, as the superstitious often see healers. He travels surrounded by heavy guard, but in the company of the leader at the head of the convoy. Lling they move in chains, as befits the armed guard of their prisoner."

Pig, he thought, his hand sweat-tight on the pearls tha
had fallen from heaven, *how does your mistress allo*
such torment? Of course, the goddess was herself a pris
oner in her heavenly gardens.

Kaydu hadn't mention Hmishi, would have let tha
slide into the misdirection that he suffered the sam
harsh but honorable fate as Lling. Llesho remembere
the cries in his dreams, however, and rejected the non
answer.

"And what of Lling's partner, Hmishi?"

"Not well." Kaydu closed her eyes, whether to call t
mind more clearly what she had seen or to blot the imag
from her inner vision he could not immediately gues
"He lives. We all need our rest now—more can wait."

"I need to know."

Kaydu looked to her father, for permission to spea
or, perhaps, for permission to withhold this informatior
He returned only a narrow shrug. Not his call, or her
She sighed.

"In Hmishi, they must believe that they have capture
the prince they were looking for, and wish to bring hir
properly chastened to their master."

"And so?" Llesho asked. Absently, he slid his han
inside his shirt and wrapped his fingers around the littl
sack of pearls, caught between his dreams of danglin
in Master Markko's clutches and the waking chaos tha
awaited them all if the Harn should kill the empero
of Shan.

"And so," Kaydu continued, "the others ride, bu
Hmishi walks. Chained, as Lling is chained, but with
rope around his neck. When he does not keep up, th
rope tightens, pulling him off his feet and choking hir
When he loses consciousness, the raiders drop him ove
the rump of Lling's horse, then set him on his feet agai
when he comes to." There was more she wouldn't sa
but he knew it, had known since he heard the scream
of his companions in his dreams, and he didn't press he

"Evil rules the waking world," he muttered, and felt the thought take root in his own heart. He would risk all to free his companions, but in his most secret soul gave thanks that this time someone else bore the torment in his place. Not for long, of course. If Hmishi survived the journey, Master Markko would know they had brought him the wrong Thebin boy. Then Hmishi would die for the crime of not being the prince of dreams, and Markko would send more raiders to search for Llesho again. But for a short time, Hmishi suffered and he did not.

"We have to get him out of there."

"All of them," Habiba agreed. "And before they cross into the Harnlands."

"Here," Harlol traced a route that intersected the raiding party on the road a good twenty li from the border, and east of where they now rested. "There are no roads through these hills, but natural defiles and hidden passes easy enough to find as the bird flies—" He sneaked a nervous look at Kaydu, as if she might peck at his eyes for suggesting such a thing.

"Can be done." She nodded her thoughtful agreement. "Do you hunt with eagles, Wastrel?"

"None so beautiful as my captain," he said, and smiled at his own temerity to give her compliments and put himself under her command.

"A warrior with flattery," she softly teased him.

Llesho wondered if either of them knew what game they played at, here at the edge of the world. "How long till moonrise?" he interrupted this strange courtship.

"Three hours," Harlol answered promptly, and Llesho nodded, suddenly more tired than was reasonable. He hadn't wanted Kaydu for himself, but he felt, as he had when Lling chose Hmishi, the exhaustion of being alone in a world where everyone else came in twos.

"Sleep," Habiba insisted. "Let others keep watch."

As if the magician saw a future in which he could no

longer defend his charge. *Oh, help me,* Llesho thought. *I am falling through a crack in the world, and no one can save me.*

He let Bixei roll out his blanket, and made no objection when Habiba trimmed back the lamp to the least glimmer. But he did not sleep. In that dim light he checked his pack, drawing out the gifts Lady SienMa had given him. Cross-legged on his sleeping blanket, he set the jade cup before him and meditated upon its green depths. A marriage cup, he knew it to be. In lives past, he had loved and married, perhaps had children, joys and sorrows. A life.

He'd died, but more to the point, his time had come again. What lessons was he supposed to learn from this life? What had he learned in the past of the jade marriage cup? A priceless object, he knew it to be—it would have been even then. Was he always a king or a prince in all the lives that he had lived in the kingdoms of the waking world? Or did the cup have some other tale to tell? Perhaps a poor soldier had reached too high, touching lips to exalted honey before the bitter gift took it all away. He reached into his pack and took out the short spear that whispered death to him, felt the weight of it settle easily in his hand. Once this spear had killed him, but it was *his* spear, no doubt of that, worn to familiarity in his grip and steeped in more blood than his own.

The coming battle would be fought on horseback. Luck had brought Llesho up against his enemies on foot until now, but that wasn't how the raiders of the grassland preferred to carry out their campaigns. The Lady SienMa had taught him, with Kaydu and his Thebin guards, how to shoot a bow from the back of a horse, how to bring the attack in close, with spear or sword. His wrist still hurt from his fall in Ahkenbad, but he reached for his bow and strung it in the near dark, with fingers that had almost lost the knack of it. When he had done that, he polished the short spear, laying them both nearby before he let his head fall back upon his pack for an hour's rest.

In the hard dark, without even the light of the lantern for comfort, Llesho woke screaming. "They are killing him. Oh, Goddess, they are killing him!"

"What?"

"Who are they killing?"

"Llesho, wake up!"

Of all the voices calling to him, Llesho responded to the last, Habiba's.

"Help me!" he cried, and sprang up, both arms wrapped around his middle. But his heart was beating out of time and he couldn't make his legs hold him. The ground rose to meet him and he let it, curling in on himself and rocking, rocking against the pain. Soldiers tortured him and abused him for pleasure and to vent their anger that their raid had come to nothing, so they thought. Broken, and bleeding inside and out from his many wounds, still they made him walk, until Hmishi had fainted in the dust. Then they tied him to a horse and laughed at his groans and his agony. Now his fever rose unchecked. With two sacred healers in their train they would let no one tend the wounds.

Callused fingers brushed the hair from his forehead "You are with friends, you're safe. He can't reach you here." Habiba called him out of the dream, and Llesho hiccuped, and wiped at his eyes with the heel of his hand, trying to quiet the erratic thunder of his heart that sent shudders throughout his rocking body. Habiba lied. Ahkenbad proved that Master Markko could reach him anywhere. But it wasn't the magician who was torturing Hmishi to death on the road to Harn.

"He knows it isn't me."

"Not yet," Habiba told him. "Time means little in the land of dreams. But soon perhaps, if we do not reach him first."

Something in the way he looked at Habiba made her ladyship's magician flinch and look away.

"He's angry because they caught the wrong one. He doesn't even care what Hmishi knows or could tell him—he thinks he's got Lling for that when he's done. He's just angry and wants to hurt him for pleasure, but he's gone too far . . ."

"Master Markko?" Kaydu asked, softly, as her father spoke, trying not to panic him again.

Llesho thought a moment, going over the dream in his head. "He isn't there. I don't know how he knows." He wouldn't say any more. Finally his heart and his breathing settled. His own stink, stale fear-sweat drying on his body, embarrassed him but he couldn't do anything about that now. Gradually, when his silence made it clear that there would be no further revelations, his companions drifted off to their own disturbed rest. Only Habiba stayed, stroking Llesho's hair back with a soothing rhythm that belied the tears falling absently from unseeing eyes. So only Llesho heard the magician's whispered prayer, "Dear lady, why? They are only children."

Habiba served the mortal goddess of war. If she were listening, she would have understood Llesho's thought. *We are not children. We never were.* But he was too tired, too heartsick and still aching from his dream. Habiba, he decided, would have to figure it out on his own.

Moonrise cast ghostly shadows over the army stirring out in the cool of night. Llesho shivered, not from the temperature, but from superstitious dread of the images moving like a dream in his head. Armies of the dead. In the moon-washed night, it seemed that he led armies of the dead. Blanched of life and color, his companions readied themselves for battle. Habiba rode at the head of their forces. Lluka and Balar had sorted themselves out amid the protection of their few countrymen. Kungol had hired mercenary guards because Thebin had turned away from war long ago. Now Kungol and heaven itself needed Thebin warriors, and skills long practiced as royal arts showed their military bones. His brother-princes would be as safe among Shokar's Thebin recruits as any soldiers could make them.

Harlol stood waiting with Llesho's horse. "Dognut rides with the baggage," he said. "I've assigned two Wastrels to stand guard when the battle comes." Two at least who might be saved, this much he gave the prince of dreams.

"Thank you."

Llesho set his bow and arrows in their saddle quiver and shifted his shoulders to bring the short spear to a more comfortable rest at his back. His place was at Habiba's left, flanking the magician-general, except that Harlol, respectful but determined, would have ridden in front, to take the first wound for his Dinha. Llesho glared him down. At his side, then, in the first ranks as befit the envoy of Ahkenbad.

Kaydu rode to battle in the shape of an eagle, seated on a hunting perch set up for the purpose on the pommel of her father's saddle. They would need her special skills soon.

"That's really her?" Harlol muttered as he settled his horse next to Llesho's.

"Probably."

At a flick of Habiba's hand, horses moved, carrying their riders into a landscape of broken shadows. The path they followed between naked hills scoured by wind erosion carried them higher, to the elevated plains of the Harnlands. Llesho's horse set a steady pace and he let Harlol distract him from reliving his dream with questions about Kaydu.

"It might be someone else, or even a real hunting eagle. But if you know what to look for, you can usually tell. The general her father always has that funny line next to his mouth when Kaydu is performing a transformation. I've figured it half for pride and half for terror that she'll forget how to change back."

With a horrified start, Harlol jerked on the reins of his

horse. The animal sidled nervously until brought under control again.

"She hasn't forgotten yet," he reminded the Wastrel, and shifted the pack that rode in front of him on his saddle. Little Brother peeked out at the passing scenery but made no comment for a change, which was some relief. The monkey had objected loudly when Llesho tried to hand him off to Dognut. No amount of argument had convinced Little Brother that he'd be safer riding with the dwarf among the baggage. And no amount of dread and foreboding could withstand the foolishness of a fight with a stubborn monkey.

Harlol watched Kaydu's familiar for a moment. Finally, he subsided into his own thoughts, perhaps trying to judge if Little Brother was more than he seemed as well. Llesho had wondered that on occasion, but he'd never seen a sign of anything but monkeyness. If Little Brother were some prince or magician, Llesho figured he'd long ago forgotten his way back to human form.

Habiba would never let that happen to Kaydu, so he, too, held his peace. He didn't mention a fear—question, really—he'd carried since Shan and the fight in the market square. Was his captain human in reality, or was that shape as false as the eagle? Her father had fought as a roc and, Llesho suspected, as one of the dragons who had come to their aid in that battle. The Dinha had called Habiba and his daughter her children, and the Dun Dragon had said the same of the Tashek people.

She wouldn't be the first dragon he'd befriended in human form, but he wasn't sure what he felt about following one of them into battle. Dragons didn't, he had concluded, quite grasp the concept of death. No reason to trouble Harlol with his questions, though. They were too complicated if you hadn't met a few of the creatures for comparison.

He'd thought Habiba preoccupied with the battle

ahead, but when he surfaced from his musing, Llesho found the magician watching him sharply.

"Deep thoughts, Llesho?"

"Not really." He lifted a hand open-palmed, not to deflect the question but because words failed him. "I was thinking about Kwan-ti," which, it turned out, was more of the truth than he'd realized when he said it.

Habiba said nothing, and in the invitation of that silence, Llesho added, "She wasn't what I expected of dragons."

"Was Golden River Dragon more to your liking?"

"I liked Kwan-ti fine. At least *she* didn't eat the people who tried to help me." He'd loved her, in a way. Not like his mother, but more than anyone since the Long March. During the years of his enslavement in the pearl beds, the healer Kwan-ti and his father's minister had been his only comfort. He hadn't known what she was then, of course. Not even when she'd saved his foolish life the afternoon he'd tried to escape Pearl Island the hard way.

"Pearl Bay Dragon is young, as dragons go—much younger even than Golden River Dragon, who is younger by far than Dun Dragon. So she hasn't withdrawn so much from the world as they. And she is a mother. Her instincts would draw her to protect a youngling whose magic was just emerging."

It was Llesho's turn to nod that he understood. Not personal, Habiba warned him: his magic, not himself, like a mother duck takes stray chicks under her wing. But that didn't answer the question that disturbed him as he rode beside the magician. "I had thought the dragons left this world a long time ago. Now I've met three of them—are there any more of them still out there somewhere?"

"Not many, but a few."

"Have you met any of them?" A sneaky question that, and one for which he would have chosen his own answer if he could. *No more dragons, and certainly not me,* it would have been, and nothing else to worry about but a magician who could sneak into a person's dreams and kill him there.

"Not many, but a few. Their day is past: mostly they sleep now, or tend to their own business." Habiba let him set the pace of the conversation, offering no more than Llesho directly asked.

"I wonder if it's a good thing, to meet a dragon day-to-day?" Llesho asked. He was thinking of Kwan-ti, and wondering about Habiba, both the dragons the magician had met and the dragon he might himself be. "One can admire Golden River Dragon, but one never mistakes him for a friend."

"Friendship may be asking too much of a dragon," Habiba conceded. "Loyalty, however, is a well-known trait of the species."

"And is Habiba the magician, her ladyship's general, also a dragon?"

He'd disconcerted the magician, and ruffled the feathers of the eagle on its perch. Llesho would have felt smug about that if not for the fact that he was shivering like he had the ague, out of fear that Habiba would actually answer him. "The Dun Dragon said . . ." he began, as if he could guide the magician's answer.

"The blood of Dun Dragon flows in the veins of the Tashek people," Habiba repeated what the dragon had said, and then reminded him of the Dinha's greeting, as if he could forget: "And I have Tashek blood."

Which didn't exactly answer the question, but was maybe as much as Llesho really wanted to know. That wasn't the end, however. "All magicians have a touch at least of the dragon in them."

"Master Markko?" Llesho didn't want to know.

"Certainly, though not as much as you may think," Habiba hastened to ease his fears. "He seems more powerful only because he has honed his skill in the arts that will do the most harm, and he turns the focus of his attention on the one task of finding and stopping our advance."

Llesho's advance, though it was kind of Habiba to share the blame around. His own magician seemed to read his face, if not his mind, however.

"You are not the center of the world, Llesho," he admonished. "When the forces of death rise up in power, all who practice life are called to battle."

Llesho studied the general's stern countenance, and saw in it the memory of more battles than his own short life had sunsets. "Then I'm nothing but a pawn."

"I wouldn't say that." Habiba tugged on his reins, readying his horse to move out of the range of Llesho's questions. "That part about not being the center of the world? I lied."

There was no time for further sparring of wits with the magician, however. Bixei had returned from a scouting expedition with a brace of Gansau Wastrels.

Chapter Eighteen

WITH a hand raised above his head to signal the troops who followed, Habiba called a halt to their line of march and signaled Bixei to report: "What did you see?"

"Tents," Bixei saluted and continued with a grimace. "Black felt domes, like poison mushrooms. I counted half a hundred of them going up not more than an hour distant."

It made sense. The sun had reached zenith. Half the distance they'd made since Ahkenbad had been straight up. If not for the altitude, they'd have broiled in their saddles by now. The Harn had come out of a cooler climate into the Gansau Wastes; they had little choice but to rest through the heat of the Great Sun. Common warfare would have pulled their own troops off the road to wait for the shadows to return. Habiba said nothing of this, however, but asked: "Did they see you?"

"No, sir." Bixei answered properly for all three scouts, but the Wastrels' indignant snorts at his back would have said enough. No outlander was going to catch a Tashek wanderer if he didn't want to be seen. "The raiders sent scouts back along the way they came. They would report that Bor-ka-mar follows, and will know that the imperial troops will have to rest from the sun as well. But they don't suspect an attack out of the Wastes."

Habiba squinted into a sky bleached white with sun glare and scratched absently at the ruff of the eagle in front of him. He might decide to stop here, Llesho figured, watching the magician take the temperature of more than the air. Or they might press on and catch the enemy while they still had the element of surprise in their favor.

"Did you see any sign that Master Markko has joined with the traveling party?" Habiba asked, his gaze fixed in the elsewhere.

"No, my lord magician. And we looked for him." The first of the Wastrel scouts, who introduced himself as Zepor, spoke with such elaborate courtesies and bows that Llesho wondered if the man was mocking them or actually terrified of the general. Bixei didn't rebuke him for it, so he figured it was terror.

"The camp remains divided in two factions as Kaydu described. Those who hold the Thebins hold the forefront, but there seems to have been fighting among the rear guard, where Shou is held."

"And the emperor?"

"We didn't see him." Bixei gave an apologetic little shrug. "They have put Master Den to work carrying water to the cook tent, with just a single guard accompanying him. The healer Carina met him at the entrance. She looked anxious but unhurt."

Bixei paused, but the Wastrel scouts who flanked him made no move to step into the silence. Rather, they looked to Bixei with worried glances, leaving it to him to report the conclusion they had drawn together.

"Some want to murder the hostages as a hindrance to flight, others would negotiate with their pursuers even this close to battle, a ransom being less costly than a fight no matter the odds."

"Bor-ka-mar won't negotiate," Habiba commented.

"No, sir," Bixei agreed. Kaydu had already tried, and failed, to dissuade him.

"But," Llesho interrupted, recalling Habiba's assurances of the night before, that Hmishi's deadly torment hadn't happened yet. "As long as the Harn believe they've captured me, they don't dare murder their Thebin prisoners. Master Markko would have their heads on pikes. Or worse. So they are slowed down whatever they choose to do and may decide to hand Shou to Master Markko as well—to get the problem of the extra prisoners off their hands."

"If Master Markko doesn't know that he has Hmishi instead of you, he will soon." Bixei clearly hated what he had to say—like the others, he had awakened to Llesho's screams, and had heard the prophetic dream—but he straightened his shoulders and made his report. "I saw Tsu-tan the witch-finder heading away from camp, to the slit trench. You knew him when you worked the pearl beds. He belonged to Master Markko even then, and must have recognized all of your party who came from Pearl Island: Hmishi and Lling, and Master Den as he was among the gladiators—a laundryman and teacher of hand-to-hand combat."

"But Master Markko won't find out until a message reaches him—"

Habiba flicked his eyelids, calculation passing in the flash of that tiny gesture.

"What the witch-finder saw, Master Markko already knows," Habiba informed him.

"Then the things I saw in my dream have begun—" Somewhere in that camp of black tents, Tsu-tan was torturing to death the most loyal friend he had.

"Perhaps." Habiba accepted the rebuke of Llesho's frown. "Probably."

Bixei's hopeful expression faded into a soldier's impassivity, but Llesho could see past the training. He, too, had ridden with Hmishi and Lling, and would fear for his friends.

Harlol cleared his throat then, a Tashek way of gaining his companions' attention. "Does this Tsu-tan also know Shou?"

"No," Bixei answered.

"The magician will pluck from the witch-finder's eyes what he needs to see," Habiba reminded them; and, "Master Markko does know Shou as a general in command of Shan's provincial forces."

They had fought against each other in the battle that had killed Master Jaks, Llesho's weapons teacher and military adviser. What would Markko do to crack the mystery of a high officer of the empire traveling alone so near the Harnish border with only a handful of Thebins and a simple laundryman?

He looked across at Kaydu, wondering what she made of this news and shivered, unnerved by what he saw. Little Brother had gone very still, studying his master as a careful student might. And Kaydu, in eagle form, ignored everything else and studied Little Brother as if he were lunch.

"We have to move now," Habiba decided, as Llesho knew he would. "Can you bring us around the flank without being seen?"

"Yes, my lord magician." The Wastrel Danel gave a short, sharp dip of his chin in affirmation. "The Harnishmen believe these hills protect their backs, but the road from here to there is an easy grade and the passes are wide and free of pitfalls. Our warriors will rain down on them like heaven's retribution."

Not yet, Llesho thought. The goddess remained locked behind her gates in her heavenly garden, from where even her tears could not reach them. But they could do the next best thing. How he was supposed to cross the Harnlands in secret after waging a pitched battle on their very frontiers he couldn't imagine, but with his brothers Adar and Shokar so close, with Lluka and Balar in this very train, and with the pearls of the goddess warm against his breast, he could believe they would succeed.

The only question that remained was the cost, and if Hmishi—and Shou—would be paying it with their lives.

Habiba was saying nothing in haste, however. Thoughtfully he watched the sky and scanned the road ahead. "The road tends to the east," he finally said.

True enough, and their intended direction, to intersect the Harn heading west and south. Ah.

"We press on," Habiba decided, "at an easy pace, not to tire the horses."

Llesho shivered in spite of the heat as they set their horses once more upon the trail. Too many would die among those Harnish tents. For the sake of the empire, he hoped Shou was not among them. For his own sake, he thought of his brothers, and the companions of his cadre, which led his thoughts to the eagle riding near enough to take a piece out of his ear without leaving her perch. Could he follow such a creature into battle and trust its strange mind to bring him back out again alive? Habiba lifted her, a flinging motion with his arm, and she took flight, circled high on an updraft, and wheeled out of sight above them. Or, Llesho mused, would he even have the chance to test the question?

And what was he supposed to do with her damned monkey?

Habiba spread his army in a thin line across the hills that overlooked the Harn encampment. With Bixei on one side and Harlol on the other, Llesho waited for Habiba's signal while the sun beat down on their backs. That was part of the plan: the Harn would face a double disadvantage with a surprise attack coming out of the sun on their unguarded side. Screaming shadows would pour down on them out of the blinding light, driving them back before they had rightly figured what was attacking.

His brothers, skilled in self-defense but with no training in the military arts, had withdrawn to the rear and waited with the baggage handlers and the grooms. They wanted to take him with them to wait out the battle in safety. He'd refused, with language that shocked Lluka, who was prone to ease his tensions in prayer. To Llesho's surprise, however, Habiba agreed with them, and they had argued the matter while they rode.

"The situation has changed," the general pointed out. "We don't need to flaunt you on the front lines as bait for Markko's taking this time. He knew when he attacked Ahkenbad where you had been, and that his raiders don't have you as they thought. Through Tsu-tan's eyes, however, he has discovered that they bring him valuable hostages. It would be better to force him to negotiate than to offer yourself in battle."

"And would you negotiate such an exchange? A deposed prince for a wandering emperor disguised as a lowly merchant?" Llesho gave Habiba a long, calculating look of his own. Would the Lady SienMa's magician, he wondered, prove any less powerful an enemy than Master Markko if it came to a conflict between them?

With just a flicker of an eyelash Habiba seemed to read his thoughts and brush aside his questions. Which Llesho took for a yes, but at the same time, a distaste for the skill. Just another reminder that little stood between the renegade magician and their own, except for the thing that Habiba had tried to explain to him on the road. Loyalty. Maybe he was starting to figure the size of that with a man like Habiba. Bigger than he'd ever thought, that was for sure. But ultimately pledged to the mortal goddess of war—not to the Emperor of Shan or a Thebin prince—which also bore thinking about.

The general, however, hadn't stopped talking just because Llesho had hit a crisis of trust. "Markko will expect you to advance with the forces sent to free the prisoners. And they've already caught a bigger fish than they know with Shou. It's a fool's mission to give them a chance at you."

"You trained me to fight." With his faith that the magician would not exchange him for the emperor restored, the giving of his life came into Llesho's own hands again. And while he would rather live and be free, once again he found the limits to what he would surrender to stay that way.

"Worlds stand or fall around Emperor Shou, but as you pointed out, I have brothers with the baggage. Either one can take my place in the Palace of the Sun if something happens to me."

"You are more important than you know," Habiba began, but shut his mouth with a snap around whatever he had nearly said.

"Don't expect me to hide when the lives of my brother and my friends—and that includes Shou—are in jeopardy." Llesho resettled his bow against his saddle with an expression that dared the general to order him off the attack.

Habiba glared back at him. "I expect you to take orders. And not to take foolish risks."

Llesho froze. This was more the magician he knew, but it reminded him how stupid it was to fling a challenge on the edge of battle. He could lose it all for them right here, split their small force along lines of loyalty—Shou's men, Thebin's and the Dinha's Wastrels. They needed to work together, under one leader, to win.

If the general gave the order, he'd be sitting out the fighting with Dognut and the monkey. But he could make his case until the order was given, and he could use the emperor in his defense: "Shou would say that you need to take the risks to understand the dangers, for later."

"And we see where it got him, don't we?" Habiba drew irritably on his reins and his horse startled and skittered in place.

Llesho had waited until he settled the animal, and then pressed his defense. "He's right, though, isn't he?" Which seemed a pretty stupid thing to say with Shou a prisoner, if not dead already. That didn't make him wrong, though.

Habiba gave him a look that peeled and dissected him for hidden motives, but he finally relaxed into a long-suffering sigh and a muttered comment about bad role models that Llesho didn't quite catch.

"Can I trust you to depend on the army at your back, and not to take it on yourself to rescue the Thebin prisoners singlehandedly?"

"I'm a soldier, trained under your own eye, sir." It cut right to his heart that the magician would doubt him, but something at the back of his mind squirmed under the demand for his promise. How much of a martyr was he willing to make of himself? Llesho decided not to look under that particular rock; better to admit the obvious.

"Do you think they'd let me?" Truth. The Wastrels and the Thebins in their party had arranged themselves as his personal army. At their head, Bixei and Harlol rode to his right and left. They might have been comrades in arms except for the tension that kept their eyes coming back to Llesho. Neither had seen the other in combat. Each doubted the wisdom of trusting Llesho's life to the other. But neither of them would let him get in over his head.

The general wasted no more time on him, but speared his self-appointed guards with a baleful glare. "The Harn don't need any more hostages," he warned them, "nor do the Thebin people need more martyrs."

Ouch. Habiba was using the deadly forms of argument after all.

"No, sir," Bixei saluted with more enthusiasm than Llesho thought was absolutely necessary, and Harlol gripped the hilts of his swords in the Wastrel posture of ready defense. He would have laid the blades at Habiba's feet in pledge of his good faith if they hadn't been traveling at the head of an army on horseback.

The general had acknowledged their pledges with a nod, and Llesho had marched with the army. Now that the waiting had come, Llesho admitted to himself that he was scared. He'd always carried a bit of fear into battle, of course, sensible considering he'd been wounded twice: once, in an ambush. He didn't remember much of that one—had slept through most of it thanks to the healer Mara, Carina's mother. Afterward, he'd gone back into battle no more scared than he'd ever been, but with the experience to know that sometimes in a fight you hurt your opponent and sometimes he hurt you.

But the wounds Master Markko had put on him scant months ago in the battle for the Imperial City of Shan had torn his body apart. Llesho still felt the scars pull when he overreached himself and likely would for the rest of his life.

When the Harn had attacked the inn at Durnhag, he'd been too surprised to be more than the usual amount of logically scared. Then his brother had hit him over the head and he'd missed the rest. Poised in the hills above the enemy for the signal to advance, however, his fear went deeper than logic. He could feel a nest of dragon kits frolicking in his guts, where his brother Adar had stitched him up.

After arguing himself into this position, he realized that only one thing held him to his place in the line: an irrational determination that his brother Adar, held prisoner below, could not die as long as Llesho was trying to save him. He was, as Habiba had suggested, a fool. He hadn't realized until this moment that he was a coward as well.

"We'll get them out." Bixei sounded more than determined—as if he were reciting a known fact. They'd never quite been friends, but that didn't mean they weren't loyal to each other and to their cadre beyond all reason. Bixei had been at Shan, and he looked like he knew some of the things going through Llesho's mind.

"I know." Confidence in his companions he meant, not a boast about their success. He was feeling damned small in himself right then, and the world seemed upside down.

"I'd always thought battles that decide the fate of worlds would be bigger," he commented, revealing a little of what he was thinking. "There are so few of us, so few of them."

Harlol, on his other side, snorted his disapproval. "That's what happens when kings play soldier. Empires stand or fall, and no one is the wiser until they count the dead and kings are found among them."

He was risking Harlol's life. Spending it, if the Dinha saw truly. Llesho hadn't thought to ask, until now, why Harlol himself had come with them. Now wasn't the right time, but he could answer the Wastrel's charge at least.

"Kings are murdered sitting in their palaces, too. Better even for kings—or princes—to die fighting than to be slaughtered on their knees." He didn't think his father would have begged, but he knew enough now that he wouldn't think less of him if he had. And thought maybe that was Harlol's answer, too, or the Dinha's.

"Better not to die at all," Bixei reminded them both sharply. Unlike the Wastrel, he'd been through battles and unlike Llesho, he'd survived them relatively unscathed. Hurt worse in his single bout in the arena, he often reminded his less fortunate comrades. With none of Llesho's morbid dread, his common sense seemed to reach out and steady nerves. Llesho twitched an eyebrow to mark the hit his companion had made, center target.

But Shou was Habiba's problem. Against the rear guard of the Harnish camp the general led imperial troops who would die to the man to reach their emperor. To Llesho and his division fell the task of finding and releasing the Thebin prisoners. Hmishi had suffered torture in Llesho's name. They owed him rescue and they had to be quick about it. The Harn now knew he wasn't the prince Markko was looking for, which made him expendable in their eyes. They also had a prince their master didn't recognize. The trick was to reach Adar before the raiders could threaten to kill the hostages. Because Habiba had made it clear they would not surrender, not even to save Shou.

Chapter Nineteen

THEY waited, soldiers and warriors together, in the shelter of the hilltops until Habiba's signal came down the line. Then the battle cries of Thebin and Tashek and mercenary and imperial trooper rose with a terrifying roar as warhorses flew down the hillsides. Infected with the heat of the charge, Llesho's mount took off with the others. Llesho gritted his teeth and held on with his knees while his horse carried him at breakneck speed into the bowl of the Harn encampment.

The raiders had thought themselves protected by the hills at their backs. They'd posted guards who looked back along the road they had come by, but still sent no scouts ahead to warn them of trouble from that direction. Habiba's army took them by surprise, as planned.

That surprise lasted only seconds. Some few of the raiders rested in their tents, and these scattered to their horses like bees smoked from their hives. But many Harnishmen remained mounted even in rest, and these wheeled and banded into groups, ready on the instant to fight. Habiba had timed his attack perfectly, however. The raiders, from their position below the attack, were forced to stare up at the advancing army which, coming out of the west, fell upon them as shadows against the blinding white light of the falling sun.

When Habiba's forces reached the encampment itself, the sun remained an ally of the magician: sparks flashed off armor and weapons, driving the Harn raiders back in confusion. Raiders on foot ran for their horses and weapons but were cut off on every side. Llesho felt the battle fever surge in his veins, drowning his fear. He knotted his reins over his pommel and fitted an arrow to his bow. Lifting up on his knees for a better angle as her ladyship had taught him, he let his arrow fly. Fitted another before he had fully registered his man down and shot, again, and again. His battle-nerved horse plunged into the fray, using teeth and hooves to drive away any who approached too near.

A squad of raiders regrouped and took the offensive, galloping into the attack with bloodcurdling screams and raised battle axes. Llesho directed Harlol to take his Wastrels to the rear of the fighting, to cut off a Harnish retreat and panic the horses. Bixei stayed close, forming his mercenaries into a circle of swords defending an inner core of Thebin bowmen grouped around Llesho himself. Firing over the heads of their own defenders, they drove the Harn back with bow and arrow.

Llesho fought with the logic of mathematical simplicity foremost in his thoughts: a Harn raider down couldn't kill his brother. A Harn raider dead couldn't stab him in the back as he drove past. He shot and he shot, until he reached into his quiver and found no arrows there. The spear at his back fairly vibrated with its own urgency to bring the fight closer. But his teams, with Bixei and Harlol at their heads, had driven the advance guard of the Harn back, where they fell into the clutches of Habiba's imperial troopers.

And then, with a shock like a door opening when one had given up all hope but the pounding on it, he realized that the battle had ended. Marching toward him, he saw more Thebins on the field than he had come with, and Bor-ka-mar, striding among the tents.

"We have to find Hmishi!" Llesho shouted. "Where is Adar?" Maddened by the dream and goaded by the weapon at his back, he slid from his mount, the short spear coming to his hand as if he been born with his fingers wrapped around its shaft. It wasn't his brother he longed to see, however, or any of his friends once he took up the short spear. He wanted Tsu-tan, wanted to pluck the witch-finder's heart out and return it to his master on a platter. With that bloody thought he broke through Bixei's defensive formation and dove toward the first tent. Nothing. When he came out again, Bixei was leaving the next tent, and his Thebin troops had scattered in the search.

From a tent larger than the others at the center of the camp, Harlol joined them, a bloody rag in his hand. Llesho recognized it as a strip torn from one of the militia uniforms they had worn in their masquerade as caravan guards to a Guynmer merchant.

"The witch-finder is gone." the Wastrel handed him the bloody cloth. "This was all we found."

Hmishi's, Llesho figured, and felt his stomach twist with memories of the prophetic dream. Was he still alive at all, or had they killed him in their rage that he was the wrong Thebin orphan? Harlol was waiting for an answer, so he nodded to show that he'd heard, but didn't trust himself to speak. Didn't know what to say to Bixei, who had come up beside them and was looking at the evidence in the Wastrel's hand with grim foreboding. Wherever Hmishi and his companions were, they could do nothing more for them here.

"Burn them," he said, with a jerk of his chin to indicate the round black tents. "Leave nothing."

Harlol stared at him for long moments, wondering what to do. Bixei, however, shared some of his loss. He had trained and fought with Lling and Hmishi, depended on them as mates in a fighting cadre, and he looked at the bloody cloth with a bleak anger of his own. He said nothing, but grabbed a tent peg and held it to a small cook fire until it burst into flame. Then, he jammed the burning spike end into the felt of the witch-finder's tent and walked away. The tent itself would be fuel to fire others.

The snapping flames fed something dark in Llesho's heart that grew without slaking. With blood in his eyes, he turned to his commanders. "Bring me prisoners," he said. "I will know where the witch-finder has taken my brother."

At that, Bixei eyed him uneasily, and Harlol would not look at him at all.

"Is this one of the times that Habiba expects us to protect you from yourself?" Bixei asked him, uncertainty in his voice.

"It's not me I plan to hurt."

Harlol hadn't sheathed his swords yet, but he rested them with their points to the ground. "You're hurting yourself with every word. If you do what you plan, I don't know if you will ever recover. And if you can massacre your enemy and walk away unmoved by the act, how will Thebin be better off with you in the palace than it is now?"

"You dare—" Llesho turned the cold heat of an inexplicable rage on the Wastrel. *He's meant to die for you,* whispered in his head. *What matter if you do it, or the Harn?*

"It's that spear," Bixei reached out and plucked it from his grasp. "I don't know what it is about the thing, but the Lady SienMa did you no favor when she gave it to you."

"Returned it," Llesho corrected, but he stumbled against Harlol with a frown, fighting a sudden dizziness that passed slowly, like clouds parting in front of his eyes.

The sounds of battle were giving way to the moans of the wounded. A horse squealing in pain was suddenly cut off as a rider put him out of his agony, but there were others crying out all around them. There were too many dead, too much blood spilled into the dry ground, though most of it looked to be the enemy's. He might have brought himself to care, if he'd found Adar and his cadre. Llesho shuddered when he remembered what he'd asked Bixei and Harlol to do, however. He was a soldier, but not yet a torturer.

He reached for the spear. When Bixei reluctantly handed it over, he returned it to its sheath at his back. "I'm all right now."

"Llesho." Kaydu, in human form, walked toward them out of the reek and stain of blood and carrion released on the battlefield. She still twitched with lingering birdness, but she'd stopped at the baggage train for Little Brother and carried him clinging to her neck. His face solemn and anxious, the monkey watched his mistress as if he expected her to transform into a bird of prey and sweep him off for dinner. Llesho sympathized. He also wondered what task she had completed as a bird, and when she had returned.

"Habiba said to bring you. He's taken the cook tent as his command post. Your brothers are with him."

"Adar?"

"No." She looked away for a moment, afraid to let him see in her eyes what he was already thinking. "But Shokar has come."

He'd known that, and was relieved to hear her say his name that way, to know that his brother had survived the battle. He followed her, picking his way past the living who moved over the ground gathering spent arrows like gleaners after a harvest. Harlol followed at a slight distance, to give them the privacy of their conversation.

"Has Habiba found Shou?" He dreaded to hear that it had all been for nothing. "Is the emperor safe?"

"Shokar found him, yes. Master Den and Carina are with him."

She'd only answered half his question and offered nothing to reassure him. "Alive?"

"Yes." She wouldn't say any more, and he wondered what he would find when he entered the tent. Shou was more than a political ally or even a friend, he realized while he waited to see how much of the man Markko's creeping spy had left them. The emperor was the only model Llesho had for how a king behaved, what he owed his people, and how he kept an empire safe as peaceful Thebin hadn't been. If Tsu-tan had conquered Shou, how did Llesho expect to defeat the witch-finder's master?

He had other greetings first, however. Shokar met him at the tent flap with a bear hug and a roar. "Little brother!"

"Don't call me that, please." He settled his clothes and his dignity, but softened his rebuke with a wry twist of a smile. "It confuses the monkey."

Only slightly chastened, the eldest prince cuffed him gently on the arm. "We thought you might be dead in the fighting."

"I had excellent teachers," he assured his brother. "I'm good at staying alive."

Balar joined them with Lluka, ready to continue his protest begun before the battle. "You have brothers to protect you," he insisted with a sweep of his arm that included Shokar and Lluka, their expressions of relief and disapproval so familiar that it hurt.

Brothers. In case they had not yet heard, Llesho told them. "We didn't find Adar."

Shokar tried to put an arm around his shoulder. "We know, Llesho. It's one of the reasons we're all so worried about you."

Too late for that. Llesho slipped out of reach, unwilling to accept any comfort. "Habiba needs to see me."

"I should think you'd have had enough of magicians leading you into danger," Lluka scolded. "We've talked about it, and we want you to come back to Shan with

us, where it's safe." Lluka seemed to think he'd taken
the round, but Llesho just looked at him as if he had
truly missed the point.

"There is no safe place. I would think that the dead we
left behind in Ahkenbad proved that if nothing else did."

Kaydu winced as Little Brother shrieked indignantly in
her ear, but added her own support to Llesho's example.
"Harnish raiders in the market square at Shan proved it
to me."

Llesho gave a superstitious shudder as new scars
twitched in his gut. Shokar, too, seemed to be remembering. In defense of his protectiveness, Shokar added, "I
would rather not see you hurt again the way you were
in that battle."

Llesho agreed heartily, but he wasn't going to say it
out loud when any admission would sound like weakness.
Instead, he asked, "Why do you, of all people, think that
there is any safety to be had in Shan?"

When his brother hung his head, Llesho repeated his
earlier question. "Where is Habiba?"

"With Shou," Shokar held aside the flap and pointed
to the center of the tent.

Habiba presided from a folding wooden chair over a
handful of raiders on their knees in front of him. Shou
sat on a simple camp stool in the magician's shadow.
Llesho saw a bruise or two, but no obvious wounds.
Shou, however, sat with the look of a man pressed beyond his endurance, who has escaped into the land of
mazes in the mind. Many, he knew, never returned from
that place.

Bor-ka-mar stood at attention at his emperor's back.
Only someone who knew him, as Llesho had come to
do, would know that his rigidly correct posture hid a
personal anguish that he had failed his emperor. He wondered if someone had reassured the soldier that it wasn't
his fault, but figured Bor-ka-mar wouldn't believe it no
matter who told him so.

Master Den and Carina sipped tea in the corner of

the cook tent. Nothing in the way they had distributed themselves gave the raiders any clue to the relative importance of their former prisoners or their rescuers.

"Tell me what happened to them," he asked, meaning the Thebin prisoners. His voice cracked, refusing him the power to say the names. The sound drew Shou's attention.

"I'm sorry," Shou said over the prostrate forms of the prisoners.

Llesho's heart froze. *They're dead,* he thought, an image of Hmishi lifeless in Lling's arms so sharp in his head that he gasped from the shock of it. Master Den must have seen something of that in his face, because the trickster god rose quickly from his place at tea.

"They're alive, boy. Alive. That miserable witch-finder escaped as your armies entered the camp. He's taken them ahead, into the Harnlands."

"I'm sorry," Shou repeated, and passed a hand across his forehead. "I didn't mean you should think—" he gave a little half laugh, caught on a deep indrawn breath, before his mind seemed to wander again.

"What happened to Hmishi?" Llesho asked the question of Carina, who hadn't moved, but watched them all with quick, anxious eyes. He feared for his brother, but he needed to know if they'd reached them in time to stop the dream.

"This Tsu-tan didn't see your attack coming through the Wastes," she answered him. "His spies reported that Shokar had joined forces with Bor-ka-mar and they were not far behind. The witch-finder ran for the Harnlands, with Hmishi and Lling, and your brother, in his custody.

"He realized they had the wrong boy right away," Carina added. "He knew Hmishi and Lling from Pearl Bay. Master Den he recognized, of course, and threatened his master's tortures for withholding the truth from his raiders. When he learned that I was a healer, he promised that Markko would burn me at the stake. But his prejudices led him to dismiss me as having no consequence, just as he dismissed Den for a laundryman. Lling he preserved for his master's questions, but he handed Hmishi over to his soldiers. They did terrible things to him. I don't know how he lived."

She stopped with a choked cry, and Master Den picked up her sorry tale. "The damage was extensive, but ill-thought. Master Markko raged within the witch-finder's own mind for putting the boy beyond questioning. He left with Hmishi on a stretcher and the healer Adar to tend him."

"And Shou?" They spoke in whispers as the emperor listened to Habiba's questioning of the prisoners, neither letting on who commanded whom, or what force had taken the camp.

Carina opened her hand, as if to let go of some truth. "Tsu-tan could not identify him, but his master made a puppet of his lieutenant's body, and even at a distance saw through the merchant's disguise."

"If Markko saw him through the witch-finder's eyes, he would have known him." Llesho told her what the rescuers had already discussed. "They met after the battle on the outskirts of Shan Province." Shou had worn a different disguise then.

"Tsu-tan called him 'General,'" Carina confirmed Llesho's observation. "Shou insisted that he had lost his post for smuggling. Markko, through his witch-finder, tried for a day and a night to force the truth from him, but Shou resisted both physical and mental attack. At the end, he admitted to spying for the empire, but never gave away his secret."

"Timing worked to our advantage," Master Den added. "The Harnish raiders who tried to force a confession from Hmishi had no reason to suspect that Shou was more than he professed. Tsu-tan believed Hmishi and Lling were simple slaves as they had been on Pearl Island. He knew nothing of Adar or Carina. Markko knew Shou as the emperor's general, but none of the other prisoners. So he accepted Tsu-tan's conclusion, that the provincial general and imperial spy had taken advantage of a chance encounter to use as decoys a pair of traveling healers with a couple of Thebin slaves. It never occurred to either of them, at that point, to question the Thebins about *Shou's* identity."

"They never would have given him away." Their companions must know that, of course, but Llesho thought it needed saying anyway.

"They didn't," Master Den assured him softly, "But Tsu-tan made him watch what his soldiers did to Hmishi, and through his witch-finder, the magician attacked Shou's mind."

Habiba had finished with his prisoners, and he called for guards to lead the captives away. When they had gone, Llesho went to the emperor and knelt on one knee. Looking into Shou's eyes for a sign of the man he knew, he whispered, "Have they broken him?"

"No," Shou answered for himself, in a whisper, "but I'm afraid for Tsu-tan's prisoners. Markko will take a long time killing them to get what he wants, and they don't have it to give." Llesho, that was. The Thebin king and whatever else he was to Markko.

"Then we have to get them back first." Llesho kept his voice low, in keeping with the almost secretive mood the emperor had drawn about them with his voice. The power of his will, however, gave force to each word. "And we will. Get them back."

"There is another," Shou nodded, as if listening to inner voices. "His name is Menar."

"Menar?" Llesho asked, unprepared to hear that name.

"A prince of Thebin," Shou said from his waking dream, "A blind poet, who mourns his brothers after many years."

"Menar is alive? Did you see him?" Llesho pushed the hope and the fear down, down. Blind. And Shou was looking at him as if he were some curious artifact he couldn't quite puzzle out. The emperor wasn't the best witness at present.

"I can't see him," Shou answered in the tone one takes with the dull witted. "He's blind. But I hear the wind in the grass, and the heavy cadence of his poems in my head. They weep, weep, for his brothers. Shokar and Lluka, Ghrisz and Adar, and the youngest, Balar and Llesho."

Wind in the grass. Menar was somewhere ahead of them, if Shou truly had some knowledge of the Thebin prince. But Shou knew about his brothers, and his weary brain might have stirred the tale out of its own longing for rescue. Llesho had not talked about Ping, however. "Does Menar also mourn his sister?" he asked as a test.

Shou shook his head. "For Ping, anger." His eyes, focused on some unseeable distance, flicked into the now again with a wince at their corners. "My head hurts," he said, with the same expressionless voice that had channeled some vision out of the grasslands.

Carina pressed a finger to her lips, silent warning that the conversation was over.

"I know," Llesho soothed. He rested his head on the emperor's knee for a moment, a gesture that in other circumstances would mark him as the emperor's man and Thebin as a vassal nation. In this hour of torment, however, he wanted only to give and receive the comfort of a son or a brother. "But it will get better. Let the healers help you."

He rose and left the tent, leaving the emperor to the ministrations of Carina, whose drawn face reflected her own worry about the prisoners still in the hands of Markko's minions. She cared about Adar, he knew, and couldn't find it in himself to begrudge his brother that loving concern. It was all getting far too confusing, how he felt and who he felt it for, and he wondered when feelings had become such a responsibility. He didn't have answers, but he took the questions out into the camp with him.

Chapter Twenty

HABIBA, acting as general of the combined armies, had ordered the remaining Harnish tents torn down and their own camp set up in its place. The dead they had taken a little apart and burned in a pile with the round black tents for fuel. The stench of burning felt and crackling flesh rose to heaven on a pillar of black smoke. Llesho watched until the flames had smoldered down to coals. "This my gift to you, Lady Wife," Llesho whispered bitterly to the rising smoke. So many had died— how many more would he add to his count before Thebin was free and the gates of heaven opened again? During the day, he could believe they did the right thing.

But night had come upon them while Habiba sorted out the prisoners, questioning some, and allotting guards to accompany others back to Shan. Carina had gone off to work with the wounded, both Harnishmen of the Uulgar clans who had followed the witch-finder and the few of their own who had need of her services. For a change, none of his friends had been injured during the fighting. If you didn't count Shou, who'd suffered in the waiting, not the battle.

Llesho had tried to rest as they urged him, but frightful dreams drove him out again into the darkness to hide.

Wandering the encampment, he found a three- legged folding stool plundered from a Harnish tent and settled himself to watch the dying of the coals that used to be his enemies. The dead couldn't tell him where Tsu-tan had taken his Thebin hostages, but he found himself asking them anyway.

"What are you doing alone out here?"

Balar's voice, that was, edged as it hadn't been when they were young and Kungol ruled over a peaceful Thebin. *War changes everything,* Llesho thought. It made fighters, if not warriors, of musicians.

"Thinking," Llesho answered. He wondered what war made of poets, of their brother Menar left in the hands of the Harn all these years. The very idea of it made him shudder.

"It isn't safe out here."

Safe. Llesho snorted rudely at that. Habiba's scouts spied out the Durnhag Road and looked ahead to Harn. Guards posted throughout the camp and along its perimeter watched for any sneak attack, but Llesho didn't expect one. The raiders had lost too many of their number in the fighting already. They couldn't count on their Harnish countrymen along the Gansau border to help them either. While they might be inclined to look the other way at the strange coming and goings of the raiders, the border clans would resist efforts to draw them into a stranger's conflict. Like not fouling one's own tent, the locals wouldn't pick a fight they'd have to live with long after Master Markko's henchmen were gone.

So Llesho was as safe here by the cooling pyre as anywhere in the camp. That didn't mean a picked team of assassins couldn't reach him any time they wanted, of course. Master Jaks had worn the marks of six such kills on his arm. The magician himself could be watching in the shape of some animal or bird of prey. He'd felt those sharp talons before. It seemed like Master Markko wanted him alive this time, though.

"What's safe?" he asked, shaky enough in his sanity not to care about the answer.

Balar seemed to take his meaning, or part of it at least. He scrounged a low stool from the ruins and dropped down beside his brother. "I'll grant you that. Nowhere is really safe. But you would be safer inside the command tent."

"No. Later, maybe." He ought to be in there with Habiba, making decisions and rewarding his own followers with his praise and encouragement, not out here sulking with his clothes reeking of the dead. While Shou tossed in restless sleep in that tent, though, he just couldn't do it.

As if he heard his name in his sleep, the emperor cried out, a heart-stopping wail that sent a chill through the camp and raised the hairs on the back of Llesho's neck. He wondered if Master Markko, through his witch-finder, had broken something vital and soul-deep in the man. Carina said not. Shou agreed with her, or said he did. But Llesho had never seen eyes as empty as the emperor's had been tonight.

According to Carina, he hadn't cried out like that during all his mental tortures. She didn't know why he did it now. Dreams, he could have told her, while he shivered in a cold sweat remembering Ahkenbad. The magician could kill even in dreams. Was that the plague of Shou's sleep even now?

"You should talk about it," Balar said. "We can help you."

"From the baggage?" Llesho snapped, and then wanted to call it back.

"With someone, then."

Balar didn't come back at him, which made Llesho even madder. He really, really wanted to fight with somebody, the kind of fight where he *could* spill what was bothering him, at the top of his lungs and spewed out along with a lot of meaningless stuff. Nobody would die and nobody would guess what of the fight was the important part and what was just noise. Balar refused to argue, so he was left alone with the dream that had sent him escaping into the night.

Wastrels lay dead in tall Harnish grass he hadn't seen since his seventh summer, their eyes wide open to the sun. Except that, instead of eyes, each orbit held a single black pearl. In his dream, Llesho went about the grassy field plucking pearls from dead men's sockets. When he came to Harlol, the Wastrel was still alive, though dying, and he reached up to his own eyes and plucked them out, handing them to Llesho as a gift. There'd been no more rest after that.

"Where's Pig when you need him?" he muttered under his breath, a formless complaint he hadn't meant his brother to hear.

But Balar was paying close attention. "Why don't you ask him? He's hanging around your neck, if we're to believe your stories."

Which might have been Balar taking the question seriously or being snide. Either way, it reminded Llesho that some things only seemed difficult until you realized they weren't. Maybe Pig was like that. Or maybe the person he really needed to talk to was Master Den.

"I'm going back." Balar seemed to realize that he wasn't going to get an answer. He stood up, his worried frown shadowed in the dim light. "Is there anything you need?"

Adar. Hmishi and Lling. Kungol. Menar. And his brother Ghrisz, whose name he hadn't heard in all his travels. Pointless to say those things to a brother who would hand them all to him on a plate if he had the power. Like Llesho's dreams, however, his heavenly gifts seemed of no earthly use. Balar was as helpless as he was to give him back what they had lost. And he confided in Lluka, whom Llesho didn't trust.

"The washerman, Master Den. If he will come." Not knowing who might be listening outside the dim glow of the funeral pyre, he didn't say aloud, *ChiChu, the trickster god, my particular adviser.*

Balar nodded, hesitating as if he might think of something at the last minute to persuade Llesho back under cover. Llesho fixed his attention on the pyre until he heard his brother walk away.

He expected the solid tread of his teacher to follow, so the short shuffling steps of the dwarf took him by surprise. Dognut dragged his own low stool behind him, and Llesho smiled in spite of himself, reminded of the first time they had met. "No ladder today, Dognut?" he asked, half expecting the little man to look at him as if he were mad.

Dognut took the question for an invitation and settled himself next to Llesho. "No camel this time." He almost smiled, but a different memory slipped across his face. He sighed instead. If Llesho had it figured right, the dwarf was Shou's personal spy as well as his musician, and maybe more. The emperor looked to varied advisers, he was slowly discovering, and the people around him were never quite what they seemed.

"How is your master?" he asked.

Dognut hesitated only a moment in his answer. "He's well enough when the sun shines." He pulled a flute from the quiver at his back. The lesser moons had risen, shedding a faint light on the instrument as the dwarf ran his thick fingers along the stops. A mournful tune rose on liquid silver notes and fell away again. "But, Goddess knows, he can't stay awake forever."

Llesho said nothing. He had firsthand experience of the torment Master Markko could inflict, but he hadn't been with the fleeing Harn. He didn't know what Tsu-tan had actually done to the emperor or what dreams the magician visited on his sleep. Dognut wasn't settling for stubborn silence, however.

"You could help him."

"I have my own dreams to worry about."

"Ah, yes." Dognut sighed. "The stone men of the

grasslands. They find the hearts of men a particular delicacy, or so the stories say, and leave a bit of a fingertip behind when they've plucked the living organ from their victims."

"I saw no stone men," Llesho objected. The dead he had seen plucked out their eyes, the pearls of the goddess in the orbits, and not their hearts.

"They are only stories," Dognut let it be known with the tone of his voice that he didn't believe his own words. "And from very far away. No one has ever seen one of these stone monsters, of course."

Had the dwarf seen such monsters himself? Llesho wondered, but Dognut wasn't through with him: "Shou is here, now, however, and he needs your help."

"I'm not a healer."

"You know Markko."

That was too close to Llesho's own thoughts. He refused to answer. Rescue arrived in the shape of a dark body that planted itself between Llesho and the pyre, eclipsing the faint moonlight. Master Den sat heavily, blocking the morbid view. He sometimes forgot how big the trickster god was; they were face-to-face, with Chi-Chu settled like a great stone pyramid on the ground and Llesho perched on his borrowed stool. He gave the musician at Llesho's side an almost imperceptible nod and Dognut returned the greeting with a bow from the waist. Then the teacher turned his attention on his pupil.

"They're not your dead," he said.

Llesho wondered if everyone had been reading his mind tonight. "Who else's?" he countered. "How many people have to die so that one exiled prince doesn't have to dive for pearls?"

"As I recall, one old man died of the fever. The rest belong to Master Markko. Don't confuse shame for surviving with blame for the acts of your murderers."

"What is that supposed to mean?" Llesho stood up slowly, his hands stiffening to rigid blades at his sides.

The fight that Balar had denied him surged in his blood-stream. He glared at Dognut, wishing the dwarf would go away so that he could yell if he wanted, make a fool of himself against the safe harbor of his teacher. Dognut didn't move, just sat watching him out of eyes that seemed to grow older the deeper Llesho looked.

So he stopped looking, took a wild swing that Master Den brushed aside with a negligent swat. Den shifted to his feet with a dangerous grin on his face, reminding Llesho that he fought the trickster god ChiChu, a master at the forms. Llesho knew he should be afraid, but he grinned back, reassured. He could beat himself to death against the mountainous figure of the god and do no damage in his turn.

"Come on, boy." Master Den circled carefully, his arms relaxed at his sides, palms out, his fingers curling an invitation. "Take me if you can."

Dognut snatched up his little stool and drew apart from the combatants. His eyes darted, measuring the battleground, cautious against sudden movements in his direction.

Llesho hooked a foot under the camp stool he'd scrounged and flipped it over the head of his teacher, providing a split second of distraction until it sailed out of sight behind him and clattered to rest on the pyre. Then Llesho attacked.

At first, he fought with deadly art, raining lethal blows upon his teacher in all the combat forms he knew. A leap, and the kick that followed it should have crushed his foe's throat. Master Den brushed the foot away a whisper before contact. The heel of his hand nearly landed on the breastbone of his teacher, but this, too, was deflected with a slapping blow.

Master Den countered with a sharp jab of pointed fingers that stopped, completely controlled, short of killing him. It hurt, and Llesho rubbed at his breastbone, circling cautiously while he caught his breath. Den waggled

his brows with a predator's baring of teeth. "Is that all
you've got, boy? A killer of multitudes who can't even
bruise the washerman!"

It wasn't the taunt about his skills, but the reminder
of the dead that finally drove Llesho into that space he
needed to find.

"I'll kill you!" he screamed. "I'll kill you!" and he
waded in. Art forgotten, desperation powered each blow.
He didn't know if he was trying to forget, or to reach
past his brain to the place he'd lost in the aftermath,
where surviving counted more than the deaths it cost
him.

When he finally grew aware that Master Den was returning none of his strikes, not even with the lesser blows
of a teaching bout, he realized that he was held safe in
the arms of his teacher, who absorbed the blows to his
huge body without a word of reproach. "I'm sorry,"
Llesho whispered, his hands relaxing into fists that
clutched at the master's coat.

"He's not the least bit sorry for trying to kill you, old
friend," Dognut noted wryly from the sidelines.

"Nor should you be." The trickster god took Llesho's
chin in his hand and gave it a little shake for emphasis.
"When the gods ask more than you can give, you are
within your right to take from them what you need to
go on. But you've got to stop taking the credit for other
people's stupidity. Particularly Shou's."

"He's right, Llesho. I've know the emperor since he
was a boy, and no one could ever talk sense to him."
Dognut opened his folding stool and sat down again,
figuring, Llesho supposed, that the danger had passed.
When the dwarf had made himself comfortable, he
picked up his argument again, sharing his exasperation
with Master Den over Llesho's head. "Doesn't get the
concept of a wall until he's beat his head against it a few
times and knocked himself out learning. The empire is
no different than that wall to the revered Shou, but it's

bigger. It's not you that put him here, it's the damned idea of being an emperor he's trying to work out with his fists instead of his brain. The Lady SienMa will not be pleased with the rest of us, but I think she meant Shou to get his head rattled. He's known the exhilaration of battle and the remote loss of troops, but war has never left its mark on him the way it has on you."

"And what of the Wastrels?" Llesho threw back the challenge. "They're going to die, and for what? It's not their fight."

"True?" Master Den asked.

The dwarf shrugged, unhappy but not denying it. "So the Dinha says."

Master Den sighed deeply, his shoulders drooping like a massive building settling into the ground. "That's not your fault either."

He didn't sound as sure as Dognut had been about the emperor. Now that he was thinking a little more clearly, Llesho could see the dwarf's point about Shou. But the Wastrels were all his.

"You have to understand about the Wastrels." Master Den cast around looking for something, then retrieved Llesho's stool from the pyre and patted out the sparks that had caught on the legs. He took for himself the other stool that Balar had used. It was too small for him, but he balanced himself over its three wobbly legs anyway, whether to retain the advantage of his greater height or because Llesho'd actually managed to land an irksome blow he didn't show. Rather, with his elbows propped on his knees, and his eyes turned away from the fire, he sank into a storytelling reverie. Llesho remembered another time, and other teachings. He prepared to pay close attention.

Den started with a question: "What do you know about the Wastrels?"

"They take their name from the Gansau Wastes. They are a religious fighting order, sworn to the Dinha as her

children." He recited what he knew like a lesson, and
Master Den gave him a little nod, gentle encouragement
to continue.

"They travel throughout the known world, mostly
alone, though they move freely from land to land by
taking on lesser roles, like drovers. Since they don't seem
to show any inclination to work more than they need, or
acquire any possessions, outsiders think the name comes
from the common usage for time wasters. But they learn
about the outside world that way, and return home to
report what they've found to the Dinha."

He stopped, surprised. Somehow he'd thought he knew
more than that. Did, in ways that he couldn't exactly say,
about loyalty and pride and survival. Strung all together
like that, though, he sensed a hole in the middle of his
understanding.

"There's another meaning of 'waste,' " Dognut hinted.

Master Den raised an eyebrow, daring Llesho to answer. But he didn't have an answer he liked, so he waited
for Master Den to fill his own silence.

"Their birth families don't depend on them for survival." Den filled in what he'd already seen. "They make
no families of their own and, in a land of dreamers, they
seldom give themselves to dreaming."

"Expendable." Llesho got it. Hated it, but he'd had
it figured.

"They're not the squeal of the pig—" the only part of
a pig, some would say, that no one has a use for, "—
but more like a handful of copper pennies." Master Den
pantomimed the weighing of coins in the palm of his
hand. "Not useful in themselves but valuable when
spent."

"The Dinha knew they would die, and meant me to
spend their lives when she'd already lost all of Ahkenbad. Why? What does Thebin mean to Ahkenbad that
it would spend its warriors for our freedom?"

"If freedom it is—" Dognut waved his flute like a
magic wand in emphasis, "—to replace a foreign tyrant

with a local monarch. But then, I've heard that freedom is highly overrated, especially by the Tashek."

"I would be no tyrant—"

"You would be no king at all, if given half a choice," Dognut chastised him. Llesho winced. He'd thought his misgivings had gone unnoticed.

"Perhaps Thebin means nothing to the Tashek," Master Den didn't look at him right away. "Perhaps everything. The Dinha would have known the outcome before she ever sent for you, but you'd have to ask for yourself why reading your dreams was more important than her own life."

He didn't bother explaining that he'd done that and didn't understand the answer, except that it had hurt Kagar more than death to offer up her cousin like a sacrifice to willful spirits. Master Den had reached the end of his patience with a reluctant student, however, and ChiChu, perhaps, never had any patience to begin with. It was time to move this conversation past the quicksand of self-pity.

"What about Shou?"

"What about him?" ChiChu tossed back the question, challenged him to start thinking again. "Aren't we out here among the dead so that you can avoid dealing with the living?"

Definitely out of patience, and cutting right to the bone. Shou wasn't a mystic, so Markko probably couldn't kill him that way. Maybe he just needed to know that he wasn't alone, that someone else dreamed horrors that night and survived with him.

"All right." Llesho stood up, dusted off his coat and breeches, and headed back.

He nodded as he passed Harlol, who lounged with his Wastrels, pretending to off duty socializing while they watched the rear of the command tent. Dognut stopped among them, his offer of a song for a cup of tea accepted with enthusiasm. He'd play a soothing melody, Llesho knew, to sweeten Shou's troubled sleep.

Bixei and Stipes had guard of the entrance, and Llesho whispered a greeting as he entered with Master Den at his back.

Habiba acknowledged the newcomers with a flick of the eyes but Bor-ka-mar, who stood at attention at the foot of his emperor's bed, showed by not a twitch of a lash that he had noted their entrance.

Carina had returned from her work in the camp and she gave them a fleeting smile before she, too, quickly returned her glance to the man on the camp bed. Shou was awake, sitting on the bed with his feet on the ground and his fingers sunk deep in his hair. His sleep had given him no rest: he was pale around the mouth, his eyes sunk into dark pits. In the chancy light of a single oil lamp, he looked like a mummified corpse.

"Emperor," Llesho said, dropping to one knee, more to meet the emperor's gaze at eye level than to offer obeisance.

"I'm glad you're here." Shou straightened his back and dropped his hands to his thighs. "We have to talk." His expression was bland.

If Llesho didn't remember what it felt like to be under Master Markko's instruments, he might have believed the act, that nothing preyed upon the emperor's mind. But he had been in that place, and his eyes bled memories. The emperor flinched away, then his face grew more unyielding. He wasn't going to talk about it, and Llesho relaxed a little. He hadn't wanted to recall that time, and didn't think Shou would appreciate the sympathy anyway.

The emperor seemed to read in his face that Llesho had joined him in a conspiracy that was more than denial but less than fortitude. He closed the subject with a quick nod and shifted his attention to the material present. "I'm going back."

It made sense, but Llesho found nothing to say that would make things any better.

"There's nothing more I can do here." Shou gave his head a shake: apology, and to clear the mist from his eyes. "Guynm is at risk. The empire is slipping away, and SienMa is waiting for me." Not just back to Guynm, but to take back the reins of his empire.

Llesho knew that, thought it was past time for it. "An empire can't survive on its own."

He hadn't meant to chastise the emperor, but it came out sounding that way. Shou, however, agreed with him.

"I finally figured that out. It's time to leave the adventuring to those with fewer obligations."

Like the Wastrels, Llesho thought, his lips pressed closed against some unpleasant truth he didn't want to look at. No responsibilities, except that they took on the dangers so that others would have the knowledge to guide their people. Like Hmishi and Lling, expendable. Maybe some day he'd come to the same realization that Shou had finally reached, about where his duty lay. At the moment, he felt more in common with the Wastrels than with the emperor.

With his decision made, Shou was finally able to admit, "I'm afraid of him."

Llesho gave a little twitch of his shoulder. "So am I. But that's not why you're doing this." They understood each other. "Try to sleep."

"You do the same." Shou actually smiled at him, not much of one, but enough to signal the quieting of some inner storm, for now at least.

Llesho did sleep. When he awoke, the emperor was gone.

Chapter Twenty-one

"SHOU'S gone." Kaydu broke off her discussion with Lluka and Dognut over the morning cook fire. Fumbling awkwardly with the strings of the quiver tied between her breasts, she rose to greet Llesho with the news. "The imperial troops went with him."

"I can see that." He blinked in the morning sunlight.

More than half their forces had packed up and vanished while he slept. Those who remained had gathered in rows on a patch of flat road at the outskirts of the camp. Master Den was leading them in morning prayer forms to the seven mortal gods and Llesho watched, frozen where he stood by a wash of conflicting emotions. The patterns twitched in his muscles with a comforting familiarity even while he felt a distance both physical and spiritual from the soldiers who performed their prayers.

With their numbers gathered under Master Den's watchful eye, Llesho managed a quick count. Thirty in Thebin uniform with Shokar in their lead. A handful of Farshore mercenaries, with Stipes among them and Bixei at their head, also followed Master Den in the exercises. With these forms his soldiers honored the mortal gods and all the mortal earth that shaped the Way of the Goddess. A slight change in the style, Llesho knew, shaped the hand-to-hand combat of the Way. Bixei had learned the forms with Llesho in the gladiators' compound at Pearl Island and he had passed on that knowledge to the Thebin troops he had trained in Shan. Master Den looked pleased with the results.

Another ten, Tashek under Harlol, kept to themselves and performed their own rituals. He couldn't be sure at this distance, but it seemed that Balar was among them, not as skilled as the more highly trained Wastrels but striving gamely to keep up. With Lluka, he reckoned there were about fifty in all. Kaydu wore the only imperial militia uniform anywhere in the camp; he hadn't decided if he should count her among their number or not.

"Drink, it's good for you." Dognut handed him a cup and Llesho took it, scarcely knowing what he did.

Absently, he took a sip. It made his nose run and his eyes water, but, more importantly, the spicy shock snapped him out of his immobility.

"Thank you," he gasped. He sat next to his brother and took another sip.

Lluka relaxed a little, as if Llesho had overcome some crisis more calmly than they'd expected. They were wrong about that, but a fit of temper wasn't going to bring the imperial militia back. Kaydu would not quite meet his eyes. She remained standing, as if braced for a blow, and Llesho figured it was better to get it over with.

"Habiba?" he asked.

"Gone," she answered as he knew she would. "To carry a report to her ladyship, in Shan."

"Why didn't you go with them?" He didn't mean it as an insult, but she jerked as if a blow had indeed fallen.

"The Lady SienMa made us a unit." Reflexively, her hand gestured at Bixei, performing his prayer rituals in front of their little band of troops. "You think Hmishi and Lling are your responsibility because they're your countrymen and pledged to your cause. But I'm their commanding officer, and I don't abandon my forces in the field."

She had stayed behind with her father when Llesho had ridden out with Hmishi and Lling. Now, when all their efforts had come to disaster, she wanted to call back that decision. Too late for that. He wisely kept the words to himself, but the anger he held behind his teeth spilled into eyes gone suddenly cold. He'd been glad for her help when she'd ridden into Ahkenbad, but her father's absence with all Shou's imperial troops reminded him how little he could depend on anyone who wasn't sworn to his hand directly.

"I'll find them, and I'll get them back." Kaydu held her ground. He supposed she meant it as a pledge, but her words goaded him past good sense.

"I don't need a nursemaid to find my lost toys. I certainly don't need someone at my back who will fly off at the whim of a magician whose loyalty lies elsewhere."

He heard, at his left, a sudden indrawn breath—Dognut the dwarf, that was—while Lluka urged him, "Calmly, brother," in his most annoyingly soothing tones.

Both combatants had passed the point of calm, however, and Lluka just made him madder.

"Take it back." Kaydu stood up to him, glaring, and Llesho gulped air, preparing his next sally.

While they engaged in a contest of guilty consciences, however, Master Den had ended morning prayer forms.

"Take what back?" he asked, joining them with his cup outstretched for tea. Llesho hadn't seen or heard him approach. Common sense, belatedly kicking in, told him that the master had made no effort to sneak up on them. He'd been too wrapped up in his argument to notice a force of soldiers—this time, fortunately, his own—come up on his flank. If they'd been raiders, they could have killed him before he knew they were there.

"Words," Llesho answered his master's question, unwilling to give up his righteous anger. Fighting in their own ranks would accomplish no good for any but their enemies and he knew that, so he added, "Too many of the wrong ones," as an apology of sorts.

"We have enemies enough out there," Kaydu agreed, an apology of her own as she pointed in the direction of the grasslands. "I don't want to be your enemy, and neither does my father. But he owes a higher allegiance, and I—"

The thought of fighting two magicians chilled his blood, but Master Den interrupted before Kaydu could go on. He spoke quietly, but with no gentleness about his tone or expression.

"You, Captain, must choose: to follow, or to lead."

Llesho had expected his teacher's disapproval, so it took him a moment to grasp what Master Den had said. Kaydu, for her part, had taken approval as her due and she drew breath in the instant, to object. Then, understanding moved in her eyes, as if she looked into the argument and saw a stranger where her own self had stood.

"Time to choose," Dognut encouraged her. "We need an ending to the tale I am composing."

"I can't."

Llesho had never seen Kaydu at such a loss. He wished their troops, surrounding them now, would go away. *Leave us in privacy to settle our grievances and move on,* he thought, but that wasn't happening. Shokar joined Lluka, with Balar at his side. Harlol, with agony in the very set of his bones, left Kaydu's side and joined them at his back. With leaden tread and bitter unhappiness drawing their mouths into tight lines, Bixei and Stipes stood uneasily between, unwilling to accept the breach at all.

They could lose the war right here, their forces dividing along the lines of an argument that could, perhaps, have waited until they had grown more secure with each other again. But Master Den, miraculously, had seen their case as Llesho had. Wherever Habiba had gone, to whatever purpose, he was no longer a part of the search for the Thebin hostages. And Llesho could not cross the grasslands wondering when a sudden call would send his captain flying off in another direction, to another fight, leaving a hole in his plans and a deeper one at the center of his own cadre. The weak links must be reforged or discarded before they cost more lives.

"You're with us, or you're not. We're in too deep for divided loyalties. That's why Habiba left." He understood that now, and wondered if Kaydu did, and if she would find her answer in the fact that her father had left her behind as well.

"My father—"

He didn't think it would ever happen, but the thought of fighting both magicians at once made him queasy. Llesho reached out to her, grasped the arm still raised to fiddle with her quiver strings. "I will never send you against him."

"Then, I guess I am yours."

"You think you mean that, but you don't. Not yet. But you will."

Kaydu bowed her head, acknowledgment and something more, the beginning of making it true, he thought. Around them, soldiers and brothers did likewise. Only Master Den looked him straight in the eye. With an ironic twist of a smile, the trickster god said, "Spoken like a king. They have you now."

"I know." It hurt to say it. He never wanted to be king.

His brothers, raised longer than he in the royal court of Kungol, seemed to understand what had transpired in those few words, but Lluka appeared less than satisfied. "I'm sorry," he said, but Llesho didn't acknowledge his brother's perception. Still didn't trust it. *Divided loyalties,* he thought, *but not about the throne.* Lluka could have the title for the asking—he knew Llesho didn't want it. So what fealty did Lluka truly give to him, and what of his loyalty had he already sold, and to whom, or to what?

He couldn't afford another challenge right on the heels of his contest of wills with Kaydu, however. He resolved to let it go for now, but to keep an eye on this brother of his. He sat, his back to the Tashek Wastrels who had set about striking the command tent.

"Is there any more tea?" he asked. The mundane request put an end to the standoff, releasing the company to go about their business. Llesho waited while his officers and advisers joined him one by one around the breakfast fire.

Tensions eased in the filling of cups. When the newcomers had settled around the kettle, with Kaydu on his right and Shokar at his left, Llesho picked up where he had meant to begin: "Where did they go, and what impact does it have on our mission?"

"Shou has taken his imperial militia to Durnhag." Kaydu shrugged, a gesture to say she delivered the message, but claimed no responsibility for its content. "The empire requires his attention, and preparations must be made for the coming war."

"He cannot mean to fight for Thebin," Llesho grabbed at the hope with both hands even though common sense denied it. The emperor had his own affairs to consider, and his own damage to repair. Thebin was far off on the other side of the Harnlands, and no great concern of Shan.

"Not for Thebin, no. For Shan. Remember, the goddess of war sits in Shou's court now. If the Harn turn their eyes on the empire, however, they must turn them away from Thebin, no?"

"The Harn may see rich pickings on their border," Llesho agreed, "but that doesn't answer what Markko wants." Llesho remembered his dream, all of heaven in disarray, its gardens all untended. What part of the demon's siege of the gates of heaven was the magician's doing, and out of what malice?

"Markko comes from the north," Bixei reminded them. "He's not Shannish, but comes from my own people, who lived in Farshore before the coming of the empire. He wants Farshore back, and all the empire with it."

"Maybe." But Llesho had feared Master Markko before he'd ever done anything against him, and he'd gone on the defensive from his first dealings with Bixei as well. "But there is something about you that reminds me, a little, of the Harn. Not your actions, which have proved your loyalty beyond question. Mostly you don't look like any of the Harnishmen I've seen lately either. But I'd like to know where your people came from before they found themselves in Farshore."

"So would we," Bixei agreed. "A past among the Harn would be pretty bad, but anything is better than a history that records nothing but slavery."

Llesho could see his point. Even Master Markko had been a slave, though high in Lord Chin-shi's confidence. Kungol, at least, had been free until the raiders came.

"It would explain the magician's choice of allies," Shokar suggested. "And maybe even his interest in Llesho? He could use a legal heir to take Thebin from his allies."

Shokar sipped and choked appreciatively on his spicy tea, but it was Stipes who cleared his throat. The former gladiator squirmed under the scrutiny of the others in their circle. He'd known Llesho as a slave boy, and couldn't hide his discomfort with this transformation into royalty. Llesho knew he wouldn't draw attention to himself unless he had something important to say.

"Speak up. It won't be the first time your advice kept me alive, Stipes."

Suitably encouraged, Stipes bent in an attempt at a seated bow. "It's just, your princeliness—"

"It's Llesho, Stipes, the same as always."

"No," Lluka interrupted with a shake of his head. "He's right about that. We are gathering our army now, we can't go on as if we are beggars at the door. The proper term of address for a prince who is a husband of the goddess is, 'Your holy highness'."

"Among friends and sitting as we are in the dirt, I would still want to be Llesho," he insisted. "But whatever you call me, I want to know what it is you have to say."

"Just this, your holy," and that shortened form of his title seemed to satisfy Stipes in ways that Llesho couldn't begin to understand. "Master Markko took an interest in you before he knew you were a prince. When he learned about your birth, he took no special notice other than his usual pleasure at tormenting his betters. But he never used you in a political way."

Bixei agreed. "He's right. If he'd valued you politically, he'd have protected you more, until he could make use of you. Instead, he almost killed you with his poisons. He may have come later to include you in any plots he may have hatched to take Thebin from the raiders and hold it for himself, but he wants you first for what you can do."

"My powers, whatever they are, have proved useless to help anyone so far."

"Not true." Kaydu hadn't been there, but she'd heard the stories. "Master Markko always knows more than it seems there is to know. He wants to bring down the Shan Empire, but I think that has only ever been a step in his real plan. He sees something in you—not your heritage, not your relationship with Shou, but you yourself—as a tool."

Master Den raised his teacup in appreciation of a trickster scheme. It made Llesho ill. "What will Shou do?" he asked, wondering if he was just another tool to the emperor as well.

"He said very little before he left," Kaydu warned them, "and didn't include me in his counsels. But this much I know: the emperor will bring his capital to Durnhag, a courtesy about which he plans to give the governor no option. Habiba has gone to summon the court, and to beg the Lady SienMa to join the emperor on his war council."

Stipes, at Bixei's side, perked up at that news. "With the mortal goddess of war on his council, Shou cannot lose."

"If that were so," Kaydu pointed out glumly, "the governor's compound at Farshore would not now lie in ruins, and her ladyship would govern Thousand Lakes Province."

"The question," Master Den explained, "is not 'can the lady win the war for the Shan Empire?' but 'will she win the war for Shou?' Even I do not know the mind of a mortal goddess well enough to answer that one."

Not even another mortal god had the power of prophecy where the goddess of war was concerned. But Llesho wondered about the question left unspoken: Did Shou ask the goddess to fight his war, or did the goddess of war use the emperor of Shan to fight a war of her own? The first test, of course, was Habiba's message. Would she come to Durnhag?

Bixei, relieved that he did not have to choose between obedience to his captain and the rescue of his companions, had his own question. "And what of us?"

"Frankly?" Just minutes ago it might have come as a challenge, but Kaydu shrugged, liking her answer less than the question. "I think Shou hopes that Master Markko's eyes will be on our efforts to free the hostages. If we are successful in at least that much, it will give Shou the time he needs to prepare for a greater war on his own borders."

A tool, or a ruse. Llesho hadn't wanted to know that, but Kaydu continued her explanation anyway.

"Shou has a problem of strategy. The Shan Empire extends for more than a thousand li to the north, but it meets the Harnlands only a day's march from Durnhag. The Gansau Wastes extend for twice that distance to the west, but share much of their eastern border with Shan and this, their southern border, with the Harnlands. And the grasslands of the Harn stretch even farther to the south and west."

Llesho remembered another time, a map of the world spread on rugs in a silk tent. The Lady SienMa had tutored him in the facts of political geography even as she had questioned him to learn all he knew about the Harn. "I know they've sent raiders into Shan, but would the Harn risk a full-scale war with the empire?"

Shokar shrugged, answering, "If they'd won at the imperial city last year, they might have carried the empire the way they conquered Thebin by taking Kungol."

He gave a little shudder, remembering, no doubt, the wonders and terrors of that battle. Shokar was a quiet man, like their father, and a warrior only by dire necessity.

"Master Markko will doubtless assure his followers that they have allies in the provinces to the north," Bixei pointed out. "But how many of the clans will follow him?"

"He will attract the bandits and free-roaming warrior class," Lluka offered. "The family bands will likely resist, at least until they see how the wind blows through the grass."

Llesho wondered how his brother knew, and regretted the suspicion. Lluka had a subtle nature, a slyness to his expression that hid unspoken calculations, but he would not take common cause with the murderers of their parents, and their sister.

They all, brothers and companions, offered what advice they could, but none of them had seen the gardens of heaven in their disarray. "Master Markko may have fixed his gaze on the Shan Empire, but the demon who lays siege to the gates of heaven came from somewhere. What is Markko's connection to that?"

"A question worthy of a king on a quest." Dognut added applause to his praise, setting down his teacup to clap his hands.

Llesho thought he ought to be angry, but he could find no sign of ridicule in the dwarf's open face. A question surfaced like flotsam in his mind—why had the dwarf,

Shou's own minstrel, stayed behind when his master had
marched?—and vanished again as their circle began to
stir for departure. Master Den threw the dregs of his tea
into the fire, and stood up, his eyes searching out the
grasslands still hidden by the distance. "I think that I
will find myself a likely trench."

They all knew it was time to ride, then, and followed
the trickster god to their feet, if not to the shelter of a
likely rock. With a nod to Shokar and Harlol to follow,
Kaydu went off to set the troops in motion while Bixei
and Stipes added their muscle to the task of striking
camp.

Llesho would have gone to ready his own pack, but
Lluka stopped him with a firm grip on his arm. "I don't
know what I have done that you distrust me, Llesho, but
I swear I wish no harm to you."

Balar watched them both, shifting uncomfortably from
one foot to the other. "I'm the one who told Kagar to
hit you," he agreed, "If anyone deserves your distrust, it
would be me."

"And yet," Llesho told him, "I trust you completely
to do what you think best in as direct a way as you see.
Your complexity is logical; music has taught you respect
for each string of your instrument, but that a string, to
sound, must indeed be plucked."

For Lluka, he could only shake his head. "There's a
twist in your thinking I can't see around. I don't believe
you want to hurt me, but we may disagree on what
that means."

"Is it because I have lost my gifts?" Lluka asked him,
"or because you do not accept what my gifts have to
show you?"

Llesho shook his head and returned his brother's grip
on his arm. "I don't trust your conclusions. You would
lead us into blind retreat because you confuse the darkness and chaos of your vision for the death of all possible
futures. But there are more possibilities than no future

at all on the one hand, or no ability to see the future on the other.

"Fear of what you see, or don't see, has clouded your judgment. If we are at the center of actions that create the future, we won't be able to see what we've made until we make it. That's not the same as having no future. I worry that you will trade away the choices I need to make to keep things the way they are now rather than risk an uncertain outcome. And I think that if you do, you will fulfill your own prophecy."

Lluka pulled his hand away as if he'd been stung. "I will not hurt you," he said, "I will never hurt you." And he ran.

"I don't understand him," Balar admitted. "But I know he loves you."

"It's not his motives I distrust." And he realized that was true.

Balar sighed. "I wish I still had my instrument," he said. "Music helps me think."

On the verge of a tart remark about the relative value of their losses, Llesho stopped himself. He knew the cost of his own: a life of slavery and flight, Master Jaks dead, his brother and his friends in the hands of his deadly enemy. Adar was brother to both of them, however, and he did not know what the musical instrument had meant to Balar, or what connection it had to his gifts. He only knew one thing for certain.

"It's going to get worse before it gets better." With a nod of parting, he went in search of his pack.

Chapter Twenty-two

THE riders of the Harnlands were said to keep to the saddle from birth, eating and sleeping on the backs of their swift, sturdy horses. They wore soft shoes, their feet never touching the land they wandered as they followed their herds of horses, until they died of old age in their saddles and toppled to the ground.

Llesho had never seen a Harnishman die of old age in his saddle. He didn't know if their shoes were hard or soft. During the Long March, however, his captors had paced their prisoners on horseback, never leaving their saddles even to separate the living from the dead. He had crossed the grasslands on foot, or in the arms of his countrymen, and hadn't ridden again until the Lady SienMa had picked him out of the practice yard at Pearl Island. She'd found in him a skinny excuse for a gladiator-in-training and put him on the path that Lleck had set for him. Now he spent so much time on horseback that he wondered if the condition of being Harnish was something you caught through your saddle, from the land. Effortlessly adjusting his weight to the shifting gait of his horse, Llesho figured he was becoming more of a Harnish rider with each passing hour.

But if a Thebin prince was becoming a rider, what had

the Harnishmen become who had invaded the Palace of
the Sun to kill the king? What did it make of the spies
and saboteurs a thousand li from Thebin, who left their
horses behind to swarm the narrow streets of Shan? And
what did a magician from the North have to do with any
of it? What hold did Master Markko have on the grasslands, and why did the raiders follow him? He needed
answers to those questions before he sent an army
against the magician—had to know if they faced him at
the center of his power, or far from the source of his
energy. And they were running out of time to find out.

There was no line in the dirt, with wasteland on one
side and grasses on the other, but they had left the Gansau Wastes for the Harnlands sometime during the afternoon. Llesho wasn't exactly sure when: the hills had risen
but never seemed to fall again. The grasses had thick-
ened and the air had thinned. One moment the horses
walked past tough sedges, the next they trod patchy
grasses growing more tender as the air took on a sweet
smell, cool with water.

They pushed their way through a dense thatch of knotted roots with grassy stalks brushing their heels in their
stirrups, onto an expanse of tender green cropped close
by grazing sheep and horses. Llesho tried to keep his
mind pinned to the moment, but past and present mud-
dled themselves in his head. He didn't know this route.
The Long March hadn't come this way, but the smell of
the air over the grasslands was like no other. He'd forgotten the taste of water in the wind, the balm of it on
the skin tight over his cheekbones. After the parched
heat of the Wastes it should have been a blessing, but
the child of his memories quaked inside him.

Now, he reminded himself, *not then.* Kaydu rode beside him, one hand on the reins and the other wrapped
around Little Brother. The monkey was uncommonly
quiet, his own face as drawn with worry as that of his
mistress. Dognut, surprisingly, had refused his place in
the baggage and reclaimed his camel and the small saddle

the Tashek had provided when they left Ahkenbad. He rode up on Llesho's other side—the better to record the tale of their quest, he'd insisted—and Llesho had not objected. A dark look, however, put an end to the cheery tune the dwarf had started on his flute. As had become his habit, Master Den walked with his hand on the bridle of Llesho's horse, making soothing clucking sounds; whether he meant to calm horse or rider wasn't clear. Lluka and Balar rode behind them. Llesho felt like he rode with a target painted on his back, but Shokar followed after, with Bixei and Harlol leading their small forces.

They had sent Wastrels to scout the way but had no need of an advance guard. The grasslands were flat enough that a rider with sharp eyes could see almost to the end of the world. Not even Harnish forces had the skill to move unseen against them in daylight.

"We'll find them and get them back safely," Kaydu insisted, as if she could draw him out of his memories with her certainty. Her doubts leaked around the edges of her dark, serious eyes, but he wouldn't tell her that.

"We'll find them," Master Den agreed. He made no promises of safety, and Llesho wondered what he would have to pay for his brother and his friends.

"Just another piece of your soul."

Llesho stared hard at the trickster god who walked beside him. He knew he hadn't spoken aloud, and Kaydu looked too confused by the trickster's words to have heard the question. But Master Den had answered his thoughts, so there seemed little point in hiding behind silence.

"Haven't I paid enough?"

Master Den shook his head. "You haven't even begun, child."

"Why does it have to be that way? You're a god. Why can't you help them?"

"Them?" he let the persona of the washerman fall

away and asked the question as ChiChu, the trickster god. "By 'them' do you mean the healer-prince, Adar? Or your sworn fighters Lling and Hmishi? If you could choose, who would you have me save?"

"Can't you save them all?"

"The gods who find you interesting aren't in the saving business. The best you can hope is that they'll keep an eye on you as long as your quest amuses them."

"A little harsh, don't you think?" Dognut muttered under his breath, but he subsided into silence at the trickster's raised eyebrows.

But Dognut was right—ChiChu's words did not ring true. Lady SienMa had suffered losses of her own, and she had not seemed amused. Heaven itself lay under siege: sometimes, in his dreams, Llesho thought he heard the Great Goddess weep.

"I don't know why, but you're lying. Nothing about this, from the moment I walked away from the pearl beds, has been that simple." What part his own struggle played in the battles waged above his head he didn't comprehend yet, but he knew he did more than prance and caper for the entertainment of the gods.

"Maybe." Master Den gave a nod to concede the point, but he smiled, satisfied, with it. "That's what a trickster god does best."

"I hope that's not the best ChiChu can do. A simple pearl diver has seen through the lie, after all."

"No more a simple slave than a simple lie," ChiChu returned the challenge. "Perhaps a trickster would hide a lie within truth with the appearance of a lie. Beautiful sky, isn't it?"

That, at least, was a truth, though not the one Llesho wanted to hear. Master Den shut his eyes, letting his grip on the bridle of Llesho's horse guide him as he turned his face into the sunlight. Llesho trailed his fingertips across the silver chain at his throat but passed it by to close his hand around the pearls that hung on a plain cord around his neck. The trickster god had ended the conversation, but maybe Pig could be made to talk, in the interest of his mistress.

Until he figured out how to summon the Jinn into the waking world, however, he would have to puzzle out his fate alone. Like what had drawn the mortal goddess of war and the trickster god ChiChu to his cause? Why of all the pantheon of gods mortal and immortal, these two? Why, of all the magical creatures in heaven and earth, had he drawn the attention of dragons? Out of all the pantheon of deities, he could have done better for his cause.

But maybe not. Lacking the strength of great armies, he needed cunning and the ruthlessness to prevail. If he won, he might call on Mercy, Peace, and Justice to teach him to be a wise ruler, but they would be no use to him now. That wasn't true, of course, if he were judging honesty here.

"In spite of everything, I trust you," he admitted to himself and his teacher.

"Then I haven't taught you very well." Master Den's eyes opened with a sly smile that rearranged his features into something that harbored deep secrets a washerman never could have kept.

"You will teach me how to perform the duties of a king in an age of magic and war, as you taught Shou and his father before him."

"Hope I do a better job at it," Master Den muttered under his breath. They both remembered the way Shou had looked when last they'd seen him. Devastated, his soul a barren land swept by scouring winds, Shou's ordeal had left him too empty even for remorse. Llesho knew the strength of the emperor, however, as well as he had come to recognize the mistakes he made. He had, after all, survived his captivity, and he would do what he must to hold the empire together, even knowing that nothing would remain of him when the task was done.

"Like Shou, I won't thank you for what you've done," he confessed. Like Shou, he knew that he would pay dearly for the favors of the gods. "But I'll use you when I must, to save my people and the Great Goddess who weeps in my dreams."

"I take it back." The god gave him a little bow. "I'm not the only one who has taught you well."

An image cleared in the mist of Llesho's mind. He saw himself stretched at the feet of the Great Goddess, an offering, not quite alive, not truly dead, but emptied of the world.

"What did you see?" his master asked; sharp eyes had marked the moment when Llesho left him for that other world, and gauged the slow drift of his return.

"I don't know." Llesho shook his head, and repeated, when a worried frown escaped Kaydu, "I don't know what it was."

Both would have had more from him, but this time he ended the discussion himself. Out of the uneasy silence that descended, Dognut skittered a song, "Merciful Wisdom," softly across a tiny flute. He knew the tune, and thought he could use more of what the song promised on this quest. For now, he'd make do with what he had and appreciate the sunshine.

Master Den had been right about the day. If he could not enjoy it, exactly, he could at least steal an hour for peace and beauty. Perhaps that was mercy enough, for now. After a long moment, Kaydu released him from her sharp scrutiny. Master Den seemed himself again, but Llesho knew better than to believe in appearances. Neither of them would forget, but for a while they rode on with nothing to disturb the silence but the call of the birds overhead.

"Riders on our flank!" The voice from the ranks drew them to a halt.

Llesho wheeled his horse around and located the blur

of riders still far in the distance. The Harnishmen had
likewise seen Llesho's party; he could tell by the blur of
their dust that they now closed the distance at a gallop.
With a quick kick of his heels, he urged his own horse
to speed, leaving behind the voices calling for him to
wait until it became clear he would not stay his course.
Then he heard powerful wings beating the air, and a
great hunting bird passed overhead. Kaydu, in the
shape of an eagle, caught a thermal and spiraled high
above them before streaking away to scout the strangers. The sounded of drumming hooves followed. He
looked back, found Harlol and Bixei gaining on him,
and he let them.

"Wait!" Bixei made a grab for Llesho's horse, to keep
him there. "Let Kaydu find out if we are facing peaceful
herdsmen or Master Markko's raiders."

Harlol watched him, wondering, it seemed, if his Dinha
had mistaken this quest and cast her Wastrels at the feet
of a madman. But Bixei eyed him with real fear for a
headstrong prince.

"I don't want to die," Llesho reassured his companion
of too many battles. "That's not what I was trying to
do—"

Bixei didn't look reassured. "Then why did you ride
out alone to meet the thing that tortured the emperor
of Shan to madness?"

Shou was, for both of them, the model of a heroic
king, a warrior prince. That he could be so brought down
in heart and soul boded ill for all of them, but most of
all for Llesho, who was the magician's special prey.

"Master Markko isn't out there. I feel it when he's
near, when he sees me. And right now, he doesn't."

He couldn't explain it, but Harlol seemed relieved by
the words anyway. He nodded to confirm Llesho's observation. "When Ahkenbad turned the evil magician away,
Prince Llesho knew. Later, when Habiba brought an
army to his rescue, the prince felt the approach of his
allies from afar."

"So much for no special powers," Bixei noted, then asked the practical question. "If not Tsu-tan, or Master Markko himself, who are they?"

Llesho shrugged. "I don't know." He almost laughed with relief and Bixei gave him a nervous look. "But they don't know me either."

They rode through a land of evil memories, into danger with yet more terrible danger beyond, but the thin air blew constant breezes on the great grassy plateau, reminding him of home. Their desert clothes rippled and snapped smartly, like banners in the sun. A smile sneaked back onto Llesho's lips His mount had wisely ignored the debate for the joys of the juicy grass and the wildflowers that nodded everywhere. Llesho could take a hint even from a horse.

"Does that mean we can wait for our side to catch up with us?" Harlol squinted into the distance, watching the advancing shadow that would resolve itself into riders soon enough.

With a reassuring slap on his horse's neck, Llesho slipped from the saddle. "We wait," he agreed.

He faced into the press of the wind and imagined the cool hand of the goddess wiping the sweat from his brow. Hunger growled in his belly, a simpler demand than any emotion, and he dug a roll of Tashek fruit leather out of his pack. Tearing off bits with his teeth, he chewed energetically, enjoying the tastes of dates and figs and apricots blended into the pounded fruit paste that the Tashek dried in thick, nutritious strips for the road. Bixei tossed him a salty round of flatbread and by unspoken agreement they threw themselves down to enjoy the fragrant carpet of grasses beneath them and the flavors that rewarded diligent chewing. And if his companions thought about them, they did not mention the names of their missing comrades or the prince held hostage by a power-mad magician.

Without realizing he was fading, Llesho drifted into sleep.

*   *   *

"On your feet, young prince. Who taught you to greet
a messenger from heaven on your back?"

Llesho cracked open an eyelid and peered up at the
Jinn who nudged at his side with one clovenhoofed foot.

"Where have you been?"

"In a sack hanging from your neck. It would help if
you would put me on that silver chain the dream readers
gave you, by the way. I could give you a jab with my
elbow when I want to get your attention."

When Llesho was awake, the pearl that Pig had become didn't have elbows, but he resolved to do as he
was asked at the next opportunity. Who knew what the
Jinn could do, given the chance? With a wave of his
front hoof, Pig dismissed the discussion. "I want to introduce you to someone you will soon meet in the waking
world."

A stoat looked up at him out of paralyzingly still eyes.
It bared its sharp, small teeth to chatter something at
him in stoat language, and reached a too-human paw to
touch Llesho's foot. He let the creature do what it
wanted, though it took an effort of will to resist the urge
to jump back. Pig gave him an approving nod, and answered the stoat in Pig language, which the shrewd little
animal listened to carefully, with appropriate nods of its
own. The creature patted Llesho on the ankle, a gesture
he would have taken for comfort if the stoat had been
human. In a beast, especially in a species so sly, he half
expected to find his socks were gone when he looked
down again.

After a moment more of conference between them,
Pig bid his friend farewell, and the stoat turned and vanished, running through the grass.

"More company," Pig said, and vanished just as a
human hand grabbed Llesho's shoulder and shook it.

"What?"

"Who were you talking to?" Bixei released his shoulder, but didn't move away. He looked worried.

"No one. It was a dream." He reached inside his shirt, the familiar gesture to reassure himself that the pearls still rested there, and found that, on his own, Pig had somehow found his way onto the silver chain Llesho had worn since Ahkenbad. There were, however, no feet or elbows jutting from the nacreous jewel.

Bixei didn't look happy with him, but he wisely kept his peace. The sun had crested and begun its slow fall into night while he slept. Their small army had rejoined them, scattered in resting groups in a guarding circle around the place where Llesho had fallen asleep. Master Den snored softly nearby while Dognut reclined at the side of his camel, trying to teach Little Brother how to play on a reed flute. The monkey didn't seem to get the idea, preferring to brandish the flute wildly about him like a battle baton while he encouraged himself with hops and leaps and wordless chatter.

Within the circle, Shokar stood nearby with Lluka and Balar, watching him with lines of concern carved in his face. Worry had aged him even since Llesho had seen him last in the imperial city. He trusted Shokar with his life, had from the moment he set eyes on him in the slave market of Shan. But he wasn't sure if he could trust any of his brothers with his truth. Wasn't even sure he knew what that was yet. Kaydu, though, he thought would understand, when she truly gave her loyalty. Until she threw her heart into her choice, however, he could only trust her head so far.

She had returned from her reconnaissance and watched him from Harlol's side, her head bent to accept the comfort of Harlol's fingers on her hair. She noticed Llesho's gaze on her, and gave herself a shake all over as if settling feathers or scales, though she wore her human form again. He remembered feeling jealous of her attention, and wondered that her interest in the Wastrel had ceased to matter to him.

"It's a small band of herders, armed to drive off wolves, but not for battle," she reported. "They have

come ahead of their herds to challenge our presence
here, but something has slowed their pace. Perhaps there
are more of us than they had realized, or perhaps their
own scouts have returned, and only now they learn that
we are prepared for combat."

Llesho considered his options. The grass smelled
sweet, the fading sunlight fell like a caress on his face,
and even the horses' satisfied whickers signaled their con-
tentment with the afternoon. He'd give the herdsmen
any ransom they asked if it meant they would not soak
this ground in blood before the day was out.

"I don't want a fight if I can help it." He hoped the
clan chief felt the same.

Bixei stared out beyond the circle of their defenses to
the small band in the distance. He calculated something
that didn't take the land into account, but his answers
brought him no more joy than Llesho's did.

"It wouldn't be a fight."

A massacre, he meant. Fighting, once started between
two such unequal forces, could only end one way.

"No way to begin a holy war." Llesho had already
decided. Now he needed the herdsmen to know it, too.
"They will see we mean them no harm if I go out to
meet them alone."

"No!" Balar stepped up to stop him. "Your life is too
valuable to throw away on a rash gesture."

"I'll go with you," Shokar volunteered, his features set
and grim.

"Yes," said Harlol, who understood, as a Wastrel
must, that battle might be waged in numbers, but reaching out must be done one hand to one hand.

"I'm with you," Bixei would hear no objection. He
still felt guilty for the disaster at Durnhag that had put
their comrades at risk.

Llesho nodded, accepting Bixei's determination to
clear his conscience of something for which no one
blamed him but himself. "Bixei will come with me. How
much threat can two men be?"

Harlol snickered. Yes, that much. If the herdsmen were what they seemed, they two could probably account for all of them before their chieftain knew they had been attacked. Llesho left his unstrung bow in Balar's hands, and mounted his horse. Small white clouds bloomed overhead like silk cocoons, and Llesho felt like he was one of them, moving with the wind across the flat plain of the high plateau. Who could fear a cloud? The short spear at his back reminded him that to be fearless meant to be foolish.

"You can die out here," it whispered. "You will die out here." He would have given it to Shokar to keep for him, but it had burned Adar—not that prince, but this one—it had found its true owner. Even if his brother could hold it, he didn't trust the spear itself enough to leave it behind.

Seeking a safe haven, he found that his hand reached automatically to the pearl that now hung on its own chain around his neck. Pig seemed an unlikely protector, but Llesho realized the Jinn was the only one with the will and the ability to do it, at least in the land of dreams. ChiChu, the trickster god, had the ability, of course, but always one had to question his intentions.

His troops parted for him, watching silently as Llesho left their circle. Bixei, at his side, was equally quiet so that the sound of hooves seemed to come out of a different world.

"I'm coming, too," Harlol announced. "It will be just like old times."

"Would that be the time you kidnapped Llesho and dragged him halfway across the desert?" Bixei wanted to know.

Harlol laughed. "That, too. But I stood at the Prince's right hand when he waited outside the protections of Ahkenbad to lead the army of the magician Habiba to the Dinha. Once was a task, twice is a tradition!"

Before Bixei could answer the way his frown promised, Llesho raised his hand for peace. "A mercenary from Farshore, a Wastrel from Ahkenbad, and a prince from

Thebin riding together will, at the least, confuse them
enough to give us time to explain," he said.

"You're succeeding on the confusion part," Bixei confirmed with annoyance. "You've already confused me."
But he subsided into his saddle with no further challenges to the Wastrel. Which was just as well, because
the herdsmen had kicked their horses to speed to meet
them. Llesho kept to a leisurely pace, to show that he
posed no threat. When they had ridden close enough to
see the glint on the herdsmen's rough weapons, he
stopped and waited for the men who belonged to this
land to draw near. Their horses scarcely startled at all
when an eagle circled overhead, and swooped down on
them. Harlol held out his arm, and Kaydu settled on it,
rustling her feathers into order. Together they watched
the riders approach.

The leader of the Harnish riders seemed about middle-
aged, his hair a mix of gray and black that he had
straightened with the fat of a sheep and twisted into one
flat braid falling from his nape to the middle of his back.
He was almost as tall as Bixei, but broad in the chest
with thick arms showing below the short sleeves of his
woolen tunic. Dark eyes narrowed over high cheekbones
jutting sharply in a broad, flat face. His hands crossed at
the wrists over the horn of his saddle to show that he
harbored no hostile intent, but he returned Llesho's
study with a sweep of coarse lashes lowered to a brooding thoughtfulness.

"Yesugei," he finally introduced himself, "A chief of
the Qubal clans, who graze this land." The Harnish language rolled low and guttural from the chieftain's throat.

Llesho understood little of what he heard: the word
for land, which sounded like a badly formed version of
the same word in Thebin, and the names by the man's
inflection. The challenge in the glance and tone stirred
an answering aggression in Llesho's bones, however. He
straightening his spine in the saddle, tilting his chin at a
regal angle, but he couldn't debate the man in the little

Harnish he knew, not when the outcome would decide whether they left the field as allies or corpses. So he answered in Thebin. When Yesugei showed no sign of comprehension, he tried again in Shannish: "Llesho, Prince of Thebin, asking your leave to pass this way in peace."

The chieftain's eyes widened briefly. "Dreams spring to life and move among us," he muttered under his breath, but in Shannish. Clearly he wanted no misunderstanding that might lead to bloodshed. Casting a glance at the mercenary and Wastrel at Llesho's side, Yesugei said aloud, "You travel in strange company, Prince of Thebin. But be at ease, we mean you no harm. Your guide has simply lost his way. The season forbids a return to the Wastes, but my clansmen will lead you safely to the Guynm Road."

Harlol bristled at the slight, but Llesho cut the air with the blade of his hand, warning him to silence. If it came to a fight now, they had no chance of winning. They might delay a battle with talk until their troops arrived, but he didn't know what forces might be riding to join Yesugei as they spoke.

"We mean you no harm, honored chief, and ask that you grant us safe passage." Llesho answered with a formulaic plea for hospitality that he hoped would cool tempers growing chancy. "We will respect your herds and travel lightly across your land." The horses would graze the clan's pasture land as they passed, he meant, but Llesho promised they wouldn't steal any horses or inflict any deliberate damage on the clan or its land on their way through.

Yesugei shook his head. "Impossible."

Llesho waited until the chieftain had given him his full attention again, and locked gazes. Yesugei frowned and drew a speaking breath, but Llesho didn't let him continue.

"I follow raiders who would deliver my brother, a blessed healer, and my own sworn guardsmen to the tortures of an evil magician who has fled into the South.

Not all the forces the Harn may bring against us will
move me from my course."

"My ulus does not treat with the South," Yesugei said.

Llesho didn't know what an ulus was. He read the
distaste on the chieftain's face well enough to judge he
might find any ally here, against a common enemy if in
nothing else. But he had to convince Yesugei to trust
him. Slowly, he opened his own soul to the Harnish rider's gaze, with all the turmoil and the strength of his
dawning power.

Yesugei gasped, as if he'd been struck. "Truly," he
muttered, drawing himself together, "dreams walk in the
waking day."

"Then we may pass?"

"I don't have that authority." The chieftain's eyes
slanted away from him when he said it, but not before
Llesho caught the sly calculation there. Yesugei lied.
What did he want to hide?

"I'll take you to the khan of my ulus. You can present
your petition to him."

"The clans elect a chief of chiefs among those who
share a common range," Harlol explained. "He is called
'khan.' The clans of such a leader among leaders are
together called his 'ulus' and may petition the khan to
settle disputes. Each chieftain pays a tax in horses and
young men who serve in the khan's army."

There seemed to be a lot of that in the world—even
the religious Tashek of Ahkenbad cast their extra young
men out into the world to explore or fight or die, as long
as they didn't disrupt the peaceful order of the homes
that would never be theirs. Llesho wished for the bite of
Master Den's trickster wisdom to draw him out of the
shadows of his thoughts.

"It's not exactly the Shan Empire," Harlol continued,
"but it seems to work for the clans most of the time."

"You know a lot about us, Tashek spy," Yesugei commented, deep suspicion etched in the dryness of his
drawl.

"No spy." Harlol shrugged, at a loss to explain to an outsider what seemed obvious to him. "Just a wanderer with eyes."

Llesho nodded agreement to Yesugei's condition. "We'll present our case to the khan, then," he said, and hastened to make clear the urgency of his mission. "I would honor your khan and beg his indulgence. I urge speed, however. Each moment that we delay takes my brother, and my sworn guards, a step closer to horrible death."

He couldn't stop the shudder that passed through him as memories of Master Markko's poisons racked his body.

Yesugei shivered in his saddle, as if he, too, felt the clench of dying muscles in his gut. "A messenger can take your word to your forces, instructing them to follow."

"No need," Llesho gave Harlol a nod, and the Wastrel flung his arm upward, casting the hunting bird skyward. Kaydu pumped her wings with a harsh cry, wheeled to gain altitude, and flew back the way they had come.

The Harnish chieftain watched her pass out of sight. He said nothing, but his face seemed to close up against the wonders that moved unseen around him. Llesho read the set of his shoulders and the lines of his forehead: not angry or frightened, but very thoughtful. Not at all like the raiders who had laid waste to Kungol. He reminded himself not to underestimate the man. This Yesugei might not be an enemy, but no Harnishman could be considered a friend.

"This way," Yesugei said, and raised his arm in a signal to his followers. "The settlement of the ulus is only a double hand of pais from where we stand." He turned his horse with the pressure of his knees on the animal's flanks, but Llesho wasn't finished yet.

"How far is that in li?" he asked, but the chieftain shrugged.

"I have never measured the grass in Shannish terms.

But we will reach the outskirts of the khan's encampment by nightfall."

Another day lost. They would lose as much time and more fighting over the detour, however. With a glance to either side, Llesho gave his own sign for his two companions to follow, and they set their course in the path of the Harnish riders.

Chapter Twenty-three

THEY rode toward nightfall at a leisurely pace so that Llesho's forces could catch up. Before too long had passed, the line of march arrived and flowed around them, led by Kaydu in her human form. Little Brother traveled with Dognut in the baggage wagon, unwilling to abandon the dwarf's shiny flutes, so his mistress rode without benefit of his monkey commentary. She nudged her horse closer and gave Llesho an informal salute. If he hadn't already figured out what was going on, he'd have thought she'd come up close on Harlol's side with no special purpose. The Wastrel, who fought for his position at Llesho's side under most circumstances, shifted to make room for her. The little smile they exchanged left no doubt about their feelings. Not at all like the sappy glances between lovers in the ballads, Kaydu and Harlol seemed to see in each other a prized weapon once lost but now fitted to its proper place.

In his dream, Harlol had died with the other Tashek, had offered up his dead eyes to Llesho on a grassy plain much like the one they now traveled. Llesho's feelings about Kaydu confused him, but he knew he didn't want the Tashek dead over them.

For all that she wasn't much older than he was, Kaydu

was his teacher and the captain of his cadre. She'd kept
him alive on a few occasions and nervous on others, a
part of his personal landscape since he'd left Pearl Island.
He didn't want that to change, but Kaydu had always
served the Lady SienMa, through her father's command.
Now she had a new tether on her heart.

Fortunately, the Dinha of Ahkenbad had put that
tether, Harlol, into Llesho's hand. He figured he could
work with that.

Catching the Wastrel's eye, he gave a clench-jawed
jerk of his chin, unwilling acceptance. "Don't you die on
her." He made it an order.

Kaydu looked at him like he'd lost his mind. "Are you
listening to me?" she asked. "Because I don't know what
you're talking about."

Llesho gave a guilty start. He hadn't heard a word
she'd said. Harlol had been watching him, however, and
he'd heard the Dinha's prediction. The Wastrels were
Llesho's to spend, as the dream readers knew he would.
"You can't change fate," he said.

"Yes, I can." Llesho brought his fist down on the horn
of his saddle to emphasize his point. "Changing fate is
what this quest is about."

"Maybe," Kaydu interrupted, "but right now, Master
Den wants to see you. He rides with the baggage."

Llesho nodded an absent acknowledgment. "Nobody
dies," he said with a last glare at Harlol, and pulled
his horse out of the line of march. None of his own
captains followed.

Yesugei, however, pulled out of line with a gesture to
his men to stay where they were. The wait wasn't long.
Carina, deep in conversation with Balar, flashed him a
little smile in greeting as they passed, but his brother
didn't notice him at all. Lluka, however, latched a pierc-
ing stare on the Harnish Yesugei, turning full around in
his saddle rather than let go of that scrutiny.

"That one is trouble," the chieftain pointed his chin
as Lluka moved away.

Llesho had to agree, "To the Harn, probably. He resents the loss of his country and his family."

"Warn him that your numbers are few and the armies of the Northern Khan are great. It would not serve his dead, or his king, to make war against an ulus that has done him no harm."

By coincidence, or so it seemed, Shokar was passing with his tiny band of Thebin fighters as the Harnishman gave his warning, and Llesho took his meaning to heart. No harm yet, but he didn't know how strong Yesugei's ulus was, or how his khan might respond to even their small threat. His host was quick to tell him.

"No army may enter the ulus of the Chimbai-Khan," Yesugei said. "However, an honor guard suited to his station may accompany any visitor of rank."

"How many for a king?"

"Fifty will do." The number of Llesho's troops, said with a wry twist of a smile to his mouth.

"And if I crossed your khan's attention with a thousand?"

"That, too, for a king," Yesugei acknowledged. "More would be asked to wait their king's pleasure on their own side of our border."

Llesho judged the khan's might by what he considered a threat but the numbers always came out the same. He hadn't had even a thousand troops in his service since he'd tangled with Master Markko's forces on the borders of Shan Province, and that had been more Shou's battle than his. Without the empire's backing, what did he have? Nothing, compared to the numbers Master Markko could throw at them. But their numbers would grow, somehow. Why else had the gods dragged him halfway across the known world? Why else sacrifice the dream readers of Ahkenbad, if they didn't intend that he win?

He looked away so that the Harnish chieftain didn't see the despair wash through him and spied, at some distance, a small flock of sheep and a greater herd of horses grazing in the still of the afternoon. Harnish outriders kept a careful watch, unmoving as statues on their short horses while herdsmen patrolled among their animals, gathering strays with the expertise the raiders had shown when driving their human stock to market on the Long March.

The grass was too short, and had been the while they'd traveled, for so small a herd to have cropped it. Llesho wondered what army awaited them whose beasts had cleared the land down to the bone for all the li around. Fingers clenched pale against the dark leather of his reins, he held to his nerve by a thread. The Harnish chieftain at his side made note of his sudden tension, though he kept his opinion to himself.

I'm not afraid right now, he would have told the man; *that other time sneaks up on me at inconvenient moments.* But words refused to come. Presently the baggage cart rolled into view with Dognut's camel, which Harlol had named Moonbeam a lifetime ago it seemed, tied to its side. Among the guards who surrounded the wagon, two each of Tashek and mercenary and Thebin, he recognized the Wastrels Zepor and Danel, but not the others.

The end of the cart had been let down. Master Den, in his usual garb that served him as well in the laundry as on the march, sat facing the way they had come. His back rested comfortably against a heap of red tent cloths and his legs hung off the tail of the storage bed, his toes nearly dragging on the ground. Seemingly unaware of the picture they made together, Dognut perched at his shoulder on a sack of clean bandages, his back to the side of the cart. Little Brother slept peacefully in his lap as he played a marching song known for its scandalous verses on a small silver flute. The baggage guards knew the song well, Llesho guessed. They hid their laughter with little success behind their battle-callused fingers.

"Master Den." Llesho swung off his horse and joined his teacher at the back of the cart. Reins held loosely in his lap, he let his legs dangle in unconscious imitation of the trickster god.

"Master of the washtubs, I surmise," Yesugei jerked his shoulder in a Harnish gesture at the supplies in the baggage cart. "I didn't know that launderer counted itself a higher rank than prince among the Thebin people." His tone clearly suggested that such ordering of the ranks went far to explain why a Harnish bandit sat on Kungol's throne.

The insult raised the hackles on Llesho's neck, and he would have returned an acid reply, but Master Den patted his leg, as if he calmed a spirited horse. It should have made him angrier, but to his chagrin it worked. He actually found himself settling again. Much changed in his world, but Master Den remained a sun around which Llesho planned his seasons. At least until he pulled the saddle blanket out from under him. ChiChu, the trickster god, would do that. It was his nature. As the nature of a Harnish chieftain made him prod for the weaknesses of a potential enemy.

"Even a prince can learn a lot from the right launderer," he answered.

"Washing shirts. A useful skill for a warrior prince," Yesugei scoffed, though with a question in his eyes. His seat on a horse should have given him a height advantage. Llesho's head came only to the chieftain's knee, but Master Den met his gaze on an equal level. The launderer's eyes, Llesho observed, twinkled with secrets.

"That, too," Master Den answered. "When a prince has been sold into slavery by enemies he had no part in making, he can do worse than learn to wash a shirt."

He can test poisons for a witch, Llesho thought to himself. Unaccountably ashamed of the time he'd spent chained in Master Markko's workroom, he kept that behind his teeth.

The trickster god continued, however, with a wry smile. "When he reaches beyond his unjustly reduced station, a prince can be taught many things."

"Master Den instructed the gladiators of Pearl Island in hand-to-hand combat," Llesho explained.

"A gladiator, a washerman, and now a warrior prince. You have been many things in such a short life." Yesugei jested with a sweeping bow to Dognut, "And this must be your swordsmaster."

The dwarf stopped his playing to raise his hands, warding off any fight between them, a gesture at odds with his stature. "Just a lowly musician, kind chieftain," he said, "who would record the tale of this quest in song. I am no warrior. This monkey, however, has seen much of battle."

Little Brother chittered fitfully in his sleep, and Llesho smiled. "He saved my life at least once," he remembered fondly, and tickled the creature under its chin.

Yesugei laughed, disarmed by the seriousness of the curious little man and the monkey in the uniform of the imperial militia. "My khan will have my head for bringing before him such a motley jumble of madmen."

"And yet," Master Den countered with a familiar smile, "your shaman dreams just such dreams, does he not, Yesugei?"

"He does," the chieftain agreed. He spent a long moment studying the gently smiling face of the trickster god, and finally nodded, as if some unspoken question had been answered, though not to his liking. "The dreams of the shaman never foretell good fortune."

"In troubled times," Master Den agreed, "fortune good and evil often travel side by side."

Yesugei rightly took this for a prophecy. "A matter for the khan to sort out," he decided. With a bow of more respect than he had shown to that point, he left them to regain his place at the head of the line.

Llesho had almost forgotten why he had dropped to the rear in the first place. When Yesugei disappeared among his own small band of clansmen, however, he remembered Kaydu's message.

"You asked to see me?"

"Mm-hmmm." Master Den closed his eyes and let his head fall back onto the folds of tent cloth.

"Did you want to tell me something? Or ask me something?" Llesho prodded gently. It didn't pay to be too demanding with the trickster god.

"Mm-hmmm." Master Den gave a little wiggle that set his whole great bulk in motion and taxed the springs of the wagon. Llesho realized he was burrowing more comfortably against the cloths at his back.

"And that would be?"

"It's a perfect time for a nap, don't you think?"

Great Sun was fading, and just looking at Little Brother, lying in boneless ease, sapped the tension out of his shoulders. A cool breeze off the grass teased lazily at Llesho's hair and the sound of Dognut's flute in a wistful lullaby took the threat of old memories out of the creak of saddle leather and the smell of the grasslands. Llesho decided that, yes, a nap sounded very good. It seemed there ought to be more to it, though, so he asked.

Master Den shrugged, quaking the wagon they were in. "I wanted to check out this Harnish chieftain you found for us. Now I have."

A question started to form—what had Master Den concluded?—but his teacher knew his mind.

"A good man," he answered without being asked. "He'll do."

"I thought so, too."

"Do" for what, he hadn't figured out yet, but he was already falling under the spell of Dognut's lullaby. Master Den took the reins from his hand and tied them to the latch at the end of the wagon. Freed of worries for his horse, Llesho curled up at the bottom of the cart and fell asleep. Under the watchful protection of the trickster god and the dwarf musician, he did not dream.

A small foot tapping insistently at his ribs brought Llesho awake just as Great Sun fired a horizon dotted with a scattering of white felt tents. Between sleepy blinks he noted that they were smaller than he'd expected: pale mounds huddled like nervous sheep on the grassy plain beneath a bowl of hard indigo sky turning purple at the edges.

"Are we there already?" He stretched as he mumbled his question, and only opened his eyes when Balar's voice answered.

"Not yet. We are on the outskirts of the Chimbai-Khan's tent city. The chieftain Yesugei says that we can camp here for the night. He's sent word ahead to the khan; by morning we should know whether we go ahead or die in our bedrolls."

"What are you talking about?" Llesho needed to be at the front of his forces when they entered the camp of Chimbai-Khan, so he untied his reins and hopped down off the wagon. "Has Yesugei been making threats?"

"Not threats, exactly," Balar admitted.

Master Den still slept—already he had expanded into the space Llesho had left, sprawled in untidy relaxation on the wagon floor. Dognut, however, followed the conversation with bright, eager eyes. "Leaving us so soon?" he asked. "I am curious about these not-exactly threats."

"My brother calls me to duty," Llesho answered. "If you want to eavesdrop on your betters, you need to saddle Moonbeam and ride in state among the warriors, not rattle along in an old wagon."

"Moonbeam and I have decided that, for our mutual comfort, we should spend some time apart." Dognut rubbed his backside to emphasize his point.

"Take what comfort you can, dwarf. For myself, I can't remember a more uncomfortable journey." Llesho could, of course. Riding with an arrow lodged in his shoulder, trying to escape Master Markko's scouting party came immediately to mind. It had hurt more, but nothing had humiliated him quite like bouncing across the desert slung over the camel's hump with his face buried in her rank- smelling flank. Not one of his more heroic moments. It hadn't turned out well for anybody, but he didn't think Dognut had had much say in his kidnapping, and Llesho was inclined to forgiveness. "An hour in your wagon has made up a part of the bill for that experience, and I thank you."

He didn't mention the precious gift of dreamless sleep, but the dwarf read him well enough to know it.

"Any time." Dognut gave a little bow of his head and picked a bamboo flute from his quiver by way of dismissal.

With Balar riding nervously at his side, Llesho eased his horse forward, toward the head of the line. The soldiers they passed stole glances at him with cautious wonder when they thought he wasn't looking. He pretended not to see.

"What has Yesugei done to distress Lluka now?" He couldn't believe he'd misread the chieftain, and Balar's next words reassured him on that account.

"Yesugei has behaved with all proper hospitality. Lluka is worried about this Chimbai-Khan."

Llesho waited for his brother to explain. Eventually, he did. "When you retired to the rear, Lluka took your place among the captains."

"Shouldn't that have fallen to Shokar?" Shokar, after all, led their Thebin troops.

Balar fidgeted in his saddle, spooking his horse. When he had settled the beast, his gaze slid away, seeming to count the soldiers they passed.

"What are you trying not to tell me?"

"Shokar doesn't want the position. You know that. Lluka does want it, but can't have it. What more is there to tell?"

Llesho blew an exasperated sigh. "I didn't ask to be king." He was feeling decidedly put upon by his brother, and not in the least blessed by this quest visited upon him by a dead adviser.

Balar shrugged. "We all know that. Lluka doesn't even want the kingship. He just . . ."

"Doesn't trust my judgment?"

"You're very young, and . . ." Balar gave an apologetic shrug. "Don't take offense, but from what we've seen so far, this quest of old Lleck's has been a disaster. The dream readers of Ahkenbad are dead, the emperor of Shan, by all accounts an adventurer with nerves of adamantine, has left the field in a state of shock. His magician, who might have given us a chance against the allies of this Master Markko, has left the field with his master. And who remains to support our cause should the Harnishmen in our company prove as villainous as their brothers who laid waste to Kungol? A washerman, asleep in the baggage wagon, who may be mad or may be the trickster god himself!

"I went to a great deal of effort to rescue you from the very fate that so unmanned the emperor of all Shan—the Harnish raiders would have taken you at Durnhag if Harlol and I hadn't got you out of there. Now I find that I am tagging behind you, with weapons sheathed, as you lead us to the very outskirts of a Harnish tent city about which we have no good intelligence. Your Yesugei has seen to that; he turns back all the scouts we send out to take the measure of our position. I think that warrants a bit of concern."

"Yesugei assures me that his khan means us no harm. I believe him."

"Excuse me for believing him not at all. The emperor of Shan did not fare so well as a guest of the Harn, and yet you put less faith in your own brothers than you do in this stranger from the race of Thebin's enemies."

Llesho had his own doubts, and couldn't really blame his brothers for their concern. Master Den asleep in the baggage wagon seemed little to wager their lives on, but it firmed Llesho's resolve that he'd made the right decision. Master Den had entered every battle alert at his side. He would do no less if they faced treachery now. But Balar had raised the specter of a greater threat, and he didn't know how to answer it.

"It's not that I don't trust you to do to what you think

is right." Llesho paused, working through his misgivings. Balar didn't wait, however.

"You just don't trust my idea of 'right,'" he complained. "You're as certain of Shokar as if he were the ground under your feet, and I can tell when you are thinking about Adar because of the longing that crosses your eyes when you think of him."

"It isn't you—" Llesho meant to say, "It's me," but Balar gave a little laugh and answered for him.

"I know. It's Lluka. I just want to know why."

And suddenly, Llesho did know why. "Why is Shokar here?" he asked.

"He brought your Thebin soldiers to fight against the Harn." Few enough of them, for a start, but he'd come.

"And where is Adar?"

"Taken prisoner on your quest." Balar got it now. Llesho could see the pieces falling into place, but he asked the next question anyway.

"And why are you here?"

Balar studied Llesho's face as he considered his answer. "I thought I knew," he said, while allegiances shifted in his eyes. Llesho didn't press him for an answer, but let the questions simmer in his mind.

"And who does Lluka serve?"

They both knew: his intentions might be honorable, but Lluka had placed his own will above Llesho's quest, and the Shan Empire might still fall for his decision. Adar might die.

"He wasn't alone." Balar defended their brother, as he must. They had spent years together studying at the feet of the Dinha. "The dream readers of Ahkenbad wanted me to bring you to them as well."

"And now they're dead." He couldn't help it, the anger he'd been ignoring since they'd left the ruined city spilled out like acid, burning him as much as it burned his brother. "Shou knew the danger he was facing. He's courting the goddess of war, for mercy's sake! But none of you had any idea of the destruction Markko is capable of. You interfered anyway, and now Ahkenbad is dead. Harlol will be dead soon, and the Wastrels who ride with him, who never would have left the Gansau Wastes if Lluka hadn't decided his will was more important than Lleck's quest."

"He wanted to protect you."

"I'm the king. It's my quest. If Lluka wants to be regent, let him fight ChiChu for the privilege. And if he should win against my combat instructor, let him take it up with the Lady SienMa!"

"Do you hear yourself, brother?" Balar reached over and grabbed the bridle of Llesho's horse, nearly losing his seat in the process. But he was determined to have his say, and Llesho was growing as skittish as his mount. "You consort with the most dangerous of mortal gods and are surprised that we worry—"

Llesho's answer was a brittle laugh with no joy in it. "Mischief and war have trained me with a harsh hand across all the li between the grasslands and the sea, brother. What do you think they have made me, if not dangerous?"

"What they have done can be undone," Balar pleaded, "I want my baby brother back."

Eyes bleak with the suffering he had seen, Llesho shook his head. "That child is dead." There was nothing left to say, so he kicked his horse into a canter and left his brother glaring at the dirt.

"Welcome, young prince," Yesugei greeted his return with a solemn nod, and "Good evening," Llesho answered as he fell in at the chieftain's side.

Lluka said nothing, but with a clenched jaw challenged the captains for his place at Llesho's right hand. Neither Kaydu nor Bixei would give ground, however. With a venomous glare, Lluka fell back to ride with Balar who seemed, after his recent conversation, to have grown thoughtful in the face of his brothers' anger.

As they rode, the tents grew bigger, but the distance never seemed to lessen. Llesho shot a wary glance at his host, who returned it with a knowing smile.

"Few outlanders have seen the tent city of the Chimbai-Khan," Yesugei offered by way of explanation, "Tales judge us by what the tellers see of us: our grazing parties, and the hunt."

"They judge you by your raiding parties, too." Llesho shivered in the rising chill. The Harnish chieftain had tested him among the baggage handlers, or so he thought. Now, with the hidden might of the Harnish clans eating up more and more of the horizon, Llesho brought out his grievances for an airing.

"The horror in the eyes of the dead and the weeping of the slaves you carry away speak louder than the songs of wandering herders."

Yesugei's head snapped back as if he had been struck. "Not every ulus rides against its neighbors," he reminded Llesho, "But peaceful folk rarely inspire songs."

"Thebin did, until Harnish raiders laid it waste." Llesho returned cut for cut in this duel of words.

But Yesugei had the sharpest return, an almost lethal blow:

"A Harnish riddle asks what prize for a man who raises his head too high above his neighbors. The answer is an ax at his neck. The Cloud Country set its sights above the concerns of smaller men, breeding miracles the way the clans breed horses."

Llesho had never heard Thebin called the Cloud Country before. The name conjured images of the clinic Adar had kept high in the mountains. He remembered waking from a fever to a window laced with clouds. The memory hurt, but his heart opened to the name and took it in. Yesugei saw the pain that flitted across his face, misguessing its cause.

"Chimbai-Khan does not concern himself with the South," the chieftain claimed in defense of his ulus' honor. "If he'd been the Gur-Khan of the Golden City, however, he would have set a watch for axes at his neck."

The Golden City was a common name for Kungol, carried with the legends wherever the caravans passed.

According to the tales, the city was so rich that even the houses of the lowest street sweepers were made of gold. They weren't, of course: not that rich, and not made of gold; the color came from the plaster on the houses. The plasterers had more work than they could handle during the season when the caravan road was open, repairing the corners of buildings where the foolish had broken off pieces to spend.

"There was no gold," Llesho said, No one had profited from the legend except the plasterers, and even they did not escape the Harnish raiders. "It was just yellow mud."

"And the miracles?" Yesugei asked.

Llesho smiled, no humor in it, but no bitterness either. More like the serendipitous discovery of wild nettles blooming in the snow: too beautiful to ignore, but too painful to touch. "Yes, the miracles were true."

His answer didn't seem to surprise Yesugei, but it didn't please him either. "Outlanders see all the Harnlands as one country, with one scattered people in it. But that isn't so."

"No." He accepted that Yesugei believed what he said, answering questions Llesho didn't know to ask. Llesho had to find the truth for himself, but he wondered why Yesugei was giving away what he could trade. Impulsively, before Yesugei could continue, he asked a question he should have been figuring out on his own: "Are you a teacher?"

"To teach a dream?" Yesugei eyed him thoughtfully. "Perhaps, in a small way. Your masters would make you a king. The gods would make you a miracle. Who will make you into a human being?"

"I thought I was one of those already."

Yesugei ignored his retort. Weighting his words with importance, he asked, "Do you know where the term 'Harn' comes from?"

Llesho's formal education had ended in his seventh summer, and this was something none of his masters since had bothered to teach him. He shook his head, again reserving judgment on the explanation Yesugei gave.

"'Harn' is a name the Tashek have given, and which they take everywhere the caravans go. It refers to the wind blowing on the grass, and names us not for who we are or where we come from, but for the fact that we never settle, always following our herds as they graze. In the South, the Uulgar people share that name, but are no friends to the North."

Llesho had heard of the Uulgar before. The explanation came as no surprise, therefore, though he didn't believe it was that simple. "These Uulgar killed my parents, my sister? Sold my brothers and me into slavery?"

Yesugei shrugged. "I don't know. The ulus of the Qubal clans never travels the Southern Road. I wish you only to remember, when you meet Chimbai-Khan, that he wasn't there at the death of the Golden City."

That sounded like something Master Den would ask of him. "I'll remember," Llesho promised. He would have asked more questions, but with a jerk of his head, Yesugei signaled a rider from his band to come forward.

"We stop here for the night," he said, and added, for the rider, "Take word to the khan's tent that we bring the stranger of old Bolghai's dreams."

The rider bowed his head in salute before wheeling his horse and galloped away toward the distant tents.

"Who's Bolghai?" Llesho asked.

"You will meet him in the morning." Yesugei let his horse amble away toward the small band setting out the frame of a felted ger-tent. He hadn't answered the question, and Llesho wondered why.

Chapter Twenty-four

IN a dream, Llesho sat at a low, mahogany table set with tea things under an arbor twined with vines from which heavy purple grapes hung in bunches bursting with juice. It didn't feel like a dream. The breeze, heavy with the scent of warm grapes and honeysuckle, swept his cheek while sunlight played hide-and-seek between the grape leaves and the arbor slats. But he had seen no arbor, no grapes, in the vicinity of their camp. Emperor Shou, two days' gone in the opposite direction, sat at his right pouring spiced tea into small jade bowls, while on his left, Pig snuffled daintily at a dish of plums. Across from Llesho at the table a large white cobra curled its body into the seat of a basket chair, flared hood swaying above its long neck.

"Is this a true dream?" Llesho asked. He hoped some jumble of memories and old stories had stewed the strange visions in his tired mind, but the emperor dismissed that notion with a soft unhappy laugh.

Pig looked up from his plums in surprise. "Of course it's a true dream, Llesho. The question you have to ask is, who dreams it?"

"You?" he asked Pig. It seemed unlikely, but Shou stared into his wine as if it were a scrying bowl that might tell him how he'd arrived at this tea party hosted by a serpent. Llesho didn't want to think about the alternative.

"Not mine." Pig confirmed what he didn't want to hear.

The snake fixed a cold and deadly eye on him. "Lleeeshhhoo," she hissed in a high, clear voice he recognized even from the throat of a serpent.

"Lady SienMa," Llesho bowed his head to honor the mortal goddess of war in the form by which she appeared to him in the dream. At the same time, he muttered a little prayer under his breath that the great white snake keep to her side of the table. Lady SienMa had taught him to pull a bow at her own hand and had fed him fruit from a silver bowl at her feet. She made him nervous at the best of times, though, and in her present form she scared him nearly to death.

"Whyyyyy are you heeeeeerrrre?" Her ladyship slithered in undulating waves against the rich grain of the mahogany table. Her flicking tongue glanced off his cheek and Llesho shuddered, frozen with dread while a frantic little voice in his head gibbered at him to run, right now, as far and as fast as he could. But she was too close. If he moved, she would strike and he would die. He knew that, just as he knew Shou couldn't and Pig wouldn't stop her. Fresh out of escape plans, he answered her question. "I don't know. Where is here?"

"Mmmmyyy Dreammmmmm."

"Oh." Llesho'd figured that out for himself, much as he hated to think it. He remembered her face in the waking world, white as the scales of the serpent and framed with hair black as the serpent's dead eyes. But which was her true form: the woman or the serpent of her own dreams?

"Both. Neither."

He hadn't actually asked the question, only thought it. Fine. She was a mind reading snake and the god of war, and he had invaded her sleep to muck about in her dream. Instead of leaving like he properly ought to do he was asking questions in his head that he didn't really want answers to at all.

"Aaaasssskkkk," she said, again reading his mind. Or he wondered, was he reading hers? The forked tongue flicked again, touching his lip in a mockery of a kiss and he barely held himself from a shudder.

"What happened to Shou?" He didn't mean just now in the dream, but what had happened to him in captivity that had left him moving dreamlike through horrors only he could see.

Pig cut an uneasy glance in his direction. "The magician," he said between slurps at the dish of plums.

"Poisons?"

Pig shook his head. "He invaded the emperor's dreams in captivity and stole his memories for clues to where you had gone."

"Ahkenbad is dead." Llesho stared with barely contained horror at the emperor. How had Shou survived when the dream readers of Ahkenbad had died of Markko's attack on their minds?

However he'd done it, all that courage and determination seemed about to be lost to the venomed tooth of the white cobra. The Lady SienMa, in her serpent form, had coiled glittering loops of her white body around the emperor. Shou seemed not to hear the conversation going on around him but absently stroked the scales of her back as the goddess of war writhed against him, around him, tongue darting over his face, her fangs never far from his neck.

Llesho held his breath, afraid to even think of weapons when the snake had read his mind already in this dream. *Don't kill him, don't kill him,* the prayer ran through his head as he considered seizing the snake in his bare hands to free the emperor from her deadly coils. She would strike him dead if he touched her; he knew that and could only sit very still and hope that she would hear his plea.

"Her ladyship would never hurt Shou." Pig snuffled up a plum and added, as an afterthought, "She loves him."

"And Shou?"

Pig gave a little shrug. "Who better to love the goddess of war than a soldier?" he asked.

"Does he?" he whispered back and meant, *How can a mortal man, even an emperor, love the goddess of war.* It felt like an unspeakable breach of the emperor's privacy to be here, in this garden, seeing something that he'd never wanted to know. But he knew better than to ignore a message from the Lady SienMa, even in dreams.

As if responding to Llesho's question, Shou turned his head and laid a gentle kiss on the back of the serpent where it lay in a coil over his shoulder.

So that was . . . love . . . not murder he was watching from across the mahogany table. Between her coils, the emperor's armor had taken on the texture of living shell, marked all over with the patterns of a turtle, but Shou didn't seem to notice his transformation.

"She has an odd way of showing it." Too sharp. Llesho winced, waited for the poison tooth to strike, but the lady merely pulled herself back to her basket chair, leaving the emperor of all Shan bereft of her chill comfort.

"Fiiiind hiiiiim. Killllll him," she hissed.

Master Markko, of course, who had turned her lover's mind inward. He thought to tell her, "I'm trying," but it came out, "I will."

Stretching the flared hood of her head high on her tall neck, the lady opened her snake mouth wide. Out of it came the most terrible scream that Llesho had ever heard. Trembling, he fell from his chair onto the loamy ground and covered his head with shaking hands. "Goddess, save me!" he cried, though jumbled in his heart he also meant, "Save us all, it hurts me, too." He woke bathed in sweat to the bloody light of the false dawn stealing through the red tent cloth.

"Wake up, Llesho, wake up!" Bixei shook his arm.

His voice sounded raspy and hoarse, as if he'd been calling for a long time.

"I'm awake." Llesho freed his arm and half-sat on his pallet, but he wondered if he had awakened all the same. The dream remained too vivid, and his flesh crawled with the memory of the great snake caressing Emperor Shou. "Oh, Goddess, please,"

he muttered, but couldn't say what he asked for. *Peace,* he thought. *Only peace, for one night.*

"What is it? Was it a dream?"

"I saw Shou with the Lady SienMa." He couldn't tell what he had seen, the lady as a white cobra, and Shou with the shell of a turtle where his armor ought to be. But the the meaning of it—"Pig says she loves him."

"Oh, that." Bixie didn't seem surprised. "I hope she can bring him back to his senses."

"She's the mortal goddess of war!"

"I prefer a more peaceful partner myself," Bixei conceded, "Of course, I'm not a general or the emperor of Shan.

"But come outside—you have to see this. You won't believe what happened while you were sleeping." Bixei drew a little apart to give him space to roll off his pallet and scrub the stiffness out of his face.

He wasn't sure he was ready to confront any more surprises—Shou with the Lady SienMa was more than enough. Bixei was waiting, however, so he straightened his spine and walked with more firmness than he felt to the open tent flap.

On what had been an empty plain when he went to sleep, a town of white felt tents had grown up and surrounded their little stand of red. This close, he realized he'd been as wrong about the size of the tents as the legends had been about the towers of Kungol. Not gold, in the khan's city, but white felt, the same matted wool used in the raiders' campaign tents but without the black dye that made the raiders' tents so ominous. These were immense, with round roofs banded with elaborately woven eaves, and draped all around with walls of heavy felt. Here and there a column of smoke rose through a hole in the center of a great round roof.

In front of Llesho's camp a wide avenue ran, with Harnish riders passing with brisk purpose or returning weary from some task that kept them busy during the night. Huge white tents squatted on either side, like glowering giants over a game of dominoes. Lesser tents scattered widely to left and right covered all the land to the horizon.

"How is this possible?" Llesho muttered under his breath. It didn't seem to be an attack, since weapons remained sheathed. Like a dream, the tents had come out of nowhere, however, and unknown magics made him nervous.

"The great khan has come to call." Master Den stood to the side of Llesho's tent, his legs planted and his elbows jutting out at his sides, his huge fists resting at his waist. To his right and left were Llesho's three brothers and the emperor's dwarf, and after, Llesho's captains. Behind him, all his small band of troops waited nervously to see what command he would give them.

"By what spell?" Llesho asked.

Before his advisers could comment, a stranger darted into sight around the corner of his tent, with Carina, the healer, following him. Llesho had seen many unusual things in his travels, but the little man was by far the oddest in human form. He was clearly Harnish and, though taller than Llesho, he was short for his own people. He wore his hair not in one plait or two, but in too many to count, all springing from his head at every angle. From the tail of each braid hung a talisman of metal or bead, or the tiny bone of a bird or small animal.

He wore robes cut in strips to show many layers over rough leather breeches that ended above boots wrapped close to the legs. Bells and amulets hung from silver chains sewn onto the layers, and from the collar around his neck the pelts of stoats hung by their sharp little teeth. When he moved or shook his shoulders, which he did in quick, jerky gestures, the pelts flew about in a little stoat dance. In one hand he carried a flat skin drum and with the other he reached for the thighbone of a roebuck that Carina held out to him.

Carina herself wore a costume similar to the stranger's, with many silver utensils and embroidered amulet bags hanging from fine chains sewn to her waist and shoulders. The end of a long hide belt hung down in back, finished at the end with a thick black fringe like the tail of a jerboa.

The stranger peered into Llesho's face, as if he could read the Way of the Goddess there. Then he gave a little nod.

"Small as my thumb, yet he carries a stinging barb," he said, as if confirming something for himself.

"I'm sorry, but I don't understand." Llesho figured he wasn't meant to, but Carina seemed to think highly of the odd creature, so he tried to be polite. Lluka, however, sniffed as if he scented something rank in the air. Probably the stranger, who smelled of old sweat and rancid fat.

"He's a shaman," Lluka explained, "A riddler."

"A healer and teacher," Carina corrected him softly as her fingers busily investigated the stranger's talismans. "This is Bolghai." Her nose nearly touched a tiny bone that she held up for inspection. "He's an old friend of my mother. Bolghai, this is Llesho."

Bolghai gave a little nod. "By the light of Great Moon the pack goes hunting in dun-colored boots."

Llesho sensed the shaman had just answered his question, but once again he didn't get it. Carina, however, seemed to have no trouble interpreting the strange riddles.

"The first, 'small but with a stinging barb,' is a wasp; In spite of his size, Llesho has the power to bring down a great man with his sting. The second compares the tent city to a wolf pack, which has travelled by night to find Llesho."

There had to be thousands of people—tens of thousands—in those tents. Llesho wondered if he didn't prefer magic to a khan who could mobilize so great a force in so short a span of time. The working of magic left the magician vulnerable, but a field marshal as skilled as the khan's gave few openings for defense.

Bolghai seemed to be paying no attention as Llesho worked to absorb the changes that had sprung up around them in his sleep. The strange little man slung his drum over his shoulder by its thong. With his free hand, he untied from his hair the bone that so interested Carina. This task was made more difficult because he continued to bob his head in the manner of a small animal in the grass. Llesho caught him stealing a glance out of bright, inquisitive eyes and an answering grin escaped before he could consider an appropriate response.

"Don't tell me you take this creature seriously!" Lluka glared from his brother to the shaman, the color rising in his face. "He practices the lowest religion, using tricks and riddles to amaze the ignorant."

Lluka was going to get them killed if he didn't shut up. Llesho kept his voice under control, but the temper snapped in his eyes and flared his nostrils. "The Chimbai-Khan moved a city of tens of thousands to surround us during the night. I would be cautious of calling him ignorant."

"I didn't mean the khan—" The color so recently risen now fled Lluka's face.

"Then treat his servant with respect." Llesho turned his back on his brother and the stunned silence of their company. This was, he realized, the crux of their problem, and he thought he had not handled it well. He couldn't back down to his brother, however, so he returned his attention to the visitor with as much calm as he could muster. Neither Bolghai nor Carina were paying

the argument the least bit of attention, though Llesho
suspected that nothing had escaped the shaman's notice.

Bolghai held the tiny bone on the palm of his outstretched hand. "A swan came drinking from the silver
river, then returned again to graze on the holy
mountain."

Carina took it with a smile. "Mama always loves your
letters," she said, which must mean that the swan repre-
sented correspondence of some kind, and possibly the
silver river meant the ink. Llesho hadn't seen any writing
on the bone, but he had no doubt that Mara the healer
would find it more informative. He really was getting the
hang of this riddle thing.

"We are accompanying Llesho on his quest," Carina
continued her explanation while she tucked the bone into
a little bag that hung from a silver chain on her costume.
"Raiders attacked us at an inn on the outskirts of Durnhag, hoping to seize the prince for the magician who has
ridden to the South. I'm afraid they've stolen his brother-
prince and others of his friends. We've come from the
destruction of Ahkenbad, and hope to rescue the hostages before the raiders reach their master."

"Deadly birds fly in the meadows before you, birds of
death fly where you have gone."

Llesho understood that one as well—deadly birds must
mean arrows, and birds of death the carrion eaters that
followed any battle. The longer he spent in his company,
the more familiar the shaman seemed. Could he have
accompanied the Long March to the slave markets? But
no, Yesugei had assured them that this group of Harnishmen had no part in the raid on Thebin. He reminded
Llesho of a meadow, though—and a conversation with
Pig.

"Have we met before?" he suggested, unwilling to ask
the man outright if he had visited Llesho's dreams as
a stoat.

The strange little man went still as a statue, then he

patted Llesho on the shoulder. "A sharp knife cuts deep."

The compliment made him blush. He did remember then: The stoat in the grass. Pig had told him to trust this man. Before he could say more, however, Master Den cuffed him gently on the side of his head.

"Prayer forms," the washerman said, "The Chimbai-Khan will want to see you when Great Sun rises." He led them all, captains and lesser soldiers, into the bit of grazing space left for the horses near their camp.

Setting himself a little apart, Bolghai watched with bright, eager eyes as they sorted themselves into rows with the princes and captains at their head. Carina followed the shaman, shaking her animal-skin robes into order about her as she went.

Master Den began the forms with "Red Sun" and Llesho stretched slowly, easily, reaching skyward to greet the morning. "Flowing River" followed. The master called "Wind through Millet" and moving into the form, Llesho became aware of the wind in his hair and the scent of the grass crushed beneath his feet, and the beat of a drum as insistent as the surge of the blood in his veins. He glanced up to see Carina hopping and leaping madly, like a jerboa, while the Harnish shaman darted in zigzags and circles like a stoat while beating on the skin drum.

The sight so amazed him that Llesho stopped in the middle of his form and took a step toward this new sound. No one else seemed to notice the pull of the music that took hold of him, filling him so full of the beating drum and tinkling bells that there was no room for will. He didn't have control over his feet or his arms, but could only watch them move on their own with a part of his mind that recorded memories but took no part in the ordering of his actions.

The drumbeat tingled all over his skin, tugging at his scalp until a part of him floated away, separating body from soul. Carina and the strange Harnishman danced, and Llesho danced with them. Bolghai spun in a circle, and Llesho felt himself spinning, spinning. His feet no longer touched the ground and he rose fearlessly into the air while the breeze held him as securely as the waves of Pearl Bay.

Suddenly, the music stopped. Llesho crumpled like a puppet whose sticks had broken. He could not move, not even to close his eyes against the growing light, but he didn't care. A pain that had lived inside of him for so long that he scarcely noticed it anymore was gone, gone, and he settled into its absence like a child. A whisper drifted through his mind on a breeze of thought—"Is this a true dream?"—and scattered like a drift of smoke on his blissful smile.

"Llesho?"

Something came between Llesho and the brightening morning. Ah, Master Den, and Dognut whose name was Bright Morning. He thought he might have forgotten the dwarf's given name once, but how peculiarly apt it seemed with his dwarfish self blotting out the light of his namesake. The stranger, too, and Llesho's own brothers crowded his vision. Shokar looked like he wished only to know what had laid his brother in the grass so he could kill it, and Lluka stared down at him as frozen as a Southern winter.

"Llesho? Are you awake in there?" Den called to him sternly, and he wondered what he'd done wrong this time. But they weren't on Pearl Island and Master Den hadn't spoken to him in that tone of voice since the arena at Farshore Province.

"He's not breathing," Shokar insisted, angry and scared and with his hands balled into fists. "Why isn't he breathing?" He was looking at Master Den, and Llesho wanted to warn him not to punch the trickster god in the mouth.

First he'd have to do something about the breathing thing, which wasn't quite working at the moment. He would have liked to tell Carina, but ah, there she was. He heard her voice clear as a lark's and insistent as a magpie's.

"He needs attention. Let me see him." She knelt over him, her expression severe. With deft fingers she felt out the bones of his neck, reaching around the back of his head to tilt him so that his throat seemed stretched for the slice of a blade and his chin pointed sharply at the sky. And just when he was wondering if he would ever remember how to breathe, she leaned over and kissed him. No, not a kiss; she was blowing air into his mouth. It filled his lungs and then, with a gentle hand at the base of his ribs, she forced the air back out again. Another, and he remembered how to do it himself, sighing the breath out of himself for so long that he thought all his internal organs had turned into air and were escaping through his mouth. Finally, when he felt flat as an empty waterskin, he blinked, and drew breath again. "What happened?"

"You fainted, but you're going to be fine." Dognut reached around the healer to reassure him with a squeeze of his stubby hand.

Llesho smiled back at him, warmed by the comfort that washed over him like sunshine. Dognut was wrong, though. "I was awake the whole time. Did you see me fly?"

"Maybe not so fine," the dwarf amended.

Carina dismissed Dognut's concern with an airy wave of her hand. "Of course he flew. It's common when just learning the skill to forget to breathe. He'll get better at it in time."

"But does he *have* time?" the dwarf muttered darkly.

Bolghai rose from his crouch over Llesho's body and peered up into Master Den's stormy face with a stern frown. "Three are tied to a tree, but one limb is still free."

Llesho had thought that he understood this strange riddle-language, but now he wondered. The image was

clear enough—a horse, with its feet hobbled—but he
wasn't a horse, didn't have four feet, and had escaped
imprisonment a long time back. Master Den said nothing
to contradict the Harnish shaman, however. With a frown
that carved a crease between his eyes, he directed the
disposition of Llesho's body onto a stretcher and called
for tea to be brought to his tent.

"I can walk," Llesho objected. When he tried to sit
up, however, Bolghai pressed him down again gently,
with a finger to the center of his forehead.

"Rest." Carina added her voice to the weight of advisers treating him like an invalid. He settled back with a
growl, but his rest proved shorter than even he expected.

"Young prince!" Yesugei rode toward them down the
wide avenue that had appeared while they slept. Around
the chieftain, an honor guard of armed riders jostled
Llesho's small band of fighters, shouting challenges back
and forth.

"The Chimbai-Khan expresses amazement at the presence of four princes of the Cloud Country in his humble
camp, and begs the company of these guests at breakfast," the chieftain announced. "I am to bring the princes
and their captains, with the khan's greetings." He seemed
not at all surprised to see Llesho on a stretcher, but
waited patiently for the prince to rise from his bed and
follow.

At Master Den's commanding gesture, the soldier who
carried the bottom of the stretcher lowered Llesho's feet,
while the trooper at his head raised that end up. Llesho
was on the verge of a smart remark about Harnish tents
growing up like mushrooms after a rain when Master
Den dropped a large open hand across his mouth.

"Of course," Master Den answered for him.

That probably worked better than Llesho's answer,
considering how few their numbers were next to the
khan's many thousands. When the tension drained from
his muscles, the hand left his mouth. Freed of the trickster god's restraint, Llesho discovered that, like his lungs,

his legs remembered how to walk and he stepped off under his own power. He wondered briefly whether the chieftain brought him to Chimbai-Khan as a prisoner or a supplicant, but the lack of an answer didn't worry him much. He'd traveled with gods and battled at the side of the emperor of Shan, so he was well prepared to face a khan with dignity. The little he knew of Harnish customs, however, told him that for a proper introduction, he needed a horse. With a minimal bow, polite without landing him in the dirt again, he gave the chieftain his reply.

"It will only take a moment, friend Yesugei, to greet the khan properly mounted."

His answer seemed the right one; Yesugei returned his bow with a calculated gleaming in his eyes. Assured that the Harnishman would wait, Llesho turned to Harlol, whose Wastrels soon had them mounted and ready.

PART FOUR

THE TENT CITY
OF
CHIMBAI-KHAN

Chapter Twenty-five

WHEN the horses were brought, Yesugei quickly sorted them as Harnish protocol dictated.

"The princes of Thebin will greet Chimbai-Khan together." As Yesugei spoke, he pointed here for Shokar and there for Balar at the right and left of Llesho. Lluka he set on the far side of Balar. With a gesture in the direction of Llesho's mounted forces, he added, "Your honor guard will wait for you outside the palace of the khan, but a servant is expected to attend each member of your party of rank. I suggest that your captains attend you in this way."

Kaydu didn't look happy with the idea of leaving their troops behind, but she quickly sorted out the captains, Bixei at Shokar's side and Harlol by Balar. She took her own position watching Lluka, who sniffed indignantly at Little Brother. The monkey had returned to his mistress and now rode in the sling on her back.

Yesugei looked over their arrangements with a frown. "If I may make suggestions, young captain?" When she nodded permission, he went on, "The khan appreciates amusements, as any man of discernment must, on the appropriate occasions. An audience to bring news of war brewing in the Harnlands would not be considered such an occasion, however."

"And for that reason, Dognut remains behind," she agreed, leaving the chieftain searching helplessly for a diplomatic rejoinder.

"But the creature, young captain—" he finally managed, though the words seemed to strangle in his throat.

"Ah, you mean Little Brother. He can cut a caper well enough in the cause of spycraft, but he serves his emperor best as a courier, and I value his judgment in matters of character."

She raised a brow in challenge, but Yesugei let it go with a shake of his head and tried again, to make a more urgent point with her.

"Have you set no warrior at your prince's back?"

"Master Den watches Prince Llesho," she answered, as if it should be obvious.

Master Den took this as his cue to step up and loop his hand in the bridle of Llesho's horse in the familiar way he had of walking at Llesho's side. "As always, young prince."

Not always. He'd chosen to follow Shou in Durnhag. But he was here, now, and Shou was still alive, which maybe the trickster had a hand in. The chieftain cast a doubting glance at the washerman, the only one among them on foot. Something passed between them, however, a whisper of laughter behind Den's bland expression, that left the Harnish chieftain shaking his head. "And the Lady Carina, friend of our own shaman, will make a welcome ninth," he said, dismissing Little Brother from his count. "A proper number with which to greet the khan."

The number of their party having met some sacred requirement in Yesugei's mind, he led them onto the grassy avenue that had come into being during the night. Young riders had gathered in their path, boasting and jostling as the chieftain led them out. With his guard arrayed around him, Llesho's way remained clear until one rider eluded his defenses and came too close, whistling and hooting derision as he aimed his horse to cut Llesho from the herd. In a countermove too fast and subtle for Llesho to catch, Master Den tipped the rider's foot from its stirrup and dumped him to the ground. And in a move that everyone could see, Little Brother leaped from the sling at Kaydu's back and landed on the boy's chest, berating him with the high, chittering complaints of his monkey kind.

The boy on his backside, taken down as it seemed by a monkey in an imperial uniform, drew the laughter of his Harnish companions, but the anger sparking in his eyes could easily become a weapon in the hand. Llesho considered his options, and dismissed them one by one. It would be just his luck to kill the fool and discover he was some favored son of Yesugei or a relation of the Khan himself. Instead, he set his chin at an arrogant angle and gave Yesugei an ominous warning. "If your children want to yap at my warhorses, they'd better be ready to get stepped on."

A condescending smile began on the chieftain's lips— the monkey, after all, traveled in Llesho's company—but he quickly recognized the dead light of too many battles glinting in Llesho's eyes. *That's right. Don't mistake me for the innocent child I have never been,* Llesho thought. When he was certain he had shaken Yesugei's complacency, he completed the warning. "Your unblooded warriors are playing a game with wooden swords against men and women who have come through fire and storm. We have stood in the rubble of Ahkenbad and seen legends spring to life, and we come to you fresh from battle with your Southern kinsmen. Our nerves are short and battle reflexes sometimes outrun good sense. I don't want to start a war with your khan over a misunderstanding."

They could not win against so many, but more than Llesho's troops would die in a fight here.

"My pardon, Prince Llesho." Yesugei snapped a command at the young Harnish riders, who answered the

command to order with some resistance. That challenge
would have to be met, Llesho knew. If he were to make
an ally of the khan, they had to find a way of settling
warriorly precedence without killing anyone. In the
meantime, however, Kaydu collected Little Brother with
an insulting sniff and older horsemen rode to meet them,
offering joking insults while they expertly herded the
younger men to the fringes. Harlol's Wastrels kept them
there. The Tashek warriors held to no formation but
rode with fierce expressions, their hands on their sword
hilts in a familiar gesture of readiness even the Harnishmen knew better than to cross.

With so many horsemen milling in the space between
the ranks of mighty tents, the avenue didn't seem so wide
anymore, and Llesho was glad to see the youthful riders
fall to the rear of the cavalcade, away from trouble.

"The Lady Bortu sent us to welcome the child prince,"
the eldest among the newcomers explained with just
enough weight on the words to suggest that the lady
considered them all children.

A delicate sop to his pride, Llesho noted, while the
elder statesmen taking their places as his wardens assured that cool heads would rule. This lady had some
power in the Harnish tent city, then—at least until the
Chimbai-Khan decided his honor had been crossed.

"This child of war thanks her ladyship," he answered,
and gave too much away in the smile at this man who
looked like a grandfather.

The man pressed his lips together, doubting. "This is
the one?"

Yesugei raised a hand, open-palmed, with a shrug.
"That remains for Chimbai-Khan to discover." He
sounded sure in spite of the words, and the old rider
shook his head. Llesho had the feeling he had ridden
into the middle of an argument that was about to sweep
him up whether he wanted it to or not.

The tent of the Chimbai-Khan stood across the far end
of the wide avenue, watching them, it seemed, down the

grassy cut through the center of the wandering city. They rode in silence for longer than Llesho would have thought possible, while tents rose up on either side of them and passed behind.

"It's bigger than Kungol," he muttered under his breath. He hadn't expected anyone to notice, but of course Master Den heard everything.

"Probably," Den agreed, and added, "The North is on the move."

Chimbai-Khan had not moved his city overnight to impress a deposed boy-prince or his small band of followers. War between the clans meant opportunity for a khan as well as bloodshed for his people. Llesho was quick to grasp what that might mean for his cause. Absorbed in considering strategic outcomes of his coming meeting, he scarcely noticed the white ger-tent at the end of the avenue growing larger in his field of view until it had filled the horizon.

They had come to the farthest reach of the city, beyond the tents standing guard over the alley. Yesugei halted at a broad grassy square where riders held races on horseback in front of a ger-tent large enough, Llesho estimated, to hold hundreds of people in council. It had looked as white as its companions from a distance, but close up, Llesho realized that the thick felt of Chimbai-Khan's ger-tent and its roof flap were covered in silver embroidery. The camp had been arranged so that the rays of the Great Sun, rising, flashed and glittered blindingly on the polished threads.

"By the Great Goddess, it's a palace," Llesho breathed.

The chieftain gave him an inscrutable look. "That's exactly what it is," he said. They picked their way slowly across the playing field to a small band on horseback ranged across the entrance.

"I bring suppliants to beg the Chimbai-Khan's favor," the chieftain announced. "Carina, friend to this ulus and beloved daughter of the healer Mara, brings to the khan's tent the Prince of Dreams, as prophesied by our shaman, along with his brothers and servants."

"Enter." The centermost horseman of the small band of guards raised his hand in a gesture of welcome, and the warriors parted, leaving a path open to the door.

"Your honor guard will receive welcome from the khan's warriors," Yesugei assured Llesho, who gave a signal for his forces to stay where they were. He dismounted, a sign for their party of nine to do likewise, and held out his reins for a Tashek warrior, who took them, in the manner of their Harnish hosts, without leaving the saddle. When the horses had been led a little apart, Yesugei likewise dismounted and directed them through the tent flap that covered the open door on the great khan's traveling palace.

As large as the ger-tent looked from the outside, it seemed even larger from the inside. Following Yesugei they trod thick furs and dense carpets. Llesho caught glimpses of tent walls hung with thick tapestries, with mirrors in elaborate frames and sculptures in bronze and silver inlaid with coral and lapis. Obscuring his view of the decorations were ranks of the Harnish nobles and chieftains. The youngest among the nobles, the guardians of the khan in their deep blue coats and cone-shaped hats, stood at attention with their backs nearly touching the circular wall. Their hands never strayed to their swords or to the short spears in the scabbards at their backs, a grave insult in the greeting of friends, but they watched with fierce glares on their faces as the khan's guests moved toward the firebox at the center of the tent.

In front of the khan's personal guardsmen, the nobles of middle age and greater sat in an inner circle with one leg tucked under them and the other bent so that the knee nearly touched their chins. Men and women together watched with grave eyes beneath elaborate headdresses, their hands lost to sight inside their long, brightly patterned sleeves.

Centermost of all, and closest to the fire, chieftains of

the many diverse clans of the Qubal people sat in uneasy alliance. These struck Llesho as the most thoughtful, and the most wary, of the khan's retainers. As he passed through their circle, Llesho felt eyes tracking his party, judging him by his demeanor. He'd have to convince every one of them if he wanted the khan's help. It looked like he had a lot of work to do there, and he figured it started now. Stiffening his spine, he puffed out his chest and sharpened each step into a challenge.

Balar noted his change in posture with a quick nervous glance, as if he'd suddenly lost his mind, but Shokar followed his lead, only more impressively because of his greater years and bulk. He didn't have to worry about the impression his captains made. The three of them shadowed the princes like hunting cats; Kaydu and Bixei with the forthright stalk of tigers, and Harlol, slinking with the desert grace of a leopard. Master Den, like a mountain on legs, had dropped the open simplicity of the washerman. His sly glance cut from side to side with the narrow-eyed calculation of a butcher measuring a flock of sheep. Young warriors on the fringes stirred uneasily. Though Master Den carried no weapons, Llesho felt infinitely comforted to have him near.

Carina, however, reached up and smacked the trickster god hard on his shoulder. "Bolghai is my teacher and a friend of my mother," she reminded him. "Don't give him cause to report ill of me."

He hadn't seen Bolghai in the khan's tent yet, but Carina's chiding reminder warned him of the shaman's presence. Master Den seemed not at all surprised at her words, but summed her up with mischief in his eyes. "The lady shames me," he said, and bowed to acknowledge the hit.

"As if I could!" Carina laughed at him, but Llesho was not feeling amused.

"Have I met even one person on this quest who is who they say they are?" he grumbled under his breath.

Carina looked at him with surprise. "I am the daughter

of my parents, both of whom you know, and a healer in my own right, which you also know. I've had teachers just like you have, and Bolghai the shaman is one of them. That makes me a good healer, not a liar."

Llesho didn't know what to say to that. It was true enough, but he still felt betrayed. "He's Harnish," he said, though he knew it would only make her madder.

It did. With a disgusted "tsk" she shook her head at him and scampered away, her shaman's garb giving her leave to act the part of the jerboa it mimicked.

"You handled that well."

Master Den was laughing at him and Carina was mad at him. Could his life get any more embarrassing? Apparently so, Llesho discovered. Just ahead, the khan sat amid the royal family on a raised platform, watching every shift in the Thebin prince's expression from across the central firebox. A little older than Shokar, perhaps, Chimbai-Khan held the same pose as his lords, his arms crossed over his raised knee. He wore a full caftan of red-and-yellow brocade under a dark blue sleeveless coat woven with intricate patterns in it: waves at the hem, dragons floating at his knees, and clouds scudding to the waist. Diagonal stripes banded his breast. His cone-shaped hat and the ornate scrollwork that edged the fronts of the coat were heavy with gold threads.

At the right of the khan sat a woman of middle years dressed all in shades of green as rich as the Khan's garb in spite of the simplicity of her color. A towering head-dress of silver foil covered in large beads of coral and turquoise obscured all but her eyes with hanging jewels. At first glance, her smile seemed to welcome them warmly. On closer inspection, Llesho trembled at the ser-pentlike calculation in her hard dark eyes. She reminded him of the Lady SienMa, not as a woman but as the white cobra he had seen in his dream. *What are you?* he wondered. With a nervous shiver, he let his gaze pass on.

On the left side of the khan, both a little lower on the platform and a little behind the royal pair, an old woman

in equally gaudy attire watched Llesho. Her probing examination seemed to peel his soul in strips, searching
each layer for his hidden truths. *This must be Bortu,* he
thought. The one who called him here, and by her age
and her place on the dais, the khan's mother. Without
her goodwill he would fail with the khan, and he opened
his soul for her to read as deeply as she wanted. If she
read him truly, she would find the goodwill he held for
her and for her son.

As if she heard his thoughts, the old woman spoke,
not to Llesho but to Yesugei.

"You have brought strangers into the ulus of my son.
Who are these foreigners, and what do you intend about
the danger that engages them in mutual pursuit?" Her
words made it clear that she knew who they were and
why they had come. She still demanded a formal introduction, however.

Yesugei knelt on the thick pelts at the foot of the royal
platform and dropped his head to his knees. When he
had performed his obeisance, he lifted his head but did
not rise to his feet. Sinking back on his heels, his eyes
on the mother of the khan, he answered her command.
"I bring you the healer Carina, who is a friend to this
ulus. With her travel four princes of the Cloud Country
with their servants and a small guard suited for the
journey."

The chieftain had cleverly shifted the blame for the
armed trespassers to a known and welcome guest. Bortu
nodded her appreciation of the tactic, giving permission
for Yesugei to introduce the unwelcome but foreseen
visitors. "Prince Shokar—" he waited until Shokar completed a deep bow, and then went on, in descending
order by age, "Prince Lluka, a younger prince of the
house of Thebin, and Balar, his brother, who have re-
sided with the dream readers of Ahkenbad since the fall
of Kungol."

Lluka gave a tight incline of his head suitable for one
of superior rank to give a ruler of lesser station. Bortu

narrowed her eyes, but the khan made no immediate
demand for a greater show of respect. Balar seemed unable to decide which brother's example to follow until
Llesho kicked him in the shin and glared ominously at
him. That was enough to decide Balar, who made his
bow even deeper than Shokar's. The khan gave a bland
and welcoming smile that didn't reach his eyes.

"Prince Llesho," Yesugei finished the formal introductions. Llesho bowed as deeply as Balar, but no more so.
He didn't want to look ridiculous, after all, and bending
any farther might land him on his head. Together, the
princes and the chieftain straightened and waited for an
acknowledgment of the visitors.

"Boy." The khan addressed Llesho with an edge of
icy condescension that brought his chin up at an arrogant
tilt he had never quite learned to control.

Before Llesho could speak, however, Lluka put himself
between the combatants. "Leave him alone."

Chimbai-Khan shifted his focus to Lluka, taking him
in with a cold, distant gaze. "Who is King of the Thebins?" he asked, but he wasn't talking to Lluka. Everyone
in the tent, including Llesho, could see that he didn't
care at all about the angry prince in front of him.

Another damned test, Llesho figured. All right, he'd
give him the answer he was looking for. "Kaydu," he
said, and flicked a finger, barely, in the direction of his
brother.

She needed nothing else. With a move swift as a
pouncing tiger, the first of his captains stepped up behind
Lluka and landed a chopping blow between his shoulder
and his neck. Lluka fell like a stone. Balar stared from
one brother to the other in horror, but said nothing. With
vague distaste curling his lip, Shokar looked down at his
unconscious brother. He, too, spoke not a word, but
turned to Llesho a look of cool contemplation, as if he
had witnessed something strange that didn't exactly dis-
please him.

For himself, Llesho gave the felled prince a brief glance

just to make sure that he would stay down until Llesho
had finished what he had to do. With another slight dip
of his head, he signaled Kaydu to step back again.

"I am King of the Thebins." he said. "And I beg the
assistance of the khan in defeating the dreadful power
that has seized the healer-prince, my brother Adar." He
didn't think this cold-eyed warrior cared much for the
lives of his guards, so he didn't mention Lling or Hmishi.

"I see." The khan saw entirely too much, and so did
his entire court, it seemed. None of the guardsmen had
reached for a weapon or moved from their places, but
the nobles and chieftains began to stir at his pronounce-
ment. At a gesture from the khan, they rose in muttering
groups and thoughtful pairs and headed for the open
door. Apparently he had performed according to plan.

A snicker drew Llesho's attention from the departing
chieftains. Damn! At the foot of the khan's raised platform, Bolghai slapped Dognut on the back with a trium-
phant grin. Well, he'd thought he'd left the dwarf behind,
just as Yesugei had anticipated no entertainment.

"A day ends, a new day dawns in fire," the shaman
said and picked up a silver flute from among the instruments that the dwarf had laid out before him.

Dognut shook his head. "But at what cost?" he asked,
and Llesho understood the riddle to mean, "He'll do."

"The usual, if he truly is the one," the khan answered.
Dognut didn't look happy, but like the khan and Lady
Bortu at his back, he watched the tent flap, waiting for
something.

And damn, again. The young rider Master Den had
unhorsed burst in and strode down the center of the tent
as if he owned it.

The younger of the two women on the platform let
her lips shape a forced smile. "I see you have survived,
my son," she said, and he gave her a flourishing bow
from the waist.

"I have, Lady Chaiujin."

"And will you not call me mother as I have requested?" she asked him, with a simper in her smile and a predatory gleam in her eye.

The young warrior bowed again. "As you will, Lady Mother." Addressing the khan, he added, "I stand before you with all but my pride intact. That hulking great servant of his put me in the dirt with a move I have never seen but sorely wish to learn."

"Sorely indeed." The khan gave him a quick laugh, but grew serious again as quickly. "He offered no threat or harm?"

More tests. If Llesho didn't need the khan's goodwill, or at least his free passage through the northern grasslands, he would end these games right now. The khan's thousands were an impassable obstacle against him, however, and an equally valuable resource as allies. So he schooled his face to a bland coolness that showed none of his feelings.

"To the contrary," the young prince of the Harn smothered a grin that made his face a mirror of his father's. "The Thebin hides nothing—his eyes showed every calculation as he considered his options and the consequences of acting on any of them."

"We had noticed," Lady Bortu agreed, and Llesho winced. He *thought* he'd been getting better at keeping his thoughts hidden.

"The servant is nothing of the sort, of course," the Harnish prince continued. "No thought came between the impulse and the action—he perceived me as an annoyance but no great threat, lifted me by the scruff of my neck as if I were a cub, and dumped me with no ceremony and less injury at the feet of my companions. And this one—" he pointed at Kaydu, "—Attacked me with a wicked creature who scolded me as if he were my own old Bortu. I am not sure who deserves my vengeance more—the captain who carries this secret weapon, or my saddle-mates, who will pay, I vow, for their laughter."

His father cuffed him affectionately on the side of his head. "I'm sure you will devise properly horrible punishments over your cups, and forget them again when your head clears," he said.

"Mare's milk lubricates the imagination," the young rider retorted, and flung himself at his father's feet.

"You ought to see the monkey, Father," the boy continued with a jerk of his shoulder to indicate the sling at Kaydu's back. "He's better than a dancing bear!"

That wasn't exactly true. Llesho wasn't ready to share the story of his travels with Lleck or the bear cub's death defending him, so he kept quiet on that point. Kaydu was craning her neck to see over her shoulder, however, and she gave a little shrug. "He's sleeping," she said. "Discipline is hard work for a monkey. Perhaps later, when he is rested, Your Excellence."

The khan accepted this answer, though Llesho could see that the monkey was very much awake. He crouched down in his sling, peering with nervous fixity over his mistress' shoulder. His wide monkey eyes never left the khan's wife, who in her turn, eyed her son with something like calculation.

"Come, Father, I've done my deed for the day, and I've seen a wonder before breakfast. Don't you think it's time I had my reward?"

The khan responded to his son's plea with a clap of his hands, and an invitation: "Princes, join us for breakfast—someone should wake the officious one—and let your captains dine with my guards."

"Hold off a moment more, my father. This one—" the Harnish prince pointed at Bixei, "—bears a name and a face out of the South."

At a gesture from the khan, Yesugei dropped a hand on Bixei's shoulder and pushed him forward a step. Chimbai-Khan examined him from top to toe, as if he were a horse he was deciding to buy. "Looks a bit like a Southerner," he agree. "Tell us your name, boy."

"Bixei, Your Excellence," he repeated the honorific he had heard, and bowed as low as the princes had to show his respect.

"And where did you come by such a name?" the khan asked.

"I don't know, Your Excellence. I was born a slave in Farshore Province and sold to Pearl Island for the arena. Until Master Markko started his war against Llesho, I had never been outside of the two provinces, though Llesho has noted a passing resemblance to his enemies in the South. For myself, however, I have no knowledge of the grasslands and don't know how that could be."

Bolghai interrupted then with a shrill note from one of Dognut's whistles. Putting it down again with a guilty start, he used the attention he had gained to suggest, "He must be one of the lost tribe."

"What lost tribe?" Llesho asked, since a guardsman didn't have the right to question a khan.

"Ages past, before the Shan Empire existed, the Harn wandered all the world, from the Pearl Bay to the Marmer Sea, to the foot of the Cloud Country itself." Bolghai related the tale in the singsong voice of a lore-master. "During the barbarian wars the Harn withdrew to the grasslands and left the Northern clans of Shan to build their walled cities. Some tales say that a clan of hunters settled between the mountains and the sea, that they remained in the barbarian lands and survived as outcasts, cut off from their brothers and lost to their own heritage. This boy may be one of them."

"I don't know," Bixei admitted, "Even slaves tell stories, but I never heard any about lost clans of Harnishmen."

"And who," asked the khan, "set a boy from Farshore with a name out of the grasslands to guard the princes of the Cloud Country, across thousands of pais and several hands of adventures, to fetch up at my door?"

"Not princes, Your Excellence, but Prince Llesho only, if I may beg your pardon," Bixei answered, while Llesho reminded himself to find out how far a pais was compared to a li. "We found the brother-princes along the way. The Lady SienMa formed a squad of guardsmen around Prince Llesho. I am one, and Kaydu is our captain. Among the prisoners we hope to rescue are two of our companions."

"You travel with the names of legends on your lips." The khan studied Bixei with a troubled frown. "The lady of whom you speak would demand the safety of your prince above all your party. She knows that the personal guards of a great prince must gladly give their lives in defense of their charge."

Bixei hitched his shoulder in a little shrug. "Convincing me isn't the problem. The witch-finder has Llesho's brother, Prince Adar, as well as the mates of his cadre."

"I can see the difficulty," the khan agreed gravely, although Llesho felt he was being mocked behind the solemn nod. "Very well. I can see that you have earned your breakfast and then some with your tale. But take this with you, that your face is your passport here. The Harn never turn away one of their own."

"Your Excellency." Bixei studied the khan's face with a wonder that raised the hackles on Llesho's neck. "Yes, Your Excellency." Bowing very deeply again, he followed his companions to a place nearer the door to share breakfast with the Harnish guards. *Just breakfast,* Llesho wanted to tell him. His companions would have a home in Kungol; this stranger had no business trying to lure a favored guardsman—his friend—away with the one thing Llesho couldn't give him: people who wore faces that whispered of his own.

The Chimbai-Khan watched him thoughtfully, but said nothing when Llesho's chin came up the way it always did when he felt embattled. Instead he turned to the guard who had challenged them at the door.

"I have missed you by my side, brother. Come, and you, Prince Llesho, who would be King of Thebin, sit by my side. My seers have kept me abreast of your journeys, but I want to hear it from your own lips."

The guardsman bowed and did as he was told, curling in the Harnish style at his brother's back. When he had settled, and the princes of Thebin had likewise found places on the step below the royal platform, the khan turned to a child carrying a tray with a single soup bowl filled with thick, rich broth and fat grains of toasted millet.

"Food," he said, and waited while his guardsman took the first sip. After sighing contentedly and smacking his lips to express his satisfaction with the fare, the man offered the bowl to the khan, who took it and drank. With that, more children appeared with bowls of soup for all, and mutton fat pies to follow.

Shokar gave the khan's guardsman a thoughtful look, then, plucking a pie from Llesho's fingers, took the first bite and chewed. "Good," he agreed on a swallow, and returned the pie to his brother.

In his own court, where his cooks were both loyal and watched, tasting the king's food had the value of ritual and courtesy. But in the camp of a potential enemy Llesho wished that no one would risk themselves on his food. He was, as Master Markko had often reminded him, an expert at handling poisons as his brother was not. Shokar suffered no immediate harm, however, and Llesho took the second bite with as much grace as he could manage. He couldn't rebuke his brother without looking foolish in front of the khan, and it wouldn't do any good anyway. Shokar would do whatever he thought necessary to protect him.

"Second son," the old woman said during a pause between bites of her own pie, "our guests must wonder what we are."

The guardsman looked to Chimbai-Khan for permission to answer and, receiving it, made a bow to each as he introduced them.

"Bortu, mother of our khan."

He'd guessed as much. The old woman measured Llesho with her stare and did not give away her conclusions.

"Chaiujin, beloved second wife of the great Chimbai-Khan."

"First wife now," the woman dressed all in green reminded him with a tragic sigh. She dropped her gaze in
a polite display of respect for her guests, but not before
Llesho caught again the hard and empty stare like an
echo of the white cobra in his dreams. Not the Lady
SienMa, he knew. But a whisper in the back of his mind
warned him, something very like. Was she the khan's
creature? At her correction the khan's mouth had tightened, as if a knife had opened a poorly healing wound.
If not his, then whose?

The guardsman had continued with his introductions,
however. "Tayyichiut, eldest son of the great khan," he
announced.

The young warrior had been shoveling meat pies into
his mouth with the steady determination of one who had
approached starvation too closely or, perhaps, like a
young man who had grown four inches in the night. He
acknowledged the introduction with a nod that lost much
of its courtly manner when he stuck his thumb in his
mouth and sucked the meat juices from it. Cleaning his
fingers each in this way, the Harnish prince turned his
lively eyes on Llesho. "Everywhere in the camp they
are saying you are on a quest to kill the magician of
the South."

"We go south." Llesho hesitated to say more about
his plans, and was saved from rudeness by the guardsman
who sniffed to signal his displeasure at the interruption.

"Mergen," he said, with a hand at his breast to indicate
himself, "beloved brother to our khan, trusted general
and most humble servant." The way he lounged in his
lord's presence, nibbling bits of broken pie from his
plate, gave the lie to the last.

As if to emphasize whatever Mergen's actions meant
to say, the khan dropped a hand on his brother's head
and stroked it as he would a loyal hound. Llesho tried
to imagine stroking Shokar's hair in that way, and trembled at the thought. His brother would drop him on his
chin. Still, that must be part of the lesson, for both the

khan and his brother were watching for his reaction. Not knowing what else to do, he bowed his head over his upright knee and let his gaze wander to the Lady Bortu, who demanded of Carina, "What have you learned of these men who would be princes of the clouds?"

"These two, Princes Balar and Lluka, I know very little about, except that they kidnapped their brother Llesho while abandoning their brother Adar to the raiders." She glared at the brothers, each of whom met her accusation in predictable fashion.

"We meant no harm." Balar had twisted his legs in a semblance of the Harnish style, but could not work out how to bow politely in this position, and rolled off the step in his attempt. Lluka sat in the Thebin style, legs crossed and with the feet tucked into the crooks of his knees. He managed to express his disdain even while he performed a perfect seated bow. The khan returned it with a measured tilt of his head, but his lips fought to control a smile while he waited for Balar to right himself. It seemed a perfect demonstration of their dilemma, Llesho thought. The brother with the power to balance the universe could not even keep to his own seat, while Lluka, the brother who should see all futures, showed no understanding of his own actions. He sighed, wrapping his arms easily around his knee in the Harnish manner learned on the Long March. The memories worried at his composure, but his body didn't care about that.

The gesture, small as it was, drew Carina's eye to him. "As for Prince Llesho, I have treated his wounds and traveled in his company from the imperial city to the very borders of the Shan Empire, and yet I cannot say that I know him. It's true what Bixei says, though. The magician makes war against him, and those who stand between them die, or worse."

Worse, Llesho knew she meant, like the Emperor Shou. But the Long March had taught him better than that. "The living can be healed, the dead must try again," he reminded her, and Carina dropped her eyes, acknowledging the rebuke.

"But is he the Prince of Dreams?" The khan had put aside the dregs of his breakfast, and he leaned forward to study Llesho more closely, raising his hand for Carina to continue.

Logically, Llesho knew that the ruler of the gathered clans of the grasslands had no intention of striking one of his guests down over breakfast. Logic didn't enter into the automatic response to the hand of a Harnishman raised over his bent body—he ducked his head in the Harnish mark of submission, the flinch as automatic as the way he adjusted his weight to keep his balance. No one who remained in the ger-tent of the khan could mistake the gesture; it seemed as if those closest to him held their breath, the distress at their center working its way out to the guardsmen in a ripple of reaction brought quickly under control. There was an enemy here who needed defeating, only they couldn't tell who it was or where they were supposed to strike.

"I'm impressed that you can sit so calmly among us, Prince Llesho."

Llesho straightened his neck, surprised by the gentle voice into meeting the khan's eyes. He wished he hadn't. The pain in them reminded him of his father when Llesho'd been sick or cut himself in weapons practice—as if he would take the pain into himself rather than see his child suffer. But Llesho wasn't the khan's child, his own father was dead at the hands of Harnish raiders, and he didn't want this man's compassion. No, not at all, and he especially didn't want to be caught with tears on his cheeks, which would happen at any moment—

Chimbai-Khan read all of that in his eyes and let his gaze drift away, cool again and as remote as the mountains, but with his question unanswered. "And this one?" he said, looking Shokar up and down.

"I like him," Carina gave her opinion with a shake of

her hair and a sly smile, shifting the mood among the guards who had responded to their leader's distress with tense confusion. "He is the eldest of the seven princes of Thebin."

"But not its king?"

"I have no gifts, Your Excellence." Shokar, who sat sideways with his legs hanging down as if the step were a chair, twisted himself still further to give the khan a bow. He didn't see the quick glance at the corner where Master Den took his ease at Carina's side, with Bolghai the shaman and Dognut with his flutes, but Llesho did. The four sat companionably together, as different as people could be. But a common wisdom beyond race or sex or costume bound the two shamanic healers. And something he could not name, beyond stature or the color of their flesh, told him that Master Den and the dwarf shared more in kind than a baggage cart on the march. He knew what Master Den was; now, he began to wonder what Dognut was as well.

"He does, of course," Bolghai answered his khan, face wrinkled up like a stoat sniffing the air. "Have gifts. Loyalty is but one of them; he serves his master well."

Llesho bristled at the description of his brother. "Prince Shokar is servant to no one, least of all to me."

Mergen, the brother of the khan, asked with a look for permission to speak and received it in a glance.

"The brother of a king, or a khan, must be his most loyal servant. To whom else will lesser folk look for their lessons in devotion?" He frowned his disapproval at Lluka, the faithful brother of the khan to a brother he clearly thought took too much upon himself.

The priests will show the way, Llesho would have suggested, thinking of Kungol and the Temple of the Moon. Then he looked at Bolghai hunkered in the corner with juice from the meat pie dribbling from the corner of his mouth, and he changed his mind. Still, it troubled him to think of his brothers serving him, not least because he wanted to be the one looking for comfort, not giving it.

He found himself watching the khan's son, who met

his gaze with a level one of his own. "It's true," that look seemed to say, and Llesho wondered where his brothers were. But mischief lurked in Tayyichiut's eyes.

"We are of an age," he noted, wiping a greasy hand on his backside. "Do you play jidu?"

"I don't know that game," Llesho admitted. Wisely he did not add that his Harnish captors did not teach slaves the games of their own children when they took them to be sold at market.

"You know how to use that?" Tayyichiut pointed to the short spear at Llesho's back. His tone had just enough doubt in it to prick at Llesho's already frayed nerves.

"Only a fool caries a weapon he can't use."

"Then we'll see if you can ride." With a laugh, the khan's son snatched Llesho's spear and ran, leaving his own behind in the rugs.

Temper flared. Llesho jumped to his feet to pursue him with fire in his eyes.

"Gently, young prince," the khan advised him levelly, but with a hard hand grasping his shoulder. When the rage cleared from his vision, Llesho saw that the guards who lined the ger-tent had every one of them drawn their swords. More frightening, however, Master Den had moved between Llesho and the closest line of attack, his muscles relaxed in the loose readiness that preceded violent action. And Dognut had turned very pale.

"It's a game, not a killing match. Reclaim your weapon, but let there be no blood shed here." Chimbai-Khan gave him a little shake and let him go. "Here—" he held out Tayyichiut's abandoned spear. "In the game you throw the weapon, and your opponent has to catch it. In that way, weapons will be exchanged again—he never meant to keep it. But remember, the goal is to catch the weapon in the hand, not in some vital organ."

The khan's reassuring smile faltered under the dismay of his visitors. "That may not be possible," Llesho explained. "The weapon is cursed, and it wants me dead."

"It can't be!" Slowly the realization leached the color from his face. Holding out his son's less dangerous weapon, he repeated his exclamation, but this time as an order. "It can't happen. Do what you must to stop it."

Llesho took the spear and weighed the heft of it in his hand. "I won't kill him." It was in his mind to say, "He's just a boy," but he held the words back.

The khan read it in his eyes anyway, and accepted the cost of his son's impetuousness. "There can be no shame in saving the world, even at the cost of a foolish boy's life."

"You can't save the world by killing children." Llesho was very clear on this. He'd been there, seen it before, and had taken the measure of evil on the Long March across these very grasslands. "All you do that way is exchange the tyrant you fight for the one you've become."

"I'm not sure a king can survive such fine sentiments," the khan admitted, "but I would not have your death on Harnish hands."

There was nothing to say to that. Llesho gave a tight nod of the head, as much of a courtly leave-taking as he could manage, and wheeled on the ball of one foot to find the guardsmen of the khan massed between him and the door. Where were his captains? He didn't see any of them in the ger-tent. Master Den was watching, not with the dismay that Llesho expected but as if he'd anticipated this very thing and awaited an outcome long ordained. There would be no help from that quarter. Once again Llesho was reminded of the danger in placing his faith in a trickster god.

"You defy your khan?" he asked of the warriors who surrounded him, and balefully stared through their leader until the man let his shoulders fall and parted a narrow path between them. Neither side offered challenge, by weapon or word, but Llesho felt their unhappy eyes on him until he stepped over the threshold.

Chapter Twenty-six

LLESHO squinted in the light of Great Sun, bright after the dim interior of the khan's ger-tent, but he didn't see the Harnish prince. Nearby, his sturdy little warhorse pawed the beaten grass in the care of Danel, one of Harlol's Wastrels. The khan's taller mount, a roan with a bristly blond mane and elaborately decorated saddle-cloths dripping gold beneath the tall saddle, tugged impatiently at the reins held by two grinning youths. This must seem like a joke to them, Llesho figured. He might agree if so many lives didn't hang on the outcome of the prank.

"Where are my captains?" Llesho grabbed his own reins from the nervous Danel. His one slim hope—to survive without killing Tayyichiut in the process—was looking more remote by the minute. He didn't even know how to play the stupid game, and—

"There, Prince Llesho." Danel gave a Tashek gesture, a tilt of his chin at the playing field. Two hundred riders all Llesho's age or younger made up two long columns shouting taunts and laughing curses at each other across the expanse of churned turf that separated them.

"Captain Kaydu rides to warn the Harnish princeling of his danger," Danel reported, "I don't think your other

captains have considered their actions as thoroughly as
they might."

That was an understatement. Kaydu had found a
mount and galloped toward the contending columns as
fast as her horse would go. Bixei and Harlol ran after
her on foot, gesturing as wildly as madmen at the riders.

"Come out, Prince of Clouds! Prove your mettle
against real warriors!" Tayyichiut seemed to take the
advancing captains as a grand addition to his prank.
Brandishing Llesho's short spear, he laughed at the
strange visitors and set his own horse in motion, escaping
among the assembled riders.

Already the first of the columns had turned and thundered away from their opponents, who jeered at their
flight. Lifting himself into his saddle, Llesho tried to
make sense of the fleeing youths, but a shake at the
bridle under his hands drew his attention from the playing field. Not Master Den, as he'd assumed from his
position, but Mergen. The khan's brother had come up
beside him; worry carved his face, but no blame for
bringing so deadly a threat into the home of the khan.
The man hadn't come out to kill him then, in defense of
his impetuous nephew.

"Note the markers on the field," Mergen instructed
him in quick, clipped sentences, pointing out first one,
then another of the three yellow stakes that had been
pounded into the dusty ground. "The first marks the
starting line. When the fleeing column reaches the second
stake, the pursuit column takes chase. At the third stake,
the fleeing column turns and the pursuit column throws
its short spears at them.

"It's a contest of skill played in pairs. Each rider has
but a single opponent, his teammate, so you needn't concern yourself with anyone but Prince Tayyichiut. The goal
is to find the hand of your partner, who plucks the spear
out of the air before it can overshoot its mark. It's a game,
remember, not war. The teams practice their throws and
catches for months before joining the game in earnest.

You won't have the advantage of long practice to help you, but Tayy is skilled at hitting—or not hitting—his target. He'll aim at your hand, not your heart."

Llesho wouldn't have to defend against a flurry, then. But the spear had its own sense of direction. It would find his heart if he let it.

"It is a mark of humiliation if a player lets his partner's spear overshoot him without making the catch," Mergen gave him a meaningful look, though Llesho wasn't sure what he was supposed to make of that bit of information. "He must dismount and retrieve the spear, taking the team out of the game and suffering the insults of his friends."

Ah. A way out. Llesho got the message. How many times had Bixei dumped him on his backside in hand-to-hand training? He could do humiliation. Easy, if the spear gave him the chance.

"Some foolish youths put their bodies in the way of the spear rather than lose their seat," Mergen cautioned, "I can trust the prince of the Cloud Country not to be foolish?"

Master Den would doubtless have had words to say about Llesho and foolishness if he'd been a part of the conversation. Fortunately, he wasn't. And on this point, Llesho didn't have any doubts.

"I would guess that even a Harnish youth would only try that once," Llesho answered, and casually nudged his coats aside to show the scar where an arrow had embedded itself in his breast. Mergen's suggestion—to miss the catch and trade his pride for the safety of all—made much more sense.

It wouldn't be that easy, of course. Mergen didn't take into consideration the spear's own desire for his death. The khan's brother nodded acceptance of the tacit agreement between them, however, a little pride for a little peace.

"It's a teaching game," Mergen explained, "None who have been blooded in battle play."

Llesho's heart turned over. They really were just boys.

The game trained them for war, but he didn't want to
be the one to put that training into action. "I have seen
an ocean of blood, and will swim in it up to my eyes
again before I am done. But I won't add any more to it
over a joke."

It was a warning of some sort, but a promise as well.
Kaydu would be bound by his promise not to start a war
if the spear killed him. He refused to think about the
ache that pulled at old wounds as he gave himself up to
the possibility of death, nor would he wonder at the pain
quickly suppressed in Mergen's eyes.

Chimbai-Khan had reached his mount and watched
from the saddle while his brother negotiated for the life
of his son. Glimpsing the impassively controlled features,
Llesho felt a surge of rage so overpowering that it nearly
took him from his horse. A Harnishman had killed his
father, his mother, his sister, and he wanted this man to
suffer as he had suffered, to feel the loss of love and
security that he'd lost when just a child. But he wasn't a
child anymore. Hurting the khan would serve no useful
purpose and cause more deaths down a path as dark as
any Llesho had yet ridden. So he gave a quick nod to
seal his unspoken oath and heeled his horse to a gallop
in pursuit of the spear that had been the bane of his life
since the Lady SienMa had put it in his hand.

The open ground fell behind with the drumming of his
horse's hooves. Llesho passed Bixei and Harlol, who had
shifted course and now ran back along the great avenue
toward the cook tent where his soldiers watched the contest, unaware of the danger the Harnish prince had set
in motion. Kaydu had been forced into the line of riders
when the column had turned and couldn't reach him. So
Llesho did the only thing he could. Letting go a high,
ululating battle cry, he flung his steed into the ranks of
the fleeing column, standing high over his stirrups as the
Harnish riders did.

Through the dust and the galloping bodies and the flash of sunlight on the sharp metal blades of upraised spears, Tayyichiut saw him and joined the pursuit, brandishing the short spear high over his head. Kaydu was among the pursuers now, and she pulled out of the column, cutting behind the charging horses and pressing her fine gray steed to bring her close to the prince. She was going to try and bump the boy's horse, Llesho saw; if she could unseat him, she could disarm him, no question.

Catching him was going to be impossible, though. The start peg was there, in front of him; Llesho's column turned to meet the pursuit. Laughing, Tayyichiut raised up in his stirrups, and Llesho braced himself to follow Mergen's advice. Just let the spear fly past and take himself out of the contest. It would teach the Harnish prince a lesson if he had to hunt for the weapon in the grass with the less skilled of the Harnish boys. Give the warriors-in-training a joke to tell about the king of Thebin for the rest of their warring lives. It would be worth it to get them all out of here alive.

But the spear had other plans. He could feel its malevolence reaching for him across the wide playing field. It would kill him, turn the innocent prince into a murderer, and in spite of all his protests to the contrary, would start a battle on this field that would very likely wipe out the royal house of Thebin.

He couldn't let that happen, so Llesho turned with the rest and steadied his knees against the back of his horse. All along the advancing column, young warriors threw to the hand of their carefully schooled opponents, who caught or missed the catch as their skill and familiarity dictated.

As Tayyichiut took aim, however, the short spear seemed to come alive in his hand. Liquid fire ran the length of it like lightning caught in his palm. Something terrible twisted his face into a mask of hate and hunger. Llesho remembered the sick longing for murder that lay behind the snarl and the fiery eyes; he'd felt it himself, had fought it and the spear for control in a way that the young warrior was only just beginning to comprehend. With a terrible scream like the vaults of hell screeching open, Tayyichiut let fly the short spear on its deadly course, straight for Llesho's heart. He knew it, felt the weapon looking for him in the chaos of the game.

Control. It was all about control. "Come to me," Llesho murmured soothingly. "And be still."

The sound of the contest faded from his hearing in a frozen, eternal moment. Then he opened his hand, stretched out his arm, and reached with his soul to take the weapon back as it hissed through the air, seeking his heart.

—And snap, he wrapped his fingers around the shaft and held on tight as the spear pulled him up, out of his saddle and into the tumult of a mock battle gone horribly wrong. Falling, rolling to absorb the shock of the fall on one shoulder, he used all the force of his tumbling momentum to plunge the head of the spear deep into the matted grass and deeper, into the loamy earth beneath. And then there was nothing he could do but flatten himself in the grass with his free hand covering his head while the ground shook and horses reared and threw their riders, running in all directions.

Fire spat from the wounded earth like firecrackers going off. Or like a spoiled and dangerous child in a fit of temper. Llesho was sick and tired of carting around an ill-tempered weapon so set on his death that he could trust it neither at his back nor out of his hands. He'd had enough of the whole stupid curse.

"You're mine." And he staggered to his feet.

"You go where you're aimed." And he set both hands on the shaft.

"You don't get a say." And he drew the blade out of the earth. It gleamed dully, pale sparks fading all along its length.

"And you—"

Prince Tayyichiut had dismounted, whether in the

usual way or thrown from his horse when the earth moved, Llesho couldn't tell. Either way, he was trembling on his knees, pale as the mane on his father's horse. His arms curled around his belly, he tucked his hands up in their crooks as if it were midwinter instead of late summer.

"I *saw* things," he said, with loathing in his voice. "It made me feel—I hated you. I tried to kill you."

Llesho wondered if he'd ever felt that bewildered innocence. Master Jaks would have said so, he figured, and Master Den probably thought he wasn't much better even yet. With a sigh that was part exasperation with Tayyichiut and part surrender to the truth that he wasn't more than a turning of a season or two from where the Harnish prince now sat, he dragged himself to his feet. Some lessons were best learned all the way—

Willing the short spear to spark just a little to make his point, Llesho glowered at the horrified boy. "Don't ever touch another man's weapons without an invitation. You *don't* know what magics he may carry, or what grudges those magics may hold. You're lucky the damned thing didn't kill us both."

"I know, lord prince." Tayyichiut bowed his head, still uncertain of his composure. He was young, though, and more resilient than Llesho could remember being. After a moment more he lifted his head, already recovered sufficiently to let out the reins on his curiosity.

"What manner of weapon is that?"

Llesho considered his answer while he willed the fire of the blade to dim. The last blade to come to stormy life in his hands like that had been drawn from the stores at the governor's palace at Farshore Province, when he'd fought Master Markko in a rage that had overpowered wisdom and fear both. He had to wonder if the hatred lived in the blade or in the lives of the soul that breathed within him.

"It's just a spear," he said at last. "The magic is always in ourselves."

Tayyichiut didn't understand, but that was just as well. He allowed his attention to drift to the circle of people who surrounded them. Kaydu and Bixei and Harlol, each looking guilty for not having stopped either of the princes. Half a dozen Harnish youths as shaken as Tayyichiut. Llesho's brothers, their horror still pressed into the clay of their faces, mostly for what might have happened but some for what Llesho had revealed of himself in the contest. The khan, eyes dark with the knowledge of disaster averted by a hair's breadth, bowed his head in gratitude while his brother Mergen studied Llesho with sharp, fierce curiosity so like his nephew's that for a moment—but such a thought dishonored him and he quickly set it aside before facing the mother of the Harnish prince.

"Thank you for sparing the life of my child." She bowed deeply with all show of submission. Her eyes were cold as agates in a face as still as death and Llesho wondered if she had hoped for a different outcome, and why.

The boy's grandmother said nothing. She alone seemed unsurprised, save the god and healers who stood a little apart, watching with varying degrees of satisfaction in their smiles.

"I told you he'd do," Dognut reminded the company with a smug sniff. Out of a flat pocket that would seem to have had no room for it, he drew a pipe shaped like a sweet potato and played a riff of notes on it. Carina's smile seemed to agree, though Master Den reserved his opinion, waiting, it seemed, for something more to happen. *Sorry to disappoint,* Llesho thought, *but I am all out of tricks today.*

"Well," Bolghai announced, "I think we can begin now. I'll need him for four days."

That bore thought for a variety of reasons. Why had the shaman given up speaking in riddles? But, of course, he hadn't. While his remarks seemed straightforward on the surface, they left only questions in his mind: Begin what? Four days for what?

"We don't have four days to spare," Llesho objected, just as Master Den answered, "Yes," with a slow inclination of his head. He seemed to be thinking hard. Not uncertain of Bolghai, rather he calculated the consequences of their actions like so many points on a line. "But only four. The boy is right. We're running out of time."

Bolghai took his arm to lead him away, but Lluka stopped them with a sneer: "And so the fate of Thebin will be decided?" Lluka snarled, "You trust a trickster and his Harnish madman above your own brothers?"

"Enough," Llesho interrupted before Lluka could say more, cutting off the insult with a sharp gesture. He'd almost forgotten that he held the damned spear in his free hand until his brother's eyes widened in what looked like fear. More than boys were parading their foolishness today. Perhaps he could make use of that fear to make his point. . . .

Slitting his eyes, Llesho willed the short spear to life. Unearthly fire gleamed in sullen menace under his hand. "We need to make new alliances here, not break the ones we already have."

Torn between his fear and his objections, Lluka said nothing. Llesho turned away, letting the arcs of light dim and go out as they flickered the length of the short spear.

"Good," Bolghai approved with a mysterious smile. "Now we find out who you are."

Llesho would have told him that he already knew that, that he had ever since Minister Lleck had appeared to him as a ghost at the bottom of Pearl Bay, but that wasn't what the shaman meant. He knew a little more about what he could do, but he didn't think Bolghai meant that either. Riddles and more riddles. The shaman's smile promised he'd find out soon, however.

The spear dulled to its usual appearance; no sign of its magical properties remained to warn the unwary of its danger. Absently wiping dirt from its flat blade on the skirts of his coat, Llesho followed the shaman off the playing field.

Chapter Twenty-seven

"**W**HERE are we going?" Llesho asked.

"This way," Bolghai answered uninformatively.

The deadly game of jidu had ended as the sun reached its zenith, with no lives lost though Lluka had made it a near thing. Llesho was hungry even before the shaman had taken him by the arm and led him away from the tent city of the khan. He was used to coping with privations during battles, but only Shou, he decided, could equal the Harn for turning diplomacy into survival training.

At least Bolghai had abandoned the annoying habit of speaking only in formulaic riddles. "Clients seek out a shaman for the healing lore," he explained with a shrug, "but they pay for the mystery."

That made a certain amount of sense, but Llesho didn't understand the shaman any better in plain Shannish than he did in riddles. When speaking with Llesho, the shaman included more words of Harnish than the khan or his court had done, which didn't make understanding him any easier. Gradually, however, Llesho began to get a sense of meaning as a rhythm rather than as a logical explanation.

Bolghai had led him around the khan's great palace

of a ger-tent, where the wagons began, ranged in a wide circle around the huge tent city. Long ropes joined the wagons together and served as a tethering place for the beasts that had taken injuries in the chaos of the game. The young Harnish warriors in training picked their way among them, looking for food for their animals and caring for their wounds. The camp was so vast, however, and the wagons so numerous, that the young combatants seemed hardly to trouble the sense of abandonment that ruled beyond the tents.

When they had passed outside the ring of wagons, Llesho saw why the khan had chosen this place for their meeting.

"The Onga," Bolghai said, addressing his comment to the river that flowed nearby. The ground was flat and dry almost to its bank on the side of the camp, but across the river a broken landscape began. A forest of trees slim as wands grew between tumbled boulders and out of the cracks in the rocks themselves.

"How do we get across?" Llesho asked.

"We fly," the shaman answered him, and smiled when Llesho's eyebrows pulled up in disbelief. "In the meantime, we'll walk on this side for a while, and begin your lessons when you are ready.

"Master Den said you only have four days."

"The question you have to ask yourself is, 'What does "four days" mean to a trickster god?'"

"He wouldn't hurt me."

Bolghai cast him a pitying glance. "The sad thing is you actually believe that. You've already been hurt in countless ways, large and small, since you met him."

"That's Markko's fault. If it weren't for Master Den, I'd be dead now, or insane."

The shaman gave him another one of those looks, as if he was missing the obvious, but made no comment. Llesho stumbled on, his mind leaving questions of politics for the concerns of his stomach as day faded into dusk. Han and Chen, the brother moons, chased Great

Sun out of the sky in the nightly ritual that painted red and purple on the horizon, and still they had not stopped to eat or drink. Then suddenly, out of the silence, sullen on Llesho's part, Bolghai spoke up.

"Come inside for some tea, then we can begin."

"Are you reading my mind?" Llesho asked suspiciously.

"Not your mind, no. Your stomach, maybe."

On cue, his stomach growled angrily. No point in denying that he'd eat a whole sheep, on the hoof, given the chance. He could see no tent or other habitation on the increasingly rocky and scrub-infested landscape, however. It made him wonder how sane he actually was, to follow a Harnish madman into the wilderness, until he stumbled over the umbrella roof of a Harnish tent sitting close to the ground. Shaking his head as if despairing of his new pupil, Bolghai circled the tent roof and gave a tug on the rope that lifted the felt covering from the fire hole. Then he disappeared.

"Where—?"

There. As he traced the footsteps of the shaman, Llesho saw the path cutting down into the earth like a burrow. He followed it to a door covered in a tent flap, and went in.

Inside, the fire hole at the center of the roof let in the last light of day, sparkling in a lazy dance of dust motes. The burrow seemed to have the same construction as the great ger-tent of the khan, but was a tiny fraction of its size and sunk into the earth. Felt batting wrapped the lattice of crossed branches that framed the sunken tent and gave some protection against the damp ground. Around the firebox were the skins of small animals sewn together to make soft rugs. Richly furred pelts of stoats hung on the lattice walls between the rattles and drums and an instrument that looked like a fiddle. From the frame of the roof hung bunches of herbs and an assortment of brooms, and on the one narrow chest at the back of the tiny burrow were heaped the skulls of rodents and other small creatures of the plains. Not all the skulls were entirely cleaned of flesh, and the buried tent smelled of their rot. Although he didn't fear the shaman, exactly, the decorations of his house made Llesho shiver. He didn't touch any of them on purpose, but in passing bumped into a broom made of sticks bound to a long polished handle that hung from the roof.

Bolghai noted the small accident with lively interest. "Come, have tea." he said, and swept half the tiny skulls onto the floor to make room on the chest for two cracked cups. From a kettle that sat warming on the banked fire he poured the tea, and then added salt and a tiny pat of butter to each. "Fortify yourself. You have much to learn before you sleep."

"I'm ready to sleep now," Llesho admitted, falling gracelessly to sit by the fire. He didn't like the shaman's smile at all.

"No sleep today, young king, or tomorrow either." Bolghai handed him a cup, and drank from his own. "We have four days to find your spirit and teach it to dance. So drink up—the faster begun, the faster done."

The tea tasted like old underwear. He grimaced but finished as good manners dictated. "My spirit is much happier on a full stomach and a night's sleep," Llesho protested, but his plight brought him no sympathy.

"If you give it comforts and demand nothing in return, your spirit will have no reason to reveal itself. We must call it forth instead with dancing, and command it to reveal itself before we give it food or rest. Are you done?"

Llesho handed him the cup. Given the tea, he was pretty sure he didn't want to share the shaman's supper. The confined burrow was already making him nervous. The damp ached in the scars of his old wounds reminding him of the dangers of consorting with magicians.

"What do I have to do to get out of here?" he asked, meaning more than the buried tent.

Bolghai gave him a little shrug and handed him the

broom he had bumped on entering the burrow. "Cross
the river. Then we'll see."

There were no boats, of course. Llesho could swim
like a sea-dragon, and he could probably hold his breath
long enough to walk across the bottom if he had to.
Against the swiftly flowing current that rippled down the
center of the stream, however, even the skills he had
learned as a pearl diver didn't give him a chance. With
a put-upon sigh, he went outside to sweep the path in
front of the shaman's burrow.

"One thing I'm sure of already," he muttered to himself. "My spirit doesn't live in a hole in the ground."

"What are you doing!" Bolghai followed him outside,
still brushing the crumbs of some hasty supper from his
mustaches.

"I'm sweeping. If you want me to do something else
with a broom, you'll have to be more specific!" Llesho
stopped, leaning on the broom handle, and glared at the
shaman who glared back at him, one hand carrying the
fiddle and the other planted on his hip.

"It's your partner! You were supposed to get to know
each other!"

Bolghai took the broom out of his hands and flipped
it around, so that the twigs were on top, and the handle
pointed at the ground.

This was one madness too many. Llesho dug in his
heels and refused to budge. "I trusted you!" he yelled
in frustration, "I left my brothers and my guards and I
followed you until my feet were ready to fall off. I drank
your tea even though it smelled like you'd been doing
your washing in it, if you ever *do* washing, which I doubt,
since your burrow smells like a slit trench in the rain. I
have tried to be patient and polite until my teeth hurt
from clamping my mouth shut. But I will . . . not . . .
get to know a broom!"

Bolghai blinked at him for a moment, as if absorbing

the complaints of his student, then he held out the broom. "Out here, where the grass is sweet," he instructed, and walked away from the burrow.

"Did you listen to a word I said! I am not going to dance with a broom!"

"ChiChu said that you were stubborn," the shaman noted, which confirmed that he knew more about their party than they'd told him, at least in Llesho's hearing. But the shaman relented a little, enough to give a word of explanation. "Of all the sacred objects in my burrow, only this broom called to your spirit. That means you must be connected to it in some way. How, we will find out. But not until you dance."

"It didn't call me. I bumped into it. A clumsy accident."

"You're not a clumsy boy." Bolghai waited, one eyebrow cocked.

"This is humiliating," Llesho grumbled. The whole day from start to finish had been one embarrassment after another. "Can you at least tell me why you want me to dance at all, let alone with a broom?"

"Many of your companions—your brothers Lluka and Balar, Carina, whose word I trust, ChiChu and Bright Morning—believe you to be the Prince of Dreams. So far, however, your dreams come and go as they choose. You don't control them; they control you."

The Dinha had said much the same, but the one thing he had learned good and solid during this quest was never to trust a simple answer. "What does that mean?"

"We don't know yet. There have been prophecies known to the shaman of the grasslands and the spirit guides of many distant lands and neighbors. But they say even less than prophecies usually do." Bolghai bared his teeth in a gesture that owed more to the warning snarl of the stoat than to a human smile. "All we know for certain is that the Prince of Dreams will stand between heaven and earth and the Great Dark. And the Great Dark is coming soon."

Llesho didn't like the sound of that. It occurred to him, as it doubtless was meant to do, that this Great Dark sounded a lot like the absence of a future that his brothers described as the loss of the powers granted them by the goddess.

"Lluka and Balar say their gifts have deserted them."

"Or maybe they haven't," Bolghai agreed.

If Master Den thought that learning to dance with a broom could somehow hold back the end of the world, he would have to try. But not before he made a last effort at understanding what he was at the center of.

"So, if I dance with the broom, it will call forth my spirit, which will learn to fly. In my dreams?"

Bolghai nodded.

"This is all to teach me to control my dreams, so that I can hold back the Great Dark and keep the end of the world from happening."

"More or less. You won't have to save the world alone." Bolghai half suppressed a smile, and Llesho had to admit the idea sounded absurd to him as well. "The dream readers of Ahkenbad would have taught you how to dream travel at rest, but their methods are too passive for a young man on a quest to save the world. For the battle ahead, you will need to control your travels while awake."

Llesho had enough trouble with dreams while he was sleeping. He didn't want them to infest his waking world as well. If he learned to control them, maybe that wouldn't happen. It struck him that coincidence was the comfort of the mindless, however, when he asked, "How would I have learned all this if Master Markko had gone in a different direction and we hadn't followed him into the grasslands?"

"You carry the answer to your riddle in your own party. There was never a doubt of the magician's direction."

Bixei. He'd noticed the first time he'd seen them to-

gether—not father and son, maybe not even clan relations. If Bixei was Harnish, though, so was Markko.

"Goddess," Llesho breathed. "He's come home to
lead the assault on heaven." It had been bad enough
when he'd thought all Master Markko wanted was the
Shan Empire. And he was in deep trouble if he could
say that with an "only" in front of it.

"Seems likely," Bolghai agreed. "But first he must
take the grasslands. Shall we dance?"

Chimbai-Khan must have known Master Markko's intentions all along, and would have fought him with or
without Llesho's tiny band. He'd been prepared to lose
his son for the shaman's prophecies and, as much as Master Den, he'd been responsible for sending him out to
learn what Bolghai had to teach him. When he added it
all up, Llesho didn't see that he had much choice. He
took the broom.

"What do I have to do?"

"Just dance."

The shaman started to play on his fiddle, choosing an
old folk tune from Llesho's childhood in Kungol. On the
feast day of the goddess, his father and his mother had
led a thousand dancers in the wide public square that
lay between the Palace of the Sun and the Temple of the
Moon. The king and queen had worn wide pantaloons in
the peasant style, but of a cloth that shimmered when
they moved, with coats narrow to the waist and split
from ankle to hip on both sides. His mother had worn
ribbons fluttering from her formal headdress and on her
shoulders, and his father had carried a three-tiered umbrella with which to shade his partner when they came
together in the dance.

Though he hadn't danced since the raiders had come,
Llesho saw the steps from that long ago festival in his
mind, and he followed them—step, twirl, half turn, step,
step—over the sweet grass. The broom came to his hand
as a partner, and he bowed and swept it along with him

through the night, imagining the twigs were hair, and the handle a slender waist.

Bolghai changed the tune, and he danced faster, though weariness dragged at him. His feet ached like two huge bruises at the end of his legs, which knotted up with cramps in the calf muscles and his thighs. His breath grew short and his mind grew distant, but still he danced. Looking toward the sound of the music, he saw that Bolghai danced as he played, leaping, and darting here and there with the quick movements of the stoat at play. Llesho struggled to keep pace, but the dance, which fit the shaman as hand comes to hand, so entangled him that Llesho wondered how he managed to trip himself so frequently with just two legs.

"Not a small creature, then," Bolghai muttered, and changed the tune to one more stately, like a camel or a horse.

Llesho moved, experimenting with the rhythm, his feet leaving bloody prints behind him as he picked carefully over the ground he had broken with his dancing through the night. In spite of the exhaustion that wept in his bones for rest, Llesho's heart beat more rapidly with anticipation, as if it waited only for the magic of the perfect song to take flight. And then the tune shifted again, and the world seemed to vanish, leaving him alone in a place of such profound stillness that he would have cried out for the peace of it. The pain was gone: he felt lighter, springier, as if mind as well as muscle had broken free of the restraints that living placed on them. And in that painless place, he leaped and curvetted, tossing his head against the unaccustomed weight at his brow.

Shocked, Llesho froze and sniffed cautiously at the night. The music was suddenly full of tones he hadn't heard before. He lost the sense of it, couldn't make out the tune or the rhythm with the distraction of air grown rich with strange new smells pungent with the tang of hidden memories. Great Moon seemed to cast a brighter light about her of a sudden, while all the things awash in her glow had grown soft and vague in their outlines. When he opened his mouth to call Bolghai, only the high call of an animal escaped his throat.

"Easy, child."

Bolghai stopped his playing and approached with cautious steps, but the movement startled Llesho. He ran for the river and freedom on the other side.

Up, up, he flew. The river was beneath him, but he did not fall, sailing across on the bounding leap of four strong legs that seemed to have discovered the skill of running on air. When he landed, he dashed away into the forest. Branches hit him as he passed and he changed his course as they struck him, plunging deeper into the wood, until he had no sense of where he was or where he was going, except away from a threat that . . . was no threat at all, but the shaman.

Somehow, it had worked. As the false dawn filtered through the trees, Llesho realized that he had left his humanity on the far shore of the river and become a creature of the forest. Its king, the roebuck. He stood, his head held high under the many-pointed antlers he now sported, and waited for the shaman to find him.

It didn't take long. A rustle in the carpet of fallen leaves warned him of the approaching stoat, and Bolghai was there, shaking the water off his thick fur with a series of huffing sneezes. He blinked his eyes and his outline grew hazy and expanded until he stood in front of Llesho in his man-shape again. His clothes, with their totems of his animal spirit hanging from his neck, were damp from his swim across the river in stoat-form, but he showed no other signs of his transformation.

The clothes were a good sign. If he could figure out how to change back to himself the way Bolghai had, Llesho figured he wouldn't do it naked, which would have just about·capped the most humiliating week of his life. Only, he couldn't do it.

"Don't panic," Bolghai soothed.

Too late. Llesho shied away when the shaman reached

to touch his shoulder. He waited, trembling, just out of
the shaman's reach and ready to flee. Animal sense, he
fought to control it.

"Think of something you keep on you all the time, that
you can use to anchor yourself when you spirit travel."

His Thebin knife—but he had no waist to hang it from.
The pearls, three in a pouch that hung by a cord around
his neck, and a fourth, Pig, who hung from a silver chain.
Weight settled around his long and slender neck, and he
skittered, the animal part of him trying to escape it while
the human part tried to wrap a hand he didn't have
around the heavy pearls.

And then he did have a hand. His neck shortened and
his head felt lighter as the antlers faded. Suddenly his
balance was all wrong and Llesho tumbled forward into
the leaves that had massed among the trees where he
had sheltered as the roebuck.

"Very good." Bolghai grinned down at him. "Now we
can begin."

"With a nap?" he asked hopefully. False dawn tinted
the sky with gray shadows. Llesho was so tired that he
shook with wave after wave of fine tremors—he hadn't
even made it to his feet yet.

"There will be plenty of time for sleep when you've
learned to control your dream travel."

Bolghai offered him a hand up. He took it, and
brushed the leaves off his clothes with distaste. From
head to toe he wore the dirt of the night of mad dancing
and the day's game of jidu.

"Do I have time to wash my face in the river?"

"And defile the Onga?" The shaman sniffed with distaste. "If you learn your lessons well, I'll let you draw a
cup from the river to use as you please," he said.

Llesho had the feeling that he'd have a choice of washing in it or drinking it, but he wouldn't get water for
both. He sighed, thinking back with fondness to the one
thing that Pearl Bay had offered in abundance: water.

But Bolghai's words reminded him that they were now on the wrong side of the Onga.

"How do we get back across the river?" he asked.

Bolghai gave a little shrug, as if to say it was a minor thing. "When you control your dream travels, you may go anywhere, and return anywhere. If you want to be on the other side of the river, you will just go."

Exhaustion was making him giddy and almost as light as the air. In that state, the shaman almost made sense.

"Then I suppose we should begin," he agreed with a careless wave of a hand that didn't feel a part of him. He followed the arm it was on back to his shoulder to be sure it was his own.

"Good boy." Bolghai had left the fiddle on the other side of the Onga, but he shifted the collar of stoat pelts at his throat to reveal a loose wooden ring, which he lifted over his head. Set in carved niches at regular intervals around the ring were little cymbals, and hanging from the front were little bells. When he shook it, a sound like temple bells rang out in the forest.

"If you want to travel in the material world, and you have no camel, what do you do?"

Riddles again. This one was simple enough though. "I walk."

Bolghai began to walk in a tight circle. "And if you want to arrive at your destination more swiftly?"

"I run."

Bolghai nodded and beat the rim of the wooden ring against his palm in a rhythmic tempo. "How soon do you want to reach your dream goal?"

"Now. But it's almost daylight—"

"Run, then, before Great Sun rises." Bolghai laughed. He kept to the path of his tight circle, but now he was running faster, pumping his arms in the air so that his wooden ring jingled with the beat of his step.

Llesho figured that was a riddle, too, and meant that he could travel not only across distance, but in time as well. He followed the shaman's lead. Though he had no instrument to keep his time, he found that the pearls at his throat beat the rhythm against his breast until it absorbed his mind and his feet and his arms, which he raised and lowered in the way of the shaman. As he ran, he considered where he wanted to go, and what he wanted to see, and how he was going to find it. Adar, of course, and Hmishi and Lling, but he shied away from there. Better to practice with a safer journey first, make sure he could find his way back before jumping into the fire.

When he thought of safety, Shokar's face rose up in his mind to meet him. Llesho followed his brother back to his dreams in the tent city of the khan.

Shokar was leaning over a teakettle hung from an iron rod over a fire in a cleanly dressed stone fireplace that Llesho had never seen before. He was in a room with a low ceiling crossed by round logs for beams overhead and a long plank table with benches on either side at the center. Llesho was dimly conscious of shelves on the wall, though he couldn't see them clearly in the dream. Mostly what filled his mind was the rocking chair sitting by the hearth, and the woman who watched his brother with wide liquid eyes as she nursed the baby on her lap. Neither man nor woman seemed aware of Llesho's presence, though the child tracked his every move as if she saw what her parents did not.

"I know you have to go," the woman said when Shokar faced her with his arguments. Llesho could see in her eyes the desire to reach out and hold her husband, to bind him tight to hearth and farm. She dropped her gaze to the nursing child, however, to hide her feelings away. "They are your brothers, and if you stayed here safe with us and they died, you would never forgive me. What would we have together then?"

"I wouldn't," Shokar protested. Llesho saw him reach a hand to her, but the woman kept her attention focused on the child until he closed an empty fist around the comfort he had meant by offering it.

"Not on purpose, no," she agreed, "but it would eat at your mind and your soul until there was nothing left of them for me." She did look at her husband then, fiercely, as if she were fighting a battle for his soul right there in her peaceful farmhouse. "I want better than that, for me and for my children. Your children. So deliver your soldiers and rescue your brothers. Just don't you forget us. Come back when it's safe again. And bring this prince, your brother, home for a visit when he's done with his wars and visions."

Shokar set his hands on either arm of her chair to still her rocking. "I will." He leaned down to drop a kiss on the child's forehead, then took the lips of his wife with more passion than Llesho wanted to know about in his brother. He turned away, guilty to have invaded the privacy of the dream; he'd known Shokar had a family. Why hadn't he considered what his brother would be leaving behind when he dragged him halfway accross the known world? Before he had more than a second for regret the door opened behind him. Three boys and a girl tumbled into the room.

"Who's the guy in the corner?" the oldest asked with a casual flick of a glance in Llesho's direction. The boy looked enough like Llesho's lost mother to blur his eyes with a mist of tears.

Shokar looked through him. "Han and Chen, fallen from the sky?" he asked, taking the boy's question for a joke.

"No!" the little girl giggled and hid her face in her skirts. "The man!"

"Llesho? How did you get here? I thought you were with Shou?" Shokar blinked, shaking his head to clear it of the vision of his brother. "No. Shou's on his way back to Durnhag. What am I doing here?"

"It's a dream," Llesho muttered, torn by the devastation that crossed his brother's face.

"No—"

And Llesho was gone, pulled back across the river and dumped on his backside at the feet of the Harnish shaman.

"I can't believe what I've done," he said, and buried his head in his hands.

"And what is that?" Bolghai quized him.

"I've torn my brother out of his home, left his farm with no one to tend it, his children with no father to teach them, and his wife with no husband to protect her against the coming war. And then I invaded his dreams and exposed the comfort he took from his sleep." As an answer, he thought it was one of his better ones. Concise and complete. So he didn't understand why Bolghai was snorting at him like a horse with a fly up its nose.

"Okay, sneeze it out before you give yourself a fit," Llesho insisted. "What did I say wrong this time?"

"Just the usual. Taking the blame for all the ills of the world, and all the decisions made around you. In all the ages men have gone to war for their own reasons—honor or glory or wealth or the right of crossing another's pasturage. To defend loved ones or to punish enemies. They didn't need Llesho the boy king to make their decisions for them, and neither did your brother."

"He wouldn't be here if it weren't for me."

"If it weren't for you, Shou would still be more a general than an emperor, and the goddess of war would still have taken him as her favorite. What do you think that would have meant to a brother who tilled the land in the empire of such a match? Ultimately, soldiers will fight because it's all they know. And emperors will bring their subjects into battle whether they wish it or not, because that is the way of warrior kings. Are you such a king, Llesho, Prince of Dreams?"

"I never wanted to be," Llesho shrugged, denying both the charge and his answer. "It seems that's what I'm becoming, regardless of my own wishes."

"Well, you learned something." Bolghai combed a twig

out of his hair and brushed off the bits of leaves he'd got on his clothes while he waited for Llesho to return from Shokar's dream. Great Sun hadn't moved very far across the sky, however. Llesho figured it wasn't much past breakfast. Which reminded him of his empty stomach. As if it heard his thoughts, his gut roared a loud and angry growl.

"Enough of that," Bolghai chided him. "Four times sets the lesson. You have more dreams to visit before you feed the beast in the belly. And this time, perhaps, we can get farther than our own longed-for sleeping tent? We still need to cross the river."

While among the dream readers of Ahkenbad, he'd dream traveled in his sleep and woken far from where he'd gone to bed. Llesho figured that, if he could move his body through the dream world while he slept, it ought to be easier when he was awake. But the shaman wanted more than a simple crossing of the river, and Llesho knew who he had to see. Taking a deep breath to steady himself, he fixed the Emperor Shou in his mind and started running, faster and faster in his demented circle.

Llesho's throat lengthened and roughened with a shaggy red pelt. Antlers sprouted from his head and his arms stretched into the legs of the roebuck. Delicate hooves touched ground and leaped, carried him out of his circle in an explosion of animal speed. The forest disappeared.

Chapter Twenty-eight

SUDDENLY, Llesho was high above Durnhag, coming down hard on the roof of the governor's palace. Roebuck hooves hit rounded terra cotta tiles and turned into hands and feet, tumbling him before he could catch his balance in either form. At his breast, the pearl that hung from the silver chain had grown limbs and distracted him with pinprick stabs of its elbows. They landed in a heap of boy king and Jinn covered in bits of broken roof tiles. Pig regained his footing first, brushing bits of tile from his tunic.

"Are you getting up from there, or do you plan to ask the emperor to attend you on the roof?"

"He's here, then?"

"In his bedchamber, but I'd have myself announced before barging in if I were you."

"Is he any improved?" The dream magic that brought them to Durnhag had deserted him now. Llesho wandered over the rooftops of the governor's palace looking for a way in before the soldiers who were supposed to keep watch started lobbing arrows at him.

"You will have to ask the Lady SienMa," Pig answered primly.

"The mortal goddess is in Durnhag?"

"In Shou's bedroom, to be exact." The Jinn gave Llesho a meaningful look. "Surprising them would *not* be a good idea."

"Oh." Slowly wrapping his mind around this new information, Llesho worked his way to the only conclusion that also explained Pig's nudge and wink. Llesho shuddered at the thought. His dream of the cobra and the turtle had already told him something of that, however, and Bixei had known before he did. Still, dreams were one thing and bedrooms something else entirely. Or so he'd thought. "They're—when did that happen?"

"Certainly not during the lady's marriage to the governor of Farshore," Pig answered slowly, as if mulling over the evidence before he spoke. Theatrics. The Jinn had probably been snooping on the emperor's business since before he'd turned himself into a pearl and rolled out of heaven. "In the imperial city, I think, they found they had much in common."

They. The roofline of the governor's palace had many breaks for incomplete stories. As Llesho climbed from one lower level to a higher by means of a low dormer eaves, he considered the intelligence Pig had offered. The mortal goddess of war and an emperor who fought as a general in his own battles.

The Lady SienMa had been good to Llesho. She'd plucked him out of Lord Yueh's clutches in the arena at Farshore and taught him how to shoot a bow. When Markko had attacked the governor's compound, she had helped him to escape. In the midst of their flight, she had returned to him the precious artifacts of his family: the jade wedding bowl and one of the Great Goddess' lost pearls; and, less welcome, the spear that wanted to kill him. She even risked her own fleeing party to lead their attackers astray, giving him time to reach safety.

Her ladyship had saved his life on numerous occasions, but she was cool and remote and dangerous. And older than Shou's many times removed grandfathers, whose ashes had long since taken their place in the temple of state that adjoined the imperial palace. Bixei had spoken of her ladyship's feelings, but her presence in the emperor's bedroom indicated that Shou felt some attraction for her as well. Shou *couldn't* be that foolhardy—the very thought of it clenched the muscles of Llesho's guts.

"Has she cast a spell on him?" Llesho asked. It seemed the only logical explanation.

Pig barked a laughing snort. "Ho, boy! What makes you think the lady needs a spell? Better to ask what spell our Shou has cast on the mortal goddess."

Bixei had spoken of her ladyship's feelings, so he tried to reverse his thinking. Women were attracted to kings, he'd heard, though it hadn't ever worked for him. Maybe his love of the thing she served drew her to the emperor. Shou could have—probably should have—stayed at home in his palace tending to the peaceful ordering of the many provinces under his hand. Instead, he sneaked out the back way to fight battles hand-to-hand with Gansau Wastrels and meet with spies in low and dangerous places. As a general, he planned well to save as many of his soldiers' lives as he could. Llesho figured he should have noticed the man's attraction to the dangers of war before this. It scared him to the soles of his shoes to realize it now.

"Be careful!" Pig shouted as Llesho slipped on a loose tile.

"Whoa!" He slid, falling, and grabbed at a red clay tile that came off in his hand. He let it go, flinched when he heard it crash to the courtyard far below, but gave it little thought as he reached for a more secure handhold.

"Halt!" a voice below shouted, quickly followed by the whiz of an arrow passing near enough to rasp across the top of Llesho's ear.

"Don't shoot! I'm a friend!" he cried out, and realized that his grip was slipping— "Help!"

"Ouch." Thank the goddess, the face of the palace was cut everywhere with balconies. Llesho finished his fall onto one of them and rolled to his knees sucking on a cut that bled freely on his thumb. Tall doors decorated with trailing vines of colored glass stood open. Habiba, just inside of them, watched Llesho with his eyebrows raised nearly to his hair.

"What are you doing in Durnhag? And how did you get on the roof?"

"Would you believe I'm not really here?" Limp as a banner on a windless morning, he dragged himself to his feet.

"I'd believe a great deal about you, child." Habiba looked him over like he was a lame camel at a thieves' sale, but he moved out of the way to invite Llesho into the workroom. "You'd better get in here before one of the local guards finds you out there and hauls you off to a dungeon or something. That seems to have been a favorite vice of the former governor, and I don't think we've quite broken his minions of the habit."

When Llesho entered the room, however, the magician examined him with narrow- eyed concentration. "Who have you been listening to now?"

"His name is Bolghai. Lluka hates him."

"He would." Habiba closed the doors. "I would have suggested him myself, but I doubted your ability to put aside your natural distaste for the Harnish people."

Inside, the room was warm and well lit, the walls turned a soft buttery yellow in the light from the many candles in holders at the corners. An oil lantern hanging from the ceiling lit a silver bowl filled with water on his workbench, and sweet herbs perfumed the air on which music drifted softly from somewhere nearby. Llesho found a cushioned sofa and dropped onto it, rubbing his eyes wearily. "They're not that bad. At least, not Chimbai's people. They've got their own trouble with the raiders from the South, so it looks like we may have an ally there."

"And what do you think of Bolghai the shaman?"

"He's very strange, and so are his lessons. I'm dreaming all of this, you know. Awake, or so he tells me, and

I must be, since I'm so tired I could drop where I stand—
or, well, sit. You can't ache for sleep while you're sleeping, can you?"

"You're dream-walking," Habiba confirmed. "Is this
your first trip?"

"Second, really, if you don't count the sleeping ones.
Bolghai says the first one doesn't count, though, since I
never left the khan's city and Shokar was still asleep
when I visited his dream. Pig was with me, but he seems
to have wandered off. That or he's still on the roof somewhere. Is the emperor about?"

"I'll take you to him." Habiba covered the silver bowl
with white silk cloth. Llesho wasn't sure what it symbol-
ized, since he'd never figured out where Habiba came
from, but he knew what a bowl and water meant in a
magician's workroom at— How had it come to be night
here, when he'd taken this journey at dawn?

"Dream-walking doesn't always follow the sun in normal hours. Time and distance seem tangled somehow.
The farther the travel, the more unrooted in time you
can become."

Habiba led him into a hallway as broad as an avenue
and once again answered his question without Llesho
having to ask it. That was probably the most unnerving
thing about consorting with magicians. He was about to
ask *when* he was, since he knew where, but Habiba had
a sort-of answer to that as well:

"We could be having this conversation in your future,
or in your past, but it is just the evening after the day
before to me," he said, which was about what Llesho'd
expected.

They had come to a double door of figured panels
worked in gilt, and Habiba rapped sharply on a drum
worked into the center of one panel. Llesho heard soft
voices, and someone stirring in the room.

The Lady SienMa opened the door. She wore a rich
robe of white satin tied with a gold belt. Her hair had
come down, and it flowed over her shoulders like a velvet

sea. Llesho tried not to wonder what, if anything, she wore beneath the robe, or what had left her hair in such disarray. Looking down didn't help, because then he noticed that on her feet she wore just a pair of embroidered slippers suitable for a lady's bedroom.

"He's here," the lady said, and stood aside.

Llesho hesitated, blushing to the roots of his hair, but the lady gestured with her open palm.

"Come in. He will want to see you." The way she said that, as if the emperor didn't know who was at his own bedroom door, drew him through it. He wondered if that was a good idea when she closed the door behind him with Habiba still on the outside.

The room was very large, rich with hangings and furnishings of gilt and lacquer work, though not as sumptuous as the royal palace in the Imperial City of Shan. The empty bed stood on a raised platform with its curtains drawn back to reveal disheveled covers. Clothed in the informal breeches and coat he wore indoors, Shou stood at the window with his back to the door. Llesho tugged the reins of his runaway imagination, but the blush stained his face with heat anyway.

"Is this your dream, or mine?" Shou asked, and only then turned away from his reflection in the glass.

"Mine, I think," Llesho answered. "Bolghai is teaching me to travel in waking dreams."

"A Harnish name. You have strange teachers, Prince Llesho."

He'd grown so accustomed to the magicians around him knowing his business before he did himself that it surprised him when Shou didn't recognize the name. It made him less like a sheep—or a slave—run through a counting shoot by omniscient masters.

"No stranger than your own," he answered, with a pointed look at Lady SienMa. "Was I wrong to be worried about you, or more right than I knew?"

Shou passed off the question with a raised shoulder, but Llesho didn't let it slide. "What happened with Tsu-tan? I'm not just prying. We are going after Adar and Hmishi and Lling, and I have to know what has been done to them."

"Put Hmishi out of your mind. He is dead already and waits only for his body to realize that fact and cease pumping blood to his heart."

"I won't accept that."

"Then don't. What you do or do not choose to believe will make not one bit of difference in the outcome." Shou crossed the room so quickly, and with such purpose that Llesho took a step back, expecting an attack. But the emperor merely brushed his elbow on his way to a low table where he picked up a bottle and poured a foggy liquid into a bowl.

"He's given Hmishi over to the torments of his followers, but fears his master if he harms a more valuable prisoner," Shou said after drinking the contents of the bowl. "Adar should still be safe from physical hurt, at least, until Tsu-tan reaches Markko's camp in the South. What Markko will do to him then I cannot say, but the witch-finder spoke much of burnings at the stake."

Llesho shuddered. He had time yet to rescue Adar. In his dreams he heard Hmishi's cries of pain, but he refused to believe that his friend couldn't be healed with time and the skills of the healer-prince. He wasn't as certain about Shou, who refused to acknowledge his own hurts.

"And you? What did the witch-finder do to you?"

"A simple beating, to put me in my place." Shou waved a hand to dismiss his tale as if to say the blows had meant nothing. But he reached again for the drink.

With a hand on the stone bottle, Llesho stopped him from pouring himself another bowl of the liquor. "Master Markko, then. From afar?"

Lady SienMa watched with distant interest as the emperor shook his head, no. She neither encouraged him nor gave any sign of disapproval, so Llesho continued his struggle for the emperor's story.

"He murdered the dream readers of Ahkenbad in their dreams," he reminded Shou, "and has visited my own dreams with threats of death as well. I know some of what he can do, but I don't have enough information yet to see the shape of his spirit."

Understanding clicked in Shou's head. Each story added to the picture, not only of Markko's powers, but also of his limitations.

"He raised my dead," he said. "In my dreams, he brought their torn and bleeding bodies rotting from their graves and pecked by birds to curse me for their suffering. Vast wastelands filled with the moldering corpses of soldiers killed in battle. Villages emptied by diseases that grow in the fields of unburied dead. Grandfathers starved to death after the armies had eaten all the villagers had grown for the winter, so that even the worms could find no food on their bones. Children and infants and old women and their strong young sons, all dead so that generals and emperors might trade a few li of ground. Each came to me and showed me deadly wounds and scurvied bones and flyblown sores, and cursed my part in their tortured dying."

"It's a trick," Llesho started to say, but Lady SienMa stopped him with a little shake of her head. Her wide, unfeeling gaze never left the emperor, however, and Llesho shuddered, praying that she never looked on him with such predatory interest. If this was love, he wanted no part of the emotion.

"If it hurts so much, why haven't you gone home? Why don't you just stop?"

"Because I love her." Shou whispered the confession that meant not just the Lady SienMa but the act of war itself, the struggle and the test of arms and the plotting of strategy against a worthy foe.

The lady went to him, a smile on her blood-red lips. He took her hands in his and she raised them to her face, put kisses on each fingertip and rested a cheek white as pear blossoms on their clasped hands.

"One good thing has come of this." Shou dropped a kiss on the bowed head of his lover, the mortal goddess of war. "My anguish serves as a warning to the khans along our borders, who now must fear the magician will attack them as well. It seems that, like yourself, we make allies where we once looked for enemies."

"And what of the governor of Guynm Province?"

Shou gave him a terrible smile, full of sadness and endurance and satisfaction. "He has joined my importunate dead."

"Oh."

Shou rested his cheek over the kiss he had placed on the Lady SienMa's head. When the lady freed her hands to raise his face to her again and run her fingers through his hair, Llesho slowly backed away, not wanting to see any more.

"I guess I'll be in touch," he stammered, at a loss for words.

Shou nodded, not really paying attention to him anymore. "I have moved my court here to Durnhag, to be closer to the fighting."

The emperor put his his arms around her ladyship and Llesho decided that was definitely more than he wanted to know. Remembering Bolghai's lessons, he began to run in a tight circle on the thick carpet. Thankfully, the emperor's temporary quarters vanished just as Shou lifted the goddess from her tiny feet.

Llesho closed his eyes tight, but that didn't stop the sensation that he was falling from a great height.

"Ohhhh," he groaned as the bottom dropped out of his stomach. He knew this feeling, like Lord Chin-shi's fishing boats on a stormy sea, and had even grown used to it during his years in Pearl Bay. He'd lost the knack of it, though, and prayed only for it to end quickly, before his stomach turned itself inside out ridding itself of a breakfast he didn't have.

Then the bright light of full day was beating against his eyelids. He was back in the waking world again, his surroundings unyielding, as he rediscovered when his ankle turned on an outcropping of rock.

"Ouch!" He fell on his backside, grabbing his booted ankle and squinting against the light. Well. He was on the right side of the river, at least. There was the shaman's burrow, and Bolghai himself in human form, which reassured him that he'd landed in the right time and reality.

"Did you have a good trip?" Bolghai stared down into his face with a sly grin.

Llesho wasn't sure if he meant the dream-walk to Durnhag or the twisted ankle. He grimaced his displeasure with the question and struggled to get his legs under him.

"How is Durnhag?"

"Dark."

Bolghai gave him a reassuring pat. "We'll work on the 'when' of dream-walking later. For now it's remarkable that you went where you chose, when you chose to do it, after only a day and a half of lessons."

So he'd been gone only a matter of hours by the reckoning of the waking world. Llesho accepted that with relief. He had only four days, after all, and he had places to go and time to harness in his dreams. In the meantime, and in case the next exercise didn't work out as well, he made a report.

"If something should happen and I don't get back, tell Kaydu that the emperor has negotiated a truce with Tinglut-Khan on his eastern border. Together, they make plans for war against Master Markko in the South."

"And the governor of Guynm Province?"

"Dead," Llesho answered

"So I should think."

Llesho nodded his agreement. Bolghai didn't need telling; he'd already figured that the governor must have been involved in the plot that had made Shou a prisoner of Markko's lieutenant, Tsu-tan.

"Chimbai will need to know this," the shaman continued with his musing. "There is no love between our khan
and the East."

"Nobody says he has to marry Tinglut's daughter, but
Chimbai will doubtless need all the human allies he can
muster when the magician moves against the grasslands,
which Shou believes he must."

"That's the problem, though," Bolghai answered with
a snort. "Chimbai *has* married a daughter of the Eastern
Khan. The lady has proved . . . of questionable value as
a wife."

Llesho remembered Lady Chaiujin's agate stare and
shivered his agreement. The shaman's explanation made
sense of the diplomat's war between the husband and
wife that he'd felt in the ger-tent of the khan, but there
was more at stake than an unhappy marriage.

"Markko is getting stronger. He couldn't kill in dreams
before. I know. He tried." That was a memory he didn't
want to revisit; he'd thought he was dying, and more
than once, but Markko hadn't carried through.

"He's Harnish, and from the South by blood if not
upbringing," Bolghai reminded him as if this made a difference in his powers. When Llesho showed no sign of
understanding his point, the shaman explained. "Magic
comes from many places, but always it grows strongest
where our roots grow deepest. Your abilities grow
stronger through training and exercise, but also because,
as you near the source of your power, it flows through
you with greater force and vigor. The same holds true
for the magician. I would be surprised if he meant to
murder the dream readers of Ahkenbad. He knows the
legends, and would not want to call on himself the wrath
of the Dun Dragon. But he is trying to control too many
distant fronts, and he cannot have learned to harness the
force of home soil in his magic yet."

"They're still dead."

Llesho didn't need the reminder. It ended the conversation about his dream journey to the emperor, however.

Discretion demanded that he remain silent about Shou's relationship with the Lady SienMa. The mortal goddess of war required more than romantic attention from her suitors. He needed to think about that more, sort out what was private and what was military intelligence vital to their struggle.

Being a god himself, Master Den would know what this new aspect of Shou's devotion to her ladyship would mean in the coming battle. He would understand the debts and allegiances between gods and the humans who received their attentions. Llesho might even learn something about Shou's relationship with the trickster god, and by the emperor's example, what he might one day be required to pay for the help he accepted from the gods in his quest. But how much did he have the right to tell the trickster god? He wasn't going to talk about any of it with the shaman.

As if he heard Llesho think his name, Bolghai gave his arm a shake. "Ready to go again?"

"Again?" But he already knew where he wanted to go.

"Four times to set the lesson," Bolghai asserted, "two more to go." He began to run. With a groan, Llesho followed, loping painfully on his sore ankle and blistered feet. Gradually, his forequarters lengthened, his scalp itched, erupted in horny antlers covered in a soft furze. With one bounding leap, and another, he landed in a camp of round black tents. At his shoulder rose the largest of the tents, and on either side half a hundred formed a ragged circle several tents deep. At their heart, a central commons had been eaten down to dust by the animals that wandered the encampment. Harnish raiders on their mounts laughed and joked as aimlessly as their beasts.

"Come in, witch." Tsu-tan, the witch-finder of Pearl Island and Master Markko's lieutenant, stood beside the largest tent. Hidden in the shadow of late afternoon, pressed dark against the black felt, he cocked an arrow in the bow he pulled.

Llesho, in the shape of the roebuck, quivered in all his muscles, but otherwise remained completely still. Behind the witch-finder, moving stealthily and with murder in her eyes, Lling crept nearer. She wore the rough pants and tunic of a slave and a smudge of grime crossed the bridge of her nose. In her hand she held a knife poised to strike.

"Come, boy. You remember what it is to be human. I won't hurt you."

"You can't hurt me," Llesho realized, "because I'm not really here."

"You're here, all right." Tsu-tan let the arrow fly and it brushed past on a breeze but didn't touch him. "The questions is, *when* are you?"

As if in answer to that mysterious statement, Llesho stepped painfully into his human form. Startled, Lling paused, her brows disappearing beneath the tumbled hair that fell over her forehead. The beginning of recognition fought its way through layers of fog that clouded her focus. She tilted her head, as if she could see more clearly out of the corners of her eyes, but came no closer.

"It's all right, girl, go on about your work. He's not going to hurt you." Tsu-tan didn't turn to look at her, but he seemed aware of every movement at his back. Lling said nothing, but slowly lowered her knife and backed away.

"Since my master took her mind she's become a fine laundress. He bids me leave her the knife to defend her virtue—for himself, I venture—not that she needs it. The knife, I mean, though virtue, too, seems a waste in a laundress. But no one would touch her even if she walked the camp naked with a price in cash around her neck. She's mad, you see. And no one wants to catch madness. It's the ultimate social disease."

Tsu-tan turned and entered the black tent then, so he did not see the look of hatred and low cunning that crossed Lling's face. With a last sly glance, she sheathed her knife and aimlessly drifted away. Llesho watched her go, wondering how much of her apparent mindlessness she owed to Master Markko and how much to her own talented spycraft. When she passed out of sight around a neighboring tent, he braced himself for what he would see, and followed Tsu-tan.

The witch-finder had gone to a small table on the far side of the firebox at the center of the tent and watched the reunion with mocking attentiveness. "I've brought you a visitor," he announced to the figure bent over a sickbed near the door of the tent, where guests of low station must wait.

"You had nothing to do with my coming here," Llesho corrected him. "I've come to tally up the charges against you, for when we meet in battle."

At Ahkenbad his dreams had been filled with the pain of his companions, so he knew to expect no good outcome of this dream-journey. When he saw his brother leaning over a pallet near the door of the tent, however, Llesho's spirits rose in spite of good sense. His brother, at least, appeared unhurt.

"Goddess, what are you doing here!" Adar greeted him with horror. Rising from the sickbed he tended, the healer no longer obstructed Llesho's view of his patient. The sight of Hmishi, lying feverish and battered on the low cot, struck him like a blow.

Llesho resisted the step that would take him to his friend and his brother. He was worried, but he didn't want to draw attention to the fact. Instead he walked toward the firebox, demanding a higher place as befitted one of rank.

"I'm not here. Not really, no matter what he says." He gave no explanation which Tsu-tan could report to his master, but his caution didn't seem to matter.

"Your brother travels in a dream, witch. He can do nothing for you."

"You're safe, then." Adar tried to keep his voice level, but he couldn't hide the sudden drop of his shoulders. The tension he had been carrying since Llesho entered the tent seemed to bleed out of him, leaving him almost limp with relief.

"I'm fine," Llesho assured him. "And our brothers Balar and Lluka as well, though I would have Lluka less stubborn." In spite of their terrible danger, Llesho offered this small joy in finding two more of their brothers alive as Lleck's ghost had promised.

"Then you would have a different brother," Adar answered with a wry tilt of his mouth. "For Lluka has known best, according to Lluka, since he was in the training saddle."

Llesho gave a nod, acknowledging the truth of Adar's words, but keeping his own counsel about the danger Lluka's arrogance might pose them all. Adar couldn't help with that, and he was anxious to ask the questions he had come for.

"You look well," he ventured.

"This one's master has a use for princes, and would keep me alive until he discovers we will not give him what he wants."

"Your milky face may be out of my reach, witch, but the boy is not," Tsu-tan warned them. From a table littered with the remains of a supper he picked up an iron rod and tapped on Hmishi's cheekbone, already decorated with bruises.

Hmishi screamed, but the pain seemed to rouse him from his stupor. Though glazed with fever and panic, his eyes tracked with intelligence as they moved from his tormentor to Adar to the newcomer in the room. "Llesho?" he murmured. "Are we dead? I didn't think it would hurt so much."

"Not yet." Tsu-tan gave a tap with the bludgeon to Hmishi's bandaged hand. "But soon enough."

Hmishi groaned, his face glazed with the oily sweat of pain. Llesho took a step forward, and the witch-finder raised his bludgeon as a warning. "You're just dreaming, young soldier," he mocked his wounded prisoner. "Your foolish king has forgotten you all."

"That's not true." Llesho clasped and unclasped his fists, but didn't dare to approach any closer. Alone, he could do nothing but cause both his friend and his brother more pain. "I'll be back for you."

"We'll wait for you," Adar promised him. "The magician assures my cooperation with the boy's pain. He won't let Hmishi die until he has what he wants from me." He didn't say anything about Lling and Llesho didn't want to bring attention to her by mentioning her either.

There were so many things they couldn't talk about, fears they didn't have to speak out loud because they shared them already: Master Markko might realize Adar would never give him what he wanted and kill both prince and hostage. Or, the witch-finder might slip his master's reins and beat the young guardsman to death in a frenzy of the hatred he felt against all magic. He may already have gone too far—Hmishi's face was pale, and he shivered with cold in spite of the gleam of sweat. There were injuries under the blankets Llesho didn't want to think about, and Tsu-tan already had his eye on Lling as a replacement victim in spite of his master's orders. It never paid to depend on the good sense of the mad; he had less time to bring troops to bear than he had hoped.

And he still didn't know where he was. He scanned the tent as if he could get some clue from the black felt, but there was nothing—instruments of torture on the lattice walls, a lantern over the cot, and the remains of supper amid the bloodstains on the low table. Llesho felt certain that the food had not been for Hmishi. More likely the witch-finder enjoyed his dinner with torture on the side. But he appeared to have no use for maps.

Adar watched him with a frown, trying to puzzle out what Llesho saw, or wished to see. Then something clicked behind his eyes. "Due west," he said softly, "straight into Great Sun."

"Unwise," Tsu-tan said. He raised his bludgeon over his head, and Llesho felt the ground fall away beneath his feet.

Chapter Twenty-nine

LLESHO braced himself for the long drop to the turf outside of Bolghai's burrow, but when he reached for them, the grasslands to the north weren't there. Instead, he felt himself caught by a maelstrom that picked him up and dragged him far off his intended course.

"Whoa!" he called, as if he could bring the storm to his hand like a wild pony. But another, stronger mind was drawing him out past the camp where his brother tended Hmishi, away from the tent city of Chimbai-Khan where Bolghai waited for him to return from his dream-walk.

"Who's there? Who are you?"

Laughter echoed in his head, and a voice that turned his guts to water licked a poison trail across his mind.

"Just an old friend," Master Markko said with mock cheer. "We wouldn't want you to fall into bad company while you are wandering the dreaming places on your own, now, would we?"

It didn't *get* any worse than the company he was in. The memory of that voice in his dreams, calling him down into fever and death, ached in his guts where recent wounds were still healing.

"You made a bad enemy at Ahkenbad." Llesho tried

to make it sound like a threat, but Markko laughed at him.

"Enemies, yes. Of corpses and children."

"And Dun Dragon."

"Like I said. Corpses. Greater powers than you or I pulled the teeth on that old worm more ages ago than you have hairs on your head, boy. But a good effort."

He didn't know. Before Llesho could explore that thought, something plucked him from the maelstrom with a wrenching force that ground his bones one against the other. It dropped him like a sack of flour to land on the carpeted floor of a tent he did not know, except that it was a Shannish rectangle with yellow silk for walls and for the curtains that partitioned the space. He had appeared in the back of the tent. On the other side of the curtain, the shadows of servants huddled, while the call of sentries floated on the night air outside.

Watching him with a satisfied leer, Master Markko sat in an elaborately carved chair. At his elbow stood a fragile table set with steaming pots and two bowls for cups, and his feet rested on a stool covered in a cushion of silk brocade. Behind him, a rumpled bed gave evidence of recent occupancy. In fact, the magician wore only a night coat belted loosely at his waist, as if he had been roused by a disturbance of his sleep.

Llesho staggered to his feet. There seemed no point in a reminder that this was a dream. In the first place, Master Markko had entered the dreams of Ahkenbad and murdered the dream readers in their sleep. Llesho had no reason to doubt the magician could do it again if Markko wanted him dead. In the second place, he wasn't certain he *was* dreaming anymore. If Markko's magic could defeat defenses as powerful as those of Ahkenbad, how difficult could it be for him to drag Llesho out of the dream realm if he wanted to? The truth was, he didn't know enough to make a judgment on exactly where he was or how Markko had got him here, so he kept quiet.

"Sit, please. Would you care for tea?"

Master Markko moved his feet from the stool, signaling that Llesho's place was below him, and held out a steaming earthen bowl. The vapors brought stinging tears to Llesho's eyes. He remembered other cups forced down his throat and nights spent writhing in agony on Master Markko's floor and shook his head, refusing both the tea and the seat.

"I won't be staying."

"What has happened to your manners?" the magician asked with a smile that dissected him on the hoof. "Don't you know it's a grievous insult in the grasslands to refuse hospitality? You must remember our happier days, when you used to sup from my hand and I would hold your head on my knee while you moaned in the night?"

"Where are we?"

"Tsk." Markko sipped from the bowl he had offered Llesho and set it carefully on the table before delicately wiping the moisture from his lips. "Oh, yes, it contains a careful selection of poisons." He waved a languid hand, as if objections were fat green flies he could brush away. "You never understood that I have always had the best of intentions in your regard, Prince Llesho.

"You proved useful in testing the effects of various poisons for the casual trade. But that was never my full purpose with you. I sought a disciple, one who might become as strong as I one day, and rule beside me in all my conquests. You were that boy; if future invulnerability requires present agony, who am I to deny the Way of destiny for the sake of a few nights of painless rest?"

The idea that the magician thought he'd been doing Llesho a favor enraged him more than it ever had when he thought Markko just used him as a convenient receptacle for his poisons.

"You could have killed me!"

"No, no," the magician objected. He poured a less noxious tea from the second pot into a clean bowl and drank steadily until the bowl was empty. "If you had died, you wouldn't be the one. Since you are the one, I couldn't have killed you. At least, not in the testing, as the others died. I *am* still stronger than you are, as Ahkenbad proved."

Another test. He didn't know why he was surprised. Next time, however, he'd just refuse to jump over their fences and see what they thought they could do about it. Of course, Master Markko hadn't asked; he'd poured the stuff down Llesho's throat and he either fought the poison or he died. Most of the tests he'd faced since leaving Pearl Island were like that. They gave him only the one choice— play and win, or die whether playing or not—and he wasn't ready to choose the alternative yet.

"Is that what you're doing to Hmishi? A test?"

"Don't be silly—are you sure you don't want any tea?—the boy is just a diversion to keep Tsu-tan occupied until I can reach his camp with the ulus of the Uulgar clans behind me—"

"And the Southern Khan agreed to follow you?"

"Well," Markko lowered his eyelashes in a false show of humility. "He died so suddenly, you know. And the carrion crows who ate his flesh died as well, a great black crowd of them, which was a terrible omen. Someone had to step in. Since we had eaten from the same dishes and I remained unharmed, it seemed the spirits of the underworld favored me.

"But as I was saying before your manners forsook you altogether, it takes time, even for one of my persuasive skills, to bring the entire might of the Southern ulus into position. As a lieutenant, Tsu-tan has little to recommend him when compared to your gifts and talents, but he has proved himself loyal, given proper payment. I knew that harm to your brother would make the differences between us far too personal, and chivalry would demand an equal response if I let him play with the girl. Take note that I have held these two off-limits for the witchfinder's games.

"The boy is a soldier, however; a simple stone on a

complex board performing his painful duty. If you are the companion I believe you to be, you will grow to understand sacrificing a few stones to gain greater territory in the pursuit of power."

"Lives aren't stones in a game. You can't just sweep them off the board."

"Of course I can." Master Markko twitched a finger and Llesho doubled over in pain. He hadn't touched the bowl of poisoned tea, but somehow, the magician had called upon the poisons lying dormant in his body and awakened them. Llesho fell, hot and cold by turns, gripped by the combined effects of all the doses he had swallowed in that long-ago workroom. His gut clenched and turned to water and he writhed convulsively in an old agony.

A whisper of silk warned him that Markko had left his chair. Llesho tried to curl protectively around his gut, to defend against the sensation of fiery knives shredding him from the inside. But the poisons bowed his spine so that his head stretched back almost to his heels. Like an old dream, the magician took his head onto his knees and touched his hair.

"I have always loved you best this way," he whispered into Llesho's ear. With a single languorous stroke, he wiped a sweat-washed tear from Llesho's cheek and licked it from his fingertip with a gentle smile. "You are like a son to me."

"I knew my father," Llesho gasped through his pain. "You are nothing like him."

"You're right, of course. Your father is dead. And I—" the magician brushed the hair back from his forehead, "—well, I would fight dragons to keep you just the way you are right now."

"You will have dragons and more to fight when I get free of you," Llesho promised himself. Then he threw up on the magician's lap. His bowels had released themselves already, his insides forcibly rejecting the poisons that had become a part of him, and he had to suffer the humiliation of his own fouled body as well as the pain. The magician did not react in disgust, however, but dropped a kiss at his temple.

"I haven't given up hope yet of bringing you to my side in this war," he said as he withdrew to change his soiled robe. "If you force me to relinquish my dream, I will regret what I must do, of course, but I *will* relieve you of your life by painful inches."

The magician dropped his soiled robes in a heap. Naked, he called a servant to dress him. *Is that what his poisons will do to me?* Llesho wondered. Master Markko's flesh was gnarled with twisted tracks of blue and green squirming under sickly skin marked here and there with the dull gleam of scales. "Magicians," Habiba had said, "all carried the blood of dragons."

A Thebin slave, though Llesho didn't recognize him, quickly answered the call, bearing robes and soft breeches. The man gave Llesho not a single glance, as if by seeing he might exchange places with this most recent victim. He cringed at his master's touch and did not breathe until the unnatural flesh had disappeared under its luxurious coverings.

"Bury it," Markko said

The thought of smothering to death in a living grave did not distress Llesho as much as it should have. Anything was better than this. But the magician nudged with a careful foot at his discarded clothing, stained with the poisons of Llesho's body. When the servant had departed with his contaminated burden, Markko turned a calculating stare on Llesho.

"Perhaps, if you have some time to think about it, you will see reason yet," the magician said, and left Llesho to suffer alone.

It was a measure of Llesho's agony that being alone was more horrifying even than the company of the man who had put him there. He longed for the sound of breathing and the eyes of another human being watching him, more frightened of dying alone in such terrible pain than of suffering for the pleasure of his enemy. Gradually, however, that longing grew into a different shape. His heart, torn with pain and loss and terror, called to a power beyond his own, for home and love and—

Home.

"Llesho?" Pig looked down at him; a worried frown wrinkled his dark, open face.

"Am I dead?" Llesho asked him and winced at the reminder. Hmishi had asked him the same thing.

Fortunately, Pig's answer was similar to his own: "No, you're still alive. How do you feel?"

"Awful," Llesho was about to say, but that wasn't true any more. "Weak," he concluded. "Where am I?" and rolled his eyes. He had to figure out something more original to say—preferably something that didn't give away how little he knew about what he was doing.

"Same question," Pig agreed. "The answer is nowhere near as dire, but a great deal more puzzling. You're alive, but you've brought us to the gardens of heaven. Again. How did you do it?"

Llesho shrugged, discovered it didn't hurt and that he lay on a soft bed of moss under a tree with wide fronds that protected him from the flat white light. Things looked better than they had the last time he'd visited heaven, but there was nothing even the best of gardeners could do about the constant glare from the nightless sky.

"I was scared and alone and all I wanted was to go home," he said.

"Got that wrong, didn't you?" Pig joked. He made a great show of settling his sleek piggy body on the moss next to Llesho, but there was less truth than usual in his round little eyes.

If the Jinn lied now, perhaps he had about being alive as well. Llesho allowed his heavy lids to fall closed over his eyes. If it meant he could finally sleep, here in the gentle warmth of the Great Goddess' garden, he decided, he didn't mind being dead after all.

Leaves rustled nearby, but Pig remained where he was,

so it didn't mean danger. That was just fine with Llesho—it meant he didn't have to wake up. When a finger touched his hair, however, imagination dropped him back on the floor of Markko's tent, under the magician's evil ministrations. In a cold sweat he started up, gasping for breath.

"Oh, Goddess," he moaned, and covered his face with his hands.

"I'm sorry. I didn't mean to remind you of him." A beekeeper sank down on her heels beside him. At her side rested a small pitcher and two jade cups. One, he felt sure, was the jade cup he had left in his pack back in the khan's camp. Setting her heavy gloves beside her, she tucked her veils up over her hat and watched him with a worried frown.

"You didn't. Don't. Well, not after I opened my eyes. You don't look like him at all."

She bore little resemblance to the beekeeper he'd met on his first visit to heaven either. She seemed much younger and more beautiful than he remembered; not with the cold and distant perfection of the Lady SienMa or the sinewy economy of function of Kaydu, though. The best he could come up with was "complete." As she sat beside him, her hands folded calmly in her lap and her dark hair tied neatly on top of her head, she seemed to contain her whole world in herself. Even her eyes seemed to reflect not just one color, but all colors, changing as he looked at them from brown to black to green to amber. The tears that shimmered unshed in them promised home for his weary soul in that world within her.

Watching the play of concern and other emotions cross her face, he wondered how many beekeepers heaven employed, and why they should all take an interest in him. The Great Goddess, of course, could appear to him in any guise. When he put it that way, the answer was obvious.

"We've met before, haven't we?" The rush of panic

receded in a babbling torrent of words and he stopped, blushing.

"Did you find shelter from the storm?" she asked, and he knew that was the answer to his question. He had lost sight of her just as a storm had swept through heaven.

"My lady Goddess."

He struggled to rise, but she urged him to lie down against her knees with a hand placed gently over his heart. "Rest, husband."

Acceptance brought shame with it. That she had traded her unguarded appearance for one that must be more attractive to him meant that she doubted his ability to love her as she was.

"Please, my lady Goddess, don't change yourself for me. I will love you in whatever aspect you show me."

"Later," she said. "When your wounds have mended." Injuries to his heart and soul, she meant. From the pitcher at her side she poured a clear liquid into his cup. "This will start the healing."

He took the cup, discovering only pure, clean water on his tongue. As he drank, some part of the taint on his soul truly did seem cleaned away. With a contented sigh he returned the cup and let his eyes fall closed. Cool fingers stroked his forehead, urging him to sleep.

Before he gave in to her ministrations, however, he owed her his gratitude. "Thank you for bringing me here."

"I didn't," she said. "Your own dreams brought you to me."

"Home." It felt right when his heart had reached out in unspoken longing for the Great Goddess, and it felt right now, as he nestled against her homely skirts.

Heaven drew him like a warm fire burning at the very center of his being, and he gave up all his denials and pretensions to a normal life with a weary sigh. Maybe the struggle wouldn't be so bad, knowing he had love and home at the end of it. Only if he won, he reminded himself. This was, after all, a dream. He'd have to go back soon.

"Home," the goddess agreed. "For a little while yet." In her arms, he let go of his burdens and slept.

He woke to the sound of running feet, and the shouts of familiar voices. Stipes, breathless and coming closer, called to their companions. "He's back!"

"What?" That was Bixei. "Where did he come from?"

"He just appeared, in his own bed."

Bixei was next to his cot now as well. "He's been hurt. Get Carina—and Master Den!"

"Right."

Stipes was gone with a brush of cloth against cloth at the entrance to the tent. Llesho's tent, since Bixei said he was in his own bed. He wouldn't know for sure until he opened his eyes, which was proving harder to do than he'd expected. With a flutter and blink against the glow of the lantern, however, he managed it, and saw the roof of his own tent, blood-red in the lamplight, over his head.

"Don't try to move—" Bixei tailed off in confusion. "My prince, excellence, please. I think you've been poisoned. Master Den will know what to do."

"Stipes is saying that Llesho is . . ." Kaydu burst into the tent and fell silent as she spotted her quarry. ". . . back." When she spoke again, her voice had gone cold as ice. "What has that old witch done to him?"

"Poison," Bixei told her. "I've seen it before. So has Master Den. He'll fight it off on his own given time, or at least he always did on Pearl Island. But it isn't a pretty sight. I hope Carina can give him something to help— can you stay with him until she comes?"

"Where are you going?"

"I'm going to kill the Harnish witch who did this to him," Bixei announced. "And after that, my fist may have a few words for Master Den himself, for letting the

treacherous bastard take Llesho away without any of us
to guard him. Why Llesho thought it was a good idea to
follow the trickster god into enemy territory is a mystery
I will never understand."

"Wait," Kaydu ordered. "We are fifty soldiers in a
camp of thousands. Before we kill the local holy man,
we need to know what happened."

Easy for her to say, Llesho thought. She hadn't been
on Pearl Island when he was dying by inches from
Markko's slow poisons. But Kaydu didn't entirely rule
out murdering the Harnish shaman, even if it got them
all killed in the process, which it would. She needed answers first, though, and this time, she was right. He
couldn't let his people sacrifice their lives over a mis-
placed threat, so he roused himself to say, "Bolghai
didn't do anything. It was Master Markko. In a dream."

"Markko. Again. This magic business has never done
anything but harm," Bixei grumbled. He kept his voice
down and his face averted so that Kaydu wouldn't hear
him. Llesho could have told him he was wasting his effort. Before she could respond, however, they were
joined by the healer, Carina, and his brothers. Master
Den and the dwarf followed close behind her.

"Soldiers, out!" Carina flapped her hands in an imperi-
ous command. "You can keep guard better on the outside, and we need room to work in here."

Bixei shuffled out with more grumbling, but Kaydu
held her ground at the entrance to the tent. "He needs
more than spears and swords to protect him from this,
Master."

Dognut gave her his most reassuring pat on the hand.
"He has more, child." He spoke with compassion and
authority. Some message passed between them, and
Kaydu bowed her head and left the tent.

"Who are you?" Llesho asked. He might have been
willingly blind to the musician's powers until now, but he
couldn't ignore Kaydu's unnatural obedience to a lowly
servant and player.

"Bright Morning, a dwarf."

Llesho tried to find answers in the dwarf's quiet countenance. When he looked into Dognut's eyes, however, all he found was sorrow, deeper than a mountain lake but much, much warmer. It seemed easier, in his weariness, for Llesho to let his questions go. He didn't object when Carina touched his energy points and his pulse; he let her press on his belly and examine his fingertips, but he knew the answer to her inquiries before she had begun.

"I can't help him," she said at last to his brothers, who stood over him with varied expressions of anger and concern. "These are old poisons, not newly swallowed but a part of him in bone and sinew. Something roused them from their sleep, and forces well beyond my skills have banished them again. I can give him something for the pain while he heals, but he will need time and rest to repair the damage they have done to his flesh."

"I'm awake, you can talk to me," Llesho reminded her. "Where is Bolghai?"

"With Chimbai-Khan. He has been desolate since he lost you in the dream world, and has argued that the khan must take up your quest as a spiritual duty to your lost soul. He was much pleased to hear of your return, but can't escape his duties to his khan just yet."

Llesho nodded his understanding not only of her words but of Bolghai's duty. "It wasn't his fault," he assured her. "I knew the dangers when I began." *How could I not,* he thought, *after seeing the destruction of Ahkenbad?*

"I'll give the khan your message," Carina promised. "Now take this—" she filled a cup with wine and, sorting among the talismans and amulets that hung from her shaman's dress, she reached into one of the many small purses. Out of it came a small silver vial from which she counted seven drops of a thick, dark fluid into the wine. "It will help you sleep," she explained to him, and touched the cup to his lips.

He flinched away from it, wishing only for the cool

water of heaven. It was enough for Carina to see and
understand his misgivings. When she withdrew the cup,
he apologized.

"I trust you, but memory sometimes overrides common sense."

"And sometimes," she conceded, "memory rises to
warn us of unseen dangers. I would help you rest, but
perhaps the medicine would do more harm than good."

"Let me help," Dognut offered. "Music is no drug,
but it has the power to give pain or take it away, depending on the song."

"Can we rely on you to play only the latter?" Shokar
challenged him with a solemn bow.

Llesho thought the dwarf would grin and answer with
a jest, but he gave an earnest courtesy instead, and promised, "Healing voices only from my flutes, good prince,
kind shaman. I would cause the chosen consort of the
Great Goddess no more pain."

Master Den cast a warning glance at the dwarf in the
corner. For a change, however, Llesho didn't deny the
allegation. Dognut settled himself into a corner and
brought out a reed flute. Soon gentle notes were drifting
lazily on the yellow lamplight.

His expression thoughtful, Master Den stroked a gentle hand over Llesho's eyes, "Sleep, young prince," he
said, "and dream only peaceful dreams."

The trickster god's words had the power of a spell,
and Llesho followed the soft music into the gentle dark.

Chapter Thirty

"LLESHO! You're awake!" Shokar rose from where he sat in the corner listening to Dognut's soft playing. Balar had joined the music with a borrowed lute, but Lluka was nowhere to be seen. "Are you feeling better? I'll send a guard to fetch the healer."

"No need." Llesho raised himself on the bed and waited for his stomach to settle. The worst of the discomfort had passed while he slept; only the faintest traces of harmless images remained to tell him that he'd dreamed at all. If not entirely himself again, the thought that he might live came as a welcome relief instead of a curse. He owed that to the goddess herself. Silently he offered thanks, trusting the forces that guided him would carry his message to her ear.

At the tent flap, the point of a spear appeared, followed by Bixei, or half of him. With the tent flap pushed out of the way, Llesho saw not only Stipes standing guard outside, but half a dozen Wastrels and an equal number of trained Thebins.

"I thought I heard voices." Bixei cast a measuring eye over Llesho, and didn't seem to like his conclusions. "Carina will want to look at him, and he needs bread—goat

milk will help as well, if we can get it. Food soaks up
the poisons, or it did on Pearl Island."

"I'm fine—"

Ignoring Llesho's refusal of their attentions, Bixei sent
guards in all directions: one to bring Carina, and one to
inform Kaydu of the prince's condition, and another to look
for food. When his messengers were well away, he returned to Llesho's side.

"What's been happening while I've been gone?"
Llesho asked, and had a thought—"for that matter, how
long was I away?"

"You went off with the Harnish witch three days ago.
He returned two days later to report that some powerful
force had plucked you out of the dreamscape and that
he could find you in no realm of sleep or waking." Bixei
dropped heavily to the floor at the foot of Llesho's bed,
momentarily overwhelmed by the memory of the shaman's words. Though he would never admit his distress,
Llesho had no trouble reading the grief in Bixei's
drawn mouth.

"The Wastrels looked for you on the grasslands, and
Bolghai and Carina both searched the underworld in the
way of shaman. Kaydu looked for you from the air, but
no one could find you. I kept the rest of your troops to
our own camp, preparing to do battle against our host if
it appeared that his shaman had banished you to a holy
realm. We considered the possibility that the khan's son
might have killed you for embarrassing him on the playing field, but he seemed to take your absence as a personal affront."

Madness, to cast their small force against the armies
of the khan. But Kaydu was kin of the Dun Dragon, and
Golden River Dragon had sired Carina, the healer.
Chimbai-Khan might have cause to regret he ever welcomed such a band of monsters into his ulus if it came
to battle between them. Fortunately, Llesho had returned
before it came to a test, as Bixei reminded him.

"You returned before Great Moon Lun rose last night,

and the sun is almost at its height now. I thought the miserable old magician had taken you too far into death this time, but Carina said you had the mark of heaven on you, that you would recover with rest. She attends Bolghai, who answers to the khan. Kaydu has accompanied your brother Lluka who, determining that you could not speak for yourself, insisted on negotiating with the khan in your name."

"I thought we'd already dealt with those pretensions," Llesho muttered. "Why didn't anybody stop him?"

Shokar stood at attention, braced for Llesho's wrath. "When you disappeared, and the old shaman couldn't find you, we discussed among ourselves who would take your place. I didn't want it—"

"Neither did I," Balar admitted from his corner. "And Lluka said that we'd already failed you when we let you go. He was the one who hadn't trusted the shaman from the start, and it looked like he was right after all."

"It wasn't Bolghai's fault."

Shokar's shoulders lifted uncomfortably. "You say that now, but we had nothing else to go on. Master Markko entered the sleep of the dream readers and murdered them, but their bodies remained in Ahkenbad. You were just gone, vanished body and soul from the universe. We didn't think he had that power."

"But Bolghai did?"

"Not on his own," Balar curled over his lute as if he would have disappeared himself rather than face his brother's questions. "Carina had explained that you were learning transforming magics and dream travel. We thought he tricked you into a trap."

Briefly, Llesho wondered if it were true. He was pretty sure that Master Markko couldn't have taken him that way unless he had already traveled the hard part— into the dream realm—on his own. Had Bolghai tricked him into Markko's reach? But it didn't feel right.

"Pig would have warned me," he decided. The goddess would not have returned him to the accomplice of his

tormentor, he was sure of that, which meant that Bolghai
hadn't been working with Master Markko. Tsu-tan, however, was the magician's puppet. It had been a mistake
to go to the witch-finder's camp, but he'd needed to
check that situation for himself.

"What's Lluka done while I was lost?" He didn't say,
"that I'll have to undo," but his companions read it in
his tone and posture. Oddly, Shokar smiled.

"Not much."

"The khan has declared himself indisposed to visitors,"
Bixei explained, "and so Prince Lluka has waited, while
Bolghai and Carina sit in council in the ger-tent with
Kaydu and Harlol as Carina's escort and Master Den,
who comes and goes as he always does. Kaydu says that
the khan takes Markko's attack on you as an insult to
his hospitality, and he worries what such a powerful magician on his borders will mean to his ulus."

"It means desperate battle," Llesho agreed, "I have
much to discuss with this khan who would be my friend."

Shokar had crossed his arms over his chest at this last
declaration, and Bixei's chin jutted in the stubborn way
he had.

"First food," Bixei insisted, just as Shokar said, "Not
until Carina has declared you fit."

Llesho would have objected, but the smell of bread
that wafted through the tent with the arrival of both
healer and kitchen servant changed his mind. The khan
would have to wait.

Not for long, however. Kaydu joined them soon after
with an invitation to join the royal family—she empha-
sized the last part of the message: "as soon as you're
well enough."

When Llesho refused to wait, she insisted that the full
force of his honor guard accompany him to the khan.
"It's time to comport yourself like a king, your royal
holiness, instead of a boy on a lark. Kings treat with
kings, after all; boys are taught lessons."

Bixei hung his head and refused to meet Llesho's eyes,

but Harlol, as always, threw his allegiance with Kaydu. "Forgetting that might have cost your life, or that of the khan's son, on the playing field."

"I've already figured that out." He would need all the forces at his disposal— including the force of his own conviction in his position—to fight the evil that had taken his brother and his countrymen, that had enslaved his nation. That evil would grow more terrible still if he did not stop it on the grasslands of the South that were the source of its power. So he sent his brothers off to find their own princely clothes. Bixei and Stipes dressed him in the embroidered Thebin coat and breeches that always traveled in his baggage now, and set his sword and his knife at his belt. Llesho checked his knife by instinct, then placed at his back the spear that whispered in his ear of power and death.

Kaydu and Harlol had formed up his troops—who lingered suspiciously close to hand—into ranks of horse. Squads of Farshore mercenaries and Thebin recruits and Wastrels out of Ahkenbad, each in the dress uniform of his kind, blended into one disciplined square of allies. He didn't see Little Brother, and realized that he hadn't since he'd returned from the dream world. Asking about the monkey didn't seem very kingly at the moment, so he filed it away for later, another out of place fact to be accounted for.

When all was ready, Llesho accepted the salute of his forces and took his place at their head, his two brothers on either side, his captains right behind. Bright Morning the dwarf insisted on accompanying them to record the meeting for song and story, and Carina joined them to return to her teacher.

As they made their way with ceremonial gravity up the wide avenue of round white tents, they passed a scattering of riders. Some were going the other way and some just watched with the still focus of herders. Others—Llesho recognized some of the younger ones from Tayyichiut's first challenge—ghosted up next to them, never remaining more than a few moments, but never passing on until others had taken their places. Finally, when these unofficial representatives of the clans had had their chance to judge the newcomers in their stately panoply, Llesho's honor guard presented him at the silvered ger-tent of the khan.

The usual number of Harnish guards in their blue coats and cone-shaped hats were scattered on horseback nearby the royal residence. Others sat together in small groups, talking quietly and throwing the bones on a leather board. These latter stood when Llesho's party approached, but none moved to stop him or his honor guard of fifty. They might have scorned the small numbers of his retinue on his arrival, seeing no threat in so few. Since he had taken their own prince in a game of spears and traveled the hidden routes of the shaman in their camp, however, they attended him with wary respect.

At the door, half of Llesho's force broke off to stand mounted guard against dangers from outside the ger-tent of the khan. Senior guardsmen of the khan stepped up, one to each man Llesho left behind, while the juniormost of their members ran to gather the reins of his dismounting soldiers.

"Your guard can't watch the horses and their king," their captain offered.

Kaydu allowed it, except that Llesho's own horse she put in the care of the Wastrels Zepor and Danel. When the horses had been arranged, the captain stepped aside, permitting them to enter.

Llesho swept into the vast palace-tent of the khan, his head at its most regal tilt, his stride confident and with none of the boastful swagger of a boy. That took some effort, since he hadn't entirely regained his strength after his meeting with Master Markko. He had come to understand the value of theater in dealing with kings, however, and produced a carefully calculated frown when he found Lluka sitting in the lowest place, by the door.

"That is no way to treat a husband of the goddess," he said, and with a jerk of his chin, directed his brother to his side. Having delivered a message about the source and limits of his brother's status to both Lluka and the khan, he bore down on the dais where the royal family waited. Kaydu would have found out how to do the honor guard part correctly according to Harnish custom, so he left her to it, neither looking back nor giving any sign to acknowledge those who followed him.

At first the ger-tent had seemed almost empty, with just small clusters of young warriors who appeared to be randomly scattered, but who left no part of the vast room unwatched. As Llesho neared the raised platform where the royal family waited, he noticed to one side a group of men whose serious intent they made no effort to conceal. Each wore the long braid and curved knife that marked the chieftains of the clan. Among them, Yesugei kept his face averted with studied indifference, though Llesho saw his attention locked to a mirror hanging on the latticed wall. More than kings understood the theater of politics.

Nearer to the dais, a group of men and women, richly dressed and with headdresses crusted in jewels and colorful stones, rested on thick carpets of furs. The khan's brother, Mergen, sat among them, as did Bolghai the shaman. Advisers, he guessed; Carina left his party to join them.

Master Den was nowhere in sight.

"Lord Chimbai-Khan." Llesho presented himself at the foot of the dais with a nod suitable for greetings between equals rather than between supplicant and benefactor.

"Princeling," the khan answered with a condescending smile.

Twenty-five hands went to twenty-five swords to demand payment in blood for the insult. The khan's guardsmen answered in like manner, but halted when he gave the signal to stand down.

"Welcome, Holy King of Thebin," Chimbai-Khan amended his greeting with a thoughtful gleam in his eyes. "Join my family, and accept our congratulations on your coming-of-age."

As compliments went, it still sounded like an insult. That would have rankled more a day ago. But all tests weren't the same; he'd figured that out lying in his own filth on Master Markko's floor. He'd never given the magician the right to ask anything of him, but the Chimbai-Khan was another matter. A glance at Kaydu gave all the instruction she needed. With a wary glance at Llesho, she unhanded her sword as a sign that his guard should do likewise.

When the swords had vanished into their sheaths again, Chimbai-Khan continued. "Your advisers may sit with mine, and your captains join my chieftains. As for your guardsmen, be at rest. You will find no hand raised against you in this ulus."

Llesho gave an affirmative nod, directing his brothers to the gathering of advisers and his captains to the chieftains. Yesugei, he noticed, watched with cautious interest. As one who had brought to the fire a small box that unfolded unexpectedly like a puzzle, the chieftain seemed to be trying to decide what threat that puzzle might reveal.

I am no threat, Llesho thought. He knew Yesugei couldn't hear it, just as he knew it wasn't true. He bore disaster on his shoulders like a heavy cloak, but for the time being, he'd take the Khan's questionable apology in trade for the certain danger he brought to the ulus of the Qubal clans.

On the dais, with a wide-eyed Little Brother in the crook of his arm, Tayyichiut waited with impatient excitement for Llesho to speak, as he might listen to Dognut's songs, or Master Den's stories. *I am only too real,* Llesho thought, *and I would trade places with you in a heartbeat—all the adventures for my parents alive, my home intact.* The Harnish prince must have recognized some of these bleak musings in his complicated frown, for his eagerness turned into confusion and embarrassment.

A little shrug of apology seemed only to confuse the boy further. *The singers and the storytellers never get it right,* Llesho would have told him. *Bravery is just an instinctive response to desperation. Some flee and some turn and bare their teeth. Your life is better served if you never have to do either.* Tayyichiut would never believe that, of course; he'd been shaped by the stories as much as by his training. The prince would go into battle with the war cries of legendary heroes in his head, just like Llesho had.

Bortu focused her dark, sharp eyes on him, looking deeper than his skin. Llesho wondered what the khan's mother saw. Did she know what he was thinking? Did it condemn or acquit him? She said nothing, however, and showed nothing on her face to tell him her thoughts. Taking a hint from the old woman, he schooled his own features to uncompromising sternness.

In the face of this sudden, cold reserve, Prince Tayyichiut darted a quick glance from Llesho to Little Brother, as if he'd made himself foolish in the eyes of all the gathered company. Kaydu, seeing his dismay, stepped up with a formal bow and relieved him of the creature. Llesho silently thanked her for the distraction, which had drawn the attention of their audience to the monkey and away from both Thebin king and Harnish prince.

"You frighten me, Holy King of Thebin," Chimbai-Khan said. He hadn't been distracted after all.

A titter of laughter rose in the back of the ger-tent, from those who thought he jested with the foreign boy. The Khan silenced them with a hand upraised in warning.

"They are fools," he apologized, pondering the mystery of the boy king before him. "When first I met you, I said that you walked with wonders. Now I see that you are yourself one of those wonders. Come, look for yourself—"

As the khan rose to his feet, the Lady Chaiujin reached a hand to restrain her husband.

"Can I offer your guest refreshment, my khan?"

"Please, wife," he agreed, "but let our shaman advise your servants in the selection of delicacies suitable for a king lately suffering at the hands of his enemies."

No one said the word "poison," but it was in the mind and the eyes of the khan as he instructed his wife. Llesho wondered what plots exposed and hidden informed such a warning, but he had no time to consider the question. Chimbai- Khan left the dais and directed Llesho to follow. They stopped in front of a carved wooden chest suitable for storing clothes or blankets, where he gestured at the bust of a bronze head.

"My father." Llesho struggled to compose his features. *Show nothing,* he thought, *give nothing away.* "Where did you get this?"

The raid on Kungol, it must have been. In spite of his own advice, Llesho's hand strayed to his knife. Enemies, after all.

All movement, all sound in the huge ger-tent stopped, as guardsmen of both kings held their breath, afraid even a stray puff of wind might cause the very disaster their charges wished to avoid.

It was a very near thing. Old instincts stirred in Llesho's heart: the shock itself was almost enough to bring his lethal training into play. The khan seemed to know something of this, however, and made no move that could be misread as attack.

"Not your father, unless he lived for a thousand turnings of the seasons after sitting for the head." He spoke with the gentleness he might use with a wounded creature dangerous in its pain.

"You will find in this ulus no loot from the South's

raid on Kungol, young king. I didn't lie about that, though I can't say the same for wars fought between our peoples in ages past.

"I didn't show you the head because of any resemblance to your father, however. I never met him, though I might have guessed, looking at you. The face is *yours*, the stern countenance, the penetrating eye, even the angle at which you hold your head. Look."

Keeping his movements slow and unthreatening, the khan raised an empty hand and pointed at the burnished mirror hanging on the latticed wall nearby. Llesho grasped at the simple instruction as a lifeline, something to do that wouldn't instantly collapse into chaos and death. In his past, lifelines had been chains, but he turned, trusting in the voice warm with a father's concern, and saw a face he didn't recognize as his own in the mirror. When had he become this person who looked back at him? What ancestor reached out of the ages to claim him for the long-dead past?

"I didn't see it when you first came to me, but you've grown into your past." Chimbai-Khan echoed his own thoughts eerily. "I don't know what it may mean, or why your path has brought you to my tent. But your eyes have looked upon the Qubal people with a silent rebuke all the years of my life, and all the years of my father's life, and so back to the first among the khans. The time, it seems, has come to pay for the deeds done that brought this bronze into the tents of my ancestors."

Chimbai-Khan's calm and earnest tones wooed him from his rage, and gradually Llesho loosened the violent grasp he held on his knife.

"In ages past, when Thebin held sway over the grasslands, a king with your own face and bearing ruled in the name of his goddess. The king, whose name was Llesho like your own, governed sternly, but with a light hand. I know that sounds like a contradiction, but the stories say he demanded an accounting of the herds and flocks each turning of the seasons. From this account he

took only the smallest number for tribute, wishing the
submission of the clans to his rule, but not their beg-
garing. Some called him Llesho the Wise. The grasslands
simply withheld the title of tyrant."

"So far," Llesho objected, "your tale would lead one
to believe you wished to collect on a debt, not pay one."
He let go of the hilt of his knife, however, and reached
out to touch the bronze. It was his face, and he ran his
fingertips along the contours of the head, trying to grasp
the idea of a Thebin as powerful as the khan described.
The image failed him. He saw only Kungol in ruins.

"There was peace." Chimbai-Khan shrugged in answer. "Some would call the price cheap at a handful of
horses and a small flock of sheep. Not all, however.

"During the festival of the Great Goddess of the
Thebin people, when the chieftains brought their accounting to the king, this Llesho you see in the bronze
met a daughter of the grasslands. His wife had lately
died, and he wished to make this princess of the Qubal
clans his queen. For herself, the story says, the lady cared
nothing for crowns and glory, but came to love the man
for himself alone.

"The king sent presents to her father, including this
head. In the way of things when a suit is tendered and
there is interest on the father's side, the chieftain kept
the gifts. He was a simple man, my many-times-removed
grandfather, and thought only that to have so powerful
a son-in-law must mean he could forgo the payment of
his tributary horses and sheep."

"But it didn't turn out that way." The spear at Llesho's
back answered his unspoken questions, wailing in his ear
for revenge so that he thought the riders passing on the
wide avenue outside must come running. No one heard
it but Llesho, however, except maybe Dognut, who sat
hunched up as if in pain. *What do you know, dwarf?*
That question, too, would have to wait, but he vowed to
make the time later.

With an abrupt thought he meant to keep in his head,

but which expressed itself with a dismissive twitch of his hand, he refused the spear its vengeance and denied it access to his mind. He was sick of the thing, told it in no uncertain terms that he had enough enemies of his own without looking for more among the ancestors. It was just a story. If, at the end of it to pay a debt, the khan would help him, so much the better.

"What happened?"

"We cannot be certain, you understand," the khan warned him. "All we have is stories, and the bronze head. But it seems the lady had brothers, who saw in the courtship a chance to free the grasslands from Thebin domination. They seized their own sister and hid her away, claiming she had been abducted by a neighboring clan.

"It was a smart plan, really. If the king didn't rescue his bride, the clans would see him as faithless, which would cause unrest. If he did come into the grasslands in force against an innocent clan, he would be seen as a tyrant and the clans would rise against him. The brothers, riding as family and advisers, could approach him with weapons in hand without raising suspicion. They didn't know their sister was carrying his child."

Foreboding churned in Llesho's stomach, but he said nothing, waiting for the khan to bring the sorry tale to an end.

"The king came, with all his armies behind him, and met with his bride's brothers to aid in his search. As a false pledge of their unity, the brothers gave the king a short spear. They did not tell him that its tip was poisoned, or that the shaman, subverted by lies, had placed a spell on it to kill the one who wielded it.

"By then, of course, their sister's burden showed for all the world to see. Fearing that she would raise up her child to avenge his father, they held her prisoner in a tent far from the clans, where they thought no one could find her. A servant betrayed them, however, and led the king to where her brothers had hidden his love. And this

is where the tragedy has put us in your debt. The king
arrived just as his queen delivered his son, only to see
her brother snap the child's neck. In his rage and grief,
the king raised the spear the brothers had given him,
meaning to slay the murderer and rescue his wife. The
spell, of course, turned the weapon back on him and he
died, the poison of his betrayers in his veins. Their sister
could do nothing but look on in horror as the brothers
she had once loved murdered all that she had come to
cherish as a woman.''

That same spear rode at Llesho's back. The story cast
a new light on Prince Tayyichiut's innocent prank. Llesho
remembered the recognition of it that had dawned on
the Chimbai-Khan almost too late to avert disaster as
the spear itself played out an old curse on both their
ancestors. This time it hadn't won, though, he reminded
the khan with a level glance at the young prince who
watched them avidly from the dais. The khan nodded his
understanding, and finished his story.

"The brothers had their war, but they died without
winning it. King Llesho's older sons had ridden with him
and they fought with the wisdom of their father, to regain
the peace. The story ends with King Llesho's young
queen. Some say the horrors of that day drove her mad,
others that she stood her ground and refused the hospitality of her own clan for what they had done. All agree
that she remained in the tent where her brothers had
hidden her. Visitors would come to her and place gifts
at her door until, one day, she wasn't there. She had
walked away, into the woods to die some say. Others
would have it that she was the Great Goddess herself,
descended from the Thebin heaven to the grasslands in
human form to love her eternal husband in his life as a
king. In that version of the tale, she went to her heavenly
home to await the return of her husband on the wheel.

"Whatever the end of the story, it has left a mark of
sadness on this clan. For the crimes of our ancestors, the

Qubal people owe a debt to Llesho the King. Ask, and I will give it to you."

Wisdom gained in a thousand bloody li of struggle had taught him that you didn't leave an enemy at your back or start an alliance with a lie. Chimbai-Khan was hiding something. "Do you also have a daughter, my khan?" he guessed, keeping his voice very low.

All expression left the man's face, which grew pale enough to remark even in the half-light of the ger-tent. "My daughter is only a child, and fosters with a friendly clan." He didn't offer a name of the daughter or the identity of the clan but added as explanation, "I would not have the past repeat itself."

"Nor I, my khan," Llesho agreed, but gave his own reminder, "I'm not the man of the bronze head, any more than I am my father."

"No," Chimbai-Khan agreed. "Both lost their battles in the end. You have to be better than either of them."

"With help," Llesho said, acknowledging the khan's goodwill even if he hadn't quite sorted out the enormity of the debt owed. Bruised and raw of heart he rolled the story around in his mind, taking in the shape of it as well as its parts. He supposed the current line of Thebin princes rose from the elder sons and shared no Harnish blood, for which he found himself heartily relieved.

"We have two battles to consider." With a bow, he accepted the invitation to return to the dais with the khan. "If we don't defeat the witch-finder and rescue his hostages before he reaches his master, he will at the very least kill the prisoners."

Chimbai-Khan nodded gravely. If the khan could comprehend that some things Markko did were worse than death, they were already halfway there. As he moved toward the dais, Llesho indicated with a glance that he wished his captains to draw nearer so that they could contribute their own knowledge of the enemy. An array of delicate foods suitable for an invalid waited for them.

Or waited except for Shokar, who abandoned good manners, to the dismay of their hostess, and helped himself to a taste of a variety of the foods—those most suited to an invalid and that Llesho might be tempted to try.

According to Bolghai, Chimbai-Khan had a troubled marriage, but he didn't think hostilities had reached the point where the Lady Chaiujin would poison her husband's guest. Mergen, however, gave an approving smile as he, too, dipped into the dishes. Surrendering to the protection he could not escape, Llesho chose only a bowl of milky broth from his brother's hand, grateful that no one pressed him to eat more. The bread and milk that Carina fed him had helped, as Bixei had remembered it would when he recommended it, but he was unwilling to tax his gut with anything stronger. When he had drunk sufficiently to satisfy courtesy, he set aside the bowl and waited until the food had been taken away. Then he began his own story, describing what had happened in his dream-walk.

"I traveled to the camp of the witch-finder, and found there my brother Adar, who appears well, and the two of my cadre who remain his prisoners. He has tortured Hmishi and, with the distant aid of the magician, has clouded Lling's mind. Only his master's orders restrain him, however, and I'm not the only one worried that he may slip his leash. I had set my dream course to return when Master Markko snatched me from the path I walked, and carried me to his own dream encampment. While he held me prisoner there, he tried to persuade me to join him."

Chimbai-Khan shook his head, as if trying to shake the pieces into place. "This magician thought to bring you to his side with torture and poison?" he asked, recalling the stir in the visitors' camp at Llesho's return and the illness that had directed the choice of foods at his table.

"He said it was important for his plan. My brothers and I have to remain alive and fall under his control for the next step in his campaign. The poisons, I think, are his idea of training the body—against assault by poisoners, perhaps."

"This next campaign. Does he mean to attack the grasslands?" the khan asked.

"I don't think so." Just so there were no misunderstandings, he explained, "Markko wants to rule over the grasslands, and he'll fight to win that power—if you don't go after him, he'll come after you. But bringing down the Shan Empire, killing the dream readers of Ahkenbad, and even overpowering the Harn—I think that's all about eliminating opposition to what he has planned at the end of it. He wants the power, and maybe that's all he wanted at the start. Now, he needs to make sure there's nobody to stop him when he puts his real plan into action."

Shokar had locked his attention on his brother's eyes as he spoke, his focus sharp as a hawk's. "Which is?"

Llesho shrugged. "I don't know. The raiders already control Thebin. If he holds the Southern grasslands, he can move on the holy city of Kungol any time he wants. My brothers will never recognize him as their legitimate king, but he had hoped, perhaps, that I was young enough to break to his will. That didn't work."

Except for a quick glance at Shokar, Llesho had addressed himself to the khan. As he spoke of his brothers, however, his eyes strayed to Lluka, who wouldn't meet his gaze. *Not yet,* he thought, but promised himself to uncover Lluka's unhappy secrets before they cost lives.

"Hostages to heaven," Shokar thought out loud. "Husbands of the Great Goddess. Three are in this tent, and Tsu-tan has the fourth, is already carrying him to his master. Something to trade for favors or power."

It made sense, but a fine tremor passed through Lluka's body. He seemed afraid of something much more terrible than Shokar's suggestion.

"Blood." He finally met Llesho's eyes, his own dark with horror. "Master Markko will want to make blood sacrifices. A commoner will do for a small request. A prince is better for a more powerful favor. The blood of a prince who is dedicated to the Goddess, and has her favor, may move heaven itself. Resisting will do, but willing is better. Young is better still, and innocent—"

Llesho knew what his brother meant, and blushed. *Not for lack of wishing,* he thought, but that was before. The goddess waited for him, and he could do no less for her. Once he had his own embarrassment under control, he considered the full implications of what his brother had said. Balar didn't seem surprised. Terrified, but not surprised.

"You knew," he whispered. "This is the future you saw, before the visions left you?"

"The visions didn't leave me," Lluka corrected him. "The future did. This Master Markko will kill you and open hell on the mountain where you die. The gates of heaven won't hold against the army he releases against them. That's where it all ends in most of the lines. In others, you die in battle, or the magician dies of his own magics, but always the end is the same. Hell is set loose, the gates fall, the world ends."

"Balar—" Llesho looked to his brother for a denial, but Balar shrugged his shoulders helplessly. "We've come to the place where we have to be, but the universe balances on a blade thin as a camel's whisker. A breath, a thought, tips all into darkness."

"More family business than we meant to share, Great Khan," Shokar apologized. Llesho nodded in agreement, but he let his brother carry the burden of the khan's shock while he studied the reactions of those around them. His own party stirred to greater vigilance, but they had all seen too many wonders to let surprise overcome them. Harlol had known from the start; the knowledge had sent him out to find a beggar prince and hide him from harm in the caves of Ahkenbad. That plan had worked out about as well as he would have expected.

Kaydu might have guessed on her own, or with her father's help. Bixei crackled with his anger, but seemed

unbowed by the prospect of eternal chaos. Perhaps, like
Llesho, his life as a slave and a warrior had prepared
him for no other end. The tale had fired Tayyichiut with
a dangerous fervor, however; the Harnish prince would
take no warnings about the barbed edge to adventures
now. Bortu seemed unsurprised, as did Mergen, which
caused Llesho to wonder about their own sources of information. Chaiujin had fixed him with her serpent's
stare, as if she would swallow him whole and digest him
slowly for the juices of his mind. She froze the heart in
his breast, so that for a long moment he missed its beating, but he had no time to consider what plots she might
conceal. The khan turned to his shaman, demanding answers. "Is this true?"

"What part, my khan?" Bolghai replied with his own
bland question.

Llesho sympathized with Chimbai-Khan's annoyance.
While their beliefs might differ, mystics seemed to all
share a common love of obscurity when asked a direct
question.

The khan persisted. "Does this whinging prince have
the gifts he claims? Is the world about to end?"

"Gifts, yes, Great Khan Chimbai," Bolghai admitted,
and added, "Truth is a deep, cold stream, however, and
this one wades ever in the shallows.

"The underworld of the animal spirits and our helpful
ancestors remains untroubled. Sky spirits of thunder and
starlight still walk the heavens unhindered by this magician and his magics. But heaven itself has suffered, and
our worlds of dreams and waking mean little to the spirits we question in their passing."

"Does that mean the people of the grasslands will survive this master's magics?" Chaiujin asked, "or that we
face defeat in anything we do?"

"It means, Lady Chaiujin, that one should listen with
caution to the advice of those to whom the question of
life or death has no meaning. But if the khan, your husband, were to ask me, 'Do we throw our lot and our

lives with this mad boy's quest,' I would have to tell him, 'Yes.'"

"We have ten thousand gathered here in anticipation of battle," the khan said, "But even so, it will take some days to prepare for a march to the South." The indirection of his words caused Llesho to wonder what battle the Qubal had anticipated before his quest ever left Ah-kenbad. He would ask Master Den about that, but in the meantime, he had his own plan to prepare.

"First, we must secure the prisoners. The witch-finder travels with a hundred or two of Master Markko's raiders, no more. My own forces, though smaller, fight for the honor of heaven and to rescue friends and brothers, not out of fear of their master. We've won against such odds before. When we go after Master Markko, however, your thousands will be welcome."

"Your troops follow their king, like filings to a lodestone," the khan corrected. "And we would not have them wandering our lands bereft of their true south. Take half a hundred of our fighters. Let them see with the eyes of the clans these terrors of which you speak and report to their captains the truth as they learn it in the flesh of their own experience. And if they should keep the royal lodestone from the hands of his enemies, then all debts are paid. The battle for the grasslands that follows will be for us."

"Agreed," Llesho accepted the offer and with it the hands of the khan, which he held between his own as a sign of the compact between them. When it was done, he glanced up at the mirror on the wall, and caught Yesugei's relieved smile in it. He returned a nod of acknowledgment; they had both done well by their different causes.

Tayyichiut would have spoken then, and Llesho guessed what he wanted, but the Lady Chaiujin silenced him with a cold frown. As she waited for the chieftains to settle, the lady beckoned a servant who brought forward small pots of tea, and bowls for the guests and family. One pot she set by the khan's wife with particular care. Lady Chaiujin's smile of welcome never warmed her eyes as she picked up a jade bowl in one hand and the teapot by its handle with the other.

For a moment Llesho wondered if she had taken it from his pack, but the challenge in her gaze as she filled it quelled the impulse to accuse. He was a guest and would make a gift of anything he owned save the wedding bowl returned to him by the Lady SienMa and the spear across his back. But the light from the smoke hole at the center of the roof played differently at its lip than he remembered. Not his own cup—another like it that she teased him with, urging him to a thoughtless accusation.

"I have a cup very like your own, Lady Chaiujin." His smile, for the teeth only, warned her that he saw through the ruse: "Save that the rim is thinner."

"Then you must have its match." The lady smiled graciously and gave him her cup to drink. "Keep it as my guest-gift. Like the bronze that haunts my husband, this cup comes from the Golden City of Kungol. Perhaps you can return it to its rightful place some day."

Too gracious. He wondered if her poisons were compatible with those of Master Markko. She caught his hesitation, however, and drew back the cup. "It's just tea," she assured him, and sipped from it. "I will beg the khan, my husband, to take no offense if you wish Prince Shokar to taste it as well, though I fear the tea will be gone by the time we are finished testing it."

Chimbai-Khan seemed more inclined to sweep the cup from her hands than to object to Llesho's caution. She seemed unlikely to want him dead, however, and had tasted it herself. The magician's attentions had made him the equal to any poisons that might leave another unaffected, so he took the cup into his hands and drank a small courtesy draft, no more than a sip.

Not poisons, he realized too late, but a love potion that set fire pulsing through his brain and body. Gazing into the lady's eyes, he saw that the potion had set her blood racing as well, but she sat demurely, her lashes quickly hiding the fever she had set to burning with her tea.

"Your pardon, Chimbai-Khan." Llesho stumbled awkwardly to his feet. His guardsmen, too, stirred uneasily to see their young king's interest so plainly written on his face and form. They could not know the lady had drugged him into love with her, but had to seriously question both his statecraft and his manners. With a shake of his head that did nothing to clear his thoughts but set his pulse to throbbing at his temples, he drew himself to his full height and sketched a shaky bow. "No offense meant to your lady or your hospitality, but my illness calls me to my bed." At the mention of his bed the heat rose in his cheeks and he swayed toward the Lady Chaiujin.

"Don't let us keep you from your rest, young king." The khan dismissed him with a wave of a hand that Llesho didn't see. He'd already turned away, facing the long walk past nobles and chieftains and his own guardsmen to the door.

"My respects—" He started walking alone.

At his back his brothers hesitated, torn between courtesy to their host and worry for their king.

"I hope the food and drink were not too taxing on his healing spirits," the Lady Chaiujin begged with mockery in her tone. "Perhaps he needs another day of rest." Her voice embraced him like warm honey.

"Oh, yes." Llesho turned around again and reached for her, found his hand restrained by Shokar, who studied him anxiously for illness. "Or . . ." He was confused. Llesho wanted to sink into her arms, but at the same time, his own voice in the back of his head, went, *Ugh! No! Run away!* "I have to rescue Adar." Focus. The little voice in his head added that to the chant and he obeyed it, marching toward the door with a singleness of purpose on which he knew his life depended, though he couldn't have said why. "But I'll come back . . ."

"Go. See to your brother," the khan dismissed the whole of Llesho's party. "We would not lose a second King Llesho to the hospitality of the Qubal clans."

Llesho thought the khan must suspect more than he could let on about his guest's sudden illness. He didn't feel ill, though. He felt delicious, and couldn't remember why he was leaving when the Lady Chaiujin waited for him on the dais, like a dream of heaven. Focus. As he passed the khan's gathered advisers, he sought out Carina, who saw with the eyes of a healer. Drawing a handkerchief from one of the many purses that hung from her shaman's dress, she made her way to the dais and swept up the jade cup that Lady Chaiujin had offered Llesho as a gift.

"His Royal Holiness will send his proper gratitude when he is recovered," she said, and wrapped the cup carefully in the cloth. With her own bow and a muttered apology she turned and followed his brothers, who had taken up positions with his captains surrounding him and moved him toward the exit. Before they had gone far, however, the door opened for Master Den. The trickster god strode toward them with an easy grin, pretending to a cheer belied by the thunderous footsteps that shook the earth as he walked.

"Magical torments are an exhausting business," he chided Llesho, leaving the gathered company to assume he meant the magician waiting in the South, and not the unsuspected potions of their queen. With a bow to the khan and a knowing glance at the Lady Chaiujin, Master Den fell into step behind Llesho's party and herded them past the firebox.

"Wait!" Llesho reached to the chain around his neck. His hand found the black pearl that was the Pig tangled in his silver wire, and he tugged at it. "I need to give the lady a present in return!"

"You will." Master Den leaned into his ear so that they could speak privately. "Tomorrow. When you are ready to leave is the proper time for a gift to your hostess. Now might be mistaken—"

"Not mistaken," Llesho whispered in his teacher's ear. "I want her."

"I know."

"And I don't even like her."

"Not surprising. I'm sure Carina can help. You've done well to remove yourself from the lady's presence."

"I have the cup," Carina joined in their whispered conversation. "I can analyze what she gave him when we get back to our tents."

They were hustling at an unseemly rate for a king's departure from another king, Llesho judged. But the voices in his head were in agreement with his feet this time, even if other parts of his body were still in rebellion. He didn't think those soldiers following him out were going to let him go back anyway, even if they were his own personal guard. Only Carina and Master Den suspected more than a natural, if rude, infatuation with the lady. The khan's men were unhappy with his behavior but not surprised by it; they seemed willing to let the visitors leave unharmed if they just—left.

A glance behind showed him that the Lady Chaiujin had gone, but Chimbai-Khan watched as Llesho's party withdrew. Regret and sorrow and even pity mixed in his eyes in a way that confused Llesho even more. Of course, Lady Chaiujin was the khan's wife, but . . . it occurred to him, though he couldn't hold onto the thought, that the lady had wanted to hurt her husband *and* the upstart princeling on her doorstop. He'd got himself out of there without making a complete fool of himself, but she'd managed to humiliate them both without ever losing her own dignity. And that made him seriously angry.

Chapter Thirty-one

"I DON'T understand—"

"There's nothing *to* understand. It's a drug." Safely back in Llesho's command tent, Carina had unwrapped the Lady Chaiujin's jade cup and set it on the folding camp table. As she spoke, she filled it with clean water and added four drops of a brown liquid thick as mud.

"Oh, I understood that part right away."

Llesho paced out his nervous energy behind her, making a detour around Shokar but staying clear of Master Den, who had laid claim to the bed where he sat taxing the strength of the cot's joints. Llesho didn't need a bed, had slept away most of a day while the poisons sweated their way out of his system. The Lady Chaiujin's drug had a completely different effect on his system. If he couldn't get access to the lady herself, which Master Den and his brothers had determined he wouldn't, he'd race his own horse to Kungol, or climb the heavenly mountains with Dognut on his back to entertain the goddess when he arrived at her gates. Something, anything.

In the corner, Dognut started up a soft tune, and stopped again when Llesho turned on him.

"I am not in the mood, dwarf."

"So I see."

Dognut pocketed his sweet potato flute, but there was mischief in the glance he flashed at Balar who, fortunately for his skin, took no chances with Llesho's temper and a borrowed lute. Lluka was off skulking somewhere, but Shokar stood like a stone pillar in the entrance to the tent.

Llesho needed to move, so he paced, and thought, and talked.

"I know I don't really have these feelings for her. She's scared me witless since the first time I saw her. And not," he added before someone could interrupt, "because I was unnerved by an attraction to a beautiful woman. She's colder than the glaciers on the heavenly mountains, and that's not my idea of passion, however innocent Lluka thinks I am. I knew it was a trick."

Shokar shifted neatly in place to block Llesho's escape from the tent. "What I don't understand," he complained, "is why you drank from a cup the lady handed you in the first place. That should have been my place."

"And it would have served us better if the eldest prince had thrown himself at the feet of the khan's wife," Llesho snapped at him. He didn't have an answer that would please Shokar. Didn't, in hindsight, think much of it himself. "I didn't think she'd poison us until she knew more about us."

"You," Balar dropped the correction offhandedly into the debate. "Her attention was all on you."

Llesho knew that, and Master Den was challenging his statement with a raised eyebrow. No one believed him, it seemed, though they appeared willing to accept the lie as a symptom of the lady's tea. With a little sigh, he relented. The truth, after all, was easier to keep track of. Which was important when he wasn't tracking all that well. "Okay. I knew she was watching me, and I figured that she'd test me with something. But if Markko has been training my body since Pearl Island to withstand the effects of poisons, and if the Lady Chaiujin could drink the tea without any ill effects, I figured I could do it, too."

As he expected, Shokar liked the truth no better than the lie. "I can't believe you would risk your life on the good intentions of a magician who has left a trail of murder from here to Pearl Island," he thundered. "I can't believe you would deliberately swallow poison just to see what would happen. WHAT WERE YOU THINKING!" he thundered.

"It was an alkaloid," Carina corrected him with absent precision. She wiped the cup carefully, and rinsed it again with pure water. "And, I think, a spell with it. There are markings etched into the bottom of the cup."

"Of course there must be a spell as well as a potion. Why should anything ever be simple?" Llesho kicked at a bump in the floor of the tent and pulled his foot back quickly when the lump scuttled away under the canvas floor. "The Lady Chaiujin had to know I carry the jade cup that Lady SienMa returned to me—she was daring me to accuse her of taking it. A search would have turned it up exactly where I left it, discrediting me and her husband, for inviting a troublemaking stranger into his camp.

"When that didn't work, she was ready with her backup plan."

"One should always have a backup plan," Master Den agreed. He didn't laugh, but it was a near thing.

"I should have challenged the khan for the honor of Thebin." Shokar fidgeted with his sword. Not a man who chose war as an occupation, he had learned it well enough. Especially in the early stages, when sides were being taken, honor and the reputation of one's cause carried as much weight as sword craft.

Dognut, however, spoke up from his corner, common sense rising out of his usual well of compassion. "The khan had no hand in it, I'd wager, nor acts out of a deep heart-love for his cold wife. But he'd be bound to defend her pretended virtue against us. We'd be dead. Markko would soon have his hands on Adar, and possibly other royal brothers who are still missing. And the khan would mourn the loss of his own honor in murdering the innocent to protect the wicked. This way, a boy lost his head in the presence of a beautiful woman but properly retreated to clear his thoughts rather than offend his host."

Master Den agreed. "Better to appear a fool than a cuckoo in the nest of a powerful man."

"Particularly when you wish him as an ally?" Llesho already knew the answer.

"And what if it had been a poison, meant to kill you and not to make you look the fool you are in front of the Harn?" Shokar was not yet ready to let it go.

"Then I would have lived or died, as Master Markko meant me to do when he fed me his doses," Llesho answered.

Shokar seemed ready to build a full head of steam, worthy of the best of his temper explosions at this answer, but Llesho stopped him with an upraised hand. He didn't have to say, "I am your king;" it crackled in every rigid muscle. When his brother bowed his head in submission, Llesho explained what had seemed obvious to him from the beginning.

"We are at war. Master Markko may command the Lady Chaiujin, or she may battle for her own cause, but I could not back down at the first flight of arrows. If we are to win this war, we have to fight it wherever it finds us, at table or on the playing field, or anywhere else it comes to us. If we don't, we'll die anyway, on our backs if not on our feet."

Shokar trembled with his inner struggle, wishing to protect his young brother while knowing that he couldn't.

"Let it go, good prince Shokar," Master Den advised him. "There comes a point in the nursemaiding of kings when one must relinquish the leading reins and let them ride on their own, even into disaster."

"It wasn't," Llesho objected quickly, but was forced

to amend his defense: "A near thing, perhaps, but it worked out."

"And you've put up with this since Pearl Island?" Shokar gave his head a shake and added for Master Den, "I don't know how you do it."

None could misinterpret the little smile Den gave him in return. His Royal Holiness King Llesho was, perhaps, no more nor less than the trickster god had made him. Which warranted greater thought when Llesho had the time.

A stirring at the tent flap interrupted the conversation before anyone could comment. After a brief whispered word with Bixei, who stood guard outside, Shokar nodded, and allowed the newcomer to enter.

"Prince Tayyichiut." Llesho paused in his restless pacing to give the prince a bow of greeting.

"Holy King." Tayyichiut returned the bow, but did not meet Llesho's eyes. He raised a small sack of herbs so that everyone in the tent could see what he was doing, and offered it to Carina. "Bolghai recognized the effects of a potion on the khan's guest, and sends this antidote, with the humble apologies of my father, and his gratitude. He wishes you to know that he would have no harm come to you in his camp, but suggests that perhaps—"

Llesho raised a hand to stop him from committing a breach of hospitality in his father's name. "My troops prepare for departure even as we speak. I would have met with your father again, to make more detailed plans for the battle to come, but we'll have time for that after we free Tsu-tan's prisoners."

The Harnish prince let out a deep breath, as if he'd been relieved of a great burden. "My father hoped you would not forsake the alliance which he holds so near to the honor of this family. He begs you to accept the gift of a half a hundred of his best horsemen, and his son to lead them, to help you regain your companions."

Llesho's first instinct demanded that he reject the

khan's offer. He'd had only a handful of days to get used to the idea of Harnishmen who didn't mean to kill him, and Tayyichiut hadn't helped to cement that change of view. The young prince seemed to owe little of his open demeanor to his mother but Llesho wondered how innocent had been the challenge on the playing field that had almost cost him his life. If the mother knew about the cup, did the son also know about the spear? He caught a breath to reject the offer, but the prince seemed to read his objection and moved to counter it before the words were spoken and it came to backing down in front of followers.

"I want to go. Before you answer, let me assure you that I meant no harm when I challenged you to play at jidu with me. I didn't realize that you carried magical weapons along with a magical name and thought only to test your conduct in warlike games. For my foolishness you hold my honor in your hands and I would win it back in battle at your command."

That all sounded too elaborate and poetical for Llesho, who still felt the uneasy effects of the potion fed him by the prince's mother.

Prince Tayyichiut read some of this in his frown, and answered for himself: "The Lady Chaiujin is my stepmother, I call her mother out of courtesy to my father." He said nothing more, but his loathing came through clearly in his voice, and the curl of his lip.

"I would not cost the khan his beloved son in a battle that isn't his to fight." That was Llesho's second doubt, but Tayyichiut swept it away with a wave of his hand.

"You're no older than I am, but you've already proved yourself in battle and you're leading a force of your own to rescue your friends. Just like you, I've trained to fight all of my life. Now it's my turn to prove myself."

"Not like me." It wouldn't help his argument to tell the war-trained prince that, until his fifteenth summer, Llesho'd wielded nothing more dangerous than a muck-rake in Lord Chin-shi's pearl beds.

Prince Tayyichiut took the words like physical blows and Llesho knew he couldn't leave it that way between them. None of it was the prince's fault, any more than it was Llesho's. Unfortunately, it left him all out of arguments to make. "I don't want you dead," had been the big one, right after, "I don't trust you any more than I trust your stepmother," which didn't seem the right thing to say in the camp of his father.

"Drink this." Carina interrupted them with a cup of tea in which the leaves and bark still floated. He wrinkled his nose, but she insisted, "It will take away the worst of the effects you are suffering."

She didn't say which effects, and gracefully did not mention their source, but Llesho blushed a deeper wine-color anyway. He hadn't forgotten that he wanted to bed Tayyichiut's stepmother, but the prince had distracted him from the evidence that told the tale to all who might look on him. While Llesho drank, Tayyichiut carefully kept his eyes focused on the top of Llesho's head as he pressed his case.

"I would not stay behind with the women when there is glory to be won."

He couldn't have chosen a less convincing argument to join Llesho's band, nor could he have chosen a worse time to make his fatal point. Carina turned on him with an imperiously raised eyebrow just as Kaydu, returning from a scouting expedition, entered the tent.

"What's this about staying behind with the women?" she asked, shaking all over as if she still had feathers.

"I'd like to know that, too." Carina added her fuel to the fire.

"I didn't mean. I meant, Harnish women don't, or well, not often, and—" He stammered to a halt, as red to the tips of his ears as Llesho had been before he drank down Bolghai's antidote.

"Do you think you can let the boy off the hook now?" Dognut asked with a twinkle. "It would be easier to explain his injuries *after* the battle than before it!"

"Swaggering about taking on twice as many because our aims are pure sounded very good when you were bragging us up to the khan," Balar conceded, "but even for heroes, greater numbers are better than being outnumbered, especially when the enemy is one who channels powers from this dark magician."

Tayyichiut grinned at Balar. "My father agrees," he said, "Both to the prettiness of the speech and to the value of not testing it too far. Will the monkey come to war with us?"

"He always does," Kaydu assured him.

"I'll hold him for you some of the time," Tayyichiut volunteered brightly.

Llesho felt the stirring of jealousy for friendships that might be born there, between the Harnish prince and his own company. "The Harn are our enemies," he snapped, shocking his brothers and the prince, but not the companions who had known him throughout his journeys.

"It's hard to give that up," Kaydu gave a little shrug. "But we have to find out where this khan will stand in the greater battle to follow. Better to have his son under our eye than to leave the enemy at our back with no hostages to his good intentions."

"My father suggested that as well," Tayyichiut spoke up easily. Too easily.

"You've had a soft life in the lap of your family and the people of this ulus. You think you can win our forces to your side the same way you charm your own horse-guards, who are friends by decree." The effects of the potion, and his own habits of ease among his companions had relaxed Llesho's features, but now he hardened his expression as he hardened his heart. "We are not so easily won, and we—any one among us with whom you will travel—will kill you without a thought if you look like crossing the least of my commands."

He'd never tested that, but it had to be that way if he were truly king. Of course, being king also meant giving orders his people could, in conscience, carry out. But he didn't want this foolish prince to think a winning smile would protect him.

As if dropping a mask of his own, Tayyichiut let the good cheer fall away. "Lady Chaiujin was my father's second wife, until my mother died in her sleep. Then she became first wife." It took little imagination to figure out how Tayyichiut's mother had died. They had that in common, then. "That happened three years ago, and I am still alive."

Llesho understood that, too. He returned the bow, to acknowledge the battles this young warrior waged within the khan's own household. "You won't be any safer in our company, but you don't have to pretend to love your enemies."

"When do we leave?" Tayyichiut was impatient to be gone, and now Llesho could understand his reasons. "At false dawn. Say your good-byes tonight."

The prince accepted this answer with a quick nod and left without a backward glance. When he was gone, Llesho realized that Bolghai's potion had worked. He felt almost normal again. Except, he was famished.

Tayyichiut had told about half the truth, which was better than he expected. Llesho had gathered his party on the playing field that served as the staging area for the khan's encampment. Surrounded by the round white tents in the soft gray light of the little sun, they awaited the arrival of the khan's troops. He'd expected the khan and maybe his chieftains and a few of his advisers would come out to bid them luck in battle, not this turnout of old and young, men and women, who thronged the edges of the field. The crowd stirred and hummed with anticipation, so that Llesho almost missed the echo of distant horses reverberating through the ground underfoot. A cheer went up as the vague tremble of the earth turned into a thundering drive down the wide central avenue of a half a hundred galloping horsemen, each with a second horse on a lead. The warriors of Chimbai-Khan wheeled onto the playing field in a tight formation and drew to a bone-snapping halt at the dais that had been set up for the khan and his family.

With a grin, the Harnish prince at the head of the company leaped from his horse and presented himself to his father.

"The lives of your warriors are yours to command," Tayyichiut recited. Dropping to one knee, he bowed his head, baring his neck to his father's sword in a ritual display of submission. That's when Llesho saw the sling on his back, and the furry monkey head of Little Brother sticking out of it.

"Rise, warrior, and fight bravely for your khan," Chimbai-Khan answered, showing remarkable restraint at the sight of the monkey on his son's back. When he had completed the formal leave-taking for a soldier, he gave a warrior's deep laugh, wrapped his arms around his son, and lifted him off the ground in a huge bear hug that drew one indignant screech from the monkey before he curled more deeply into his sling.

"Bring home tales of wonder, and a scar or two to enchant the ladies," he instructed his son. In the khan's eyes, Llesho read the truth of his desires: for mild tales and small scars, but most of all, the coming home. Tayyichiut was his only son.

"I will." His eyes snapping with pride, Tayyichiut set his shoulders in a military bearing. "Father, bless these, your warriors, as they prepare to die in your name."

"Bring death to your enemies, take only shallow wounds to mark your striving on the battlefield."

The khan let his gaze drift over the waiting horsemen, and Llesho did likewise. Twenty-five of them were youths with not a moment's real experience in battle. When the khan's exhortation to the troops ended, the crowd descended upon his army. Mothers pressed packets on their sons with dainties for them to eat in the saddle. Fathers offered advice and the prized family sword or a quiver of fine arrows, as if these gifts of war-craft could bring their children home safe again. And more boys, swearing in an effort to seem more warlike, were unable to hide their disappointment that they had not been chosen.

With his heart in his boots, Llesho wondered why he'd been chosen to introduce the Harnish prince and his young followers to the battlefield. Perhaps he'd sounded more assured than he felt when he had talked about taking on Tsu-tan. If he'd known what Chimbai-Khan intended, he would have warned him. People he could ill afford to lose died in his quest—advisers and followers both—and the more he needed them, the more likely they were to suffer and die for it.

If the khan had seen the rescued Emperor Shou, he might have thought again about sending his son into this war, small as the coming skirmish might be when compared to the struggles that would follow it. He couldn't even tell that part, however, without risking the empire itself. Enemies, of which the Shan Empire had many, waited only for a sign of weakness to fall on their prey. Llesho didn't want to bring that down on his friend or on the people of Shan. He just hoped that by keeping silent he didn't bring disaster on the Qubal ulus and their young prince.

At least the boisterous young warriors each came with an overseer in tow. An equal number of hard-bitten vet-erans—with expressions so impassive Llesho knew they felt as frustrated as he did—followed their young charges onto the playing field, driving a herd of riderless horses on leads. As he thought about it, the strategy behind the makeup of the company started to make sense. Hard-ened warriors would balk at orders from a stranger and a boy, as they saw him. Tayyichiut's youthful cadre, how-ever, would accept the leadership of their own age-mate and ally against their own race's older generation.

The warriors charged with seeing them safely through their first battle would fight at Llesho's command to keep their children alive, and to bring them home as grown warriors who had passed through their first campaign. That Chimbai-Khan had meant to wage this war all along crossed his mind. That the khan had sent his son to draw his first blood gave Llesho both a responsibility to his ally and an opportunity to learn through his son more about the hidden agenda of the khan. Keeping them all alive was the tricky part.

When the battle-scarred fighters drew to a halt, their leader dismounted. It was Mergen.

"Gifts," he said with a bow to Llesho and a sweep of his hand to indicate the horses stamping impatiently among the riders. "We will ride to battle in the Harnish style." That meant traveling at full gallop, an extra horse tied to each rider's mount. The Harnish riders changed mounts in mid-gallop, stepping from stirrup to stirrup as if crossing a stream upon stones.

"Like the wind," Llesho agreed. His own army lacked that skill with horses, so he added, "But even the wind pauses between gusts, to blow more fiercely when it rises again."

"So the wind blows in the East," Mergen gave a wry nod of acknowledgment, but his attention from the moment of his arrival had been focused on his brother, and he waited only for the minimal courtesies before turning to the khan himself.

Discussing statecraft in the khan's ger-tent, Mergen had seemed a mild, thoughtful man. Now he confronted his leader and kin like a storm sweeping over the grasslands. Chimbai-Khan wanted to send his brother to watch over his son's small force. Mergen objected. They spoke too softly for Llesho to hear, their heads drawn together, but their views very far apart. Even from a polite distance he could see lightning flash in the eyes of the khan and thunder answer in the tight-drawn vee of Mergen's brow.

In the end, Mergen won, and Yesugei stepped up to

take his place with Llesho's captains at the side of his own young prince.

"I see you plot with my chieftains against me, brother." Chimbai-Khan's low voice held subtle threat as he watched Yesugei exchange places with his brother. It was, Llesho realized, the chieftain's horse, and Yesugei's pack. Mergen had never intended to travel with the advance force.

"As always, Great Khan, your advisers conspire to keep you alive."

Llesho wasn't supposed to hear that either, or to see Mergen's quick glance toward the dais, where the Lady Chaiujin stood with the khan's mother and his other advisers. Nor did the khan mean for him to hear his answer, "I make it difficult for you, I know." The slap on Mergen's back, however, he gave as a signal to all that the dispute at the highest ranks had ended in peace.

The remounts had to be apportioned among the various riders and the company sorted into order. As the captains busied themselves insuring the preparedness of their troops, Yesugei himself took charge of Llesho's gift. "She is a strong and a tireless lady," he promised, stroking a hand down her neck and across the mare's shoulder. "I trained her myself."

"She is beautiful." Llesho gave the horse a rub, but he raised a questioning eyebrow at Yesugei

"Mergen's no coward," the chieftain explained under cover of pointing out the finer points of horseflesh.

Leaning in as if to comment on the hardy grasslands pony, Llesho gave a quick nod to show that he had figured that out for himself. "Does Mergen really think she will try to kill the khan?" he muttered.

"What do you think?" Yesugei didn't blink. Anyone who saw them talking would think they were discussing bloodlines.

"I think, some gifts carry a heavy price." Llesho wondered if the Lady Chaiujin stewed her own plots or acted for her father in the East. Either way, she was the viper hidden at the bottom of the basket. He'd have to get word to Shou before the emperor put his trust in an alliance that might be false at its heart.

"He wants Prince Tayy out of her reach. I'll be glad to escape her eye as well."

Llesho gave a small nod, understanding well the khan's concern. An ambitious wife didn't need an heir by her rival in her way. Llesho wondered if she carried her own candidate for the role, or if she had convinced the khan that she did.

"Shall we oblige him?" Llesho asked the question lightly, but they understood each other.

Riders and horses sorted out, Llesho led the princes both Harnish and Thebin to bid Chimbai-Khan farewell. With them came Yesugei, who touched his forehead to the back of his khan's hand.

"Bring my son back to me, friend Yesugei."

"He will come back to you a man—you have my word, Chimbai-Khan."

Llesho had fought many battles, and had killed his share of men and monsters both, but he'd never understood how anyone could think him more of a man for taking a life than his older brother Adar, who saved lives. He let Yesugei's promise stand unchallenged, however, and completed his own farewells as diplomacy dictated. But he'd learned something important about the Harn in this leave-taking. More than the city that moved across the grasslands like a great bird of prey, or the food they ate or the way they rode their horses, he thought that maybe this was the greatest difference between the Harn and Thebin. He wondered how safe a peaceful nation could be with allies who bred war into the very bones of its children. That probably depended on the children— Chimbai- Khan's strategy had layers and layers.

With Harlol and his Wastrels scouting ahead and Kaydu above them in the shape of an eagle, they moved out. As Great Sun sent his first rays over the horizon,

Llesho took the lead. His brothers like a defensive wall around him, he guided them in the direction Adar had given in his dream travels: West.

They'd be in time. The raiders might share the Qubal style of combat by speed and stealth, but the witch-finder who led them did not. Nor could Tsu-tan travel swiftly with his prisoners in tow, especially with one as weak and broken as Hmishi. Llesho tried to think of that as an advantage, but still it cramped in his gut. They'd find Tsu-tan and put an end to his torments, then they'd take down his master.

More thought would have to wait until first rest, because they were going to war Harnish style. The wind slapped at his face and the drumming of hooves surged in Llesho's blood. He leaned low over the neck of his horse and urged her to greater speed, knew their hearts beat to one rhythm. The wild joy of it drove out thought and the whispers of the death-spear at his back. For the first time since the Long March, his mind was free of memory.

Chapter Thirty-two

INTO the afternoon he called a halt for rest and to await the reports of the Harnish scouts and the Wastrels he'd sent forward. They had started across flat plains, but the land rose broken and uneasy as they flanked the Onga River. Stands of slender trees clung tenaciously to hillocks streaked with flecks of mica in the stone. Llesho's mount barked a shin on an outcrop jutting out of the grass like an accusing finger or a book of rocky tablets upended in the ground. Others had taken small hurts as well. Blowing and sweaty, even the uninjured horses needed rest. So did their riders, at least among those not bred to the saddle in the Harnish way.

It gave Llesho an excuse so that he didn't have to admit how worried he was. The scouts should have returned and their continued absence raised the hairs on the back of his neck. What was happening out there?

Tayyichiut wandered over to where Llesho sat a little apart from his brothers. He held his elbow a little way from his side and watched Little Brother, who clung upside down from his forearm and watched him back. "Where is Kaydu?" he asked, rubbing at the same raw wound that fretted Llesho.

"Scouting ahead," he answered. He would have added, "in the shape of an eagle" to discourage the prince's interest, or suggested that he take it up with Harlol, but figured that part of it was none of his business.

Checking for a patch of ground free of sharp stones, the Harnish prince lowered himself to the grass. "Without a horse?"

"She has another one." Llesho sneaked a glance at the sky. She might have hidden in the pearly tangle of pink and white and the gray of coming rain to the east. Kaydu had traveled west, however; the dark shadow of an eagle riding the updraft would stand out sharply against the hard, clear turquoise of that sky. He saw nothing, and it was growing late.

"You can tell what someone thinks of your intelligence by how well they lie to you." With his forefinger, Tayyichiut idly scratched at Little Brother's head, a gesture the monkey seemed to take as comfort. He seemed to focus all his attention on the animal, seemed not to have looked at Llesho at all. Continuing in the same even tone, he added, "Judging from that one, you must think I'm pretty stupid."

"Not stupid." Not anymore. The prince had sounded him out for the khan and reported with unnerving insight, after all. It would serve him well to remember that. Llesho snapped his attention back to the moment.

"Stupid," Prince Tayyichiut insisted. "You think I know nothing of the magical world, any more than I do of battle. You don't even pretend. I thought at first we might become friends, but . . . you can treat me like an enemy if that makes you feel better, but I won't tolerate being dismissed as unworthy."

With a casual flick of his arm, Tayyichiut settled Little Brother on his back and rose effortlessly. He started off in the rolling, bow-legged gait of the Harnish riders. None of his hurt feelings showed on his face.

Llesho came to his feet but made no move to stop the

prince. He knew what Tayyichiut was feeling just below the surface, had experienced it himself often enough. Honesty wouldn't help either, the way he felt.

"What do you know?" he asked.

As an apology, it sounded more like an accusation, but it stopped the Harnish prince long enough to give an answer.

"Once, when I was very young, I surprised Bolghai at his private ceremonies. He bit me on the thumb." Carelessly, Tayyichiut stuck out his hand, thumb up as if counting off on his fingers. Each sharp little stoat tooth had left the mark of its own puncture in the fleshy pad. "So, when the terrifying Captain Kaydu entrusts her animal companion to my care, and her horse goes riderless to battle, I can pretend to be a fool, so that I don't offend the officious boy king with delusions of being better than I am. Or, I can admit that I've been watching for a small creature in the grass."

"Look up."

Tayyichiut raised a sardonic eyebrow, but understanding glinted in his eyes. Neither of them could resist a quick glance at the empty sky.

"And I *am* better than you." Llesho's taunt had none of the edge that would have made it impossible to say whether he'd meant it.

Tayyichiut puffed out his chest and struck a fierce pose. "Any contest, any time." Little Brother dented the swagger of the boast when he appeared above the prince's left shoulder to rub the top of his head on the underside of the princely jaw.

"So, you're afraid of her, too." When it came to issuing challenges, Llesho clearly had the advantage.

Tayyichiut caught the "too" at the end of it, though, and disciplined his smile to a rueful seriousness only after a struggle. "I would have thought the mighty king of the Cloud Country feared no one."

Llesho nearly choked trying to stifle the snort that escaped anyway. "Oh, please! She was my combat instruc-

tor and my first captain—and that was back when I was
the lowly corporal, and no king of any kind." Not quite
the truth, but close enough.

"You are born a khan—or a king—my father would
say. It only takes circumstances to reveal that fact to
those who would elect you."

"So you won't follow your father as the khan by right
of birth?"

"Not unless the chieftains choose me. Should I live
long enough, I'll first stand for chieftain and if our clan
elects me, I will have our vote in the ulus. Eventually,
when we need a new khan, the people will perhaps select
me for the honor, and perhaps someone else. Yesugei is
a good man, for example. I hope to be revealed as khan,
of course, as you are revealed to be the king of the
Thebin people."

"That sounds like something the Lady SienMa would
say," Llesho thought out loud. Thebin didn't have chieftains to elect a king like the Harn did, but Prince Tayyichiut was right. He'd been chosen out of all his brothers
for some inborn trait he still didn't understand, but her
ladyship had seen it all along.

"The mortal goddess of war." The prince shot him an
uneasy glance. "My father is right, you do travel with
wonders."

"It didn't feel much like a wonder when Kaydu was
pounding the stuffing out of me every day, though."

Tayyichiut puffed out a breath, his eyes on the sky
and his mind far from her ladyship. "Yeah, but she is
sooo hot!" Kaydu, of course. Only Shou could think such
thoughts about the Lady SienMa

"Yep." And she should have been back by now. It
was time to stop waiting and start looking.

"Don't do it."

"What?"

"I'm not stupid, remember. Don't go after her. Your
brothers will have my head if anything happens to you."

"That won't happen."

"At least, take me with you. I can fight—"

Llesho shook his head. "If I do anything that stupid, Kaydu will have *my* head." He didn't say if he meant going after her or taking the prince with him when he did it, but Tayyichiut didn't ask, so he didn't have to lie.

Bixei came to get them then, and they parted company with a last backward invitation— "Call me Tayy. All my friends do. Even the ones my father didn't order to like me."

Ouch. Llesho winced at his own slight. "Okay." Then, because he felt he owed him something more, he said, "Bixei and I were adversaries before we were friends." He didn't say "too" but they all heard it, even Bixei.

"You have to knock him on the head a few times, but eventually he comes around," Bixei assured the prince, then pretended to surprise. "But you already know that!"

Llesho gave him a shove, and even found a laugh to give his friend as a reward. But under the camaraderie, he was plotting his escape.

The Harnish pony he rode kept to a steady, ground-eating gait and knew the way the land fell here, so he gave her only as much attention as she needed to keep them heading west. He wasn't sure how this dream traveling worked. He knew he could reach the dream world easily enough running in a circle, but what would happen if he tried to do it while riding? For that matter, how could he transform into his spirit-being on horseback?

Whatever happened, he had to try. Yesugei would keep them on course if he succeeded, and Carina, at least, would know what he'd done and calm the others until he returned. That assumed his body didn't fall out of its saddle and break its roebuck leg when he leaped, but he had to take some risks.

If he worried about it, he'd never find his missing ~~~outs, so he let go of every consideration but the important one—how to do this on horseback. Running was running, though. He settled deep into the saddle and caught the rhythm of his pony—her breath swelling the barrel of her chest between his legs and the beat of her hooves up through his knees, and the way her neck moved, as if she reached for each step with head and heart. When he found her stride in the rhythm of his own bones, he felt himself changing, running on four legs with the weight of a rack of antlers heavy on his head.

Kaydu, he thought, and in his dream-form, searched for her throughout all the worlds. There. There. He reached, and trod the air with his four sharp hooves, lifting toward the eagle circling low over a dark cloud rising up from the ground below.

She dived and he followed. Not a cloud, he saw, but the very earth, risen up taller than the forests in rocky pillars that walked on two legs. No more than a hand's count of creatures tore up the ground on which their prey made their stand, but each was the size of a hillock. In the unnatural chaos of churned earth and shadow below, Wastrels and Harn fought a desperate, hopeless battle against creatures who used whole uprooted trees as weapons against swords and spears. The stone-men wore earth and grass like a suit of clothes, but their gray faces flashed mica in the sun. Their shadows shed a darkness over all the ground below as they fought over their catch. Llesho watched in horror as a pair of the creatures tore a screaming Wastrel in two between them and abandoned their argument to feast on his human flesh.

The smell of death quivered in his nose, and roebuck instinct trembled in his muscles. *Flee!* But he'd sent these men to their deaths—Danel and Zepor, and, Goddess forgive him, Harlol, who had followed him out of Ahkenbad to his death. It was his fault, and he wouldn't leave them to the harsh mercy of these horrors.

"Nooo!"

Lowering his head to attack as Kaydu pecked and gouged with talon and beak, he struck the nearest of the stone monsters with his front hooves. Raking a gouge across its middle with his antlers, he drew clear spring water like blood from the wound. Llesho had no time to contemplate what this must mean, but pressed his advantage. He turned and kicked out with his back legs, putting all his strength into the blow.

The creature bellowed in rage. Raising a giant hand, it swung at him with the tree it used for a club. He leaped back, evading the worst of the blow. Kaydu swooped to his rescue, pecking at its flinty eyes with a beak that could snap bone but had no effect on the glassy stone. When the stone monster turned its attention to her, Llesho attacked again, but the first wound he had torn in its flesh had already healed itself. The second must surely do likewise.

As they fought, the screams and cries of their friends on the shattered earth rose up to them, urging them to greater efforts. Llesho wished his spirit-being was a dragon rather than a roebuck—a dragon might defeat the creatures who murdered his friends and allies. He didn't have that skill. But Kaydu—

Maybe she could have done it if she'd come upon the scene in her human form, but the eagle's brain was smaller, the transformations more difficult. *We are well and truly dead,* he thought, as a giant grassy hand reached up and grabbed him around the throat. It squeezed and he choked, feeling the air passage close tight under the powerful grip. He twisted his head, goring at its wrist with his antlers. Bleeding clear, cold water, it loosened its grasp on him, and Llesho wriggled away. Kaydu was suddenly between them.

"Goooo! Goooooo!" The harsh bird cry shaped the lipless word as she beat her wings in his face.

The screams from the scarred ground below had died. Llesho hesitated, searching for signs of life, but found none. Their friends lay scattered and still, their clothing torn, their bodies ravaged, their blood black upon black in the shadows cast by their rocky assailants. He faltered, remembering the Dinha's prophecy. *Goddess, Goddess, what had he done?*

"Gooo! Goooo!"

When he did not immediately obey, Kaydu raked a talon lightly across his nose—not enough to do him any serious damage, but it jolted him out of his shock. The monsters of loam and stone were falling, melting back into the earth, but an army of crows blackened the sky, heading for the dead. Llesho threw himself among them and tossed his antlers to chase them away. There were too many. He couldn't stop them as they pecked at the flesh clinging to the gnawed bones left behind by the monsters who had disappeared into the earth again. Kaydu wheeled overhead, diving among the crows but having no more success than he at chasing the huge flock away.

Staggering with grief and the blind confusion of his animal body, Llesho drew a little apart from the feeding frenzy of the birds. Exhausted, his dream set him free and he sank to the earth as himself, with legs weak as a newborn's. His mind had grown too numb to care that the ground he lay on might rise up and rend him as it had his scouts. His dead lay picked by the crows on the field of battle, but whatever had animated the rocky plain had departed. Nothing remained but the wind in the grass and the blood soaking into the ground.

Kaydu did not settle, but landed nearby with many small hops and lifts into the air, unwilling to trust to the uneasy earth. She did not return to human form, but cocked her head and watched him out of the beady predator's eyes of her eagle shape.

Water splashed on his knee, and he looked up, but the sky was cloudless. Another drop fell and he realized, distantly, that he must be weeping, though he felt too weary even for sorrow. Kaydu inched her way nearer by small hops until she had settled in the curve of his outstretched arm. With the feathered comfort of her

nearness warm against his side, he let his eyes slide
closed. Impossible as he would have thought it, he slept.

Standing among the dead in the field of monsters, Pig
waited for him on the other side of dreams.

"You knew this would happen!" Llesho accused the Jinn.

"So did you."

"No." Llesho shook his head, denying the accusation.
"This isn't what I saw in my dream. If I'd known that
Master Markko could raise monsters out of the grass
itself against us, I would have stopped him before it came
to this."

"Maybe." Pig shrugged, shifting his silver chains so
that they clinked with the motion. "What happens when
I drop this stone?" To demonstrate, he let go of the
stone in his hand.

"It will fall," Llesho answered as it fell. He wasn't in
the mood for lessons, but knew he wouldn't get what
he wanted until he'd given the Jinn answers to his self-
evident questions.

"And how did you cause that to happen?"

"I didn't. Stones always fall when they are dropped."

"Now you begin to understand a little about the
dream worlds."

So that was the point of this exercise. It wasn't his
fault. If he believed the outcome would always be the
same, though, he was doomed from the start. "You
sound like Lluka, with all paths leading to the one end
he sees in his prophecy."

"If it doesn't happen," Pig reminded him, "It isn't a
prophecy. It's just another failed possibility."

In all of Lluka's visions, the world always ended in chaos
and despair. The Dinha had known that when she gave him
her children. In the field where her Wastrels had died, it
seemed natural that he should think of her not as the young
Kagar who had wanted to be a warrior, but as the Dinha,
mother of her people. He wasn't the only one being jerked

around by fate. Well, fate and Master Markko. He knew who had raised those monsters out of the bones of the earth. He knew what he had to do next, too. His dream—long ago, it seemed now, before Ahkenbad had died—told him that. He would have walked away and refused the task, but he reckoned Harnish warriors and Wastrels had died for this. For the sacrifice of his dead, he had to finish it.

Reality was not quite the same as the dream where he had first seen the Tashek dead on the Harnish grass. As he approached, he saw that only empty orbits remained where the eyes had been, and the birds had left little flesh on the bones.

"The pearls of the Great Goddess must be here," he said, and dropped to one knee at the side of a Wastrel he recognized only by his flowing desert coats. "Or it was all a waste, for nothing."

"Yes," Pig sighed deeply and agreed, "a waste."

He didn't want to look closely, or to touch, but he didn't have any choice. The eyes, as he had seen, were empty, and the bones of the fingers had been scattered and broken. But he remembered the story Pig had told him, of monsters who plucked out the hearts of their victims and left a bit of stone in their place. Cringing inside at what he had to do, he moved the Wastrel's torn coats a little bit and groaned, sickened by what he saw. Within the bony cage of the warrior-priest's breast, a large black pearl lay where the heart ought to have been.

"I can't," he whispered, and curled his fingers into his palm, refusing the desecration.

"You must," Pig reminded him.

"Oh, Goddess." Reaching for the pearl, he cried out against his fate. "You ask too much!"

"Not yet," Pig told him. "Soon, though."

Llesho rose, wiping the pearl on his shirt, and put it in the sack at his neck with the others he had found both in dreams and in waking. As happened when the Jinn walked beside him, the pearl wound with silver wire that usually hung from the silver chain of the dream readers was missing. It would return when the dream was done.

Now, Pig led him through the grass, from body to
body. At each, Llesho stopped and bowed his knee.
Lodged between the ribs of the second and the third, he
found not a pearl, but a small stone which Pig instructed
him to remove and fling away.

"The hearts of men are sweet to the stone monsters,"
Pig explained. "When they reach inside for the prize,
they leave a piece of themselves behind, like a broken
fingernail. It's how you know they've been here."

"No," Llesho corrected him. "You know it when they
reach into the sky and pluck you out of it by the throat."

"That works, too," Pig agreed.

They moved on, stopping again at a body with the tatters
of a long Harnish tunic clinging to the bones. It was harder
for Llesho to grieve over the khan's warriors; he kind of liked
Tayyichiut, but didn't trust him yet, or any of the Harnish he
had met. Yesugei came closest and he thanked the goddess
that the man hadn't been among the dead. Another step and
he nearly tripped over a stoat gnawing on a Harnish tunic.

"Get away from there!" When the creature didn't
scamper away as he'd expected, Llesho pulled his foot
back to give it a kick. Pig stopped him with a forehoof
on his shoulder.

"It's his son," he said.

Looking closer, Llesho saw that the creature didn't
gnaw the body as he had thought, but nuzzled its fierce
snout at the dead man's breast while tears rolled down
his furry cheeks. "Bolghai?" he asked.

Pig nodded.

They had sent only seasoned veterans out as scouts, none
of the boys who had followed Tayyichiut. Even men the
age of Yesugei or the khan must have had a father at some
time, he figured, though he'd never expected to meet one.
Pig must have seen his thoughts in the look he fixed on
the stoat and its warrior son, for his eyes gleamed with a
dark, ironic humor. It wasn't his fault he didn't know anything about the fathers of fathers. He hadn't exactly grown
up knowing much about families at all.

"What's he doing?"

"Trying to dislodge the stone," Pig eased himself down, and stroked the stoat's head with a gentle forehoof. "It pins the dead man's soul to this plane, so that he can neither enter the underworld to join with his ancestors nor return to the wheel of life to be reborn."

As if he had only then become aware of their presence, which was possible, Llesho thought, given the depth of his grief, Bolghai rested his furry head on Pig's knee. With his mouth held open for each panting breath, the stoat set up a high, keening wail that rattled Llesho's nerves and ached in his teeth. He didn't touch the animal, remembering bite marks in Tayy's thumb, but carefully eased himself to his knee.

Pig nodded, holding the stoat's attention with soft murmurs while Llesho reached into the dead breast of the shaman's son and plucked out the rock that had pinned his soul to his corpse. Llesho was beyond surprise, so it came as none that the stone was a black pearl the size of his fist. He tucked it into the sack around his neck, with the others he had collected. The act seemed to release both father and son, for Bolghai shimmered into human form, the tears still wet on his cheeks.

"I'm sorry," Llesho started to say, but Bolghai didn't seem to hear.

"Thank you," the shaman whispered as he faded into nothing on the breeze.

When the last faint glow that marked where he had stood vanished from the air, Llesho turned to Pig, who stood grieving at the side of his friend's dead son.

"I have to find Harlol."

The Jinn nodded. He seemed too caught in his own feelings to speak, but he led on, to a body with the flesh still clinging to it lying on the bloody grass. He recognized Harlol's swords, and the red sash he wore around his waist. The orbits of his eyes were empty, and Llesho fell to his knees on the bloody ground with a whimper that sounded to him like no king at all.

"I'm sorry, I'm sorry!"

It seemed as though he had said nothing else since he'd been cursed with the knowledge of his destiny. Harlol was dead, not reaching to pluck pearls out of their sockets as he had in the dream so long ago, before the Dinha had ever given her Wastrels to his quest. That didn't mean Llesho was getting off easy.

"His hand." Pig gestured with a forehoof.

"Oh, dear Goddess, no!" In death, Harlol's hand had plunged into his own breast. Beneath the cage of bone, dead fingers clenched around a pearl that rested where his heart should be.

Llesho pulled his own hands tight to his sides and rocked on his knees like a widow. "I can't, I can't, I can't," he said, over and over again, while Pig waited patiently for him to realize that, yes, he must, and therefore could.

"Can't you do this one thing for me?" Llesho asked.

"Is that a wish?" Pig asked, and all the world stilled in the moment. Not breath or breeze or beating wing broke the silence of the waiting world.

"Not a wish," he amended, "but my heart's desire, at a higher price than I can pay." With that he reached to cover Harlol's fingers with his own, and carefully pried them one from the other, away from the pearl at their center. He didn't add any more apologies. They'd been given and heard, or not, and he had nothing more to say that wouldn't admit too much. But he thought, within himself, *I will miss you. I would have learned more about you, if fate had given us more time.*

He rose to his feet, his eyes to the brittle turquoise sky, and when he looked again, it was to see the last shimmering glimmer as Harlol faded and vanished. Had he been there at all? Llesho wondered. Or was this just another dream, and he would waken to discover he had hours yet to stop the deaths, to send his party round another way. But when he turned away again, he saw Kaydu, still in the form of an eagle, watching him, and in the distance, the thunder of horses.

Chapter Thirty-three

"LLESHO!" Tayy was the first to reach him, jumping from his horse before the beast had entirely brought its headlong gallop to a halt. "What's happened here? Are you all right? I can't believe you did this after you promised . . ."

The Harnish boy had him by the shoulders, was shaking him, but his anger was a mask for the concern that sent fine tremors through him. Llesho stared into his face, wondering—

"Are you a dream? Or are you real?" he asked. He looked around for Pig, but couldn't find him. Kaydu was still there, however, watching him with the beady eyes of a predator. She spread her wings as if to take flight, but settled again when he reached a hand out to her.

"I'm real," Tayy assured him, "What are you?"

"I'm a dream," he muttered, and let himself fall into the safety of the other's arms. He knew exactly when he'd started to think of the Harnish prince as a friend. Bolghai, in the shape of a stoat, had lain his head on Pig's knee and wept for a fallen son, whom Llesho'd sent to his death. You couldn't stay enemies with a people who died for you. If Prince Tayyichiut wasn't an enemy, then he could accept his friendship. The logic had clicked in place between one heartbeat and another. He would be Tayy's friend, just as the boy had asked him. And he wouldn't let that kill either of them, no matter what. Tayy didn't know that, of course, but called for Carina in a voice high with panic.

"They're dead," he muttered into the shoulder that held him up, kept him from falling. "He raised the earth itself, stone monsters that tore them to pieces, and I couldn't stop it!"

"Gods of earth and water!" Tayyichiut muttered. "Are you talking about something real, or a dream thing?"

"Both, I think. Kaydu won't turn back."

They both looked over at her. She looked back, her intelligence dimmed to the hunting instincts of a bird. She didn't seem to recognize them at all.

"Goddess, Llesho, what happened?" Thank the goddess, it was Shokar who grabbed him away from Tayyichiut. He couldn't have tolerated Lluka's touch. "You were on your horse, riding with the rest of us, and then you were gone. How did you get here?"

"Dreams." He shivered, let his brother hold him for a moment more, then pushed himself away. He needed to be a king, no matter how bad it felt.

Yesugei watched him out of wide, wary eyes. Not the dream travel, he knew—as a chieftain of the Qubal clans, he'd seen the magic of his own shaman often enough. But he'd caught sight of the battlefield over Llesho's shoulder.

"They're all dead." Six men, on a field that had risen up against them. Carina perceived that he had suffered no injuries, and followed the direction he pointed, into the broken ground where the bodies had lain. "Bolghai's son was among them. I didn't know—"

"Otchigin." Tayyichiut nodded sadly. "He was my uncle's anda, his brother by sworn bond. Mergen will mourn him."

Bixei reached him, then, and once again he had to submit to a shaking, before Stipes could pull his companion away with an admonishment, "You aren't teammates in the arena anymore. That is no way to treat your king."

"It is when that king persists in behaving like an idiot, charging off alone into danger and doing it in ways his sworn bodyguards cannot follow." Bixei gave him one last shake, but having said his piece, he stepped back, taking up a guarding position at Llesho's shoulder.

The Harnish prince gave Bixei a look frosty with disdain. "You shouldn't let your servants talk to you that way," he advised. "My father says that familiarity breeds unrest."

"He's not a servant." Llesho thought about it a moment. "I suppose he's more like your uncle's anda, sworn to me out of friendship and a debt of honor that he has assumed from another."

Tayyichiut eyed Bixei with more interest this time. "I suppose he knows lots of stories about your adventures."

"Too many," Bixei admitted. "What's happened to Kaydu?"

They didn't know. "Harlol's dead. Killed by the stonemen. We tried to fight them, but it was no use."

"They'll be gone, then." Yesugei looked out over the turned earth with the still wisdom that had drawn Llesho to trust him from the first. "When the stone men return to the earth, they take the bones with them."

The bodies had been there a few minutes earlier, when Llesho had walked among them, plucking stones from their chests. Some time during the press of greetings, they'd disappeared, leaving nothing but the print of their bones in the blood-soaked ground.

"How will we free their souls," Tayy asked, suddenly distraught as he hadn't been by the news of their deaths. "How can I return with such a failure on my back, to have given the soul of Mergen's anda to the stone-men!"

Running to the place of blood and mayhem, he kicked at the blackened turves. When he drew his sword to slash at the exposed rocks, however, Llesho grabbed his wrist and forced it down.

"He's free. They're all free."

"You don't understand. The stone-men pin their victims' souls to the ground they died on—"

"With a broken fingertip, left in the breast where their hearts used to beat." Llesho shuddered, remembering the sensation of drawing the stones from between the bones of the ravaged bodies. Three black pearls as well, though he didn't know how they'd got there. "I know. Pig told me. I took care of it, for Bolghai."

"You're not just saying that to shut me up?"

Llesho shook his head. "I wouldn't do that. Not anymore."

"There are no souls but those of earth and air and water on this land." Carina joined them, offering comfort where she might, though what she had seen troubled her. "Evil has passed here, but it's gone now. It seems to have taken the hate with it." She passed a thoughtful gaze over Llesho, and he ducked his head, embarrassed not at the change in him, but that she had seen the hate he had carried in his heart until now.

"I saw Bolghai mourn his son and I realized how stupid I've been," he confessed. "Otchigin died in my service, just like Harlol and the Wastrels. I'd forgiven Harlol long ago for kidnapping me, and I figured it was time to stop holding a grudge against the Qubal clans, who'd done nothing to me but bear a resemblance to my enemies."

Kaydu had figured that out long ago—that's why Little Brother was peering over Tayy's shoulder now. It sometimes took him a while, Llesho figured, but he always got there in the end. Carina seemed to agree, because she gave him an absent pat and wandered off again to squat down beside the eagle that Kaydu had become.

His explanation seemed to satisfy the Harnish prince as well, though for him that just meant more questions. Tayyichiut eyed the battlefield in wary study. "Did your Tsu-tan call the stone-men from the earth? That's a very powerful magic."

"No." Llesho was sure of that. "He's a miserable

sneak with a talent for hurting people. He learned that much from his master, but he doesn't have the skill or the ability to do something like this." He needed to pay a visit to the real power behind the attack, on his own terms this time.

"Don't even think it." Little Brother screeched to be let go, and Tayy let him clamber down his long, gangly arm, but he never broke eye contact with Llesho.

"What?"

"If you don't want me to know what you're thinking, you will have to go back to being enemies, because your face is clear as Lake Alta to your friends."

"He's right," Bixei agreed. "About your face, *and* about not going after Markko on your own. After all we've been through to get here, don't let him goad you into doing something stupid that gets you killed this close to home."

Not close at all. The more li he put behind him, the farther away Thebin seemed to get. Maybe that was because of the armies that stood between, or maybe it was his own growing unease. The more he tried to think of Kungol as home, the more remote he felt. His fear of Master Markko paled beside this growing pain that Kungol was no more his home than Pearl Island had been, or Farshore Province. Perhaps he'd been wandering so long that he no longer had the power to feel at home anywhere he went.

And maybe they were right. Maybe he wanted to confront Master Markko because, when it came down to it, the battle that locked him to his enemy had become the only home he'd ever have. When had the thought of dying by a familiar hand become more comforting than that of living as a stranger everywhere? He was a fool, plain and simple.

"He's thinking again." Tayy addressed the comment to Bixei, with the question, "Does that always presage a quick leap into disaster, or does he sink into suicidal thoughts only when I'm around?"

"Master Jaks used to keep him focused."

Bixei stared out over the recent battlefield, and Llesho followed him down that thought, to another field, and Master Jaks dead protecting him from the same enemy they pursued almost to the ends of the earth.

"I didn't know him for long, but his brother Adar seemed able to calm him when moods struck. And Master Den, of course, but he's with the army your father is bringing."

"Lucky for him," Llesho remarked, "I'm running through my teachers, and my brothers, like they were water in the desert."

Kaydu sat, one clawed talon curled under her and hungry eyes fixed on Little Brother.

"What happened to her?" Bixei asked. "She's never stayed in animal form this long before. Did Master Markko—"

"I doubt he needed to. I think she really loved him, and she couldn't save him."

"Harlol? Huh."

He'd noticed, of course, but none of them had taken it as seriously as they should have. Together, they watched as the eagle's fixed stare hypnotized the monkey. Tayy was the first to speak up. "She doesn't recognize him."

"She'll kill us if we let her eat him." Bixei started forward to rescue Little Brother, but Llesho pulled him to a halt with a firm hand on his shoulder.

"Wait. If she kills him, we've lost her anyway."

Tayyichiut looked at him as if he'd just confessed to eating babies for breakfast, but Bixei nodded, and held still. Magical forces gave an edge in battle, but only if you could depend on them totally. Better to know up front if they would slip control under pressure and turn against you. Even if it cost them Kaydu, they had to find out. Carina understood that as well, even as a healer. The knowledge marked her face with deep lines of sorrow, but like the rest of them, she waited.

Little Brother sat in the trampled grass, face scrunched in confusion as he frowned at his mistress. Several paces away, Kaydu cocked her head, as though she were deciding on the most effective angle for breaking the monkey's neck.

"Ahhh," he whimpered, and stretched out a monkey paw to touch her as if he expected her to transform herself and swing him onto her shoulder the way she had so many times before.

This time, however, she snapped at him with her heavy beak and shifted her weight uneasily from foot to foot. Llesho held his breath.

Little Brother rolled forward on his butt, looking around for help from some other direction, but Llesho didn't move. Kaydu hitched her wings and took a step back without breaking the gaze she fixed on her familiar. The monkey followed with a tiny creeping step forward, and the eagle reached, faster than Llesho or his companions could act, and snatched him up by the neck.

He'd seen hunting birds, and knew what came next. A quick toss of her head and she would snap Little Brother's spine. With care she might kill him without ever drawing blood. Llesho couldn't watch her, though. Not this time. Slowly he closed his eyes.

So he missed it when she changed, only realized when Little Brother's joyous shriek told him the monkey wasn't dead after all. When he opened his eyes, his captain stood before him. The untamed hunter lurked in her eyes, but they were shifting with the human pain of memory. She hugged Little Brother close, accepted his warm arms around her neck, but said nothing. Llesho expected Carina to do something healerish, or womanly, or something, but she dusted her hands off against each other as at the end of a dirty chore and wandered off with a satisfied smile that he didn't understand at all. They needed Habiba, and anger sparked at the Lady SienMa. She might be the mortal goddess of war and his own mentor on occasion, but she didn't have a right to demand Habiba's presence so far away when his daughter needed her father.

I hope you've been scrying your daughter, magician, he thought. *I hope you've got a better idea of what to do for her than I have.*

But no dragon appeared in the lowering sky, and there was no Harlol to sidle up beside her and calm her as he might the hunting bird. Only her father had had the same knack of treating her like a woman and a hunting bird both at the same time and in whichever form she took.

Tayyichiut hid his surprise behind a cough. "I knew about such powers, of course, from Bolghai. But it's a shock to actually see the change in person."

Llesho gave a little shrug. "Wait 'till you meet her father."

"Dragon blood?"

"Yep."

"I think I'll wait. Forever, if possible. But you never answered my question."

"What question?"

Kaydu was paying attention, too, stealing glances at the empty battlefield but, thankfully, tracking the discussion with all her wits about her.

"You're not dream traveling to confront this Master Markko fellow on your own."

"No," Kaydu informed him, still not given to more than brief, imperative statements, but in full command mode. "He's not."

"My father is bringing an army of ten thousand," Tayyichiut reminded them. "He'd be very disappointed if you cheated him of battle." There was enough in the statement to assuage Llesho's pride and nudge him to accept how ridiculous the idea was. If he reached Master Markko and defeated him one-on-one at his own magics, he still had an army of Harnish raiders to contend with. That army hadn't needed the magician to take Kungol; they wouldn't let it go even if he did vanquish their current leader. He might even be doing them a favor by ridding them of the magician.

"First, we rescue Hmishi and Lling and Adar," he agreed.

Kaydu shifted Little Brother to her shoulder. "Tsutan's war party lies not more than an hour from here," she reported, and started them moving back toward where their own forces waited. Yesugei and Shokar had held their army back, giving them the small privacy of distance to come to terms with their grief and resolve their differences. Now the time had come to act. "He must have trusted to the monsters his master raised here to stop us; he's made camp by the river."

Llesho squinted into the sky, estimating the daylight that remained. The clouds that had loomed in the eastern sky now made a low ceiling almost to the western horizon, but sunlight still slipped pink and gold around the edges. He reckoned they had time, if they didn't linger. So, plan on the move, relay through his captains. And Tayy's. Yesugei would see to that.

The chieftain cut a meaningful glance at Shokar, who returned the look with confidence. Bixei paid them no attention—no one measured him against a nation he was supposed to lead. He sought out Stipes and wandered off to deliver the plan to the small band of mercenaries who had come with him from Shan. Tayy, however, gave a sigh of long-suffering irritation that found an echo in Llesho's own breast.

"Do you ever get tired of their tests?"

"All the time," the Harnish prince answered. "All the time."

"Well," Llesho decided, "now it's time we tested them." Striding over with Kaydu at his right and Tayyi-chiut at his left, he said, "We ride now, and fight before dusk. Kaydu knows the way."

"He chose his stopping place for convenience to water, rather than defense," she reported. "The ground dips away to the river and the rise on either side obstructs his line of sight, giving us the tactical advantage. There's plenty of scrub and small clumps of twiggy trees close to the river. If we leave the horses a little way off, we can sneak into the camp itself and attack before he knows we are there."

"The bush attack." Tayyichiut nodded, knowing the tactic. "Break your forces into small squads and send them in from random directions, so that if one is sighted, the presence of the others remains hidden. When you're in position, I will bring my warriors around in the lake attack."

"What's a 'lake attack?'" Llesho wanted to know.

Tayy cupped his hands to demonstrate the closing of a circle. "We'll form a ring around the camp and attack from above, on all sides at once."

Yesugei nodded approval, but pointed out, "To be done properly, you should withhold half your force at least, and attack in waves."

Llesho recognized the suggestion for the test that it was. So did Tayy, who answered confidently.

"If we had a hundred more warriors, and this Tsu-tan the same," he agreed, "But we don't, and neither does he. Besides, if we don't take him in the first onslaught, he'll kill the prisoners in his rage."

Llesho was thinking the same thing. "We'll only get one chance to rescue them."

"And if you can't save them?" Lluka asked. His complexion had gone ashy pale from some vision Llesho didn't want to know about.

"Then we'll have all the time in the world for revenge. But I don't accept that as the only option." If all ended in chaos, then nothing he did could make things worse. Llesho found that freeing in a way he thought would terrify his brothers, who put too much faith in Lluka's visions. He believed that Lluka saw what he said; Llesho just wasn't convinced his brother understood what he saw. That made all the difference.

"Captains, advise your troops. Kaydu—"

She gave him a flash of warning in eyes gone cold and predatory. He shivered, but accepted that she didn't want his comfort or his pity.

"We ride for our cadre," he finished. Not what he wanted to say, but it reminded her of earlier ties than the one she had lost. She didn't want any bindings on her heart right now, but he wouldn't let her think she was alone, not as long as any of them were alive. *We need you,* he thought. *We needed Harlol, too, but fate took that decision out of our hands before we left Ahkenbad. Before we met.* He didn't know how much of that he communicated without the words she wouldn't allow, but she held Little Brother more tightly, and mounted her horse with a lighter step. That didn't reassure him. Llesho determined to keep an eye on her during the assault.

"You're not riding anywhere." Shokar, who knew better, rested a hand on the bridle of Llesho's horse. "You're a king now. It's your job to stay alive—"

It took him precious seconds to bring himself back from the battlefield of stone monsters and dead friends, back from the anguish of his captain. When he did, he brought with him the stony darkness that had taken root in his soul.

"No." Llesho kept his voice low, which seemed to make things worse. Silence tighted around their web of whispers. Dissension among the leaders always made the troops uneasy. He had to nip this fast, before they defeated themselves in their own ranks. "I'm a soldier. My masters trained me to fight and if we don't win this war, that's the only skill I have to sell."

Bixei caught his eye and held up an arm where the thick metal wrist guard of the mercenary guild gleamed. "We will be fighters for hire together," said the challenge in his sly smile.

"That's not all they've taught you," Shokar objected, but Llesho'd had enough of listening, and he had no intention of waiting for Lluka to add more doom to the discussion.

"I'm going," he said. "We don't have time to argue, and you wouldn't win anyway."

When he slung himself into his saddle, the Harnish prince did the same. "Chimbai-Khan, my father, says that kings fight their own battles, or they soon have no battles to fight."

No more battles sounded like the best outcome he could imagine, but he figured there was more to it. Harlol's battles were over, and so were Master Jaks'. The khan was right. Kings fought their own battles, or they died anyway, like his father had.

Shokar seemed to be working toward the same conclusion. "You know, if we die, Lluka will be in charge of the next battle."

"According to his visions, it's the end of the world. How much worse can even Lluka make that?"

He hadn't spoken the thought aloud before, but it didn't rattle his brother the way he expected. Lifting onto his own horse, Shokar heaved a put-upon sigh. "I don't know which of you is more trouble."

"My way, at least there is a chance of success," Llesho pointed out. "Lluka's way will save you an hour in the saddle, but could cost the kingdom."

"Right. You've made your point. Do you treat all your brothers this way?"

Bickering meant the crisis was over. Kaydu cut them short with an abrupt nod, and gave the signal to move out.

THE ground rose gently before falling away again to the Onga River beside which Tsu-tan had pitched his tents. Kaydu signed for a halt while the terrain was still rising. Another hand-signaled command followed, and the combined force of Thebin recruits, mercenaries, and the remaining Wastrels dismounted and broke into small, tight bands. At their backs, the Harnish warriors spread out in a thin line that ringed in the valley below. Llesho's troops would find the captives and spirit them away while Tayy's Harnish riders distracted the raiders with a "lake" formation assault.

Promotion had broken his own cadre as much as the capture of Hmishi and Lling had. Llesho found himself alone at the head of a squad of Shokar's Thebins; nearby, his brother led another. He'd considered Shokar more of a frontal assault sort of person, too straightforward for his own good sometimes, and grimly distasteful of battle. But he'd taken the same training from Bixei and Stipes that his recruits received. Crouched low to take cover in the undergrowth, he ran with a smooth, sound-less grace copied by the squad that followed him. Half of them were women, like Lling.

Llesho hadn't taken the time to find out who his fight-ers were, and he regretted that now, when he was leading his own small band into the camp of the enemy. They moved together as a single organism, however, sensitive to his every gesture, and Llesho quickly adapted, trusting in Bixei's training and the strength and courage of his own people. He followed Shokar's example, crouched into a swift glide, and slipped among the clumps of un-dergrowth. Tsu-tan, or his captain, had posted guards, but they had grown lax with inattention as the days had passed and they grew more secure, thinking that no at-tack would come. A Thebin farmer-turned-soldier ghosted ahead and took out the man nearest their posi-tion, slicing his throat from side to side in one smooth, quick pass—a barnyard skill as much as a soldierly one. He let the body fall, and wiped his knife on the grass.

Llesho gave him a nod to acknowledge the service, and led his band around the smaller tents, targeting the largest, where he knew Hmishi lay with the healer-prince Adar in attendance. Off to one side, Bixei crept as silently with his mercenaries, and farther around the bowl of the river valley, Kaydu led the Wastrels. They had come to know her through Harlol, who would have led them if he'd lived.

Don't think about that, he warned himself. Don't think about the dead he'd already lost, or those who would die today or tomorrow or the next day in his battles. The black command tent was ahead, and he dropped silently to his knees and pulled out his knife while his squad followed, snugging in close under the shadows of evening. He could hear the murmur of voices inside; carefully he cut into the felt at the bottom of the tent and slid the small flap aside to peer in between the crosspieces of the lathing. Tsu-tan was there, squared off against Adar, who stood between the witch-finder and the bed on which the wounded Hmishi lay.

"He can't take anymore. He's going to die. Can't you get that through your head? He's a human being, and can only take so much abuse before the ability to heal is exhausted. He's already passed that point—"

"Then it doesn't really matter what I do to him, does it?" Tsu-tan picked up the iron rod he had used when Llesho had visited here in a dream. Adar moved to intercept the blow, and took the weight of the rod on his shoulder. Llesho heard the crack of bone, and his brother fell, groaning, to his knees.

Enough. Llesho would kill him with his bare hands and stomp his bones into powder. He started to his feet, but a hand, reaching out of the shadows, stopped him with a touch at his elbow. He thought his heart would fail at the shock, but training kept him moving until his brain could catch up. He rolled and twisted, shifting his knife from a sawing to a stabbing hold and poised, the point quivering at her throat.

"Lling!" soundlessly he mouthed her name, and she nodded, drugged hypnosis still cloudy in her eyes. She was fighting it. He could see that, and her own knife had come into her hand, as he had seen in his dream travels.

She held a finger to her lips, signaling him to keep silent, and rose lithely to her feet, folding her own knife down at her side as she did so. Then she was gone, slipping through the murk that shrouded Tsu-tan's tent.

Llesho's small squad watched him worriedly. They were supposed to wait for Tayy's lake assault before going in. Lling wasn't part of that plan, however, and Adar didn't have that much time. Llesho gestured for them to stay, and followed Lling, his knife and sword both at the ready in the deadly tradition of Thebin royalty. At the door to the tent, however, he waited. In the confusion of the coming attack, he could take Tsu-tan without fear of discovery. Now, Lling had the advantage—as long as she could fight off Master Markko's control.

Tsu-tan glanced over when Lling entered his tent, but gave her no more notice than that, his attention focused entirely on Adar. Llesho, hidden on the other side of the door flap, saw the sweat beading over the witch-finder's lip, the rapid rise and fall of his chest as the argument excited his breathing. "Do you want to take his punishment, healer?"

"Your master says no." Adar made no move to protect himself. His tone and expression made it a token protest. Like his patient, Tsu-tan had drifted over an invisible line, and there was no pulling him back now. Adar observed the forms, but did not raise a hand to protect himself. As a healer and as a husband of the goddess, he had taken an oath and would protect his patient at any cost to himself.

The witch-finder's hands tightened rhythmically on the weapon, but the reminder of his master stopped him short of raising it again. A Thebin peasant was one thing, but Markko wanted the princes for his own uses.

"Perhaps the girl, then?" he grabbed Lling by her hair and swung her body close to his. "My master will understand if I can take her instead—" He leered down into her trance-dazed face and raised the iron rod to strike another blow.

Not Lling, Llesho thought. In his seventh summer he'd

lost his bodyguard to the Harnish raiders. He was older now, better trained, and Lling was still alive. It didn't have to end that way again. "Not one more blow against my people—"

Recklessly he moved the door flap aside, ready to come to her rescue even if it did bring the witch-finder's guards. As he stepped into view, Tsu-tan whipped around, Lling held close as a shield. "You!" he smirked. "Is this another trick of your dreams, beggar prince?"

"No dream," Llesho assured him, and raised his ready-drawn sword.

"I assume you're not alone?" Adar asked faintly. Llesho figured he knew what was on his brother's mind. It was easier to get into a prison than to get out of one, even if it was made of tents.

Before he could answer, he heard the sound he'd been waiting for: the war cry of the Harnish riders rising over the pounding of their horses. Tayy had begun the attack. Llesho heard the hiss of arrows in flight and the clatter and snick as they found their marks in bodies and tents. Some, he knew, carried barbed points, some carried flames.

The thunder of their galloping horses shook the ground as they made their descent. Raiders would be spilling out of their tents, gathering on horseback to repel the invaders while Llesho's ambush troops took their signal to slip into the abandoned tents to search for prisoners. They would find few, he knew, and join the attack so that the enemy was hemmed in on all sides and within its own ranks.

"That's your rescue party now," he said, watching Tsu-tan all the while.

"Guards!" the witch-finder called, and paled when the Thebin faces of Llesho's squad appeared in his doorway.

"Excellency?" Llesho's corporal inquired. She was tall for a Thebin, approaching middle age, and the scar over her right eye made her look as dangerous as she was.

Llesho acknowledged her salute. "Don't let anyone in until I tell you."

The woman frowned uneasily at the tableau before her. She knew her job, however, and bowed her way out. No one would pass while his squad lived.

"Let her go." Llesho gestured at Lling with his sword. "You know it's over for you now."

Screams rose in the camp, muffled by the black felt that surrounded them, but the witch-finder glanced nervously at the doorway, calculating, Llesho could see, his chances for escape. So caught up was he in the threat from outside that he almost missed the life glinting suddenly in Lling's eyes.

The flash of recognition wasn't enough to save him. Tsu-tan dropped the iron rod, freeing his hands to throw her away from him. Lling held on with her free hand and with the other she rested the point of her knife neatly at the base of his sternum.

"Die," she whispered, and plunged her knife into his heart. "Die crawling on your belly, snake." She took a step back and let him fall.

"I guess you didn't need me after all." Llesho pointed his sword at the ground, but kept his knife at the ready. The sounds of battle were close, and he didn't want to get overconfident.

"Actually, I did need you." Lling glanced up at him with a curious frown knotting her brow. "I think more clearly when you're around."

"Glad to oblige. How are you thinking now?"

"Good." She stared down at Tsu-tan, absently wiping her knife on her sleeve. "Good."

The witch-finder didn't hear. Blood frothed at his lips, and slowly his eyes filmed over. When the blood stopped, he was dead. Across the body, Llesho and Lling shared a little smile. He thought perhaps he shouldn't feel that way, but his heart felt lighter.

"Let me look at him," Adar whispered. His strength

was almost gone, but still he held on. "Maybe I can do something—"

"It's too late. He's dead."

Llesho turned away from the body of his enemy and knelt beside his brother. Adar was going to fall on his face if they didn't do something, but any movement would drive more of the jagged bone fragments through the skin or deeper into his body.

The idea of his brother lying on the same floor as the man who had tormented him raised Llesho's gorge, but he didn't see any choice. He pulled off his coat and flung it on the carpets well clear of the blood that soaked through nearby, then eased Adar down, holding him while he screamed with the agony of shifting bone. He could hear the grinding of shards against each other, but had nothing to offer other than soft words of encouragement.

"Carina is with us. She'll be here soon. You just have to hold on a little longer."

Gritting his teeth against another cry that might bring the battle down on them, Adar grunted in pain, but he was down now. Panting through pursed lips, he held onto consciousness with the techniques that had worked on his patients in the past and would keep him awake now.

"Scream if it helps." Lling advised him while she pulled open drawers and pawed through dressing gowns until she found one that didn't reek of Tsu-tan's scent. "Llesho's people have the door covered."

"Fainting is okay, too," Llesho added. *Fainting is good,* he thought, *you can't feel the pain that way.* He couldn't help but notice that, in all the commotion of Adar's injury and Tsu-tan's murder, Hmishi hadn't awakened at all. *Fainting is good,* he reminded himself, but secretly he knew it was much worse than that. Adar had said Hmishi'd gone too far.

He needed Carina, and that wouldn't happen until they'd taken the camp.

"Stay with them," he requested. When Lling nodded assent, he slipped out to join his squad.

Chapter Thirty-four

INTO chaos. He'd been in a battle like this before, the other side of the Harnlands, but this time, they had more than the advantage of the high ground. Raiders would fight fiercely if they saw a profit at the end of it, or if a harsh master drove them from behind. But Tsu-tan was dead, his prisoners already taken. Llesho's bands of ambushers rose up to harry Tsu-tan's guard from their supper and fire the tents. The arrows from Tayy's ring of warriors cut off escape, pushing the enemy deeper into their own camp so that they had nowhere to go but the commons, where they were easily cut down by spear and sword.

Llesho led his own small squad into the thick of the fighting, swords bristling. He slashed and parried, stabbed and slew until his arm ached. When he could no longer lift his sword, he drew the spear from his back. Old skills learned for the arena shifted his balance and he leaped and jabbed, twirled under the guard of a raider and tore up through the muscle that wrapped his opponent's rib cage. *Not opponent,* he reminded himself. *Enemy.*

The raider fell screaming; his blood hissed and steamed as it pooled on the ground, sizzling at the touch

of old magics leaking from the spear. Llesho whirled to
defend a squad-mate whose name he didn't know, and
when he surfaced from the battle rage, the raiders had
broken. Fierce against the weak, the very savagery of the
Harnishmen's own raids added fuel to their terror of the
mighty. They dreaded the retribution of their enemies,
who they imagined were as merciless as they were themselves. At that moment, Llesho didn't blame them. He
was feeling merciless indeed, but Yesugei had taken
charge of the Uulgar captives who flung themselves to
their knees in surrender. The remains of the battle
moved off toward the river, pursued by Tayyichiut with
a band made up of equal parts of his own warriors and
Bixei's mercenaries. Llesho left them to it- -he had more
pressing business.

"Shokar?" he asked of his corporal, who watched him
with uneasy wonder as she struggled to steady her labored breath. She nodded in the direction of a burning
tent.

Shokar stood with the point of his sword on the ground
and his weight resting on the hilt. His eyes had the glassy
look of shock about them.

"Are you hurt?" Llesho touched a finger to the back
of his hand, careful not to startle battle nerves.

"I'm fine." Shokar brought his vision back from the
middle distance to rest on his brother. "You're all
bloody—"

"Not mine. Tsu-tan's dead. Lling killed him." He
didn't say that he'd been glad, or that he would have
done it himself, but Lling beat him to it. Shokar wouldn't
understand the feelings that knotted his stomach. Wrong
feelings, he would have thought, the satisfaction mixing
with the grief. Tsu-tan was dead, Hmishi was dying, and
Llesho didn't want to look at what his journey was turning him into. "Am I becoming like him?" he asked.

They both knew he meant Master Markko. He hadn't

planned to say it out loud. Now that he had, he held his breath, afraid of hearing his brother's judgment but needing it all the same.

"You're becoming a king," Shokar told him. "I'm glad it's not me. Really. If I try to guide you, it's because I don't want to see you hurt. The Harnish boy's right, though. If we protect you too much, from the fighting or the decisions, you won't be fit to rule. If we don't protect you enough—"

He'd be dead, or turned into the enemy he despised. Llesho looked out over the battleground, where his small army was doing clean up. Moving from tent to tent, they entered with weapons at the ready and came out again with the captives Tsu- tan's forces had taken as servants. Along the way they gathered prisoners of their own, the Uulgar raiders of the South, who had hidden among the slaves. He'd leave that part of the campaign under Ye- sugei's command, he decided. His own concerns had narrowed to the handful of lives he had carried out of Shan. "Don't let me be a danger to my people."

"This is conversation for philosophers. Or the gods." Shokar refused the responsibility. "If you are brooding over the death of a villain like Tsu-tan, you need the priests or that old shaman, not a judge."

"I'm glad the witch-finder's dead—this blood is Adar's. Tsu-tan had tired of beating a dying soldier, and had begun on our brother."

"How bad?"

"Not as bad as Hmishi. He needs the bones set in his shoulder."

Shokar nodded, understanding the brooding now. "You'll want Carina for that; I saw her on the banks of the Onga. Tsu-tan's guard tried to run, but they were hemmed in at the river. Some jumped. The lucky ones were pulled out by their fellows, the less lucky washed up drowned at a bend a little way downstream. Where's Adar?"

"The command tent. Like his master, Tsu-tan liked to

keep his toys close." Llesho turned away to find the healer, but Shokar's warm hand firm on his shoulder stopped him.

"You're a good man, Llesho," he said.

He wasn't sure of that anymore, but it warmed him to hear his brother say it. Shokar didn't wait for an answer, but went to attend their wounded brother while Llesho searched out the healer.

He found her among the dead who lay tumbled on the beaten grass that grew between the clumps of tall thin trees on the banks of the Onga. She wore the costume of a shaman and flitted from one to the next of the dead with the darting hops of a jerboa. With a prayer over each, she closed their staring dead eyes before moving on. At first, Llesho thought they were all Southern casualties. Then he recognized a boy among the bodies, and realized that he couldn't tell them apart. North and South, the Harnish wore the same long woolen shirts above wide leather trousers, with long coats over all. Some of the veteran Southerners wore hanks of hair sewn to their coats, trophies of their human kills as he remembered. Mostly, they looked younger than he'd expected.

Death, he had realized long ago, cured every face of its intentions. He didn't begrudge Carina's tears, but the living needed her more.

"I've found him. Adar. He needs you."

"He's hurt?" That surprised her. Which surprised him. Her mother didn't read minds, exactly, but Mara had known what he was thinking, and Carina's father was a dragon. Still, she moved fast enough when she knew there was trouble. "Please, lead me to him."

They met a party of Tayyichiut's veterans heading toward the river as Llesho and Carina left it. Among them they carried the body of Tsu-tan, taking him down to be burned with the others. Carina stopped them a moment for a prayer over their enemy. The hard-eyed warriors gave her the respect due a shaman, but they didn't encourage her to linger.

"Whoever killed him will need my attentions as well, when I have seen to Adar."

She looked at Llesho as if she expected him to confess, but he just gave her a weary nod. "I'll tell her. Adar said that Hmishi was too far gone, but I thought if you would look at him—"

"Of course. At the very least, I can intercede with the spirits of the underworld to gentle his passing."

That wasn't what he had in mind; Carina warned him away from a petition she mustn't honor with a frown. "Soldiers die," she said, "Kaydu knew that. Lling does. So do you."

They had reached Tsu-tan's command tent, so he didn't have to answer. Didn't want to have that conversation. He'd have taken it to avoid facing the inside of that tent again, but that wasn't a choice. The tent smelled of blood and other taints, but at Shokar's instruction, his squad had rolled the tent walls up halfway and had taken out the blood-soaked carpets.

Hmishi's spirit had not returned from the place where it waited for the journey to end. There was no part of his body that remained unbroken, but Lling sat with his shattered hand on a pillow in her lap, afraid to touch lest she return him to the pain of the waking world. Suddenly, the thick air in the tent was choking him, and Llesho knew he had to get out, away, before it killed him. So he ran.

Tayyichiut found him at the river. Still flushed from the battle, the Harnish prince fidgeted with flat stones he scrounged from the banks, skipping them over the water where his enemies had lately drowned.

"They sent me to find you," he said, and skipped a stone the color of a stormy sky once, twice, three times before it sank. "I told them to send a servant, but they pointed out that as a king, you had no obligation to obey a servant. As a guest, however, you must agree with your host or have the manners of your house cast in doubt. Shokar assured me you would never do that. So here I am."

Llesho sat with his back against the bark of a convenient tree and his knees tucked under his chin. Tayy was right; he owed his host not only for the protection of his camp and the training of his shaman, but also for the aid he had given in battle. Still, he found it impossible to move.

"They want you to come back. Kaydu said to make it an order if I thought it would work. Won't, though, will it?" Throwing himself to the ground next to Llesho, Tayyichiut curled his leg under him and let the couple of stones left in his hand dribble to the ground. "I didn't think so.

"Otchigin is dead, and Yurki died right over there—" he pointed to a place of rusty stains on broken grass, "—and I don't know what I am going to tell my uncle, or my father, or Yurki's father, for that matter. I always knew that people could die in battle. Mergen taught me not to value life more than honor, and Yesugei warned us all to expect death and welcome life at the end of it. But nobody told me about the big holes it left in the world when you lived but your friends didn't."

Tayy's distress held a mirror to Llesho's own pain. When the first tear slipped from the corner of the prince's eye, Llesho found an answering tear in his own.

"Since Kungol fell, you can count the seasons I've spent with my brothers on your thumbs," Llesho said. He didn't look at his companion but stared out at the river, thinking back to Pearl Island. "I met Bixei and Stipes and Master Den when I went to the arena in my fifteenth summer, and Kaydu I met when we fought each other in my first and only bout as a gladiator. But all the life that I remember has Hmishi and Lling in it. We trained together for the pearl beds, and worked together as a team until my quest pulled me out of Pearl Bay. I thought I'd lost them for good then, but fate and the Lady SienMa brought us back together again in service to the governor of Farshore Province.

"Lling was always the best soldier. Hmishi only came along because we had all been together for so long we didn't know any other way to be. He didn't want to be left behind, and now I've got him killed."

"It wasn't just you," Tayy suggested. "From what I've heard, he loved Lling, and she loved him. He couldn't have stopped her from going, and wouldn't have let her go without him."

"Now you're saying it's Lling's fault?"

"Seems to me it's this Tsu-tan's fault, and his master's."

Llesho did look at him then, locked gazes, making very sure that Tayyichiut understood. "It doesn't matter whose fault it is. He's still dead."

"Not yet." Tayyichiut dragged himself to his feet. He wobbled a little, and Llesho could almost feel the shifting of balance in his own legs. Battle fatigue was hitting, leaving muscles limp as rope and bones shaking like a newborn foal, but he managed to right himself with the dignity of a warrior prince. "He will be soon, though. Lling thought you would want to say good-bye."

"Lling knows I am bad at good-byes." He'd nearly dragged Master Jaks back from the dead, were it not for the protest of the corpse itself. He knew better now, or thought he did. Nevertheless, he doubted Lling would leave him alone with her dead lover. Who still clung to life with each ragged breath. Giving a last empty glance at the river, he clambered to his feet and turned to follow Tayyichiut.

The prince reached out and rubbed his thumb across Llesho's cheek, first one, then the other. "My father says that a khan must never show weakness," he said, and Llesho saw the tears glistening on the fleshy pad just before he wiped them dry against the side of his coat. Together, they made their way back to the camp.

Shokar was efficient, and so was Yesugei. The Harn raised their camp on the plains above the little valley where the Onga River flowed. Their wounded needed to be close to water and protected from the wind, however. As healer and shaman in the camp, Carina chose the valley where Tsu-tan had made his camp. First she had the troops clear the black tents of the enemy, then the square red ones of Llesho's army and round white ones of the khan's troops were set in their places. As much as they needed shelter, their wounded needed the clean air of their own tents.

Hmishi was still alive, though he had not roused when they moved him to the shelter of a red tent. Lling had insisted that if he wake, it must be to the red light of his own tents, to convince him that he had indeed been saved. Though all his bones were broken, Carina set only his left arm, so that Lling could hold his hand on a pillow without the ends of the long bones grinding against each other with each small shift of her position.

"He made me break Hmishi's hand," she whispered through her tears. "He controlled my movements, but not my sensations. I raised Tsu-tan's iron rod, and felt the bones break beneath it when it fell."

Her eyes had a distant look, grim and deadly, so that Llesho wondered if the magician still controlled her from afar. "Something broke inside me, too. Then you came. Slowly the spell he cast lost its hold over my thoughts."

When she smiled, Llesho realized that she was slipping into madness. His quest, it seemed, had that effect on even the most competent of those who surrounded him.

"Is he still in your head?" Llesho asked. He thought he ought to be more worried about the intelligence Master Markko might be collecting through her eyes, but he found that mattered less to him than the creeping horror of the magician's hold on her mind.

But she shook her head. "I felt him go when the witch-finder died," she said, never taking her eyes off Hmishi. "I don't think he can maintain a hold on a mind he's taken from so far—not without a willing intermediary working with him. And Tsu-tan was more than willing."

"But he's gone. You're safe." He stopped her fingers from their restless wandering over the hand she held in her lap. *You can't be broken,* he thought. *Hmishi's not the only one who needs you.* He didn't add that to her burden, but reminded her of the only duty that seemed to matter to her now. "Hmishi will need you when he wakes up—the real you, the one he loves—right here, and not hiding away safe inside your head."

"Do you think I'm really safer inside my head?" she asked, her voice rising to a keening wail, "when all I can think about is the breaking of his bones?"

"I need you whole." It spilled out, selfish as it was. *He* needed her, *he* couldn't lose them now, when Master Markko's armies stood ahead of them, so close to the final battle.

"You need too much."

Llesho had said the same of his quest to the gods and ghosts who moved him. They hadn't released him, and he couldn't let Lling go either. "Who else can I depend on to do murder for me?" he asked, and it was the right thing to say. She was no less mad, but he knew that, just as the magician had, he could pull her strings. Only, instead of magic, he would use her hatred to control her. It made him ill to think it, but he couldn't let her go.

"He doesn't have your brother."

"What?" Llesho pulled back from the brink of his thoughts to focus on what she was saying.

"When the magician was in my mind, he took what I knew, but I sensed his thoughts as well." She shuddered at a memory. Coward though it made him, Llesho was glad she didn't share it with him. "He was looking for Menar, the poet, but he hadn't found him. It's hard to track the blind from a distance; he can't see out of his prey's eyes, so he doesn't know where to look. But he hears the camel bells, and the air grows warmer."

That jibed with Shou's report. He felt a burden lift

from his heart that Master Markko hadn't succeeded in capturing the blind prince. But warmer? The high plains had already passed the height of summer and now declined swiftly into winter.

"Camel bells mean a caravan," Llesho mused out loud, "but does it cross north, down off the plateau toward Shan, or into the West?"

West, he thought. Lling didn't look away from Hmishi's wounds, but she was tracking now, and he took ruthless advantage of that. "Did he know of Ghrisz?"

"Oh, everybody knows about Ghrisz," she said in such an offhand way he wondered how the matter had escaped him.

That was Markko's imprint, however; the magician had tapped a mind somewhere Llesho's brother was well known. "Tell me, then."

"He's in Kungol."

"A prisoner?" He was plotting rescue attempts in his head when she answered with a dark smile.

"A fugitive. In hiding. It's a race now, he thinks. If the raiders find Ghrisz, they will kill him." She had gone away in her head again, and Llesho wondered who was speaking to him—Lling, out of her memories, or the magician himself, in control again and taunting him with pieces of the puzzle. She'd said he was gone, but could she have been mistaken?

"Master Markko?" he asked, softly so as not to startle her.

But when she stole a glance at him, he knew. That was Lling, the most dangerous of their cadre, but herself alone.

"He can't touch me now," she said, and he wondered if she meant more than the breaking of the spell with Tsu-tan's death. "I can't read him either, anymore. But I remember it all." And she would use even her most horrific memories in their service if it brought her closer to Master Markko's blood.

"He would have used Adar to draw Ghrisz out of

hiding, but now he seeks the last brother to use as bait, to draw you all to him. If you win through and find Menar first, he loses his leverage against the raiders who hold Kungol. And he wants something in Kungol very badly."

"But what?" The raiders had looted the treasuries of Kungol long ago, and they had mostly been spiritual anyway.

"I don't know. I never got deep enough to find out." Her gaze was clear when she turned it on him. "Find him for me, and I'll make him talk. Those secrets—what pain he feels as pleasure, and what other he fears most in the world—I know."

Llesho shivered at her grim purpose. What did it make him, knowing he couldn't do what Lling proposed, but willing to let her take that burden for him? What other tasks in front of him would prove greater than his strength? This one, for instance. Watching Hmishi die.

Carina joined them then, with a shallow dish of pungent purple water in which leaves and bits of bark floated. "He can't drink," she said. "Even if his throat could swallow, there is too much damage throughout his body. Any liquid would leak through the wounds and create infection where it pools. But this will help."

She took a soft white cloth and dipped it in the water, then smoothed it over Hmishi's cracked lips. "Sometimes, especially when the pull of life and love are strong, the spirit of one who has traveled so far on his journey to the underworld will turn back to bid farewell. This should free him from the pain, if he should rise out of his sleep to say good-bye."

"Thank you." Lling reached for the cloth, and Carina gave it to her, relieving her of the pillow on her lap so that she could move about his bed with ease.

"Bathe him carefully—he won't feel the pain where the elixir touches."

Llesho figured he wouldn't feel the pain anyway. He'd seen death on the battlefield, and it hovered thick above this bed like a dream. It gave Lling something to do, however, and a way to touch her lover without fear of hurting him. Knowing Carina, that was her intention. It seemed to be working. The healer passed in and out of the tent with a word, a touch, but left them to their vigil. Chen and Han, the lesser moons, crossed the sky with Great Moon Lun in pursuit, but Llesho marked their passing only by the dim red light that moved across the roof of the tent.

Finally, as the lesser sun spread the gray light of false dawn, Lling curled up on the floor close beside the bed and closed her eyes. Llesho resisted the pull of sleep but battle and grief had exhausted him. Like Lling, he would not leave Hmishi to die alone, but found a place on the rugs to rest. Sleep, when it came, crept up on him like a gray mist.

Pig was waiting for him in the dream world, but he didn't need his spirit guide to tell him where he was. He recognized his brother, and the woman pulling him down on the rich-turned earth with an arm around his neck and a kiss on his lips while the bright heads of sunflowers above them guarded their play. With a long, silent glance at Pig, who watched the couple moving among the tall green stems, he began walking, out of his brother's dream.

He had figured out on his own that he sought out Shokar's dreams unconsciously, for the comfort they afforded. That ought to mean that he could visit his other brothers as well, though he doubted that he would find so warm and inviting a resting place in any of their dreams. Before he went on spending lives in his quest, however, there were things he had to know. Like, what did Lluka dream that filled him with despair? He would go there before he was done, but first he brought the image of Balar to mind. This brother, too, harbored secrets. He didn't think Balar would react as badly as Lluka would to finding Llesho in his dreams, so he stepped up, into a room with walls plastered in yellow mud and lit by a branch of candles on a familiar table. They were in Balar's music room in the Palace of the Sun.

"Come in if you want to, but try to keep still." Balar turned to him with a frown of concentration pulling at his brows. In his hands he held a lute which he was tuning with small turns of the keys and small shifts of the frets. It was a smaller instrument than Llesho knew him to play: four courses of strings, he saw, with two strings per course, except for the highest string. Seven strings in all, six in pairs and one alone.

"Where is Ping?" Llesho asked. He figured the strings must be the seven brothers, but where was their sister?

"Not yet born," came the answer, "Soon, though, I should think." Not long after Ping was born, Balar had gone to Ahkenbad for a diplomatic visit and training in the mystical ways of the dream readers. In his dream, Llesho's brother had returned to that more peaceful time, but still his face was tense with worry.

"What are you doing?"

To demonstrate, Balar strummed the lute. It took no expert in music to hear the sour clash of notes. "I can't seem to bring them into harmony, no matter what I do." He shifted the frets a bit more, tried again, and shook his head, dissatisfied. "This one is the key—" He plucked the highest string, the solitary note. The string Llesho thought must symbolize himself.

"I think it's this one," Llesho said, and pointed to the lowest string, so tightly drawn that it seemed on the edge of snapping. The neck of the lute seemed to strain under the pressure of that tension.

"I've lost the key," Balar pointed to the beak, where one tuning key was indeed missing. "Still, it's all in the balance. The other strings will have to compensate. Especially—" he gave Llesho a pointed look "—the highest."

"I don't think I can stretch any farther," Llesho answered in the same metaphor.

Balar gave a little shake of his head. "Then you'll have

to find the key." He returned to his tuning as if he
were alone.

After just a moment more to breathe in the memory
of Kungol, Llesho started running in his dream. He
thought about visiting Adar, but didn't want to disturb
the work of Carina's healing herbs on his brother's sleeping body.

"You know what you have to do," Pig reminded him.
"You might as well get it over with."

Llesho did know, and he ran with a purpose, finding
his brother Lluka sleeping in his tent with a lantern glowing in the dark. He wondered if Lluka always slept with
a light, if the darkness of his mind was so desperate that
he daren't close his eyes on an outer darkness as well.

"What do you want?" Lluka opened his eyes, staring
into the corner of the tent where Llesho stood, but his
brother didn't seem to see him. "If you are a demon of
my sleep, begone. I've had enough of your torments.
They don't move me anymore."

"Not a demon. It's me, Llesho." He stepped into the
lantern light, but Lluka didn't see or hear. With a
grumble he straightened his tangled blankets and lay on
his back, staring blank-eyed at the tent cloth overhead.

No dreams here, Llesho thought, before he was swallowed whole into a directionless gray twilight. Like the
gardens of heaven, he remembered, where night never
fell. He reached to clasp the pearl he carried at his
throat. When he found them all and returned them to
the Great Goddess, light and dark would return to
heaven, and the stars would ascend to their proper
places. He didn't know how, but it was part of his quest.
This wasn't the heavenly gardens, however. In Lluka's
dream, there was no earth to stand on, no heavenly paths
or divine fruit trees. The gray dusk, aswirl in ash and
fire, rang with the clash of swords and the cries of the
dying, reeked with the sweat of battle and the fear of
horses and soldiers. And their blood, a smell that choked
him as Llesho struggled to find his way.

"Lluka!" he called through the dream landscape. "Where are you?"

"I am in hell, brother. All the futures I have seen come to this, though you are dead in most of them." Lluka took shape, came forward out of the mist.

"What has happened here?" Llesho asked. "For that matter, your answer to my first question was dramatic but not very useful. Where are we, and how did we get here?"

"The questions are impossible to answer. 'How *will* we get here?' at least gets the when of it right. This is the future of all the worlds. 'Where' doesn't exist anymore. Hell will overrun heaven and earth, killing the night and murdering the day, wiping out all that lives or grows or breathes. When they are free, the demons of hell will set fire to the air and trample the heavenly gardens under their clawed hooves. The material world will vanish, disintegrate into nothing as the forces of heaven and hell come together in the greatest conflagration the universe has ever known. All the realms of sky and earth, of the underworld and the wheel of life will fall in the fires of that battle. In all my dreams, and my waking nightmares, this is what I see."

As Lluka spoke those final words, the sounds of battle erupted in an explosion so immense that his senses couldn't grasp it. Fire swept toward him in a wall, faster than a horse could run, faster than a mind could grasp the oncoming devastation. Llesho called out in terror and threw his hands over his eyes, too late to stop the blindness as the fire swept over him. In the trembling gray of the death of the universe, he realized that he was still alive, the battle raging around him as it had before the conflagration had passed over.

"And now, we do it again," Lluka said with a grimace of a smile, mocking both of them.

"Does Master Markko do this?" Llesho asked, his voice shaky but determined. All he had to do was stop the magician, and none of it would happen.

"No," Lluka answered, "though he started it long ago. When he was young, I think, he wished to prove his power over the underworld, probably by calling the dead, though his purpose and his methods make no part of the dreams that fill my nights. What the dreams show is that he released a great demon king from hell instead. How the magician survived his own magic I do not know either, except that he must have made some bargain with the creature. Their goal is now the same—bring down the gates of heaven. When hell takes the heavenly gardens, all life will perish, all worlds will perish."

A fireball suddenly filled the sky, sucking all the sound out of the air and freezing time and motion in the moment. Llesho crouched down, cowering behind his sleeve, as the waiting havoc was released in a hurricane riding ahead of the flames. When the storm had passed over them, Lluka continued.

"Like you, I once had hope. But one by one the futures that might vie with the destruction have vanished from my dreams. Now I only see the end, and sometimes, the face of the demon raging at the gates that still stand against him. But they weaken, and there is nothing left to be done but die."

"There has to be a way," Llesho insisted, though his heart quivered in his chest. "The Great Goddess calls me to her aid. That has to mean we have a chance of winning."

"None that I can see," Lluka answered, then he squinted, as if something had obscured his vision. "Llesho? Where did you go? Llesho!"

Returning his brother's call would do no good, any more than waving his hands in his brother's face. The dream had taken Lluka past Llesho, and he wandered away, moaning as the fireball rose again, taller than any tree, tall enough to swallow Great Moon Lun in its vast maw. When Llesho brought his eyes away from the horrifying sight, he was back again in the tent city of the khan. The ger-tent of the khan lay ahead, and he felt the lingering pull of the Lady Chaiujin's potion in his blood. He entered, surprised that none of the khan's many guards stopped him as he passed down the center to the dais where the khan slept with his wife. Except that when he reached the mound of rugs and furs, an emerald- green bamboo snake raised its head and looked at him out of lidless black eyes.

"Go back," she hissed at him. "You do not belong here." And she laid her head down on the khan's breast.

Pig rejoined him then, a troubled frown curling around his tusks. He put a forehoof on Llesho's shoulder, drawing him away. "She's right. You don't belong here."

"I want—" he began, and woke up with the words still on his lips.

Chapter Thirty-five

LLESHO woke in the red tent where he had started his dream travels. Dawn had brightened the sky to the color of Lluka's dreams, confusing him for a moment. Had he really returned, or was he still dream traveling? But Lling still slept at the side of the cot where Hmishi's labored breath stuttered and fell, stuttered and fell. *Back,* he thought; it hadn't happened yet. There was still time to stop it. He gave a shaky sigh of relief and threw off his blankets.

On the cot in the corner, the breath rattled in Hmishi's throat, and died.

No! Leaping to his feet, Llesho pressed his lips tightly together to keep from raging out loud. He thought he ought to wake Lling but refused to give her up to grief; he needed her sane to keep from flying to pieces himself. But he couldn't stay here, with the rage beating at his ribs.

Low branches hit him, and vines grabbed at his legs, but he ignored them and the small injuries he collected. Llesho was running before he realized what he was doing. *No, no, no!* He needed to get away, escape to the river where he could rail at the gods for laying waste to his life again and yet again. When he was far enough

from the encampment that he thought no one would
hear, he gave himself up to the anger and pain clawing
its way out of his throat.

"I can't do this!" he screamed at the gray mist clinging
to the river. "I needed him! I needed Harlol, and you
took them both! How am I supposed to save Thebin?"
The fireball of Lluka's dream rolled through his waking
mind. "How do I stop the end of the world if I can't
even keep my own cadre alive! You may as well ask me
to empty the Onga River with a drinking cup—it's
impossible!"

He didn't know who he was shouting at, but it wasn't
the woman who stepped from between the trees. Lady
Chaiujin, dressed in green like bamboo in the spring,
answered him anyway.

"I know, child." She stretched her arms wide to him,
and smiled sadly as she said, "They ask too much and
never give you the rest you crave. But I will give you
rest. Come."

He should have wondered how she happened to appear in the woods outside his own camp when he had
just visited in dreams the tent city of her husband a hundred li away. The dream he had visited, in which she lay
as an emerald-green bamboo snake on the breast of her
husband, should have warned him of the danger she rep-
resented. But her voice crooned low, hypnotically calling
to him with promises of rest and more in the comfort of
her soft arms. She didn't inflame him as she had before
but offered the cool water of peace between her breasts.
Part of him remembered Carina's warning, that a potion
had stirred the longing she raised in him.

It should have troubled him, but his losses lay so heavily on his heart that he was beyond caring anymore. He
went to her with his own arms wide, and let her wrap
him in her green peace.

Heavy footsteps rattled in the undergrowth behind
him. Llesho sprang back, shocked to be caught with his
arms around the wife of the khan. Before he could begin

to formulate his excuses, however, Master Den broke into the clearing by the riverbank.

"I thought I might find you here."

The lady had disappeared. Den's brow furrowed when he caught sight of Llesho standing alone by the river. Coming closer, he hissed a "tsk" and from the place where the lady's arms had wrapped him, Master Den plucked a snake as green as new bamboo. "We'll have none of that, Lady Chaiujin."

With Master Den's presence, the dream state seemed to fall away from him, and Llesho recognized the snake as poisonous, with a sting as deadly as anything Markko had ever poured into him. She went for the trickster's hand with bared fangs, but Master Den caught her behind her jaws and raised her so that they were eye-to-beady-eye. "He belongs to the goddess," he said. "Your master cannot have him."

She hissed at him and lashed her tail while he held her gently, so that she hurt neither herself nor him. When she had calmed a little, he set her into the crook of a tree.

"Is that really Lady Chaiujin?" Llesho asked as she slithered away in the branches.

"As real as she was when she greeted you in the tent of her husband," the trickster god asserted. Llesho wondered, though, which visit he meant—the formal one, when she had poisoned his tea with a love potion, or the dream travel where she had greeted him as a serpent in the bed of her husband. He didn't have a chance to pursue his question, however.

"You've been busy," Master Den noted wryly, brushing at his shoulders with the discerning eye of a body servant.

Llesho waved him off, heading back toward the camp with an angry jerk of the head. He was sick of riddles, sick of help showing up just when it would do Hmishi no good at all.

"How did you get here, and why do you always arrive

just moments too late to be of any earthly use to anyone?" Llesho snapped the questions like arrows as he headed back for the camp.

"The khan traveled through the night with his army and raised his city on the plains above us." With his great long strides, Master Den quickly caught up to Llesho, who didn't indicate by any gesture that he noticed while Master Den gave the mundane explanation for his appearance. "We fetched up here shortly after false dawn, but no one could find you in the camp. Prince Tayyichiut seemed to think you might have sought the comfort of the river. And so I have come, just in the nick of time, to save you from a greater rest than you bargained for."

There were layers to that statement that Master Den's presence forced him to consider. No, he hadn't come to the river to find the comfort of death. But, yes, he had welcomed the touch of the Lady Chaiujin even knowing what she offered. And as for the nick of time—

"Maybe not." Let his teacher chew on that and see if he liked it. When a beautiful woman offered him rest in her arms, he'd be a fool not to take it, even if she meant it to be permanent.

More likely, he was a fool to think that was a good idea. It gave him pause. Maybe Lling wasn't the only one who had crossed the line of sanity. He'd seen it in her—how had he not seen it in himself?

"Carina said to tell you that Adar is resting comfortably, but will have to travel under sedation and with the baggage until he heals. Lling would not be moved, but has taken a little tea. She will sleep at least until Great Sun rises. Bright Morning attends Hmishi's body, and wanted me to fetch you."

"The mortal gods make uncommon messengers," Llesho remarked pointedly.

Master Den raised an eyebrow and sniffed his displeasure with his student. "That's what we do—deliver messages. The question, when confronting the gods, should always follow thusly: 'Who sent the message?' and, 'What was its purpose?'"

"Do I get any clues?" Llesho kicked through fallen leaves, expecting no answer. The trickster god surprised him.

"You can be sure that the gods who attend you fit the purpose."

"Then I suppose I am lucky that I've got you and not the Lady SienMa."

Den slanted him an ironic side glance. "Oh, she's on her way."

That didn't surprise Llesho at all. But Emperor Shou had her special favor. "What does Dognut want?"

"You'll have to ask him yourself."

They had come to the tent where Hmishi lay. Carina was nowhere in sight, but Bixei and Stipes waited for him in front of the tent, and Tayy stood with them, cradling Little Brother in his arms.

Bixei stirred and gave a bow of salute. "Your brother Shokar was here, and paid his respects. He has gone off to keep an eye on Lluka, who has begun muttering under his breath in a way that worries Balar and sets Shokar's teeth on edge, he says. Balar himself is inside, with Bright Morning."

"Where is Kaydu?" He didn't mention Lling—Llesho knew where she was.

Tayy answered with a wave at the sky. "She has gone to offer her report to her father. That one suggested it—" he jerked his chin at Master Den. "But I'm worried that she might become trapped in the form of a bird, as she was before."

"Habiba can handle it," Master Den dismissed the objection with a shrug. "She'll be back."

"Then if everything is in order, I'll go to the khan." Tayy cast a worried frown at the rim of the dell. On the plains above, an army ten thousand strong settled in around them. But in one tent, the key to all their fortunes lay in fever. "My father is not well," he advised them. And, because he knew Llesho would understand, he added, "The Lady Chaiujin carries a second heir."

Second after Tayy himself, Llesho knew, but her claim seemed unlikely to be true. He wondered what kind of child the bamboo snake carried in her belly, and if Chimbai-Khan had anything to do with it at all.

"There is room in my cadre for a likely warrior," Llesho offered, and darkness lifted from the prince's eyes. Almost he could forget the boy was Harnish. Without another word, the prince left them. Llesho entered the tent where Hmishi lay, with Master Den at his back.

"There you are." Dognut set his flute aside and faced Llesho with a sad smile. Curled into the corner of the tent, Balar continued to strum a lament softly on his borrowed lute. Master Den lowered himself with a grunt to the rug near the door. Llesho thought to bring him higher in the room as befitted a visiting god, but that was a Harnish way of thinking. He sat where he could guard the door against intrusion and listen to the mournful plucking of the strings at the same time.

"It was a mercy," Dognut looked up at Llesho, watched him move agitatedly around the tent. Llesho would not sit, but strayed over to stand and watch Lling, who slept beside Hmishi's bed. "The boy was so badly hurt."

"No." Llesho turned cold eyes on the dwarf who was more than he had ever seemed but, like Master Den, no use at all to any of his dead. "There is no mercy here. Evil wins again, because Mercy has gone out of the world."

"That isn't true." Dognut rested his hands on his knees, and Llesho was reminded that fate had shown the dwarf no mercy either, but still he seemed to believe. "We don't always recognize mercy when we see it. It isn't always what we want or think we need, but it's there. It's here."

A veil seemed to slip from the eyes of the dwarf. He let Llesho see what lay inside—the turning of the seasons, and the aging of the sun, and the rise and fall of empires. The smile was old, and wise, and patient, and filled with the pain and misery he had seen across all the ages. But it wasn't kind. "Is it a mercy to bring him back to suffer, not just the pain of his physical injuries, but the memory of all that was done to him?"

"That wouldn't be mercy, no. But to bring him back, mended, a god could do that."

"The universe is a place of balances, young king." Bright Morning lifted his hands, palms out, to demonstrate his point while Balar nodded his agreement from the corner.

"If a god should grant such a favor—" one small hand rose above his shoulder, while the other he dropped to his waist, "—what would you trade to restore the balance?"

"My life," he said, too quickly, and Master Den gave him a stern frown. He'd been trying to throw his life away since—it seemed—forever. Hardly a sacrifice, then, and one he couldn't in conscience make anyway.

The dwarf tilted his head, considering Llesho carefully. "Who among the thousands who follow would you trade for the life of your best friend?"

"No one," he finally admitted. He had plenty of lives to spend in the war with Master Markko, but none at all in trade for the sole purpose of seeing Hmishi laugh at him again. "I don't have anything. It's just—he's one too many, you know? I need a reason to keep going. I thought that Kungol was it—home, and freedom, a kingdom—but they're just words and a world away.

"Hmishi and Lling, Kaydu, Bixei and Stipes, they're the only home I have. Even my brothers don't feel a part of me like they do."

Balar bowed his head over his lute. He didn't protest, though Llesho saw that it cost him to keep silent.

Bright Morning agreed, however. "The mortal goddess

of war does good work, though its strength is never meant to last."

"A broken sword wins no battles."

The dwarf dropped his hands into his lap. "You ask too much," he said.

Master Den barked a short, ironic laugh. "You've been taking lessons from the student, Bright Morning. I've heard him say the very same many times."

True. He'd said the very words himself, to no avail. The gods kept asking for more anyway. Now he was asking back; he figured it was time they knew how it felt.

"Balar?"

The prince dropped his forehead to the pregnant body of his instrument. He didn't look at them as he answered the question that Bright Morning must have asked already, and more than once.

"Lluka sees disaster down every path. For myself, I cannot answer. I want to see my brother home, on the throne of our father, and I would balance that end any way I could." He did look up then, with a grim smile. "My gift has not deserted me, but I don't dare use it."

"You're right, you know. We do ask too much." Bright Morning shook his head. In the end, it came to a simple truth. "Your heart needs rest."

With that, he took up a silver flute and set it to his lips. When he played, Llesho's heart lightened. Lling stirred from her sleep, rubbing her eyes.

"What's happening?" she asked, her eyes on Llesho but her ear cocked in the direction of the music.

"I don't know," Llesho began, but the silver tones of the flute lifted him with unreasoning hope. When he looked on his dead friend, Hmishi's breast rose and fell, rose and fell, almost imperceptibly at first, then growing stronger with each breath, until his eyelids fluttered.

"Hmishi!" Lling fell to her knees and dropped her head on his shoulder, her arms enclosing him. Between her sobs she repeated his name, "Hmishi, Hmishi, Hmishi."

Llesho watched them, as if from a distance. He'd wanted this, asked for it, but in the end, it wasn't about him at all.

Hmishi's eyes roamed without focus or comprehension until they fell on Llesho, then his brows knotted. "Am I dead?" he asked.

The words echoed down the long dark corridor of memory. Hmishi had asked him that before, and he'd asked the same of Pig. This time, Llesho smiled and answered, "Not anymore."

"Good." With a contented sigh, Hmishi closed his eyes and went to sleep.

Read on for a preview of
the sequel to *The Prince of Dreams*

The Gates of Heaven

New in hardcover this month from DAW.

Llesho watched, taking in every step in the process of electing a new khan. For something so important—the khan would lead the clans, including their army of ten thousand—the method proved disappointingly simple. As the ceremony progressed, however, he found himself drawn into the gravity of even the simplest act.

Bolghai was summoned and came at the call. He wore his hair in a mass of plaits from each of which hung a talisman of metal or bead or bone. His robes, cut to show their many layers, still bore the bloodstains of the sheep he had slaughtered for the khan's pyre, but he had cleaned the pelts of the stoats that hung by their sharp little teeth in a collar around his neck. He did not walk with a stately pace to the dais as the Thebin priest might do, but scampered and pranced like his totem animal, setting the pelts to kicking at his shoulders in a little stoat-dance. His clothing jingled at each step with bells and amulets that swayed on silver chains sewn onto them.

The first time Llesho met him, the shaman had shocked and repelled him. But Bolghai had helped him to find his own totem, the roebuck, and had taught him

to control his gift of dreams for his own ends. Sometimes
at least. Now, he watched with interest as the shaman
hitched and hopped to the dais in the persona of his
totem stoat. Bolghai carried a flat skin drum and the thighbone of a roebuck that he used as a stick. He wouldn't
be creating totemic magic, so he wouldn't use his fiddle.
Rather, he'd need the drum to set the pace of the coming ceremony.

When he had reached the fur-heaped royal dais, the
shaman grasped the thighbone in the middle and tapped
with first one end, then the other, in a rapid tattoo on
his drum.

"When is a prince not a prince?" he demanded. confronting Tayy with more beating of his drum while he
waited for the answer to his riddle.

If there was no khan, there could be no prince. Tayyichiut bowed his head, accepting the judgment dictated
by custom and the sacred nature of the riddle. Allowing
himself to be ritually driven off by the beating drum, he
left the dais to sit with Bortu and Mergen of his clan.

"When is a wife not a wife?" the shaman asked next,
subtly changing the rhythm of his drumming. It wasn't
what she expected. Llesho, watching Tayy carefully, saw
the surprise in his eyes as well. Bortu's features, however,
relaxed in grim satisfaction. Her son was dead, but she
was no fool.

"I am no barren tree, but bear the khan's heir in my
belly." She clutched a hand below her unbelted waist
and spat at the shaman's feet. So, the riddle had set her
aside not as the widow, but as one who had not truly
blessed the marriage bed of the khan. Llesho figured that
much. Sort of. And she objected. He wondered not for
the first time what, if anything, the Lady Chaiujin did
carry in her womb.

Bolghai accepted her correction, more or less, with
the smallest of stoatlike gestures and adjusted his drumming accordingly. "When is a queen not a queen?" he
amended.

A wife remained a wife even at the death of her husband, but with no khan there could be no queen. Lady Chaiujin bowed, as Tayyichiut had done, but with less grace, and let herself be driven from the dais. She took a step toward her husband's clan, but Bortu turned her back, and the Lady Chaiujin hesitated, finally taking up a position alone, though closest to the dais. No one challenged her for the assumption of that right, but no one came to support her either. While few might guess her part in the death of their khan, she had made no friends among them.

Alone on the dais, Bolghai let the thighbone hang by a cord that tied it to the drum. Holding up his open hand, he asked another riddle: "Apart they are weak, together they smite their enemies." As answer, he closed his hand tight and raised it high over his head: the separate fingers were each fragile, but made into a fist, they made a powerful weapon. So, Llesho figured, the clans, joined in the ulus, became strong.

Bolghai's next words confirmed Llesho's guess: "Who here gathered would make a fist?"

A huge roar rose out of the gathered clans, aided by the shaman's drum. When he settled into a slower rhythm, the clans began the process of electing a khan. No one outside of the clans had ever been privileged to see the like before, and Llesho held his breath, his eyes darting everywhere to see everything, as two guardsmen came forward and set a low table down in front of the fur-covered dais.

Bortu came forward first and set a bowl on the table while Bolghai drummed and danced so energetically behind it that Llesho wondered how he managed not to kick it over. Bortu's bowl, of simple wood but inset everywhere with precious gems, he recognized for its great age. When she set it down, she raised her chin in challenge at her son's wife, who had no clan to bring to the ulus but must put herself forward as the regent of her husband's unborn child.

Bortu retired to sit again among the leaders of her clan, a signal for Great Mother to follow Great Mother, each rising to place her bowl before the drumming shaman. Every bowl was made of a precious material— worked silver or gold, porcelain, or alabaster, and each was elaborately decorated with some sign or sigil prominently marked to indicate the clan of origin. None showed the age of Bortu's, however. Chimbai's clan was the oldest, then, and Bortu, by chance or destiny, was the oldest of the Great Mothers. When he looked into her eyes, something moved, and for a moment the whites vanished into the hard black light of a bird of prey. Not a snake like her daughter-in-law, but he wondered what magics lay hidden within the old lady.

In a contest, he would have placed his bets on Bortu and he wondered why she had not used her skills to save her son. When he looked again, however, he saw only a sad old woman, grieving for her precious child. He thought of Lluka, his brother who saw all futures falling into chaos, and wondered if the old woman sacrificed her line to some future that none of them could see. He was pretty sure he didn't want to, all in all.

The procession of the Great Mothers had ended with seven bowls placed upright on the table at the shaman's feet, and three placed upside down as some sign to the gathered clans.

Master Den leaned over with a brief explanation that confirmed his guess: " 'Up' means the chieftain will accept the khanate for his clan if he is chosen. 'Down' means the clan has no wish to rise to khan right now. Not wealthy enough, or not united among themselves enough, or perhaps just wise enough to know they presently count no generals among their younger men."

"Or waiting out the killing before stepping in to pick up the pieces, and the wealth of the losers," Kaydu suggested. They'd both seen as much in the far provinces of Shan, where Lord Yueh had hoped to reap the benefit of Pearl Island's fall and had been gobbled up himself by Master

Markko. Llesho determined to pay more attention to those who had turned their bowls down. But now the Qubal clans focused on those who would be khan.

"One a hand may brush aside," Bolghai intoned to a slow and steady drumbeat, "Many lift their heads to heaven with a glittering crown about their brow."

Tayyichiut was the first to rise in answer to this riddle. In his hand, Mergen had placed a pebble—easily swept away, but many became a mountain with a crown of glaciers. He went to the table and set the stone inside Bortu's bowl with a bow to the shaman, who had stopped his dancing and shivered in place in a fit of ecstasy, and another bow to the ancient bowl. After him, Yesugei rose and, performing the same bows, set his stone in Bortu's bowl as well.

Master Den let go of a little sigh as their friend sat again among his clan. At Llesho's raised brow of inquiry, he whispered, "Yesugei was the most likely candidate if the clans decided against Chimbai's policies. He has signaled his followers where his own allegiances lie."

Llesho nodded. He thought he understood, but Master Den seemed unsatisfied with his reaction and added, "It could have come to war among the Qubal clans, with enemies on both their borders waiting to fall on them."

Master Markko in the South, and Tinglut, the Lady Chaiujin's father, in the East. He looked at the lady, sitting with venomous poise, her head demurely downcast, but with calculation glinting from under lowered lashes. As soon as they were done here, he'd have to find Shou and warn him. Tinglut would sign his treaty with a pen in one hand and sword held in the other behind his back.

"Would you share the thought that wrinkles your brow like an old man?" Kaydu asked him.

"I just realized that I am starting to think in Bolghai's riddles."

She rolled her eyes in sympathy and added, "If you start giving orders in battle that way, I'll thump you."

He was so happy to hear her talk to him as his captain

from the old days that he didn't even bother to point out he had never given the orders in battle anyway. That was her job.

The vote came to an end then, or so it seemed. The pebbles all looked alike. It would be harder that way to figure out who voted against the new khan once he took office, Llesho figured. That made retaliation less likely, though he was sure that some had done it in the past. His understanding of politics had grown that subtle at least. They hushed while Bolghai gave the count: three clans had stubbornly cast their votes for themselves, but seven had gone to Chimbai-Khan's line. The clans retrieved their voting bowls and each took a pebble from the little heap at Bolghai's feet.

When the table before the royal dais was once more empty the shaman declared in riddle form, "Out of many, one. Out of one, four. Out of four, one. Out of one, many." Each part of the riddle was punctuated with a flurry on his drum.

The first part made sense: many clans had voted, one clan won. What the rest meant, Llesho couldn't fathom until four figures came forward and faced the dais again. Chimbai-Khan's line, but who among the likely candidates would be khan?

If she spoke true that she carried the son of the dead khan, Lady Chaiujin might claim right to the Khanate as the regent of the heir. That presupposed the truth of two potential lies: that she carried a child of the khan at all, and that the khan had chosen her unborn babe as heir over his grown son by the wife who had gone on before him. Bold as the serpent she was, the lady pushed her way to the fore all out of order of her precedence and placed an alabaster bowl on the table at Bolghai's feet. "For my son," she said, "in the womb."

Bolghai looked like he would speak some prophecy or judgment, but his trembling overcame him and the Lady Chaiujin made her escape without comment.

Bortu, who should have been first, followed with

greater dignity and cold, bright eyes on the back of her
rival. In the death of her son, Lady Bortu had a right to
seek the khanate in her own person, but she set her bowl
upside down on the low table, removing herself from the
contest. Lady Chaiujin settled in her place with a little
gloating smile at this. Bortu returned her only a slow
blink of a predator hypnotizing its prey, before turning
away. Llesho had a fleeting vision of a hawk with a
snake's neck crushed in its mouth.

When he had cleared his eyes of the image, he found
Bortu staring at him with the first emotion he had seen on
her face since the death of her son: he had surprised her.
Read my mind, old woman, he thought. *Know me. I come for
vengeance and you are welcome to sit on my shoulder when I
ride.* But she gave him a small turn of the head, an answer,
"No," and a reason—she looked now at her other son.

As chieftain of the clan during his brother's reign,
Mergen had a rightful claim to the khanate and he drew
near the dais and set his jewel-encrusted bowl upright
next to the two that had gone before him. Tayyichiut
followed, and like his grandmother, repudiated his claim
upon the ulus. Instead of putting his cup facedown, however, he lifted Mergen's up and set his own beneath it.
When Bortu saw what he had done, she smiled and returned to the dais to do the same. Now the four cups
were gathered into two, Bortu and Tayyichiut showing
that they stood with Mergen against the outsider with
the questionable belly. The Lady Chaiujin raged behind
her impassive demeanor, Llesho could see it in her eyes,
but the chieftains nodded their heads in approval as the
pace of the drumming grew more rapid.

The contestants had no vote, since each had made
their choice in the position of his or her bowl upon the
table. One by one the chieftains, smiling or grim, followed Yesugei again to the dais and cast their pebbles
into Mergen's bowl. When the last vote had been cast,
there was no need for the shaman to make his ritual
announcement, though he did it anyway:

"When is a chieftain not a chieftain?"

To which the gathered chieftains replied in a rousing chorus, "When he is khan!"

After that came the swearing of loyalties, first, through their chieftains, the personal guardsmen who tended the khan and protected him. Then the chieftains, one by one, each dropped to one knee, fist clasped over his heart, to promise warriors at need and cooperation in counsel as was the custom of these Harnish clans. Not a king, but something else entirely. Llesho had known that with his head, but understanding shifted in his gut as he heard the chieftains give their conditional allegiance. Finally it came time for the heirs to swear their loyalty.

"I have lost my bravest son in service to the Qubal clans," Bortu mourned, and added, for Mergen, "The underworld will find my smartest son more difficult to bring home."

"I hope so," Mergen answered. By home, of course, she meant death, and Llesho suspected that Mergen would be a great deal more difficult to kill than his brother.

Llesho recognized the worry line that creased Tayy's forehead, but Mergen moved instantly to erase it. Taking his nephew's hands, he announced, "The son of my brother is my son. I beg you call him prince, and treat him as you would my own person."

"My father—" Tayy began, but Mergen-Khan stopped him with a finger touch of warning on the back of his hand. "Leave everything in my hands, Prince Tayyichiut. I am your khan."

To the gathered clans it sounded like a good-hearted reminder to a younger relative that he owed a greater deference to his uncle's new status. Llesho heard Mergen's words for what they were, however—a promise—and saw Tayy's embarrassment likewise as cautious hope and grief all roiled together. He waited to see where the ax would fall. Not on Tayy, for sure.

It came as no surprise that the Lady Chaiujin offered

no allegiance but an insult. "Among the eastern clans, a brother would offer the safety of his own hearth as husband to his brother's widow and father to his brother's child. I expect no such comfort from a man who would take his anda for a bride, but beg a small tent and a servant to tend me until my time. When I am delivered of my dead husband's true heir, I would ask only the freedom to choose a husband from among the clans."

Mergen-Khan's face became thunderous. The slight was obvious. A Harnishman, particularly a man of position, made alliances in many degrees, but anda was the closest. Blood brothers for life, sealed by gifts and held in the heart, the anda was a cherished friend. Occasionally more, which caused no trouble in the tents of a man who also kept to his wives and his husbandly duties to his clan. But Mergen had no wife, and his anda, Otchigin, had died fighting the stone giants of Master Markko.

The Lady Chaiujin threatened civil war with Chimbai-Khan's unborn son as her instrument, but Llesho didn't think that Mergen had noticed that. She'd called his dead anda a coward and a thief, stealing Mergen's duties from his clan. The khan's eyes went flat. "Better my anda than the serpent who made my brother's sleep so permanent," he said, and raised a hand as if to strike her.

She flinched, but the action didn't save her. By prearranged signal, the guards of his dead brother, newly sworn to their elected khan, came forward. Two who had been Chimbai's oldest and most valued friends seized her between them, and Mergen's own swordmaster stepped up behind her.

"Strangle the murdering witch," Mergen said, and the swordmaster wrapped his hands around her neck and squeezed.

"You'll pay," she choked out. With a twist of her neck, she turned into a jewel-green snake. Her grin exposed bared fangs she sank into the meat of her strangler's hand.

"Ah!" he screamed, and dropped her as his hand

throbbed with venom. Her captors struggled to hold on, but her arms had vanished. Slipping easily out of their grasp, the Lady Chaiujin glided quickly into hiding between the layers of rugs on the ger-tent floor.

"Everybody out!" Mergen ordered. And to his guards, "To sword! Find her and put an end to her." He reached out and grabbed a goblet from the chest that sat by the fire and raised it over his head. "This jeweled cup to the man who brings her dead body to me: snake or woman, I don't care which. Just find her!"